THE GIFTS
OF ARTEMIS

Douglas Scott

ARROW BOOKS

62–65 Chandos Place, London WC2N 4NW

An imprint of Century Hutchinson Limited

London Melbourne Sydney Auckland
Johannesburg and agencies throughout
the world

First published by Martin Secker and Warburg Ltd 1979
Fontana edition 1981
Arrow edition 1988

Phototypeset by Input Typesetting Ltd, London

Printed and bound in Great Britain by
Anchor Brendon Limited, Tiptree, Essex

ISBN 0 09 956470 X

CONTENTS

BOOK ONE

Prologue

January 1943

The room in the Kremlin was austerely furnished. Six men sat facing each other across an oblong oak table. The chair at the head of the table was vacant.

The men rose expectantly as the door swung open and Josef Stalin entered. With a wave of his hand he bade them be seated. There was a movement of chairs as the six seated themselves. Stalin took the chair at the head of the table.

'Comrades,' he said, 'before we begin, I have news from the battle-front. This morning, the commander of our forces encircling Stalingrad sent a surrender demand to the commander of the Fascist soldiers in the city. The German, von Paulus, has seen fit to reject the demand. I have, therefore, given orders to the Red Army to smash him and his troops without mercy.'

There were murmurs of approval from around the table.

The gathering was ostensibly a meeting of a Presidium-appointed sub-committee, convened under Stalin's chairmanship, to liaise on matters of mutual interest between the Party Executive and the Foreign Secretariat. In a state capital, however, where nothing was quite what it appeared to be and secret committees were as numerous as busy little groups of bees in a rose-garden, this committee was even *more* secret than most.

Its members had all been hand-picked by Stalin and their appointments simply endorsed by the Presidium. No reports of the committee's activities were ever made public. Nor were their deliberations minuted. In the intricate governing machinery of the Communist State, they were part of a secret policy-making enclave within the Party's most secret caucus.

Their job was to formulate and define the Party's and the State's long-range external policies and strategy. The men around the table were not known to the Russian public like Maisky or Molotov or Zhukov or Vasilevsky or Beria – but they each exerted control of other committees active in foreign affairs, military matters, intelligence operations, and the deployment of economic resources.

Stalin spoke succinctly about the future strategy, of the need to pursue the invaders across Europe to the Alps and the sea, and of his determination to crush all capitalist-bourgeois elements in Poland. 'The lands we gain,' he concluded, 'shall be our bulwark against capitalist-bourgeois imperialism.'

'What about our other neighbours?'

The question came from a sallow-faced bearded man wearing the uniform of a colonel in the Red Army.

Stalin smiled.

'Where the Red Army goes, governments will rise which will be in total sympathy with international socialism and our Party ideals. The workers of these countries will demand it.'

The Colonel nodded sagely.

'Yes. Yes, of course,' he said. 'But if the military effort is to be concentrated on a western push and a circling movement aimed at Germany, what of the southern flank – the Balkans?'

Stalin smiled again.

'Ah, Comrade Colonel – your own special area of interest, the Balkans. You realise that Hungary,

Czechoslovakia, Rumania and Bulgaria all stand in the path of our armies and will fall?'

'Yes, but what of Jugoslavia and Greece?' came the the reply.

'Mountains and rivers. Mountains and rivers,' said Stalin. 'The great battles will be fought in the plains. We shall push hard into Jugoslavia certainly, but we cannot divert the armour needed for our main westward advance for excursions into the mountains of Macedonia, Greece and Albania. We can seal these lands off from the north but the political destinies of these countries will be decided from within.'

'The Party is strong in Jugoslavia, Albania and Greece.' said the Colonel. 'Will the workers and guerrilla fighters not feel abandoned by us if we do not send our armies in? The Poles will not welcome us except on their terms, but the Greeks look to the East for their salvation.'

'The Greeks are strong enough to achieve their own salvation,' said Stalin. 'We have sown the seed but they must reap the harvest . . . when it is ripe, not before. The Revolution is on the march in Greece but not in Poland. In Poland, the reactionary and capitalist forces have still to be smashed and the land to be won. In Greece, the Monarchists and bourgeoisie are discredited and scattered and three-fifths of the land is held by forces loyal to the idea of socialist revolution.'

Stalin raised two hands and displayed them to the committee.

'This hand,' he said, clenching his right fist, 'is the hand that deals with Poland.'

He smashed the fist on the table.

'This hand,' he said, and he made undulating gestures with the fingers of his left hand, 'is the cunning political hand which deals with the Balkans.'

He smiled wryly before continuing:

'You crack a hard nut with a fierce blow.' Again he

11

brought his right hand down hard on the table. 'But you open a door by turning the handle.' He gently rotated his left hand around an imaginary door handle.

The bearded colonel smiled faintly.

'Tito has agreed to come secretly to Moscow for talks with Comrade Molotov. He wants our advice on how to handle the British. They actually imagine he will help them restore the Monarchy!'

Stalin laughed.

'Tito is a strong man and nobody's fool. We must watch him ourselves. But, for the moment, we must welcome him for the hero he is and do all we can to help him. What about Greece, Comrade Colonel? Churchill dotes on that country like a child over a prize toy. He regards the place as the cradle of civilisation — a land which must be kept within the British sphere of influence, even, it seems, if the rest of the British Empire falls in pieces around his ears.'

'Churchill will do everything in his power to restore the fascist King George to the throne if Rommel is defeated in Africa,' said the Colonel. 'The British have many agents in Greece and they prop up the King and his so called Government-in-Egypt. They stand in the way of socialist revolution.'

'Let them try,' said Stalin, 'while *we* make sure of Poland. Perhaps, Colonel, it would help your comrades here understand the situation more fully if you were to tell them of the revolutionary strength in Greece.'

Five faces turned expectantly towards the Balkan expert.

The National Liberation Front in Greece was set up under Communist Party direction as long ago as 1941 — in September of that year. It is organised and controlled by loyal Marxists and Leninists who have co-opted Trotskyites in the fraternal alliance of the Left. The Greeks call the Front the EAM. It is, in effect, a secret coalition government of resistance and revolution, and it commands greater popular support than the puppet government installed by the Germans or the Royalist Government-in-Exile.'

'Wait,' said one of the committee. 'When you say it is a coalition Government, does that mean it includes representatives of counter-revolutionary parties and Royalists?'

'No,' said the Colonel. 'It is totally a coalition of the Left. The Populists and the Republican Liberals would not join – but they may be regretting that decision now. Because the EAM now speaks for about two-thirds of the people. Even the middle classes have been flocking to support it.'

'Is this desirable?' asked another committee member.

The Colonel smiled grimly.

'Nearly three hundred thousand Greeks have died of starvation since the Fascists invaded. Poverty and starvation and the collapse of the capitalist economy have killed off more traditionally held middle-class political concepts than a hundred years of socialist propaganda could achieve. These people despise the collaborationist government, which has made them peasants overnight. And they get no comfort from the Cairo Government. The EAM is their only source of hope.'

'And the EAM is not toothless,' observed Stalin.

'Far from it,' said the Colonel. 'Nine months ago, EAM formed the ELAS, the army of the National Liberation Front. It started last spring with only a couple of hundred men. Now, there are more than thirty thousand under arms in the mountains. By next summer, there will be double that number.'

The grey-haired committee member on Stalin's right said:

'Such forces should be able to hold down many German divisions which, otherwise, might be thrown into the fight against the Red Army.'

13

Stalin nodded his endorsement.

'And it also gives the Americans and British something to think about if they try to dictate to us where Polish borders should or should not be. We shall concede nothing over the Polish question, saying it is our problem and ours alone – but we can afford to be flexible and co-operative over the Greek question. We shall allow ourselves to be persuaded by the British and their American friends that they have a special responsibility to give Greece military and economic help.'

'And the only way they can do that is to co-operate with EAM politically and the ELAS militarily,' pointed out the bearded colonel. 'The question is how soon can we risk a direct military confrontation between the ELAS and, say, the British?'

'That must not happen before the Red Army is in Berlin,' said Stalin emphatically.

'A direct confrontation may be inevitable before then,' said the Colonel.

'Then it must be avoided at all costs,' said Stalin. 'Let our Greek revolutionaries rattle their bayonets at the British. Let them be provocative and prickly allies – but do not let them precipitate a major conflict, one which would make Red Army intervention necessary. Let the Greeks be hostile and co-operative in turn. Let them obstruct every attempt at political interference in Greek affairs but, outwardly, they must be willing to compromise for the preservation of a common front against the enemy. If the British treat the ELAS as equals in order to defeat the Germans and Italians, then they must recognise the EAM's political strength and rights when Germany is overthrown.'

'What about the guerrilla forces in the north-west of Greece? Zervas, the Republican, is an avowed enemy of the Marxists and Trotskyites in Athens and Thessaly.

And there are Royalist bands in the Pindus Mountains who are no friends of socialist revolution.'

'Then they are the enemies of the Greek people and should be treated as such, Comrade Colonel,' said Stalin. 'If they will not accept the friendship of the ELAS in the common struggle and acknowledge EAM as the rightful political authority, they should be eliminated as fascist collaborators and criminal bandits.'

'This will mean, Marshal, that Greek will have to kill Greek.'

Stalin glared at the Colonel.

'What reward would you give to the Russians in the Ukraine who, even now, are known to be collaborating with the German invaders of our land?'

'Death,' said the Colonel.

'That' said Stalin, 'Is the merciful reward. So, let Greek show equal mercy to Greek. Greece in the long run will be won politically along Comintern policy lines, from within by revolutionaries joining forces with non-Communist radicals to form a front of the Left to achieve peaceful revolution. But they must carry a big stick to the conference table. The trick is in waving the stick often but using it sparingly. Let the forces of reaction strike the first blow at the Left so that the world will condemn them as aggressors. Let the Revolution in Greece build its muscles and preserve its strength for the final battle, the battle it knows it must win. It must not be wasted on skirmishes which postpone the final reckoning and have no hope of being decisive.'

While the supreme ruler of the USSR was dictating far-reaching policies affecting the future of a Greece which lay bleeding and starving under Nazi occupation, Winston Churchill – on that same bitterly cold winter night – was pondering over occupied Europe in the warmth of his subterranean London office. He had just had a wide-ranging discussion with Brooke, the Chief of Staff, which had swung from one end of Europe to the other.

Churchill turned to a despatch which had reached his desk. It was an intelligence report from Cairo. It mentioned rumblings of discontent among soldiers of the First Greek Brigade, which was stationed in Egypt. Agents had been trying to locate the source of leaflets which had been passing between the Greek troops. These urged the men to disown their King and the Greek Government-in-Exile and seek recognition by the Allies of EAM, a clandestine coalition in Athens, as the sole authority on Greek affairs.

So far, intelligence agents had been unable to uncover the authors of the leaflets. One theory was that they were the work of Nazi agents-provocateurs. Another was that the mischief was all part of a Communist propaganda exercise.

Churchill pencilled a cable to be sent to Middle East HQ. He wanted the situation with the Greek Brigade to be watched closely and he wished to be kept personally informed of any developments.

His thoughts turned to Greece, a country which had always excited a profound fascination in his mind – ever since he had first studied Classics and History.

> The mountains look on Marathon -
> And Marathon looks on the sea;
> And musing there an hour alone,
> I dreamed that Greece might still be free.

Churchill conjured up in his mind the glory that was Athens, and a great longing filled him. Of all the capitals in Europe, this more than any other exerted a special pull. He resolved that when freedom returned to that great and beautiful city, he, too, would return and walk again in Constitution Square.

16

CHAPTER ONE

Night Landing

February 1943

HM Submarine *Seasnipe* surfaced at 2030 hours. She was close enough to the Greek shore for the First Lieutenant to identify Castel Tornese, the old crusader fortress to the south of Killini. *Seasnipe* then proceeded at periscope depth on a north-westerly course.

Two and a half hours later, the submarine surfaced again. When the First Lieutenant sighted land to starboard, he called the Captain. A moment or two later, Lieutenant-Commander Hubert Barnard joined his Number One on the conning-tower bridge.

The wind was gusting force five from the north. Scurries of sleet mingling with the icy spray breaking over the submarine's bows caused Barnard to shield his night-glasses with the sleeve of his duffle-coat.

'I can't see a bloody thing!' he complained.

The First Lieutenant was crouched against the starboard wing of the conning-tower, his spread hands making a weather canopy over the end of his binoculars.

'That's Cape Papas almost directly abeam,' he said.

Barnard grunted.

'You must have eyes like a cat, Timothy. I can't see the land, never mind tell Cape Papas from the Cape of Good Hope. Wait a minute, I can see the land now.'

'You can make out the old lighthouse in silhouette.

There's a faint glow in the sky behind it. Must be coming from Patras at the head of the Gulf.'

'Patras will be blacked out.'

'Well, there's a definite glow. Maybe the RAF have been busy.'

He had no sooner spoken than thin pencils of light appeared in the night sky to the east, some twenty-five miles distant. The search-lights probed the low, scurrying clouds in silent show.

'Looks like our fly-boys are going to be keeping Jerry occupied. With luck we'll be able to put our passengers ashore in peace,' said the Lieutenant.

Barnard turned his back as the submarine dipped its nose into a particularly large sea and a sheet of solid water burst over the conning-tower, drenching its occupants.

A stream of oaths exploded from the submarine's commander.

'To hell with this! I'm going below, Timothy. For our guests' sakes, I hope to God it's not quite so rough at the other side of the Gulf.'

'Lovely weather, sir. Bracing! I'm only too pleased to hold the fort.'

Barnard threw the Lieutenant a look which carried a question about that officer's sanity. The Lieutenant was unaware of it.

'Shall I bring her round on the new course , sir?' he asked. 'The Cape is now bearing oh-nine-five.'

'Ten to starboard, then,' said Barnard.

The Lieutenant bawled down the voice pipe.

'Steer oh-five-oh,' he instructed. 'And give me a time check.'

'Bringing her round now, sir,' came the reply. 'Steadying on oh-five-oh degrees. The time is twenty-three twenty-nine.'

A rating on look-out moved aside to allow Barnard to open the hatch and climb below. He made his way to the tiny ward-room where he found his three 'guests' finishing off a supper of grilled mutton chops and fried eggs. Barnard threw off his wet duffle.

'Eat up, gentlemen,' he encouraged the three men. 'It may be your last taste of civilised food for some time.'

One of the three bridled visibly. He was the only one of the trio not in army uniform: a handsome man with flashing brown eyes and smooth jet-coloured hair. He was sombrely clad in a black polo-neck sweater and black trousers, which were tucked into black web anklets.

'Are you saying that we do not eat civilised food in Greece? That we are savages?'

There was a snake-like hiss to his words. His eyes were pin-points of angry fire.

'Not at all, old chap,' said Barnard, unruffled. 'I'm very fond of Greek food myself but, from what I hear, it's not very plentiful in your homeland at present.'

'Don't be so touchy, George,' said the central of the three men sitting round the table. Captain James Mackenzie was a broad-shouldered six-footer with dark curly hair and twinkling eyes. Like the third member of the party, he wore a white polo-neck jersey under a khaki battledress tunic.

'Do not patronise me,' said the man in black. 'And do not call me George. In the interests of my security, if not yours, you should obey your own order—and that was to use only my codename. This was emphasized to you in Alexandria at the briefing'.

Mackenzie laughed.

'You don't know the half of it. Know what that Welsh major said about your codename before you got to the briefing? He told Preston and me that the Greek captain we were to team up with had a codename which must have been invented by a pox doctor.'

'I do not follow,' said the Greek. 'I chose the name Cephalus myself.'

19

'But you pronounce it the Greek way with the "C" Hard, like the English "K". He in his ignorance had only seen your illustrious moniker written down, and he pronounced it with a soft "C".'

'I still do not see what this has to do with a doctor,' said the Greek.

'He kept calling you Syphilis,' explained Mackenzie, with a broad grin. 'He even suggested that Preston and I should change our codename to "Clap" and "Guns" to be in fashion.'

Barnard and the second army man – the one Mackenzie had referred to as Preston – laughed uproariously. The Greek was not amused.

'You British are like children. You think it is funny to insult a Greek officer. You would not laugh so much if you were under my command. You are stupid pigs.'

He stood up, pushing plates away from him in an angry clatter of crockery as he did so.

The smile vanished from Mackenzie's face. He stared evenly at the Greek.

'You're losing your cool again, friend. No offence was intended and I'm sorry you can't occasionally see the funny side of things. You'll have to forgive us if we don't all go around with faces like the Judgement Day. It really bothers me, Captain Cephalus, that since the day we met up you've not shown so much as a glimpse of anything that could pass for a sense of humour. In fact, you're about the moaningest bastard I've ever met.'

The second army man spoke for the first time. He had a soft American accent.

'Easy, boys,' he intervened mildly. 'Let's not all get riled up. Look, it's getting mighty close to row-for-the-shore time. What say we lower the temperature a bit and go check that we all remembered to pack dry socks and a tooth-brush? How long we got, Commander Barnard?'

Barnard looked at his watch.

'We'll be coming up on the rendezvous in about thirty minutes.'

With a graceless glower at Mackenzie, the Greek turned and left the ward-room.

'Sorry, gents,' said Mackenzie. 'But there's something about our Greek friend that makes me decidedly uneasy. All the Greeks I've known have been jolly guys who laughed a lot. That one's got so much bile in him that it worries me.'

'You never know what he's been through to make him like that,' said Barnard. 'It was us who picked him up two months ago – on the Thessaly coast. He was a bag of nerves then. Must carry a bit of weight with the top brass at Middle East HQ, though. We made a special trip to collect him and a couple of our chaps. Better not to ask what makes guerrilla johnnies smoulder. I'm just glad he's a friend and not an enemy.'

'I've never had a friend before who didn't have a sense of humour,' said Mackenzie thoughtfully. 'Not one I've been glad to call *friend*.'

'Forget it, Mac,' said the American. 'We've got to trust that guy with our lives. Better if we don't rile him. Like that man says, there's no telling what hellish things have happened to him to make him such a mean and ornery cuss. Are you all ready to go?'

'Ready – and twitchy as hell, as you've probably noticed. All I've got to do is spend five minutes in the officers' bog . . . Make sure the bowels are suitably emptied and ready for action. It would be too bad if I had an accident – of the instant evacuational sort – when we hit the beach.'

'Now, that's a thought,' said the American. 'You lead the way up the beach evacuating instantly – and Kirkos and I will just *slip* up after you!'

Mackenzie groaned.

'That is the crappiest joke I ever heard! And go easy on calling Georgie boy Kirkos. He doesn't like it, remember? His name is Cephalus – with a hard "C", as in clap.'

'Yeah, I know. Kay-phall-ass. Captain V.D. Cephalus.'

Mackenzie grinned at Preston.

'Do you get your excruciating wit from the Greek half of the family or from the Yankee Doodle side? Or have you been reading too many jokes on the backs of match-boxes?'

The American pushed his chair back and stood up. With an extravagant sweep of his right arm, he bowed in mock solemnity.

'From my father, rest his soul, I inherited the dynamic acquisitive adventurism of the pioneer Prestons, who bought Manhattan from the Indians for a box of glass beads. From my Greek mother, bless her heart, I inherited my classic aestheticism and cultural sensitivity . . . Allied of course to a high degree of peasant cunning and political acuity.'

'And that in a nutshell,' Mackenzie observed to Barnard, 'is why they've sent the bum to Greece on this mission. Isn't that right, Leo?'

Lieutenant Leonidas Theodosius Preston – erstwhile graduate of Cornell University and the training school of the American Office of Strategic Services, and currently holder of a temporary commission in the British Army – graciously agreed.

'You speak the truth, Captain Mac, sir. It was not my good looks, not my effortless urbane charm, nor even any of the dozen or so other admirable qualities of mine – which you must have observed - that got me lumbered. No, sir. It was my dual heritage . . . That union of backgrounds which joins the civilised sophistication of Democracy's cradle with its latest and biggest bawling infant in the Western Hemisphere . . . That's what landed me in my present predicament! That and the fact that I can converse in the Greek language with

22

an accent that is not quite abominable enough to be incomprehensible.'

Mackenzie applauded gently. Barnard was looking at his watch.

'I don't want to hurry you, gentlemen, but it will soon be going-ashore time.'

'If we gotta go, we gotta go, said Preston.

There was no let-up in the weather. When the *Seasnipe* hove-to off the shallow northern shore of the Gulf of Patras, the wind came buffeting from the land, making the spume leap from the crests of the short, angry waves.

Barnard conned the submarine at dead slow speed so that, on station at the rendezvous point, the vessel provided a lee for the launch of the two rubber dinghies which were to take the three men and their equipment ashore.

Four naval crew had been detailed to ferry Mackenzie and his companions to the beach. The oilskin-clad sailors were already standing-by with the dinghies when Mackenzie climbed from the afterhatch into the ferocity of the elements.

'Suffering Jesus!' he cried when the blast of weather hit him. 'If this is Greece, I take back all I ever said about Egypt.'

Preston and the Greek huddled beside him on the narrow, slippery deck while the sailors awaited the order to launch the dinghies.

'Don't put these craft into the water until I give the word,' came Barnard's voice from the conning-tower. Even through the amplifying medium of a hand megaphone, his words were barely audible as they were seized and borne away by the gale.

'Make the signal,' Barnard ordered the Yeoman, who was huddled, Aldis lamp in hand, on the weather side of the bridge. The man pointed the lamp towards the dark mass of Mount Varasovon and triggered five long

23

flashes. Five short flashes came winking back from the shore.

'They're there sir,' said the signaller.

'Good. I'm going down on deck to wish our travellers well. Take over, Number One.'

'Aye aye, sir.'

Barnard reached the afterdeck in time to hear a heated exchange between Mackenzie and the Greek.

'Hell's bells,' Mackenzie was complaining, 'you're carrying more bloody armaments than a Sherman tank! And where's your life-jacket? You'll never get one on on top of that lot!'

Barnard stared in surprise at the Greek. He was indeed bristling with weaponry. Three pistols were strapped around his waistband. He wore two bandoliers of cartridges, criss-crossed about his shoulders. Over his left shoulder was a Lee-Enfield rifle and a tommy-gun was hung from his neck by a strap.

'These guns are more important than a life-jacket,' said the Greek. 'Where I go, they go.'

'And that could be straight to the bottom of the sea, you great poultice!' shouted Mackenzie. 'For Christ's sake, ship them in the dinghy with the other stores and go back for your life-jacket!'

'No. Where I go, they go!'

'It's his funeral,' chipped in Preston. He's not worth arguing with, Mac.'

Mackenzie scowled at the Greek in impotent fury.

'Your reception committee's waiting ashore,' said Barnard, having to shout above the storm. 'And this isn't too healthy a place for us to hang around. Time you were under way, Captain Mackenzie.'

Mackenzie glanced absent-mindedly over his shoulder at Barnard.

'Sure, sure. You're right,' he said with resignation.

He turned and stretched out a hand to Barnard.

'Thanks for everything, Captain. Sorry we've been

24

such a nuisance to you. Have a safe journey back to Alex,'

While the sailors launched the dinghies and began loading most of the supplies into one of them, Barnard shook hands with the Greek and the American in turn and wished them luck.

The Greek climbed down into the dinghy, which was almost full of stores. Mackenzie and the American had no choice but to go in the other.

One of the sailors was loading a bulky canvas-bound chest into the dinghy occupied by the Greek. The small craft was rocking dangerously and the Greek was holding grimly to the side.

'Careful with that one,' shouted Mackenzie.

'What the hell do you have in this one, Captain? Lead ingots? It weighs a bloody ton!'

'Just make sure it gets ashore all right,' said Mackenzie.

It took two sailors to load the chest safely in the Greek's dinghy. When the dinghies were finally cast off from their parent, their crews paddled them along the lee of the submarine with comparative ease. It was a different story when they rounded the bow of the submarine and met the full force of the off-shore gale.

Progress was laborious. In grim silence, the submariners inched the dinghies forward across the half-mile of broken water towards the land. At a speed which filled Mackenzie with impatience, they edged towards a rocky inlet which was guarded on its western side by a spur of rock jutting fifty or sixty yards out to sea. The spur dropped from a height of twelve feet at its armpit with the land to sea level at its extremity. Breakers beyond its visible end indicated that it projected some distance further underwater.

Mackenzie's dinghy was first to reach the seaward end of the spur. The tiny craft almost came to grief on the underwater reef. The swell momentarily ran away from the shore and the flat bottom of the dinghy grounded briefly on sloping rock. The craft teetered, stranded, hanging at an angle of twenty degrees below the horizontal, tipping its occupants towards the stern, before a wave caught the spinning rubber oval and hurled it into deeper water.

The paddlers quickly regained control and made for the sheltered water of the inlet, while Mackenzie signalled furiously with his arms to the other dinghy. Couldn't they understand that they were cutting the corner of the reef much too closely? Shouting and gesticulating, he tried to warn the Navy paddlers to keep wide of the spur and enter the inlet in a wide curve.

The other crew seemed oblivious of Mackenzie's frantic signals and were suddenly obscured from his sight by the greater mass of the rocky spur. His own craft was now surfing and there was no sign of the second dinghy as the first grounded on sandy beach.

Leaving Preston and the navymen to haul the dinghy clear of the water's edge, Mackenzie leapt ashore and ran towards the rocky spur. He clambered and slithered along its length towards the seaward point. At first, he could see nothing in the angry sea beyond. Then he saw the other dinghy. And he was filled with furious dismay. It was floating out to sea bottom up.

Hope flared when he saw movement, and he realised that two men were clinging to the life-ropes of the capsized craft. There was no sign of the third occupant. His eyes scanned the water.

Again movement. He focused on a shape fifteen feet beyond the promontory end. A wave broke over what looked like a rock, partly submerged. The rock seemed to move. And again. Then the shape was recognisable as the shoulders of a man with arms stretched desperately to find a hold on the reef.

Pulling off his boots and placing them high on the rock behind him, Mackenzie faced the sea and gingerly stepped forward. With a shudder of apprehension, he launched himself into the surging water. The paralysing iciness of the sea's embrace made him cry out in physical shock. His breath seemed to die inside him as he struck out in the general direction of the struggling man.

His fore-and-aft Navy-issue life-preserver kept his head high and undoubtedly saved him from having his brains bashed out on the rocks. He felt himself carried at a great speed across a swirling pool formed within a natural bend in the rocky spur at its tip. Then he felt his legs crashing against a smooth, sloping slab two feet below the surface.

It was almost impossible to see but, during a flashing respite in the fury of wave and water, he glimpsed again a dark body being swept seaward ahead of him. He lunged towards it and was again carried by an ebbing rush of water until his outstretched fingers fastened on human hair.

It was the Greek.

His rifle had long gone but the tommy-gun was still festooned like a millstone about his neck. Mackenzie tore at the strap and pulled it over the half-drowned Greek's head.

The man was so heavily encumbered with bandoliers and other appendages that trying to keep him afloat was like trying to swim with a bag of cement wrapped in a horse harness.

Mackenzie pulled and battled his way over the reef to the quieter waters of the inlet, towing and manhandling the dead weight of the other man and continually screaming curses at him through mouthfuls of water.

Exhaustion finally made him relax his talon-like clutch on the Greek. Mackenzie made no immediate attempt to renew it even as the other man slipped slowly from sight below the surface of the water. Gulping in air, Mackenzie released the ties of his life-jacket and wriggled out from under it. He let it drift.

A shallow surface dive was rewarded when his fingers touched then held the half-drowned Greek's shoulder. He pulled the man's head clear of the water and manhandled him across the floating life-jacket.

The Greek now lay across it, the weight of his shoulders forcing it below the surface. But his head stayed clear of the water most of the time. Mackenzie, gripping the man under the chin with one hand, paddled himself and his tow shorewards with the other.

His feet touched sand. He hauled the Greek three steps out of the water and then dropped him like a sack of potatoes. He fell on his knees before dropping face down and letting his breath come in great laboured sighs.

He was dimly aware of being lifted by the arms and being dragged up the beach. Preston and the two men from the *Seasnipe* hauled him and the Greek to the shelter of rocks.

'I'll be all right in a minute,' breathed Mackenzie. 'Is the Greek alive?'

One of the sailors had already turned the Greek on to his stomach and was giving him artificial respiration. Water vomited from the Greek's open mouth. The vomiting became a racked spluttering and coughing.

'He's alive,' said the sailor. 'He'll be OK once he's coughed up his other lung. What happened to our mates?

'They're all right, I think,' said Mackenzie. 'Their dinghy capsized. It's upside down and they were hanging on to it. You'd better take our dinghy and get to them.'

The two navymen needed no prompting. They were over already moving into urgent action.

Mackenzie forced himself to sit up. He was shivering uncontrollably.

'You'll need dry clothes,' said Preston. 'What happened to your boots?'

28

'They're out there on the rocks. I took them off before I went in the drink.'

'I'll see if I can find them.'

The Greek was hunched on hands and knees, still coughing up seawater. He, too, was shivering as if he had the palsy. Mackenzie could hear the man's teeth chattering between paroxysms of retching. 'I should have let you drown, you bastard,' said Mackenzie.

'How did I get here?' spluttered the Greek.

'I went in after you. That's how! But I shouldn't have bothered. There were more important things on that dinghy than you. Lost now! The whole bloody operation's scuppered before we've even started.'

'What was so important? They can drop more radios from the air.'

Mackenzie didn't reply. He alone in the party knew what had been on the dinghy and he was under strict instructions to acquaint no one with the contents of that heavy oblong chest. That one crate and its safe delivery was the sole reason why a sea landing had been ordered for Mackenzie's group instead of the more normal drop from the air.

Mackenzie stood up and began to beat his body with his hands in an effort to get his blood circulating.

'Where are your people?' he asked the Greek. 'I thought they would be here.'

'They have their orders, too. They will not make contact until thirty or more minutes after the landing signals have been made.'

'Why wait?'

'They must make sure there are no German or Italian patrols in the area. If there are, it is their job to distract them while we make our way inland.'

Mackenzie was suddenly aware of a movement above him. A trickle of small stones bounced down the rock face and landed at his feet. A shiver of uninvited fear intensified his shaking with cold.

He looked up towards the source of the sound.

Dimly silhouetted against the sky, someone stood motionless as a statue. Preston chose that moment to return.

'I found your boots . . .'

The last word trailed away almost to inaudibility as he, too, saw the lone figure on the rock above. His right hand unclipped the stud of the web holster at his belt and his fingers closed over the butt of his service revolver.

'Cephalus.'

The one word dropped softly from the figure on the rock. The Greek on the beach moved numb limbs and struggled to stand erect.

'You,' he breathed, and there was surprise in the way he said it.

'I'll come down,' said the voice from above, speaking in Greek. Mackenzie and the American, frozen into immobility, breathed again.

The stranger above disappeared from sight, but the sound of small stones dislodged by feet indicated descent around the side of the rock.

'Hey, it's just a kid,' said Preston, as the figure – now seen to be no more than five feet four – appeared from around the base of the rock. The newcomer wore a below-the-knee sheepskin coat and the head was enveloped in a woollen cap pulled over the ears. An ancient long-barrelled rifle of Turkish origin was slung over one shoulder and a deep haversack was slung at the waist from the other.

'I am twenty-eight years old,' said the voice in English. It had a slight American nasalness and a pleasant contralto pitch.

Mackenzie and Preston realised simultaneously, although neither would have admitted being a hundred-percent-sure, that the newcomer was a woman.

The figure advanced eagerly towards Kirkos, but

halted at a barely perceptible gesture of the Greek's hand.

'There is no time for greetings, woman. Where are the others? Surely Spiro did not send you alone?'

'No others are coming.'

Kirkos swore colourfully.

'What went wrong?'

'We stayed at a village near Domnitsa the night before last. The Italians bombed it. I was the only one who was not wounded. Yorgo was not badly hurt. He took Soter and his brother back to Karpenisi. What about you? You're soaking wet and shivering.'

'I fell in the water. I'll need dry clothes if I'm to walk a step in this cold. Why did the Italians bomb the village you were in?'

'It wasn't because of us. Some fool of a boy shot at an Italian patrol not far from the village. The bombing was their way of showing how much they appreciated it.'

'Aren't you going to introduce us, Captain Cephalus?' asked Mackenzie, who had listened to the exchange in Greek with interest.

Kirkos nodded in the direction of Mackenzie and Preston.

'The English Captain is *Claymore*. The Lieutenant in English uniform is American. He is *Tomahawk*.'

'Aren't we carrying this codename nonsense too far, Kirkos?' said Mackenzie. 'We're not being introduced by radio.' He advanced towards the woman.

'I'm Mackenzie – and, for what it's worth, I'm not English. I'm a Scot. The Lieutenant's name is Preston. Call us Leo and Mac. We didn't get your name.'

'Christina . . . Christina Kirkos. My husband did not tell you that I might be here?'

'Your husband?' said Preston, shaking hands. 'You mean Kirkos here? But you . . . You're not Greek?'

'No,' said Christina Kirkos. 'I'm from Plattsburgh,

31

New York State. Some other time I'll tell you the story of my life. In the meantime, it's nice to meet somebody from home. You're the first American I've spoken to in three years.'

'Too much time is spent talking,' scowled Kirkos. 'It's time we were moving out.'

'Not before we see these sailors are all right,' growled Mackenzie, 'and decide what we're going to do about that stuff that fell in the drink. First, though, I'm going to dry myself. I'm freezing to death!'

He went to his kit, which Preston had propped against a rock next to his own.

'I've got dry clothes, Kirkos,' he said. 'What are you going to do?'

'I'll lend him some,' said Preston. 'And you'd both better take a swig of this,'

He handed Mackenzie a flask which he had extracted from inside his tunic. Mackenzie unscrewed the top of the flask and took a long swallow. He wiped his mouth with the back of his hand and looked goggle-eyed at the American.

'Ye gods, Leo!'

'Distilled by the gods, certainly,' the other grinned. 'Pure, unadulterated, full-strength, British Navy rum! You're really supposed to dilute it with water.'

'It's got a kick that would make the dead get up and walk!' exclaimed Mackenzie. 'It's like a liquid log-fire!'

He passed the flask to the Greek. Kirkos accepted it readily and upturned the neck into his mouth.

The sailors from the submarine came paddling back into the cove while Mackenzie and Kirkos were completing the process of drying off their purple bodies and donning warm clothing. All four navymen were in one dinghy. They had also, by some minor miracle, retrieved two canvas-wrapped cylinders which had remained afloat and they had salvaged the Greek's kit, which had been tangled with lines on the overturned craft.

Mackenzie examined the markings on the cylinders while Preston passed his rum flask to the sailors. As a result of his examination, Mackenzie announced that the cylinders contained food and radio spares respectively.

The two submariners who had been in the water rejected any idea of remaining to dry off, hinting that Barnard would already be three-quarters way towards a nervous breakdown as a result of their prolonged absence from the submarine. The four men climbed into the drier of the two dinghies and, with the other in tow, began to paddle vigorously out to sea. This time, with the offshore wind assisting their progress, their task was much easier.

'Let's go,' said Kirkos. 'The sooner we get away from the coast and into the mountains the better.'

'It's not as simple as that,' said Mackenzie. 'The reason I came by submarine instead of jumping out of a plane was to ensure personal delivery of one of the crates that is now lying out there in God knows how many feet of water. There's no point in me going on without it. I've got to get it back.'

'Explosives?' asked Kirkos.

'You could say so – but it's not really your business. It's my problem. Just take my word for it that without that crate, I might as well have stayed in Egypt.'

'It is too dangerous to stay at the coast,' said Kirkos. 'My orders were to get you safely to Karpenisi for the rendezvous with *Broadsword* as quickly as possible.'

'If I don't have that crate, meeting *Broadsword* will be a waste of time. It's the crate he's interested in, not me.'

'What about the American?'

'He's to get his orders from *Broadsword*. There's nothing to keep him here. Couldn't we send him on ahead with the lady as guide? You and I could hide out here until the weather improves and then try some deep-sea diving.'

'That is out of the question,' said the Greek. 'I have been away from my men for nearly two months. It is imperative that I return to them immediately.'

'You say that like you'd be happier to see them than you were to see your wife. What eats you, Kirkos?'

For a moment, Mackenzie thought the Greek was going to hit him. But Kirkos thought better of it. He said:

'War and women do not mix. She disobeyed me in coming to the mountains. She would have been more use to me looking after our house in Athens.' He shrugged his shoulders expressively. 'But she is American.'

Implied in that last statement was what the Greek obviously felt to be the entire explanation. Clearly a Greek wife would have known to do as her husband ordered her.

A sly smile – of the nearest to a smile that Mackenzie could remember – crossed the Greek's face.

'I shall go on with the American,' he said. 'That is the solution! I shall go on with the American and you can stay here with Christina. She knows the coast well and has friends in both Mesolongi and Agrinion. The American and I shall tell *Broadsword* the reason for your delay and arrange a new rendezvous . . .'

'Here, hold on,' said Mackenzie, 'Assuming we get that box out of the water, it's going to take two very strong men to carry it. It's no job for a woman.'

'You underestimate my wife's talents in this kind of work, Captain,' replied the Greek. 'It should not tax her resources unduly to acquire a mule.'

She's got the next best thing for a husband, Mackenzie thought grimly, but he was bereft of any positive answer to the Greek's astonishing suggestion. Kirkos called his wife over. She and Preston were deep in conversation in the shelter of the rock upon which the woman had first made her appearance.

Christina Kirkos, it turned out, was even less enthusiastic about her husband's plan than Mackenzie, and she said so in no uncertain terms. Kirkos silenced her with an angry outpouring of Greek and over-ruled her objections. She capitulated.

'It is isolated here and safe enough during the dark but it would be madness to hang around until daylight,' she told Mackenzie. 'We must find a safer place where there is shelter. We shall have to go north of the Naupaktos highway. It would be fatal to be caught between the road and the sea.'

'How far are we from the road?' asked Mackenzie.

'Less than two kilometres. I know a *kaliva* – a shepherd's hut . . . It's only a short distance up in the hills – but it will do as a base until morning. It's well hidden.'

Preston nudged Mackenzie in the ribs as they shouldered their packs in preparation to move out.

'It's always the same when I go on a foursome,' he whispered. 'I always get the ugly one.'

It was nearly three in the morning when the small party reached the east-west road which ran round Mount Varasovon and roughly parallel with the northern shore of the gulf of Patras. Not a thing moved along the road's length in either direction.

Kirkos and the American were to follow a track into the mountains which had the Evenos River in sight as a constant guideline. The foursome split up when, finally, the river came into view. Kirkos and Preston went north. Christina Kirkos led Mackenzie west across wooded hillside.

In addition to his pack, Mackenzie carried the food cylinder which had been saved from the capsized

35

dinghy. Preston and the Greek had taken the radio equipment. The food container on Mackenzie's shoulder had been designed for dropping by parachute - not for porterage. The cylinder itself weighed little — being of aluminium — but its contents of tinned rations gave it a weight of nearly sixty pounds.

Mackenzie cursed under his breath as he staggered along in his companion's wake. His shoulders and arms ached from his unwieldy burden, which he moved from shoulder to shoulder every hundred or so paces. The continuous uphill walking also drew from his thigh and calf muscles an unrelieved agony of protest.

The higher the pair climbed, the fiercer the wind howled. The sky overhead was now star-studded, the sleet clouds having been blown far to the south. The going underfoot was slightly easier higher up as the result of a recent sprinkling of snow which had filled up the treacherous hollows between loose stones and flinty earth.

They breasted a ridge and Mackenzie was aware of a sudden relief from the biting wind as they began to descend a twisting goat-track.

'Not far now,' the woman called back to him. He followed her through a narrow gully. Walls of stone rose on either side so that only a narrow ribbon of starry sky was visible overhead. The path was wet and slippery, the darkness almost all-pervading. Twice Mackenzie lost his footing before edging forward again with groping footsteps.

Suddenly the light grew better. The defile began to open out as they entered a natural bowl in the hills. On flat ground, at the higher end of this rocky amphi-theatre, was the shepherd's hut, sheltered against the northern wall. Lower in the bowl, the black water of a mountain tarn glinted in the starlight.

Light briefly bathed the doorway as the woman ahead of Mackenzie flicked on a flashlight and entered the *kaliva.* He followed her into the windowless hut, wrinkling his nose at the dank odour. At least the place was windproof. The floor was tramped earth and worn rock. In the centre were the charred remains of a fire.

The woman remained invisible behind the flashlight, allowing Mackenzie to divest himself of his load. He lowered it to the ground with a groan of pleasure.

The pair had exchanged less than a dozen words since they had parted company with Kirkos and the American. Now Mackenzie reached into a pocket of his capacious rucksack for a tin of cigarettes. He held the tin out towards the eye of the flashlight.

'Well,' he said, 'it's not the Palace Hotel, but am I glad to be here! Have a cigarette. Take the weight off your legs.'

The light moved as the old Turkish rifle was unslung and propped against a wall. A slim hand extracted a cigarette from Mackenzie's tin.

'Thanks.'

She placed the flashlight on the floor and sat beside him, leaning against his pack and the food container. Mackenzie studied her face as she bent forward to light her cigarette from his proffered match. He kept the match alight, watching in the flickering glow of the flame the highlights jumping along the line of her cheekbone.

She returned his stare without the flicker of an eyelid. The match went out.

'Will you know me again?' she asked acidly.

Mackenzie ignored the rebuke.

'That woollen cap makes you look like a boy,' he said. 'I have a brother of eighteen. You could pass for him.'

'Do you want me to strip off and prove I'm a woman?' There was an angry curl to her words.

Mackenzie smiled.

'I wasn't casting doubt on your femininity. I was

37

merely making an observation about your headgear. It isn't exactly a Paris hat,'

'And this isn't exactly Paris!'

He laughed.

'Paris it certainly is not!' he agreed. 'Look, I'm sorry if I sounded cheeky. This . . . this arrangement wasn't my idea. I'm sorry if I upset things. I know you would have been happier going on to Karpenisi with your husband.'

'Some husband!' she said with feeling.

Mackenzie gave an embarrassed little cough.

'It's none of my business, I know . . . But George was a little offhand with you when you turned up at the beach. He didn't seem overjoyed to see you. It rather shook me. I thought all Greeks were very passionate and possessive where their women were concerned.'

'With George, the accent is on possessive. But, like you said, it's really none of your goddamned business!'

Mackenzie held up his hands as if in surrender.

'I know, I know. I apologise for sticking my nose in. Let's forget it, eh? I just want to be friends.'

The hard set of her mouth and jaw softened. The beginnings of a smile flirted with the corners of her lips. She whipped off the woollen cap and released a cascade of raven hair. She gave her head a shake so that the hair tumbled more evenly about her shoulders.

'Sorry,' she said. 'I've been a bit on edge and there's no reason to take it out on you. I didn't mean to sound such a pain in the neck.'

She gave a sweet smile.

'Welcome to Greece, Captain Mac.'

CHAPTER TWO

Strangers in the Dark

Mackenzie lay on his back staring up into the darkness. He was shivering with cold. He had chivalrously offered one of the two blankets he possessed to the woman. And she had accepted it.

She lay only a few feet away from him, snugly cocooned in her sheepskin coat and *his* blanket. He could hear her breathing gently, but could not tell whether she was asleep or not. What a strange, disturbing creature she was. There was something absurd to the point of unreality in the unexpectedness of the situation he was in.

He seemed to have lost track of his true identity somewhere along the line, like a repertory actor who has been playing a different character six nights a week and has lost his fundamental self in a confusion of assumed roles. There seemed no sense or pattern in the turns his life had taken to lead him to this godforsaken Greek mountain-top sharing a roof with a gun-carrying woman who, until a few hours ago, had not even existed in his life.

Egypt already seemed light years away. Even further back in the misty recesses of memory was the special training-camp in Palestine where he had spent six reasonably enjoyable months learning the arts of secret war. There had been the intensively physical training – parachute jumps, commando courses, survival exercises, mountain warfare. There had been the less strenuous but demanding-enough sessions on map-reading, sabotage, radio communications, ciphers, and languages.

At the time, it had never been quite clear what it was all leading up to. Even since his series of briefings by related but quite separate government departments in Cairo during the past month, Mackenzie wasn't all that sure.

His introduction to what was called 'The Firm' was casual.

'You have special qualifications and knowledge which we can use,' he had been told by a bland Royal Navy Captain of Intelligence, prior to his posting to Palestine for special training.

Mackenzie felt that there were three different personalities rolled up inside him now – and it was difficult to determine which of the three was uppermost at any given moment.

There was the original, on which the other two had been superimposed: Mackenzie the happy-go-lucky journalist with the questing mind and the yen to travel; whose reports from the Spanish Civil War had helped his reputation but wiped away some of his romantic idealism. That was Mackenzie the civilian. After Spain, he'd had spells in Athens, Beirut and Cairo. He had been in Teheran at the outbreak of war, and had made the long sea journey round South Africa and home so that he could enlist in his native Scotland.

Commissioned in the Black Watch, he had become Mackenzie the infantry officer and assumed a whole new identity. The War Office, in its wisdom, had promptly sent him back along the route of his enlisting voyage – back round the Cape of Good Hope but, this time, to Suez.

He had arrived in North Africa in time for the long retreat from Cyrenaica and a leg wound which earned him an ambulance ride for the last two hundred miles.

It was while in hospital in Alexandria – in the next bed to a New Zealand officer – that the prospect of cloak-and-dagger operations for 'The Firm' had first arisen.

The New Zealander had casually mentioned Mackenzie's knowledge of languages and Eastern Mediterranean politics to a high-ranking friend. As a consequence, Mackenzie received an invitation out of the blue to report to the RN Captain at Middle East Intelligence HQ.

And thus Mackenzie acquired a further engrafting to his dual personalities of journalist and soldier. He became a spy. There was no other word for his new role. It demanded more than the onerous-enough task of soldiering behind enemy lines. It went a step further in that it demanded he not only fulfil an exacting function for Military Intelligence, but that he also engage in simultaneous espionage for a political department known as Section Six.

A shadowy eminence called Commander Six had spelled it out to him. Commander Six had stressed to Mackenzie the need to perform as zealously and as efficiently as possible the military assignment allotted to him by MEHQ. He was to be BLO (British Liaison Officer) to three Greek guerrilla units, each of which was known by the *noms de guerre* of their commanding officers: Cephalus, Orestes and Ionidas.

His purely military instructions would come from the British Area Commander – a full colonel called Garrow, codename *Broadsword* – who had been in Greece for eighteen months.

'Colonel Garrow doesn't know you will be working for my outfit, Section Six, as well as for him,' the Commander had told Mackenzie, 'but you will have sufficient autonomy and freedom of movement as BLO to keep him happy and do a useful job for us, too. Often you will find that the two jobs actually overlap. Your straightforward military function of co-ordinating guerrilla activities will give you an ideal opportunity to collect the special intelligence which we want.'

'What happens if there's a conflict of interest?' Mackenzie had asked shrewdly. 'What do I do if fulfilling my military obligations means having to let my work for you go by default? Or vice versa?'

'You must use your discretion,' Commander Six had advised him unhelpfully. 'Your work for us has priority as far as London is concerned, but we won't lift a finger to help you if you botch the job that is essentially your cover. Most of the people who work for Section Six do not have the protection of a military uniform if things go wrong. You do - but it's the only protection you have. There is no circumstance now or in the future in which we would admit that we employ you. You will be told of ways to contact us in certain emergencies — there are strings we can sometimes pull — but you can never let your work for the Section be used as an alibi or let-out for any jam you may get into. You will be completely on your own.'

'And how do I communicate with the Section? How do I pass on this intelligence you want?'

'You won't make any attempt to communicate with me or with the Section,' was the unequivocal reply. 'The Section will contact you at regular intervals. My assistant will brief you fully on the ways you'll be able to identify these contacts. Thereafter you will report verbally to them when they make themselves known.'

Commander Six had then asked Mackenzie a question which had taken him by surprise, if only because its relevance to the conversation thus far was unclear.

'Did you know that someone here in Egypt has been trying to incite mutiny in the Greek Brigade?'

'No. It's news to me, sir.'

'It could be the Communists. It could be the Germans,' the Commander had elaborated. 'The truth is we just don't know. But we hope that you will find some of the answers for us in Greece. We shall, of course, be making our own investigations here in Egypt, but I have a feeling that the inquiries at this end will lead us up some conveniently unproductive cul-de-sac. Do you like Communists, Mackenzie?'

'No, not particularly.'

'That's odd,' Commander Six had shot at him. 'I seem to recollect some euphoric reports you wrote about the International Brigade in Spain.'

So the Commander had done his homework.

'I was younger then, sir. Not that I take back everything I said at the time. I still have the greatest admiration and respect for some of the men who fought for the International Brigade. Many of them, as *I* certainly did at the time, believed they were fighting for freedom and justice.'

'But you have since tempered your views on what the Red Flag stands for?'

'Let's just say that I gained certain insights into Communism which gave me the impression that a dictatorship of the Left was no more desirable to humanity than a dictatorship of the Right. To tell the truth, I'm not really a political animal. My personal sympathies fly in too many different directions.'

'Good,' commented Commander Six. 'That reassures me that you are the best man we could have picked for this work. You realise that the biggest of the three guerrilla units you'll be working with is Communist-controlled. It is an ELAS unit.'

'Yes. I was briefed on that.'

'Well, your military brass will have warned you not to take sides politically. Yes, I see they must have. Well, we're not quite so dogmatic about things. We shan't mind if you hit it off with the Communists – without ingratiating yourself, of course. Your connection with the International Brigade in Spain could be helpful. If you let them think you are not unsympathetic politically, you may be able to find out what they're playing at. But don't overplay your hand. You will still be the official representative of HM Forces in their midst and I don't want Garrow to report to HQ that you're no bloody good. Understand?'

'I think so, sir.'

But now he was in Greece, Mackenzie wondered if he understood anything. Life back in the 51st Division was a far less complex thing. His Jocks were now well west in the advance from Alamein and that, he suspected, was where he really should have been, too. There, the issues were straightforward. It was the Jocks versus the Germans. Nothing more.

'Are you awake?'

The contralto voice from the darkness broke into his thoughts.

'No. It's too damned cold!' he replied.

There was a movement in the dark and the flashlight flicked on. He felt his blanket unceremoniously removed. He sat up.

'Don't get excited, Captain. There's no point in us both shivering.'

Christina Kirkos was folding his blanket double with her own. She sat down beside him and offered him a corner.

'Pull it over. It makes more sense to share the two blankets we have. Better than freezing to death independently. You don't mind, do you?'

'Not if you don't,' said Mackenzie.

'Good. I hate stuffy men.'

She snuggled close to him. A musty fragrance reached his nostrils — a mixture of damp woolly smell from her coat and a sweet body odour that was distinctly female.

'Don't be afraid to snuggle up close,' she said. 'It's the only way we're going to stay warm. I won't bite you . . . so long as you don't take liberties.'

He smiled in the darkness. He had gone tense with

self-consciousness at the first suspicion of bodily contact, but now he put his arm around her so that her head nestled just under his chin.

'This is a new experience,' he said. 'I've never gone to bed with a woman who was wearing a thick sweater and a sheepskin night-dress.'

'It's the only style of birth-control approved by the Greek Orthodox Church. My God, your hands are like ice.'

The numb fingers of the arm encircling her had touched the nape of her neck. She drew his other arm inside the covers and slipped his hand under her sheepskin coat. It rested on her sweater just above the soft curve of her hip.

'How's that?' she asked.

'I could get to like it.'

'Remember it's all in the line of duty. Now go to sleep.'

He awoke shivering with cold. The reason was soon apparent. She had gone.

Thin fingers of light were penetrating the hut through smoke-holes in the wall just under the roof and between cracks in and around the rectangle of the door. Mackenzie stood up and thumped his arms against his body for warmth.

The door opened and she was standing there, framed in it against a backdrop of grey, misty light.

'The wind has dropped,' she announced. 'And there's a hill mist. I think we can risk lighting a fire.'

'What with?'

'This,' she said – and dropped an armful of wood on the floor. 'There's what used to be a thicket of trees over by the lake. They're dead and rotten now. The wood's pretty damp but it'll burn.'

Once over the initial difficulty of getting the wood alight, they soon had a modest fire going. Smoke wraithed around the hut rather unpleasantly, but the heat from the flames was adequate compensation. Mackenzie, who had a bundle of sodden clothes from his excursion into the sea the night before, spread the garments around the fire.

'You're sure this smoke won't be seen?' he asked.

'Not a chance. Not while the mist's hanging around. If any wind gets up, we'll douse the fire.'

Mackenzie opened the food container and began to pack its contents into the special super-size rucksack which had held most of his belongings. He had decided that by carrying his blankets and some of his clothes in a roll outside his pack, most of the food would be carried more easily on his back.

Christina, meanwhile, brewed coffee from an American compo pack he had given her. With the scalding, smoke-flavoured coffee, they ate a breakfast of stewed apples from a tin and raisin biscuits.

'That's the first I've tasted in over six months,' she said.

'Delicious – even if it did come from a tin.' She read the label: 'Product of Tasmania.'

'We'll need to dispose of the evidence,' said Mackenzie, eyeing the tin. 'And that, too.' He nodded in the direction of the aluminium food container.

'How about the lake?'

'Is it deep?'

'Very. We could put all the trash in that container and fill it up with stones to make it sink.'

'Good idea. I'll also knock a few holes in the thing to make sure. Then I'll need to make my mind up what we're going to do. When would be the best time to get back to the beach?'

She wrinkled her nose.

'After dark. But you're not going to have much chance of finding whatever-it-is in the water at night.

46

Maybe now would be the best time – while we've got this hill fog. Or first light tomorrow.'

'If we could get to the beach under cover of the mist, we could make a try at the salvage work shortly before dark. And then get the hell out of it when it *is* dark.'

'That figures. George said something about me getting hold of a mule. Was he serious? I mean, is that contraption you're after too heavy for us to carry?'

'I'm afraid it is,' said Mackenzie. 'But where and how would you get a mule?'

'Buy one or steal one,' said Christina. 'They're not easy to get. Have you got any money?'

'Enough to buy a string of mules if necessary.'

'Then it would be safer to buy one. I'll get one from the Italians in Mesolongi.'

'The Italians!'

Mackenzie looked at her as if she had gone out of her mind. She grinned, enjoying his surprise.

'Why not?' she said. 'The Italians will sell you anything if you have enough money. Rifles, revolvers, grenades, food. They run the black market. Most of them are fed up and far from home. And Mussolini doesn't pay them peanuts.'

'I didn't think the Greeks would have any truck with the soldiers,' said Mackenzie. 'Didn't you say the Italians bombed the village you were in? That kind of thing can't endear them to the civil population.'

'Oh, don't get me wrong. There's no love lost between the Greeks and the Italians. There's nothing we'd like better than to boot their backsides all the way back to Italy. But they're quite a different kettle of fish from the Germans. They'll make these reprisals because some general has been under pressure to act tough and has ordered it, but the soldiers themselves have no heart for this war or chasing Greeks up into the mountains. They'd much sooner stay in their barracks or lounge around the taverns drinking wine . . . And you can't blame the Greeks for trading with them. You've no idea how desperate the food situation is. Children have been dying from starvation. People have been trading their family treasures to get enough scraps to make a bowl of soup.'

'I'd heard it was bad,' said Mackenzie with a frown. 'That's the really dirty side of war. At least in the desert it was soldier against soldier. The civilians didn't come into it much.'

'You care, don't you?' said Christina softly.

'Yes, I bloody care.'

Mackenzie snapped the words out angrily.

'Sorry,' he said quickly. 'I didn't mean to bite your head off.'

'At least it shows you're human.' She was looking at him with a soft light about her eyes. Mackenzie saw the compassion in her look and stared at her, his own expression softening. It was as if they were seeing each other for the very first time.

They had spent the night together under the same blanket . . . Held each other close for warmth . . . But this was the moment when they stopped being strangers and their awareness of each other as multi-dimensional beings suddenly intensified.

For Mackenzie, it was a moment of realisation that the turns and twists in his life leading to this mountain-top were probably nothing in comparison to the trauma and torments which his companion had suffered en route to the same location. She shouldn't be here, he thought. She should be back in some New York suburb, putting kids to bed or worrying about the price of sugar or a commuting husband's mortgage. The last thing she should be doing was living like a fox in the hills of Greece.

'You're looking at me like I'm Little Orphan Annie,' she said.

'I was just thinking how tough it must be for you . . .

After the kind of life you must have been used to in the States.'

The soft look from her eyes vanished. The curve of her lips tightened into a severe line.

'What I was used to back home! You've got to be joking. Look, Captain, don't start worrying on my account. You're looking at one little girl who knows how to survive. You're never going to find me starving . . . Not for the Stars and Stripes, not for the glory of Greece . . . Not for any man!'

There was no compassion in her look now, only bitterness. Mackenzie was at a loss to know why his innocent remark should so speedily and unaccountably cause her to lower a barrier between them.

'Famous last words,' he murmured with a note of wry regret in his voice. 'You sound so bitter and so very, very sure.'

'You're goddamned right I'm sure!' she said vehemently. 'A woman can always get by. No woman needs to starve in this stinking world. She's got something that every man wants — and if she remembers that and doesn't let the moonlight get in her eyes, she's going to get by.'

He wanted to reply angrily, but he restrained himself. He got to his feet and, in silence, began to turn the clothes he had been drying before the fire.

She watched him with mocking, provocative eyes.

'Have I shocked you?' she asked.

'Shocked me, no. Saddened me, yes. It doesn't become you to talk like some hard-bitten Cairo whore.'

'You're different from other men, are you?' she taunted. 'You're not interested in the only thing women have to sell?'

There was an edge of sorrow to his softly spoken reply.

'We all have something to sell . . . Innocence, honesty,

bodies, loyalty, integrity. I've always believed that it's what we don't sell of ourselves that matters.'

'Spoken like a saint.'

'I'm no saint,' he said, his voice rising slightly. 'But nobody *owns* me. And nobody ever will.'

Her smile continued to mock him.

'Spoken like a man,' she said. 'How self-righteous can you get! The Army owns you. Or are you a one-man army? No. The Army whistles and you jump. They say run – and you run. They say die - and you die.'

'You've got it wrong,' he said. 'The Army didn't buy me. I'm a volunteer. I voluntarily *gave* my services to the Army. If you own yourself that's something you can always do – *give*. If you don't own yourself you've got nothing to give.'

'Know what, Captain? I think you're a sanctimonious bastard.'

'That's your privilege,' he said. 'I don't really give a damn what you think. I think it's time I was getting on with the war.'

In sullen silence they went about preparing for the return to the beach. They removed all sign of their occupation of the hut.

In a far part of the bowl in the hills, Mackenzie found a dry fissure in the rock wall which proved to be an ideal hiding-place for the bulk of their equipment. He and the woman disguised it even more from casual discovery by placing loose rocks against the narrow entry. Into it, they had stacked Mackenzie's pack and Christina's ancient rifle. As she was going into Meso-longi on her mule-purchasing expedition, prudence demanded that she leave the rifle behind.

The last traces of their fire were carefully removed, although the lingering smell of smoke threatened to negate their efforts at concealing recent occupancy. It hung about in the still atmosphere and frustrated all their attempts at ventilation of the hut.

The absence of wind – which was to their advantage inasmuch that it aided the misty conditions to persist – also had a penalty clause, it seemed. It gave a clue that the *kaliva* had recently been occupied.

The descent from the mountain was a joy to Mackenzie after his back-breaking climb, fully laden, the night before. The only item from his kit which he carried on this occasion was a towel. This he wore scarf-fashion round his neck, the ends tucked into the outer of the two khaki sweaters he was wearing. A woollen commando cap was perched jauntily on his head.

They reached the east-west road without incident. From a vantage-point near the road, Christina pointed out the Agrinion-Kryoneri railway and gave Mackenzie his bearings for finding the landing-beach.

The sound of motor-cycle engines sent them scurrying for cover, German soldiers, acting as outriders, went speeding past, closely followed by a grey staff-car.

'Time I was on my way if I'm to get back before dark,' said Christina. 'I'll meet you at the beach as soon as I can. Stay well out of sight.'

He held her elbow briefly as she made to go. She looked at him with an air of impatience, eyebrows arched.

'Yes?'

'Good luck, Christina.'

'Save it for yourself,' she said. 'I know how to take care of myself.'

She covered the short distance to the road and began to walk briskly along it in a westerly direction. She had travelled less than a hundred yards when the sound of a labouring engine reached Mackenzie's ears. Heart thudding, he dropped flat on the ground. His eyes searched the road to the east.

An ancient grey bus rattled into sight. Two Italian soldiers in great-coats sat behind the driver. They cradled rifles in their arms. The rear seats in the bus seemed to be occupied by workmen.

Mackenzie knew that Christina had no chance of leaving the road and taking cover without being seen from the bus. There was *no* cover where she was. Nowhere she could run. He held his breath. His hand reached for the revolver at his belt.

Christina was still walking along the road. Surely she could hear the bus. It was making enough noise. She was making no attempt to leave the road. Mackenzie crouched, waiting, his hands suddenly clammy on the cold butt of the revolver.

To his surprise, the woman on the road turned as if hearing the bus for the first time. She turned to face it. Then she waved an arm. She was flagging it down.

The bus stopped. After a short conversation with one of the Italian soldiers who had climbed down on the wide front step, she got aboard. The bus trundled on its way. Soon it was lost from sight.

With its departure, Mackenzie experienced a strange feeling of total solitude. Nothing moved in the bleak, mist-enshrouded landscape except for a lone seagull scavenging inland and screeching its plaintive cry.

Mackenzie got to his feet. With a final glance along the empty road, he began to make distance from it. Half-walking, half-running, he traversed the lower slopes of Mount Varasovon towards the shore of the Gulf. He located the landing-beach after only a little difficulty, having reached the sea a quarter-mile away from it and not being certain at first whether he was to the east or the west of the location he wanted.

Then he recognised the spur of rock which identified the inlet he sought. In the shelter of a rock overhang above the landing-site, he paused to smoke a cigarette and take stock. The water was oily calm. It was hard to believe that this was the place where, only hours before, waves had crashed against reef in elemental fury. There was activity to seaward.

Two small coastal freighters — spewing oily smoke from their stacks to curl and hug the water — steamed up the Gulf to Patras, escorted by an Italian corvette with lines like a yacht.

The roar of powerful engines heralded the sight of a sleek German E-Boat which hugged the shallows of the northern shore as it headed west. Mackenzie watched it round the headland and disappear towards Troulis.

An hour passed. Mackenzie began to feel like the sole inhabitant of the earth. Loneliness pressed in on him and, with it, a growing anxiety for the young woman who had ventured alone into Mesolongi.

The sea mist thickened. Visibility was reduced to a stone's throw. The boring inactivity and his own impatience finally got the better of Mackenzie. He climbed down from his eyrie and explored the spur of rock. The water was crystal clear. Mackenzie could make out every detail of the seabed as he clambered along the rock. His surprise at his discovery of the water's clarity was accompanied by a surge of optimism. The optimism became a high tide of joyful excitement when — from the end of the spur — his searching eyes identified the unmistakable shape of a tommy-gun resting in sand about ten feet below the surface.

He decided to delay no longer the attempt to salvage the treasures resting on the seabed. Returning to the beach, he stripped to the skin.

The coldness of the water made him gasp. He endured it with gritted teeth and, after totally immersing himself, it became less of a physical pain and more of a constant numbness.

His first sortie resulted in the retrieval of the tommy-gun. His second produced a case containing a battery-charging machine for the radio. After this, he dried himself and pulled on trousers and sweater. His hands

53

were purple, like raw meat. He could scarcely move his finger.

He knew he would have to go into the water again, because he still hadn't found the most important case of all. It was an unnerving thought. Not for the first time, he cursed the lottery of selection processes which had picked on him to be responsible for a king's ransom in gold. He had been trained to a fine point of efficiency to drop into Greece from the sky, only to be told at the last minute that he would be landed from submarine because of a chestful of gold sovereigns needed to buy the loyalty of some very doubtful allies. From the outset, Mackenzie had been unhappy about the seemingly haphazard arrangements for getting the shipment to *Broadsword*. The powers-that-be were prepared to risk one of His Majesty's submarines and its crew to get the gold to Greece, but precautions for its safe delivery thereafter were decidedly offhand.

'We've got to trust Kirkos and his guerrillas to get you and the gold to *Broadsword*,' Mackenzie had been told, 'but they mustn't know what you are carrying, just in case they decide that possession is nine-tenths of the law. All you've got to do is keep an eye on the stuff without making a song and dance about it. Kirkos thinks that you are going by sea because he has never had any parachute training. He'll probably have about twenty men waiting for you on the other side to see you get safely to the mountains.'

Twenty men! There had been one girl! The whole bloody thing was a shambles from beginning to end. And Mackenzie's role was the most impossible of all. Whoever dreamed up the bright idea of passing off the gold in Greece as just another box of supplies had not anticipated that it would land in twenty feet of water or that a man and a girl would be left with the responsibility of portering it across sixty miles of mountain track.

54

Mackenzie was tempted to leave the gold in its watery grave. He stared at the water now, hating the thought of re-entering it.

He ate a bar of chocolate and smoked a cigarette and immediately felt better. His skin had a tingle as if his whole body was on fire. But he postponed an immediate return to the water. The day was creeping on. He would time his final effort for an hour before sunset.

As the time approached when he realised he would have to submit himself once more to the torture of the icy water, he ventured out to the end of the rocky spur in the hope that he could locate the missing case visually from above the surface.

A deepish pool to the west of the reef looked interesting. A patch of sand extended into rocky shadows. Any of the dark shapes in the shadowy section could be the box he was looking for. They could, he realised, just as easily be rocks.

There was only one way to find out.

Once more, he undressed.

Clambering as far as he could on the rocks, he lowered himself into the sea. He gasped anew at the shock which enveloped him. Several swift strokes carried him to above the sandy patch of seabed. Taking a massive gulp of air, he surface-dived.

Swimming deep, his exploring hands slithered over one loose rock, which moved slightly at his touch, then one that was immovable, then another. He half-turned as the desire to surface blotted out all other considerations. Then his paddling right foot struck against something that was not rock. He arched in a graceful half-somersault so that, now, his right hand groped in the area where his foot had been a moment before.

He touched canvas. It was the outer wrapping of a heavy case. He tried to wrestle it to the surface. It was far too heavy.

His lungs close to bursting point, Mackenzie surfaced.

An explosive gasp of sheer relief burst from his lips as he broke water and opened his mouth to drink in air.

A second noise crashed across his gathering awareness of his surroundings above water – a great roaring of noise which seemed to be almost on top of him. There was no mistaking the source of that sound. It was the fast-revving throb of an E-boat's motors, probably the same vessel which had passed so close inshore earlier in the day. Mackenzie looked around in panic but could see nothing.

He swam swiftly towards the rocky spur and clung to its craggy side. He felt so drained of energy that he was already half-resigned to the inevitability of capture. He had not the strength to pull himself out of the water. He crouched there, only his head above water, the noise of the E-boat's engines a doomful thunder in his ears. He inclined his head to seaward but could see nothing, only the wafting mist.

The roar of engines seemed to be getting nearer and nearer. Then they passed a climax of sound and, unmistakably, began to recede. They continued to fade in the distance.

Mackenzie hauled himself from the water and scrambled weakly back along the reef to the beach. He was half-crying with cold and so occupied in towelling himself with his uncomfortably wet towel that he did not hear the movement behind him. Christina's hoarse whisper of his name almost startled him out of his wits. She stood a few yards away, her face white with concern.

'When I heard that engine noise, I thought . . .' She did not complete the sentence. She was staring at Mackenzie, anxiety and uncertainty written in her eyes.

He faced her across the inadequate screen of his towel.

'It was an E-boat. It passed earlier today. I didn't

hear you come up. You frightened the bloody life out of me!'

'You're blue with cold,' she said.

'I've known better days for a swim.'

He folded his towel across his middle and pulled on a sweater.

'Do you have to stare? I'm not shy – but the cold does things to a man which I find embarrassing.'

'I didn't mean to stare.'

'Forget it. Did you get the mule?'

'Yes. It cost plenty too. Apart from the price I had to pay the Italian *caporale*, I also had to pay off four buddies. They've been commandeering every mule between here and Arta on the orders of the *Commandante in capo*. They've got a nice little racket going.'

'Have you any rope?'

'Yes – and a carrying harness. Pretty worn but it'll do. And I managed to get some feed, which is almost more difficult than getting a mule.'

Mackenzie was shivering. He said:

'I'll have to go back into the water. There's one crate I've got to get out, but I'll need the rope. Can you get it? Where did you leave the mule?'

'The mule's tethered to a tree, higher up. Do you want me to try to get it down here?'

'No. We might never get the damned thing up again. Just get the rope.'

When she returned, they both went out along the spur of rock. Mackenzie pulled off his sweater and handed it to her. He put the coil of rope over one shoulder.

'Here goes,' he said. In one quick movement, he had tossed the towel at her and slipped into the water. Marking the distance he had to go in his mind's eye, he swam out to the spot directly over the sandy patch of seabed. With a flash of hips and feet he dived. His hands closed over the canvas-wrapped box. He tried to work the end of his coil of rope through the lashing on the crate. The lashing had drawn very tight from its immersion in water. He tore his fingers trying to force the rope end between lashing and canvas. It just wouldn't go.

Although his lungs were again threatening to burst, he persevered. Furiously, he tried to make a gap between canvas and lashing big enough to get the rope end through. He succeeded in getting about four inches of rope tucked in the lashing. Letting the coil go from his shoulder, he thrust up to the surface for air. After a brief rest, he dived again. Tired, he had to swim in order to get depth. He wondered how much more he could take.

This time, he got about eighteen inches of rope end through the lashing, but all feeling had left his fingers. They refused to obey him. Every time he tried to loop the end of the rope into a half-hitch around the longer length of line, an invisible hand seemed to pluck it from his fingers. He surrendered his hold and drifted up to the surface. His legs and arms were like lead weights. It took him all his conscious thought to keep his head above water. He lolled helplessly, and what seemed like a gallon of seawater filled his mouth and nostrils and flooded into his lungs and stomach. He retched and flailed limply with his arms. Everything was going black. His head sank and nausea welled as more seawater flooded down his throat.

His arms grew weaker and weaker. He had no strength to move his legs. His chest seemed to be held in a tightening pinion of steel.

He was only dimly aware of an arm reaching round him and his chin being pushed clear of the water. A kicking leg touched his and he was being pulled backwards through the water.

He was aware of grounding on a submerged slab of

rock. The skin of his shoulders rasped over stone until he was half out of the sea, his legs still trailing in it.

He was able to breath now. He just lay there sucking in draughts of air in great shuddering sighs. He opened his eyes and saw only a dripping grey sky. He half-raised his head and a face came into focus. Wide eyes stared at him above an open mouth from which came short sharp gasps of breath.

'I thought you'd drowned.'

She was supported by one knee on the same rock as that on which he lay. Like him, she was half out of the water. Rivulets ran from her hair on to his chest.

'I couldn't tie the bloody knot,' he managed to say. 'My strength went. Christ, I'm half dead!'

He tried to sit up. The movement caused her to lose her precarious hold. She slithered over his body back into the sea. The only thought that struck him in that moment – and he was aware of its absurdity in the circumstances – was that she was as naked as he was. She had small, perfectly shaped breasts which slapped against his knees as she slithered over him. She regained a grip on the rock and trod water with her feet.

'Whatever it is you're trying to get out of the water, leave it. We can't get it now.'

'I've got to get it,' Mackenzie said stubbornly. 'I'll be all right in a minute. I'll give it one more try.'

'No you won't.'

There was a splash and she was swimming away from the reef. He watched her, his teeth chattering. She located the floating end of the coil of rope which had drifted to the surface. She dived, following the line down. A series of ripples billowed out from the place where she had disappeared in an arc of white flesh.

After what seemed an age to Mackenzie, a dark head reappeared. She swam towards him and held out an end of rope.

'Can you hold that?'

He took the rope and got shakily to his feet. He turned to help her from the water but, already, she had pulled herself on to the reef, where she stood breathing heavily. She was shivering and her skin had turned a reddish purple.

'I tied the rope.' she said. 'We'd better get some clothes on before we pull it out.'

Her clothes lay scattered on the rocks where she had thrown them. She gathered them now and began rubbing herself with what appeared to be an undergarment.

'You can have my towel,' Mackenzie said gallantly. 'I'm afraid it's not very dry.'

'I'll manage with this. It's an old undershirt – much more serviceable than a bra in the mountains. I never like wearing things tight round my chest. I'm flat-chested anyway.'

That hadn't been Mackenzie's impression a few moments before and, as she was now standing with her back to him, he felt it might be indelicate to move to a vantage-point where he could confirm or deny the statement. He said nothing. Wrapping his towel round his waist, he scrambled past her and went up the beach to his own clothes.

The feel of dry clothing on his back again was like being given a blood transfusion. For the second time that day, he began to feel his skin tingle from the top of his head to the tips of his toes.

He lit two cigarettes and crossed the beach to the spur of rock. Christina was dressed but still towelling her hair. Mackenzie gave her one of the cigarettes.

'Thanks,' she acknowledged.

'You're the one who earned the thanks. I've never been so near to drowning. I swear I was going down for the last time when you appeared out of nowhere. You saved my life.'

She blew a curl of smoke.

'You were underwater a long time,' she said. 'I thought you must have got into difficulty. That's when I started taking off my clothes. I felt a right ninny standing there in my goose pimples when you surfaced. Then I saw you *were* in trouble.'

'You're quite a girl, Christina Kirkos.'

He gave her a friendly pat on the bottom and moved past her along the reef. He picked up the coil of wet rope and began to haul in the slack. Slowly, he pulled in the canvas crate, like a fisherman landing a monster catch. Kneeling, he fumbled with raw hands at the knot Christina had tied. The wet hemp had already hardened to the rigidity of wood but he worked the end free. Coiling the rope, he slung it over one shoulder and tried to lift the box.

Its weight staggered him. The muscles of his back screamed complaint as he dragged the load over the slippery rocks to the beach.

'What in God's name is in there?' Christina asked.

'All the treasures of Cathay,' he said, through heaving breaths. 'I just hope that mule of yours doesn't buckle at the knees when we load it on his back.'

Between them, they manhandled the box up to where the mule was tethered. The last light of day had gone before the beast was loaded up and ready for the road. Mackenzie had dried the salvaged tommy-gun with his towel and carried it slung from his neck.

The overcast and the clinging mist contributed to the completeness of the blanketing darkness which descended and disoriented even Christina. The small procession blundered through it as best they could, but their pace was agonisingly slow.

After an age, they came upon the roadway without warning. The angle at which they reached it made them realise that they had been walking almost alongside it for fifteen minutes. Their arrival at the road coincided with a change in the weather. A wind gusted up out of the north, vacuuming up the mist clouds and revealing patches of starry sky.

They moved west along the road until Christina found the landmark which gave her her bearings. Walking ahead of Mackenzie, she pointed to a vaguely discernible track leading up into the hills. They began to climb.

Clear of the first ridge above the road, they were temporarily blinded by a furious snow-storm. They plodded on into the teeth of it, the snow clinging to their faces and front while their backs remained dry.

Rocks stood out like black marble tombstones on the whitescape of hill before them. Their footsteps were muted in soft virginal snow, which the wind whipped up around their knees and blew back across the tracks they made, concealing them within minutes of the imprints being made.

Mackenzie had lost all sense of time when, with a thrill of recognition, he saw ahead the narrow cleft leading to the *kaliva* hidden in the sheltered crater. He marvelled at the endurance of the woman marching steadily ahead of him.

She had the door of the hut open when he reached it. She took the mule-strap from Mackenzie's hand and coaxed the animal inside. Working by flashlight, she manoeuvred the mule to one end of the hut where some stones on the floor marked a partition of sorts, no more than eighteen inches high. She fastened the strap to a ring set in the wall – an adornment which had escaped Mackenzie's observation previously – and stepped over the low wall into the centre of the hut.

'I'll feed Hector and water him if you can unload him,' she said. 'Then, if you can get your stuff from the hole in the wall where you hid it, I'll see if I can find some more wood. I think we deserve a fire. What do you say?'

'I'm at the stage where I'm beginning to think it

would be worth getting caught by the Jerries for a mug of hot soup. I don't honestly think a fire could be seen up here unless from the air. I'm all for getting a good blaze going.'

CHAPTER THREE

Only Two Can Play

The paper wrappings from a packet of biscuits made fire-lighting easy. They dined on tomato soup, tinned steak and kidney pudding, with peach segments for dessert. Never had food tasted so good to Mackenzie and Christina Kirkos as it did that night.

Content and warmed by the dancing fire, not even the curling smoke which smarted at their eyes was able to diminish their feeling of well-being. Cushioned against Mackenzie's kit, they lay back blowing spirals of smoke from their cigarettes to add to the fire's pungent vapours.

'How did you meet George?' Mackenzie asked conversationally.

'In Paris. he was a student at the Sorbonne. I was a dancer at a club owned by a Greek. Some of the better-off Greek students used to be regulars at the club. It was the usual boy meets girl sort of thing.'

She blew a cloud of smoke.

'I came to Athens just before the war — to spend the summer with George and his folks. We ended up getting married. He was different in those days.'

'Different?'

'Well, yes. He was always intense. Serious about things — especially politics. But he was romantic with it, too.'

'I'm afraid George and I didn't exactly hit it off,' said Mackenzie.

'He changed,' said Christina.

'How do you mean?'

'His whole personality. The ideals he used to have. The way he treated other people. His personal philosophy, if you like.'

'Tell me about it. I'm curious because I'm going to have to get along with him and it's been mighty hard going so far.'

The words of Commander Six were at that moment ringing in Mackenzie's ears. Of all the guerrilla officers in whom the Section has a particular interest, George Kirkos, alias Captain Cephalus, was high on the list.

'He's a complete mystery man,' Commander Six had said. 'We know he comes from a pretty wealthy family. His family had shipping interests. We also know that he was involved with Republic factions when Metaxas was running Greece – and that wasn't a healthy pastime – but beyond that we know nothing other than that he surfaced not too long ago as an ELAS strongman.'

As he relaxed in the mountain-top *kaliva* with the wife of George Kirkos, Mackenzie had a twinge of conscience which he wondered if he could afford. This unusual, strangely volatile woman – whose relationship with him so far had run hot and cold with instantaneous and unpredictable switches of temperament – had saved his life only that afternoon.

Now, when she was off-guard and in a trusting friendly kind of mood, it was an obligation of his real purpose in Greece that he should pump her dry of every scrap of information she possessed.

He wanted to say to Christina Kirkos: 'Tell me nothing about your husband, especially if you have any love left for him, for anything you say in confidence will be treacherously passed on by me, filed in a dossier, and help earn me a special salary which not even the Army knows about.'

But Mackenzie did not voice his conscience. Instead,

he listened carefully to Christina's trusting analysis of the reasons which had brought about a seeming personality change in the man she married.

'He was different when he came out of prison,' she said. 'It seemed to make him cruel and twisted and secretive in a way he never was before. But maybe it's understandable that prison did have that kind of effect on him. If you get beaten and kicked around for no other reason than you hold different political views from the regime in power, it's bound to make you more bitter and violent yourself. George always was a terrible coward when it came to physical pain. It's a miracle he lasted more than a week in that dreadful prison.'

'How long was George in prison?' Mackenzie prompted.

'Nearly eighteen months. A lot of people were arrested when they tried to topple the Metaxas dictatorship and set up a Republic. George wasn't involved in the actual rebellion but they got round to him eventually. He was arrested in April 1939. We had been married nineteen months.'

'What charges?'

'The usual ones – trying to overthrow the Monarchy, forging documents, distributing illegal literature to university students, and so on. They sentenced him to fiteen years.'

'It must have been very hard for you.'

Christina smiled.

'Oh, I missed him at first – but it wasn't hard for me. Greek politics meant nothing to me and my life went on exactly the same as before except that I didn't have a husband around to keep me in line. I went to all the parties just the same, shopped in Paris for my clothes, went for vacations to the family villa on Melos. Oh, my life didn't change that much. I don't think George has ever forgiven me for that. He got round eventually to accusing me of marrying his family's bank balance, not him.'

Mackenzie offered her another cigarette and lit it for her.

'I'm not going to ask you if there was any truth in George's accusation,' he said affably. 'I shall assume it was a monstrous lie and that you married him for love.'

Christina turned over on her stomach and looked at Mackenzie sideways.

'Never assume anything, Captain Mac,' she said evenly. 'Especially about me.'

He studied her to see if she was provoking another argument with him. But she was grinning.

'I'll let you into a secret about me,' she said. 'The money a man has adds greatly to his personal charm as far as I'm concerned. Nothing turns me off quicker than a wise-guy with an empty bill-fold. The greatest aphrodisiac I know is the tinkle of diamonds or the rustle of folding money.'

Mackenzie said nothing. She *was* trying to needle him again. Well, he wasn't going to be needled.

'Well,' she said, 'aren't you going to say something? Aren't you going to tell me haven't I got the morals of a Cairo whore'

I'm not going to to be drawn into a silly argument with someone who saved my life only this afternoon – even if she did call me a sanctimonious bastard this morning.'

'I only saved your life because you make a good hot-water bottle. I was damned if I was going to cuddle up with a mule tonight.'

She smiled impishly and added:

'Come to think of it, there's a lot of mule about you. You've got fixed ideas about virtue and people. You like to get everybody in the right pigeon hole and label them like specimens. Once they're in their little compartments, that's it. Making you change your ideas would be like trying to move a pyramid. I bet you are ten times more stubborn than old Hector in the corner over there.'

Mackenzie shrugged good-humouredly.

'I don't think I'm like that at all,' he said. 'But if I were I'd still have a lot of catching up to do on you. You've stuck me in a pigeon-hole and got me all taped. OK, so I'll appeal against the findings some other time.

'You know, Mac,' she said sweetly, 'I'm probably the only woman after your mother who'll ever say this to you, but I could get to like you.'

'You were telling me how George changed when he got out of prison,' said Mackenzie, letting her last remark go. 'How did he get out?'

'The Germans let him out. After the invasion in 1941. They wanted George to work for them, even offered him a government post.

'What did he do?'

'He pretended to go along with them. So, they let him out, gave him his freedom. Then the first good-looking chance he got, he hightailed it to the mountains and joined up with that old bandit, General Spiro.'

'And how did his ideals change? You said his political views were different.'

'So they were. Before the war, he was a Republican – but a right-wing Republican. This didn't make him too popular with his father. Old Papa Kirkos was a great one for the Monarchy. But George and the old man saw eye to eye on strikes and getting tough with the Communists.'

'Is his father still alive?' asked Mackenzie.

'No. He died about a year ago. He just couldn't read George at all when he came out of prison. He wanted George to get the hell out of Greece and take me with him to the States. It's what I wanted to do, too, damn him!'

'But George wouldn't go? Why?'

'I don't know. He came out of prison talking Marx and Trotsky and bloody revolution. It seems that most of his friends in prison were of that persuasion. The difference between him and most of his revolutionary friends was that he got out of prison and they didn't. Most of them refused to recant, so the Germans shot them. George said that he revered them as martyrs but saw no point in following their lead. He wasn't going to be any use to Greece dead.'

'And he has been fighting in the hills ever since?'

Christina shrugged.

'Depends on what you mean by fighting. Bullying poor mountain villagers into submission and spreading the Gospel of World Revolution is more like. I've been with his cut-throats for nearly a year and they've kept well clear of the Germans in that time. The first sign of a German patrol and they move camp faster than you can say rabbit.'

'That's accepted guerrilla tactics,' said Mackenzie. 'Harass the enemy where he's weak and disengage if he shows up in strength.'

'George and his bullies haven't harassed any Germans that I know about. But they sure as hell knock the daylights out of any Greek who doesn't kow-tow to them. I saw ten of them club a poor schoolmaster to death because he wouldn't sign their goddamned enlistment pledge and pay the taxes they levied.'

'I haven't heard about any enlistment pledge,' said Mackenzie.

'George made *me* sign one of the damned things. Me, his wife! He was going to send me back to Athens otherwise.'

'But what is it?'

'Just a slip of paper acknowledging EAM as the Government of National Liberation and promising to serve in its army, the ELAS. There's also a nice little clause about death being the automatic penalty if you rat on the agreement.'

'An oath of allegiance,' mused Mackenzie. 'I suppose most armies have something of the sort.'

Christina gave Mackenzie a searching look.

'Most of the oaths I know are obscene,' she said. 'And that one isn't any different. I'll give you a friendly warning, Captain Mac. Don't expect to find yourself the centre of popularity when you get to Karpenisi. George's bandits talk about the British as Royalist dogs and imperialist scum. They are going to make your life hell. They may not lift a finger to harm you, but they are past-masters at the art of making you feel unwanted. I know.'

Her voice wavered with bitterness. For a moment, Mackenzie thought she was about to cry.

'They've been getting at *you*? he asked. 'The wife of one of their leaders?'

'I may be George's wife but I'm not his right-hand woman,' said Christina. 'It will be interesting to see how you get on with Petrea.'

'Who is Petrea?'

Christina smiled grimly.

'The sweetest bottle of poison you're ever likely to clap eyes on! That Petrea! She is political commissar for George's unit. Nobody in the outfit sneezes without her say-so. George dotes on her. Why in hell do you think he was in such an all-fire hurry to get to Karpenisi? He doesn't need me or want me when Petrea's available. God knows what he sees in her. She's as lovable as a rattlesnake. And I'd trust a rattlesnake further!'

This time Mackenzie could see tears sparkling on her face. He half-raised an arm towards her. It was a gesture in sympathy not quite carried through; an impulse to comfort which was retrained by uncertainty.

Christina read it and hurriedly got to her feet. She turned her face away and brushed a fist down her cheek.

'That smoke's going for my eyes,' she said. 'I thinkI'll get a breath of fresh air before I turn in.'

Mackenzie made to rise.

'No,' she cautioned him. 'Alone if you don't mind. I want to go to the little girls' room anyway.'

She went out. Mackenzie stared at the door. A mixture of conflicting emotions and uncertainty gnawed at him.

He smoked one cigarette. Then another. She had still not returned. He pulled on his woollen commando cap and went out.

It was a bright, frosty night. He walked as far as the lake without seeing her. He collected some firewood and walked slowly back towards the hut. Then he saw her. She was standing against the rock wall beyond the hut.

'Aren't you cold?' he called out. 'I've got some more wood. I'm thinking of hitting the hay.'

'You go ahead. I'll be in shortly.'

Inside the hut, he threw some more wood on the fire. It flamed and crackled fiercely.

He spread his poncho on the floor and shook out the two blankets on top of it. Then he raked in his kit for items of clothing big enough to supplement the blankets as coverings.

Kicking off his boots, he crawled under the blankets and lay staring at the shadows dancing in the ceiling. He heard her come into the hut. She moved about behind him, busy at her haversack bag.

He heard a sigh as she took off one boot and then the other. She moved about again, making only soft rustling footfalls. He waited.

A sleeve of sheepskin coat brushed his cheek as she clambered over his kit from behind his head and crawled under the blankets beside him. A hand sought his and gripped it fiercely. There was a desperate loneliness in that grip.

71

'I want you to know,' he said, searching for the right words, 'I want you to know that I can understand things better now . . . And I care.'

A muffled sob broke from her, as if she had been holding back for a long time. Her arms reached for him and she lay across his chest, clinging to him like a child in need of reassurance. She continued to sob but the sounds were muted by her closeness to him. Her body convulsed slightly with each sob. Each smothered sound and convulsive movement seemed to drive an arrow of pain into Mackenzie. She turned her face up to him. It was a shadowy mask against the firelight behind her, and he could feel but could not see the tears which fell from her cheeks on to the hand and wrist reaching to comfort her.

He held her close, letting the weeping spend itself. Slowly she calmed. She was the first to break the long emotion-charged silence.

'I want to be loved,' she whispered hoarsely. 'I *need* to be loved. I just want someone to love me and hold me. I've wanted someone to tell me they care . . . Even if it's a lie and they don't really mean it . . . I want to be able to pretend – if only for an hour – that somebody . . . just one person . . . cares whether I live or die . . . cares that I exist.'

'I care, Christina,' murmured Mackenzie. 'I really care. It's important to me . . . now . . . what happens to you. It's something I didn't plan or calculate. It's something I don't even want . . . But it has happened . . . God help me but I do care and I won't be able to stop caring . . . because there's no going back.'

She pressed a wet cheek on his and then kissed him on the mouth. It was a greedy, passionate kiss which sent shocks of trembling desire coursing through him. He cradled her round on to her back and kissed her with an intensity that equalled hers.

Reality intruded briefly.

'I want you, Christina,' he said, 'But it's madness. I can't help remembering you're that bastard's wife.'

'I won't tell him if you don't,' she said softly. Her fingers edged into the waist-band of his trousers and worked through until her hand was on the bare flesh of his back. She began to caress him softly.

He pressed his lips hungrily on to hers again. His own hands searched. They found the ties of the sheepskin coat. He pushed the flaps of her coat away and encountered a soft mound of naked breast. Surprise at the discovery made him catch his breath.

'I didn't wear the sweaters tonight – or anything else,' she whispered.

Until that moment, Mackenzie had believed that what was happening between them was spontaneous. He paused, checked by the treacherous thought that he was being led where she wanted him to go. But the throbbing excitement of his desire was greater than any newly arrived inhibition.

Her body was like satin. She thrust it against the exploring hand and writhed sensuously as he ran his fingers over the bulge of her hip to trail down one thigh and up the other.

Then she teased away from him and, with a wriggle which shed both blanket and coat, she stood up.

'Do you still think I look like your brother?' she asked impishly.

Mackenzie got to one knee and stood up. He grinned.

'There's absolutely no resemblance,' he said. 'And you were wrong about something, too. You're not flat-chested. You're beautiful.'

She playfully came towards him and unfastened the belt of his trousers. He tossed his sweater on to their bedding. She unbuttoned his shirt.

When they were both naked, she put her arms round him and teased her head against his chest, shaking the tendrils of her hair against his flesh. She kissed the soft

73

hair of his belly and then sank back on the blankets, where she sat propped on an elbow looking up at him.

'You have a nice body, Captain Mac. Do you mind me staring at you now? I've wanted to again – ever since this afternoon at the beach. There was something you said – and you were right. Cold water does nothing for a man's pride.'

'But you do,' he said softly.

She stretched out on her back, knees bent, legs open, and made a beckoning motion with her arms.

'Take me now. Take me.'

It was not an invitation. It was a command.

CHAPTER FOUR

Appointment in Berlin

Manfried Keller walked behind Admiral Wilhelm Canaris to the staff-car waiting outside the unpretentious offices at numbers 74–76 Tirpitzufor. The driver held the door open respectfully.

'We are going to my home,' Canaris told the driver.

Keller settled into the back seat beside the man who was the head of Germany's military secret service, the Abwehr. Canaris had been an odd choice by Hitler for the post. He belonged to the old school of German militarists and was a secret hater of the Nazis and all they stood for.

Yet Canaris had been boss of the Abwehr since 1935, a fact which testified not only to his staying power but to his cunning. The SS had never made any secret of their ambitions to take over the Abwehr and incorporate it to their own Intelligence Service. Canaris, however, had outfoxed them at every turn.

Keller was some years the Admiral's junior, but an old and trusted friend: It was because of this friendship that Canaris had invited him to dinner. In the comfortable setting of the Admiral's home they could talk in a more relaxed atmosphere than was possible at the Tirpitzufor offices.

The two men said little on the drive across Berlin. When they reached the house at Schlactensee, Canaris led the way in.

'I have something I want you to see,' he said to Keller.

'If nothing else, it will show you why I have a special interest in your work. The blacks* look on your part of the world as a backwater, you know, but that's certainly not my view. How do you find Athens?'

'Its a beautiful city.'

They were in the entrance hallway. Canaris pointed to a large painting of a proud-looking warrior wearing Greek national costume and brandishing a scimitar aloft.

'Well, what do you think of him, Manfried?'

'I am impressed. He frightens the life out of me. Should I know him?'

Canaris laughed and put an arm round his friend's shoulder.

'You are looking at one of my ancestors,' he said. 'That is the great Constantin Kanaris, hero of the Greek War of Independence. Now you know why I have a special interest in Greece and everything that happens there.'

Later, the two men relaxed in facing armchairs. They had dined well on grilled trout and were now sipping brandy.

'You know that Walther Schellenberg got Heydrich's job running the Blacks' intelligence service?' said Canaris. 'He's a clever swine. He has been tittle-tattling to Himmler about me.'

'Aren't you afraid they'll get you one of these days Wilhelm?' asked Keller.

'Oh, I can handle Himmler,' said Canaris. 'But life's not easy. Schellenberg is a persistent devil. He has been after Oster's hide for long enough and, poor old Oster, I may not be able to save him. If Schellenberg can't get the Abwehr in one fierce swoop, he seems determined to pick off all my best friends one by one. You must always be on your guard, Manfried.'

* The name given by the Abwehr to the German SS Intelligence Service

'I ought to be safe enough in Greece.'

'That's what I want to talk to you about. Hitler has been screaming in his usual maniacal way about what the Abwehr are doing, or rather not doing, in Greece. He can't understand why more than half a conquered country seems to be still in the hands of terrorists and we seem powerless to do anything about it. What *are* you doing about it, old friend?'

Keller, who was completely bald, stroked the shiny dome of his head.

'I am losing my hair over Greece,' he said with a twinkle in his eyes. 'Seriously, Wilhelm, I have not been idle. I have sown the seeds of quite a lot of mischief and some are already bearing fruit. I have agents placed now who can cause considerable damage to the enemy's war effort.'

'What we need is something spectacular, Manfried. Something which will keep Hitler amused and help keep the SS off my back.'

'Didn't you see the Cairo reports this afternoon? One arrived shortly before we left headquarters.'

'I didn't see any Cairo reports,' said Canaris. 'Not today. But then I was taken up the whole time with this distressing business over Oster. Where did you see the Cairo signals?'

'Schmidt showed them to me while I was waiting for you. They'd just been decoded. He knew they would be of interest to me because they were from my agents.'

'The damned things are probably sitting on my desk right now. What did they say?'

Keller smiled.

'The Greek Army in Egypt is in revolt. They have mutinied against the British.'

Canaris was astonished.

'*You* engineered this, Manfried?'

The other man shrugged modestly.

'One cannot make fire without combustible materials.

77

I merely dropped a lighted match where a fire hazard was known to exist.'

'Has there been fighting?'

'I don't know. The situation is not clear. The British have clamped a security blanket down on the entire area and information is apparently difficult to obtain. What we do know is that British troops have surrounded the Greek positions and that the Greeks themselves are in a fighting mood. They have been digging in and preparing to defend themselves.'

'Brilliant,' said Canaris. 'You have no idea how much time this will buy for us, Manfried. Schellenberg will be sick with envy.'

'That is not all,' said Keller. 'The British are going to think that the Communists are to blame for the trouble. The deeper they dig to find the causes, the more convinced will they become that the hand of Moscow is involved.'

'Manfried, you are a genius,' Canaris said with an ecstatic clap of his hands. He was on his feet with delight. 'You know, you should be here in the thick of things in Berlin and not in the field. Your talents are being wasted.'

'Not wasted, I hope,' said Keller. 'And you know me well enough . . . I would never be happy with a headquarters job. I like to move about – here, there and everywhere – setting things up, then sitting a little way back and pulling the strings. I could never be doing with the interference and constant battles you have with the Blacks.'

Canaris regarded his friend solemnly.

'You're not still dreaming up wild schemes to assassinate Churchill, are you? You know that I disapprove?'

The eyes beneath the bald dome twinkled.

'You always tease me about that, Wilhelm, but you always misunderstand me completely on the subject of political or strategic assassination. I know you think it's against the rules - not cricket, as the English would say – but there are no rules in our game. I'm a professional trouble-maker, remember, and it's the art of the game that appeals to me – its subtleties and bluffs and counter-bluffs, not some abstruse rule which protects a politician but doesn't apply to the politician's pawns, where the cost in lives destroyed is never counted.'

'Come now, Manfried. Admit you have a bee in your bonnet about assassinating Churchill,' said Canaris.

'I swear I don't,' protested the other man. 'Churchill just happened to be the target when I presented the idea for the operation back in 1940. But it could have been de Gaulle or Roosevelt or Stalin or Anthony Eden. The victim of the assassination was relatively unimportant to me. What mattered was the beauty of a single stroke which could never be traced to its authors and yet would cause maximum confusion to the declared enemies of the Fatherland.'

'But what does it gain in the end?' asked Canaris.

Keller sighed. They had had this argument before.

'Look, Wilhelm,' he said patiently. 'I am like you. I am a patriot. Neither of us likes Hitler and his gang but, whether we like it or not, he has involved us in a war which will either end in disaster for all Germans or great triumph and new opportunities to put our house in order. Germany has a better chance victorious than defeated. So, anything we can do in these circumstances which can save the lives of Germans is worth thinking about. The points I am making about political or strategic assassination are these . . .'

He enumerated on the fingers of his hand:

'One – the deed can be carried out by very few operatives. One man even.

'Two – it involves the death of only one man, the victim.

'Three – it has to be accomplished in such a way that

the blame for the outrage falls on the enemies of the Fatherland. The British must blame the Russians or the Russians must blame the Americans.

'Four – if the operation is successful, German lives will be saved because our enemies will be so busy killing each other that they won't be killing Germans.'

'It could go terribly wrong,' said Canaris. 'It could boomerang. It could have the directly opposite effect of the one intended. Have you thought hard about possible failure?'

Keller shrugged.

'Success or failure? I admit that these in the end are not what motivate me. One hopes naturally for success and puts everything into achieving it. But take away all the uncertainty and the game is not worth playing.'

'Damnit, Manfried, can't you see that that's a basic flaw in your whole argument!' exclaimed Canaris. 'Your motivation is what counts with you, not any of your high-sounding justifications. You are just a gambler, pure and simple! That's all this really means to you – the chance to calculate odds and then back yourself to out-think the other fellow!'

'Isn't that what life is, old friend?' replied Keller. 'Isn't that what you are doing every day of your life? You, too, are a gambler, Wilhelm. And if you'll admit it, the game only has savour when the stakes are high. The game is not worth playing if winning or losing is a foregone conclusion. Better to build roads or run railways or grow flowers, do something else altogether to pass the time between the cradle and the grave.'

Canaris refilled their glasses from a crystal decanter.

'I take your point about the game being all-important to you, Manfried. And to me, too. But that isn't and never will be a moral justification for political murder.'

'But the beauty of the game is the *only* moral thing!' said Keller. 'The weapons we use, the methods, the lies, the deceit . . . These, surely, are immoral if we do not invest them with a certain beauty of pattern and purpose. We can never be sure that the ends we achieve justify the means we use. So, why should we hold the life of a politician sacrosanct in a game where nothing else is sacrosanct? We can't afford such niceties. If it is all right to butcher ten thousand soldiers in battle and, as a result, shatter the morale of the enemy, is it not more moral and more merciful to shatter an enemy's spirit by removing the politician who is their rallying-point or the general who is their hero?'

Canaris smiled grimly.

'You argue formidably, Manfried, but your psychology is confused. You will never convince me. Destroying a public figure leads to anarchy. It is not our purpose to breed anarchy and perhaps unleash forces which we would be unable to control ourselves. We are players in a dirty enough game – but the game still has certain rules which we can abandon only at our peril. It is like a football match . . . The side which starts kicking and maiming in the hope of winning is often the side to end up with most men in hospital. Call me old-fashioned if you like, Manfried, but while I am still in control I shall never sanction political killing.'

There was a look bordering on sorrow in Canaris's eyes as he looked at his friend.

'Don't tell me you have already got some assassin-ation blueprints in your brief-case?' he said.

'They're not quite at the blueprint stage,' Keller admitted with a grin, 'but I do have two or three poss-ible candidates in mind. Just a mental exercise on my part, you realise. I haven't set anything in motion.'

'You'll never change, Manfried. You get an idea in your head and you play with it until it becomes an obsession. Who is it this time? Churchill again?'

Keller's grin broadened.

'He did come into one of my plans but there are some difficulties. I would have to lure him to North Africa

81

or somewhere in my area. Actually, I have been working out an unhappy end for the King of Greece.'

'Well, you can put it right out of your head,' said Canaris. 'I forbid it. That is not just advice from an old friend, it's an order. Do you understand?'

Keller nodded.

'I understand. You're the boss, Wilhelm. I'll dump the ideas. You have my word on it.'

They shook hands solemnly.

'I know I can depend on you, Manfried,' Canaris said. He did not let go his friend's hand. A new thought seemed to strike him.

'Something has occurred to me, Manfried. Forget what I said about dumping those mad ideas of yours. Don't throw them out. Keep them at the back of your mind.'

This change of tune puzzled Keller.

'But I thought you were totally opposed . . .' he began.

'I am. I am,' Canaris put in. 'But I was thinking of you. If anything happens to me . . . If Schellenberg and his gang finally get rid of me, things could become very unhealthy for you – for no other reason than we are friends as well as colleagues. If that does happen, it will do you no harm to have those assassination ideas up your sleeve. They're the kind of thing Hitler would like. You may need them.'

'This is no way to talk, Wilhelm. Nothing is going to happen to you. You are indestructible.'

'Keep your plans just the same. And promise me this . . . If you ever hear that the Blacks have taken over the Abwehr, send a cable direct to Hitler saying that you formulated the ideas for these special operations years ago but that I had always vetoed them. It could save your life.'

'I would not betray you like that, Wilhelm. I shall never bring up the idea of political assassination again.'

Canaris gazed steadily into his friend's eyes.

'I want your solemn promise to do as I say.'

Keller gave way before that gaze.

'Very well, if it will make you happy. I promise.'

'Good,' said Canaris. 'Now we'll sit down and you can tell me all about Athens. You are returning tomorrow, I believe?'

'I fly to Trieste tomorrow and then I'll be going by road for most of the way after that. I have several calls to make.'

'Ah, that should be quite a journey. There will be plenty of snow on the peaks at this time of year. I envy you, you know. I should like to see the Greek mountains in winter instead of being chained to an office in Berlin. Will it not be more dangerous for you going back by road? Those guerrillas are quite a handful by all accounts. You could find yourself under attack.'

'Oh, that's more than just a possibility,' said Keller. 'I can tell you here and now that we *shall* be attacked. I am depending on it. I have gone to a great deal of trouble to arrange it.'

CHAPTER FIVE

Stopover in Karpenisi

The cold light of morning brought a subtle change to the relationship between Mackenzie and Christina Kirkos. It was as if their night of love-making had exhausted for the time being all their physical and emotional needs. Each was aware of having in some way used the other to expiate some private devil. Now, they were both eager to be on their way to Karpenisi.

If, by tacit agreement, intimacy was suspended, so too was the hostility which had flared in the first twenty-four hours of their acquaintanceship. Almost a reversal of the natural way of things had occurred. They had not, as often happens, gone to bed as friends and awakened lovers. They had bedded as lovers and risen in the morning . . . just good friends.

The practicality of this arrangement was of value in the journey that faced them in the cold light of day. The trek with the mule to the rendezvous at Karpenisi turned out to be one of the most gruelling experiences of Mackenzie's life. It made him marvel anew at Christina's powers of endurance.

Their route took them along treacherous mountain tracks and along precipitous ridges. They battled the whole way against rain, sleet, snow and winds which cut to the bone.

They reached Karpenisi in mid-afternoon of the third day.

The town was in the control of guerrilla forces. These

fierce-looking men strutted everywhere: some in ragged winter clothes, some in uniforms of a kind. Most of them sported a little red star on their caps, signifying that they were members of ELAS.

News of Mackenzie's and Christina's arrival preceded them.

Mackenzie became aware of what looked like a deputation coming their way. The central figure of the group wore a British Army battledress tunic with red tabs on the collar. On his head was a Greek Army cap emblazoned with a red star. Mackenzie did not immediately recognise the officer as George Kirkos. He looked quite different in his new get-up. There was authority, arrogance, in the way he carried himself, and this was somehow magnified by the demeanour of his entourage, who formed a respectful semi-circle behind him.

He halted and allowed Mackenzie and Christina to advance the last few yards towards him. His entourage – an assortment of villainous-looking cut-throats to Mackenzie's eyes – lurched to a stop behind him.

There was no warmth in his greeting. He ignored Christina completely. His cold eyes were fixed on Mackenzie.

'You took a long time,' he said. 'We thought you had deserted.'

Some of the entourage advanced boldly and now grouped themselves around the newcomers. They studied Mackenzie with jeering, insolent faces. One made a ribald comment in Greek.

George Kirkos angrily ordered the man to be silent. He glowered at Christina.

'Go to the house, woman. You don't need me to show you the way.'

To Mackenzie's surprise, she showed not a flicker of dissent at her arbitrary dismissal. She scuttled off, pushing her way through the throng of men. Her eyes were downcast and her manner wholly subservient.

Mackenzie remained silent. The mule stood docile behind him. He felt at that moment like a lone pioneer of the Great American Plains who had wandered unwittingly into the lodges of the Sioux nation painted for war.

'Haven't you scum anything to do?' Kirkos roared at the guerrillas. The men moved off in twos and threes, leaving Mackenzie and the Greek alone to their confrontation.

'This is my territory,' boasted Kirkos. 'Look, I am now a colonel of ELAS. I outrank you, Captain.'

He strutted before Mackenzie like a peacock.

'You'll outrank me when you're a colonel in the same army as I'm in, George, not before. In the meantime, I suggest you start showing a little respect for His Britannic Majesty's representative. Where's all this Greek hospitality I've heard so much about? I didn't expect a red carpet and a guard of honour, but I did expect a more cordial welcome than I've got so far.

The Greek scowled.

'I warn you. Do not call me George. Here, I am Colonel Cephalus. Here, the names of the past have no meaning. They are dead.'

'All right, Colonel Cephalus. Anything you say. This is your territory. I certainly won't be the one to remind your comrade friends that Kirkos was a highly respected name in the nasty capitalist world until someone waved a little red flag in your face.'

The Greek's face turned white with anger.

'Watch you tongue, *Anglos!* There are some here who would kill you for that kind of talk. They know me here as a loyal Marxist. They know all about me and my family. So, just watch your tongue!

Mackenzie was already bitterly regretting the runaway sharpness of his tongue. It would hang him one of these days. What was it in him that made him lash out verbally on a personal level when circumstances

86

and the situation demanded circumspection and diplomacy, the subjugation of personal feelings?

This shortcoming, he realised, made him totally unsuited for the job he was supposed to be doing. That, he thought, and the fact that I'm tired and hungry and just can't stop myself hating this Greek bastard's guts.

'I'm sorry, Comrade,' he apologised. 'I spoke out of turn. Maybe you'll make allowances for the fact that I've been walking since first light and I'm hungry and dirty and angry enough to kick my grandmother if she looked at me sideways . . .'

He drew a hand across his brow.

'Look,' he said wearily, 'you and I have got to fight a war together – on the same side. Maybe we should work a little harder at it.'

Mackenzie had presented an olive branch. He watched the Greek's face as the other seemed to wrestle mentally towards a decision of acceptance or rejection. The anger gradually faded from those dark, intense eyes.

'You are right, of course, Captain,' he said. 'Forgive my manner. Perhaps I have lived too long in these harsh mountains. Now, you must let me conduct you to General Spiro. He is anxious to see you.'

'My orders were to report to *Broadsword*,' said Mackenzie. 'Perhaps I should see him before I do anything else, with all respect to your general.'

'The English Colonel has been very ill. He was unable to reach Karpenisi. He sent a message that you were to be brought to him after you had met General Spiro.'

'Where is the English Colonel?'

'Your American friend, Preston, has already gone to him. He is at a village some distance from here, Methravioplos.'

'I can't say I've heard of it,' said Mackenzie. 'Is is far?'

'It is well-named, eh?' said the Greek. 'Methravioplos

– the place of the day after tomorrow. It is nearly two days' march. But come, you must meet the General.

Mackenzie tugged at the mule's lead as Kirkos led the way towards a solid but attractively designed house built of timber and local stone. The roof supports were timber and a wooden balcony fringed the front of the building at first-floor level.

Two men, armed with sub-machine guns, lounged on the front steps. They nodded casually to Kirkos and reluctantly made way for him to enter the front door. The Greek waited as Mackenzie tethered the mule to one of the timber pillars supporting the balcony.

The house had at one time belonged to a doctor. Mackenzie was taken to a ground-floor room which had been the surgery. Two more guards were stationed outside the surgery door. Inside, a mountain of a man was seated behind a desk, writing. His manner suggested that penmanship was a most laborious and unnatural activity for him.

He did not look up. He was a picture of intense concentration as he carefully worked the pen in agonisingly slow movements across the surface of the paper. Suddenly, the pen slipped. With a roar of rage, the man hurled the pen down on the desk and gave voice to a string of curses. When he looked up and saw Mackenzie standing at the other side of the desk, the look of fury gave way to the nearest thing which that craggy face could muster to smiling benevolence.

General Spiro was possibly the ugliest man that Mackenzie had ever met. He had a huge shaggy head, with beady eyes which peered out from behind fat cheeks and a bulbous nose. Indeed, cheeks, nose and a fringe of forehead behind shaggy eyebrows were the only patches of flesh visible in a face covered by straggly beard and moustaches.

'Ah! *Zito oi Angloi!*' he boomed unexpectedly, and extended a podgy hand to Mackenzie.

Long live the English indeed, thought Mackenzie, as he had his arm pumped up and down like a bellows in a blacksmith's forge.

The house seemed to tremble as General Spiro came round the desk and proceeded to pump Mackenzie's hand all over again. He was massive, with shoulders like an Aberdeen Angus and legs like oaks. Mackenzie wondered if he had risen to his present military eminence by sheer force of physique and personality, or whether a warrior's brain lurked behind the small, sharp eyes.

Spiro produced a bottle and three glasses from the shelves of what had once been the dispensary. The bottle contained Haig's Scotch Whisky. Mackenzie noticed the sticker on it which read: *Available to HM Forces only*.

The General poured generous measures for all three and then held his glass aloft.

'To Victory,' he toasted. 'Death to Fascists and all enemies of the people.'

'To Greece,' said Mackenzie tactfully, and goggled while Spiro poured fifteen shillings' worth of good Scotch down his throat as quickly as the emptying of a thimble.

'I have heard all about you, Englishman,' said Spiro after the glasses had been replenished and all three men were seated on hard chairs placed round the outside of the desk. 'You fought in Spain, no?'

'I didn't do any fighting in Spain, General. I was a reporter. I worked for a newspaper.'

'It is the same – to fight with the gun, the pen.' He smiled roguishly. 'I . . . as you witnessed . . . I am more at home with a gun than a pen. But you are at home with both, eh? It is good.'

'I don't do any fighting with the pen now,' said Mackenzie. 'I am a soldier like yourself. I am flattered that you should know anything about me.'

'They said – those who told me – that you fought with the International Brigade.'

'I *lived* with the Brigade,' Mackenzie corrected. 'I starved with them. I got shot at and shelled and bombed with them - but only so I could write stories about them.'

Spiro beamed and put a hand on Mackenzie's shoulder.

'I, too, suffered with the Brigade. I was just an ordinary rifleman then. All courage and ignorance. But one learns in such a hard school, eh? Yesterday's green rifleman is today's general.'

General Spiro's goodwill was embarrassing to Mackenzie in its lavishness. He tried not to show his discomfort. It suited him admirably that one of the most powerful men in the ELAS Command should welcome him like a long-lost brother, but he set no great store by the man's warmth. There was an element of risk in being folded to Spiro's bosom. It was rather like enduring the embrace of a grizzly bear. Not too bad if you are another grizzly bear, but fraught with danger for the ordinary mortal. The fine distinction between a demonstration of friendship and the execution of a snipe-snapping hug was so marginal that the exercise was not to be indulged in without considerable caution.

It did not take long to discover that Spiro's ability to exude goodwill was matched by a capacity to expend thunderous wrath with equal facility. There had been a sign of this volatility of temperament in that introductory transformation from anger to benevolence when Spiro had broken the pen. Confirmation came when Spiro quizzed Mackenzie about the nature of his mission to Greece. Spiro had had no doubt that Mackenzie had been specially sent to him in response to repeated demands he had made to Cairo for guns and money.

'I know nothing of your requests to Cairo,' Mackenzie confessed to the guerrilla leader. 'All I know is that I am to act as liaison with three guerrilla groups and co-ordinate a series of attacks on German communications during the spring and summer.'

This was not the whole truth, but it was as much of his brief as he cared to reveal to Spiro in advance of any consultation with *Broadsword*.

Spiro promptly flew into a raging fury. He damned the British Command and the Greek Government-in-Egypt as liars and traitors and neo-Nazi imperialists. Both his wrath and his language were spectacular.

The only consolation for Mackenzie was that he, personally, was excepted from Spiro's vituperations. They were directed entirely at his superiors back in Cairo, for whom he was only an errand boy.

It came as a relief when Spiro finally ended the audience and airily dismissed Kirkos and Mackenzie from his presence. He instructed Kirkos to extend every hospitality to the British officer while he was in Karpenisi, with the rider that his stay in town would be brief, there being no reason why the *Anglos* should not be on his way to meet *Broadsword* at dawn next morning.

Mackenzie emerged from Spiro's headquarters into the chill of the late afternoon, pressed down by both mental and bodily fatigue. The effects of his journey from the coast were catching up with him fast. A panic of dismay hit him when he caught sight of the post to which he had tethered the mule with its precious cargo. The mule was no longer there.

'*Tō Moulāri?*' he roared at the two guards, who were still lounging on the steps. 'Where is the mule?'

They told him that a woman had come and taken the animal away. The beast had not been fed for more than a day, it appeared. The woman was going to feed it. There was no reason for the *Anglos* to get excited. What was a woman for but to do a woman's work?

'Christina has always been very thoughtful as far as

91

animals are concerned,' Kirkos said to Mackenzie. 'She will have watered and fed the mule and, no doubt, stabled him for the night. Why are you so concerned? Was it the explosives?'

'Explosives? What explosives?' Mackenzie's mind was reeling with tiredness.

'The big crate on the mule. I saw you had rescued it from the sea.'

Mackenzie had been on the point of denying knowledge of any explosives. Now, he hastily had to improvise.

'All my personal kit was on that mule, too. I thought it must have been stolen.'

'In normal times, anything you possessed would be safe from theft in these parts. You could leave a purse on the street and it would be returned to you. But these are not normal times. People do not have enough food or clothes or medicines, and you would be advised not to let any of yours out of your sight. Or your weapons. Any of my men would walk fifty miles on the outside chance of stealing a gun.'

Kirkos had his headquarters at a house a quarter of a mile distant. The owner was a scholarly man in his late fifties whom Kirkos introduced as the Doctor. Mackenzie never discovered the discipline of the man's doctorate, or whether it was simply a courtesy title.

He was shown to a narrow attic room unfurnished apart from a straw mattress rolled out on the wooden floor. His personal kit was propped against one wall. There was no sign of the other things which had been loaded on the mule.

'It is not luxurious,' said Kirkos, 'but it is dry and warm. Better than a bivouac in the open. I'll have some water sent up so you can wash.'

'What about the other gear that was on the mule? I'd be happier if I could sleep beside it. I've gone to a lot of trouble to get it this far.'

'I'll find out what Christina has done with it. We have an underground store shed at the back of the house. She probably had it put there. If so, it will be perfectly safe. The place is under twenty-four-hour guard.'

'I'd prefer it up here where I could see it.'

'I have told you it will be safe.'

Kirkos turned on his heel and left Mackenzie staring at the open doorway. With a sigh of exasperation he sank down on the mattress and took out his cigarettes. He felt a hundred years old from fatigue and frustration. At that moment, he would have given a year's pay to be back in the heat and dust of the desert with his uncomplicated Jocks.

Mackenzie dined that night in comparative style. After aperitifs in the form of ouzo, there was a filling meal of *kokoretsi* – a dish which he decided was the Greek version of haggis. It was a long thin sausage made from goat offal and an assortment of herbs. It tasted delicious.

In addition to the Doctor, Kirkos, Christina and himself around the table, there was a coldly beautiful blonde with a voluptuous figure. He knew, even before the introductions were made, that this was the Petrea of whom Christina had spoken in unflattering terms. She was wearing khaki shirt and slacks and, like Kirkos, she was not given to smiling.

In pre-war Athens, Mackenzie had often enjoyed typically Greek dinners in the homes of friends and in restaurants. These occasions had been memorable for the joy that had been generated with much talk and laughter.

Dinner at the house in Karpenisi was the opposite. The meal was eaten in almost total silence. They were served by a skinny peasant girl who limped and shuffled grotesquely because of the misfortune of a tubercular hip.

When the girl finally cleared away the dishes, Kirkos produced a stone jar of cognac.

'Now we shall drink!' he announced. 'The good Captain saw fit to rebuke me this afternoon on my lack of warmth in welcoming him after his long march. We much repair the image he has of Greek hospitality.

'There's really no need on my account,' said Mackenzie. 'I enjoyed my meal immensely and I'm tired enough to sleep the clock round. If it's all right with you, I'd just as soon toddle off to bed.'

'You are rejecting my hospitality?' asked Kirkos. 'You disappoint me, Captain. I thought that you were the one who said we should work harder at understanding each other. What better way is there to do that than share a flagon of brandy?'

The Greek's eyes were boring into his, challenging.

'Perhaps,' said Petrea, 'the *Anglos* has found Christina's company too exhausting these last few days and fears that ours will be dull.'

'Just what the hell do you mean by that?' flared Christina.

The Doctor, with a glance first at Petrea and then at Christina, rose hurriedly.

'Excuse me, please. There are things I must do. You will forgive me, Colonel, if I do not stay and drink. There are my reports . . . You know what it is.'

'Of course, Doctor,' said Kirkos. 'You must go. But I hope the Captain will stay just a little longer to tell us about his adventures. Christina has been so vague in bringing me up to date with their travels.'

He handed Mackenzie a brimming glass as the Doctor made his tactical withdrawal.

Kirkos raised his glass.

'To Anglo-Greek co-operation,' he toasted.

Mackenzie accepted the glass and raised it.

'I'll drink to that,' he said.

'I think I'll go to bed,' said Christina. She looked uncomfortable and panicky.

'You will stay,' said Kirkos.

Rebellion flashed briefly in Christina's eyes. She had half risen from the table. She promptly sat down again.

'Very well, if you insist.

'I insist,' said Kirkos. He studied Mackenzie with a cold smile playing about his lips. 'Well, Captain, I have to congratulate you.'

'For what?'

'Three days in your comapny has been good for Christina. It has worked wonders for her. Haven't you noticed how obedient she is to me?'

'It is always the same,' said Petrea. 'Just like the last time.'

'Shut up, you bitch!' said Christina.

'Ladies, ladies,' said Kirkos soothingly. 'What will our guest think if you spit at each other like cats?'

Mackenzie didn't know what to think. He did not like the way the conversation was heading. And he cared even less for the undercurrents between the two women. He realised he was sweating.

Petrea was staring at him as if a distinctly bad smell was emanating from his direction.

'You are the cool one, *Anglos*.' she said. 'How you can sit and drink at the same table as the man you have dishonoured is beyond me.' She turned to Kirkos. 'And how you can encourage this charade, Colonel, makes even less sense.'

'Just what the hell are you talking about?' asked Mackenzie.

'I'm talking about you and that slut!' said Petrea with an angry toss of her head in Christina's direction.

It was too much for Christina. She picked up a glass from the table in front of her and threw the contents in Petrea's face. They would have been at each other's throats if Kirkos had not thrown himself between them. He restrained Petrea and nodded towards the door for Christina's benefit.

'Go now,' he ordered.

Christina ran from the room, tears coursing down her face.

'You'd better leave us, too,' he told Petrea. The girl left the room with a final malevolent glare at Mackenzie.

'You must forgive Petrea,' said Kirkos to Mackenzie. 'She looks on all Westerners such as yourself as decadent and corrupt. She is a very puritanical woman. And, unfortunately, she sees herself as guardian not only of public morality but of my personal life.'

'She has a dirty mouth and a dirtier mind,' snapped Mackenzie angrily.

Kirkos lit a cigarette and blew a cloud of smoke across the table.

'Petrea is Political Commissar for my Battalion,' he said. 'She wields a great deal of power and influence.'

'And who winds Petrea up and keeps her ticking, in an ideological sense? Does she get her orders from Athens or direct from Moscow?' Mackenzie flung out the question boldly. Something was needed to get the conversation away from the emotional background where the two women had drawn swords.

Kirkos gave Mackenzie a searching look.

'Petrea is under my command,' he said sharply. Then he saw the disbelieving look on Mackenzie's face. He grimaced. 'You don't believe me? Of course, I was forgetting that you had experience of these things in Spain. All right, so Petrea gets her orders from Athens. It's no secret. Why are you so interested?'

'It's my job to get to know how you people work,' said Mackenzie.

Kirkos refilled his glass and topped up Mackenzie's. His aim with the flagon was unsteady and some of the liquid splashed on the table.

'I'm getting a little drunk,' he said. 'General Spiro isn't always so generous with his whisky as he was this afternoon. What else do you want to know about ELAS, Captain?'

'Who gives you your orders?' asked Mackenzie. 'Commissar Petrea?'

Kirkos flushed. For a moment, Mackenzie thought he had pushed the Greek too far. His male ego was obviously bruised by the suggestion that a woman kept him in line. But the Greek controlled his feelings well.

'Petrea's function is political,' he said. 'Mine is military. Were you trying to suggest our relationship was more personal than that?'

'Not at all.'

'Surely Christina said something to you? She is very jealous of Petrea.'

'I can't think why,' said Mackenzie.

Kirkos drained his cognac. He laughed. He *was* getting drunk.

'Christina thinks I sleep with Petrea,' he confided. He found the idea highly amusing. 'What Christina doesn't understand about Petrea,' he went on, 'is that Petrea would stop doing my bidding the minute I jumped into bed with her.'

'I'm afraid I don't understand either,' said Mackenzie.

'Surely you noticed how she dotes on me?' said Kirkos.

'Yes, I did get that impression.'

'It's not my body she loves,' said Kirkos. 'It's my politics.'

'*Chacun à son goût*,' murmured Mackenzie.

'Don't mock me, Captain. I'm telling you all this because I don't want you to get the wrong impression of my relationship with Petrea. She loves me for the purity of my political doctrine, nothing else. I have never laid a finger on her and never shall – because it would reveal to her that I am human after all and not divine. Sex to her is just a function for the procreation of little Marxists. To sleep with a man for the fun of it is beyond her comprehension. That's why she's so puritanical.

'You are being very frank with me.' said Mackenzie.

'Perhaps it is the cognac,' said Kirkos. 'Or maybe,' and he said this almost to himself, 'I have too many secrets. I have to talk to somebody.'

He splashed more cognac into the glasses, draining his own in a gulp. He blinked across the table at Mackenzie.

'My secrets are safe with you,' he said. 'Petrea will do my bidding for as long as she has this political crush on me, this Marxist-Leninist worship . . . She thinks I am a Messiah. And Messiahs can do no wrong.'

'Freud would be very interested in your relationship,' observed Mackenzie drily. He had not been keeping pace with Kirkos, drink for drink, and was now alert to the possibility of extracting more information from the Greek than could be obtained by six months' patient investigation. There was no saying what revelations he would make if he persisted in emptying the flagon of cognac.

The glow of superiority which flared in Mackenzie as a result of feeling master of the situation was brutally extinguished in the next instant. He was totally unprepared for the question which Kirkos threw at him out of the blue.

'Did you enjoy screwing my wife?' asked the Greek.

Mackenzie was caught completely off guard. He was flustered and could not conceal the fact.

'What kind of bloody thing is that to say to a man?' he blurted defensively. He could feel his guilt showing as surely as if he wore a placard around his neck proclaiming his adultery.

Kirkos was grinning at him evilly.

'Did you think I did not know?' he snorted. 'Do you take me for a complete and utter fool? I knew it the moment I saw the pair of you this afternoon. Christina always gives herself away. Surely you saw how docile she was — how I just had to wave a finger and she jumped? I saw it right away! Petrea noticed it the moment she set foot in the house!'

Mackenzie sat in silence. He felt like the gladiator, disarmed and helpless, who lies in the arena awaiting the *coup de grâce*. Why had he ever allowed himself to get involved with Christina? Why? He made a final try to bluff his way out of the mess.

'You've got things all wrong,' he said. 'Your wife wouldn't look twice at me.'

Kirkos was not buying it.

'An innocent man's reaction, especially that of a British officer, would have been much more indignant, Captain. You are a very poor liar. But you needn't look so worried. I am not going to make a big scene. I may take it out on her, but not you. You can wait.'

'If you dare harm her . . .'

'Yes? What will you do?'

Mackenzie glared at Kirkos.

'I had you figured for a bully,' he said. The desire to punch that coldly smiling face was strong in him.

The cold smile vanished. There was only malice now in the Greek's face, but his tone was almost forgiving.

'It was probably not your blame,' he said. 'You are not the first with Christina — not by a long way — but you may be the last.' The flicker of a smile returned. 'I really do hope my insatiable wife gave you some pleasure, Captain. After all you *did* save my life the other night. I owed you some small favour in return. Perhaps you will concede that the debt has now been adequately repaid — even if I did get rather the better of the bargain.

Mackenzie moved against the table and seized the other man by the front of his jacket.

'You rotten bastard . . .'

Kirkos shook himself free and stood up.

'Just how much of a bastard I am, Captain, is something you're going to have to wait to find out!'

CHAPTER SIX

Action in Prospect

The three-engined Junkers transport taxied to a halt. To the west, beyond the town of Ioannina some six kilometres away, the last light of day was fading from the sky.

Manfried Keller walked from the aircraft, pulling his knee-length leather coat tightly about him. Greece was not much warmer than Albania, he decided. He had left Tirana in mid-afternoon, having abandoned his earlier plan to travel by the murderous road which traversed the spine of Albania and the mountains of north-west Greece.

Hoffman was waiting for him at the airfield with a staff-car. Keller got into the passenger seat and expressed the hope that his younger colleague from Athens had not been waiting too long.

'Any word from our friend in the mountains?' asked Keller when they were speeding towards Ioannina.

'Yes, but nothing definite yet. More British officers have been arriving from Egypt and something is in the wind. But our friend had no details.'

'Have you see von Harzer?' asked Keller.

'This morning, just after I got in from Athens. He wants us to dine with him this evening.'

'That will be no hardship. He keeps a good table. Is he still champing at the bit for the action I promised him?'

Hoffman grinned.

'He gets more and more impatient. He is fed up with our convoys being ambushed and then wild goose chases into the hills with not a guerrilla to be found.'

'What kind of force is he putting at our disposal?' asked Keller.

'Three companies and vehicles to carry them.'

'Good for von Harzer,' said Keller. 'He thought we'd be lucky to get a couple of platoons of aged infantrymen. What are the companies? Any good?'

'They're experienced men mostly. They've been made up to strength since their Division was withdrawn from the Eastern front. One mortar company, one machine-gun company, and a company of riflemen.'

'Excellent,' said Keller. 'We'll see how good the Greeks are when the opposition isn't a couple of truckloads of World War One veterans and a handful of walking wounded.'

A new moon was throwing a streak of silver across the waters of Lake Pambotis as Keller's car entered the outskirts of Ioannina. The domes and minarets of the town's ancient mosques were grey shapes against a velvet sky.

The car drew up in the paved court of a long white building with stone-flagged gardens. Its arched windows and doors reflected an Ottoman influence on the architecture. Two sentries sprang briskly to attention as Keller and Hoffman strode into the building.

'Ah, gentlemen. You're just in time. Colonel von Harzer asked me only this minute to telephone the airfield to see if the plane had arrived from Tirana. He hoped you would be in time for a glass of wine before dinner.'

The grey-haired Wehrmacht captain who greeted Hoffman and Keller just inside the front door had a chestful of Great War ribbons and walked with a stiff leg. Clicking his heels, he bowed briefly towards Keller.

'I trust you had a good flight, Colonel-General.'

102

'It was bumpy over the mountains but it hasn't impaired my appetite,' said Keller.

Half an hour later, Keller was standing, glass in hand, deep in conversation with Colonel Franz von Harzer, commander of the German forces in north-west Greece. The Colonel was in good spirits. To him, the very fact that Keller had returned to Greece was a sign that long-awaited action was in prospect. He hated occupation duty and he seldom lost an opportunity to say so to anyone who cared to listen. For once, however, this was not his theme as he talked earnestly to Keller.

'Do you honestly think the guerrillas will throw a thousand men into this?' he was asking. 'If we could draw such an army of these bandits out into the open and make mincemeat of them, it would be worth a hundred punitive expeditions into these damned mountains. And quite a feather in my cap, too!'

Keller smiled.

'I can't promise you anything, Franz, and damned well you know it! I didn't know, remember, whether you would be able to supply twenty men or a couple of platoons for this operation. In any case, my object is more than a victory for you and your men. These guerrillas seem to want to fight each other more than they want to fight us and there's an outside chance that we'll be able to give them a helping hand.'

'The Greeks and their wretched politics!' said the Colonel. 'I shall never understand them. I would rather be in the desert with the Afrika Korps – even if they're up against it just now.'

'Don't say that too loud,' said Keller. 'If my scheme goes wrong, we could both finish up in the desert! And not with staff jobs . . . digging latrines!'

CHAPTER SEVEN

Army on the March

Mackenzie marched like an automaton. Hector the mule trotted along faithfully in his wake. Man and mule occupied an isolated position in the long column of men.

Mackenzie was about fifty yards behind the main body of a hundred and fifty guerrillas. He was about the same distance ahead of a rear-guard of more than fifty men.

Kirkos was not only guiding the British officer personally to Methravioplos, he was taking his entire command with him. Mackenzie would have been quite happy to leave the lot in Karpenisi but, since he was to be co-ordinating the ELAS battalion's operations with two other guerrilla units, there was no reason to oppose Kirkos's declaration of what he intended to do. They had set off from Karpenisi at first light after Mackenzie had spent a night divided into periods of wakefulness and tortured dreamings.

Quarantined with the mule between the two bodies of marchers, Mackenzie now coaxed on his mule with friendly one-sided conversation. This included repeated observations that the mule was a much nobler and more intelligent creature than the two-footed lamebrain doing all the talking.

Mackenzie was in a bitter, self-condemnatory mood. From the moment he had set foot in Greece, things had started to go wrong. And he had complicated matters considerably by behaving like an adolescent idiot. His orders had been to win the trust of the ELAS guerrillas. Instead, he had formed an adulterous relationship with the wife of one of their leaders and thus made an implacable enemy.

He couldn't figure Kirkos at all. If, after finding out about his wife's affair, the Greek had come at him with a knife, Mackenzie could have understood it. He would even have preferred it. He just couldn't make out the man at all.

At first acquaintanceship, Mackenzie had put Kirkos down as one of those surly boors whose character was all on the surface. But the more he saw of him the more he came to realise that his first impressions were far wide of the mark. There were twisted and concealed depths to the man which suggested a very complex personality indeed.

He was never exactly what he seemed at any given moment.

His behaviour the day before had illustrated this amply. It had ranged from hostile to warmly confidential and back to hostile again. How much of what Kirkos revealed to the world was his true self – and how little? His relationship with Petrea was beyond belief. Did it betray a man who was ruthlessly ambitious to obtain power as a politician or as a soldier, or as both? At times, talking about Petrea and Marxism, he had sounded blatantly cynical about politics. At others, he had sounded so neck-deep in dogma as to be fanatical.

Mackenzie could not rid himself of the feeling that Kirkos was a total fraud, that he was none of the things he claimed to be or appeared to be, but a sham of such proportions that there were times when even the man himself could not distinguish between his real being and the image he was projecting.

The more Mackenzie tried to figure things out, the

more his mind seemed to whirl. Only one thing was sure. Kirkos was not just the bloody-minded Greek he had at first taken him to be. He was altogether much more dangerous and incalculable an animal.

If Mackenzie had any lingering doubts about the vicious hostility which the EAM propagandists had whipped up amongst the guerrillas for direction against the British, they vanished long before the column reached Methravioplos. He found he was as welcome among them as the carrier of bubonic plague. Whether they were on orders to do so or not, he had no idea, but they treated him with such open insolence, or malicious contempt, that it became increasingly difficult for him to contain his smouldering fury.

Methravioplos was one of those mountain villages which had no apparent reason for existing. It wasn't on a road going anywhere or from anywhere: simply a collection of houses nestled on a mountain shelf. One access was a stony track which connected the village with another track, which connected eventually with the road which wound over the Pindus mountains and connected the towns of Arta and Trikala.

There was only one way the village could be approached by strangers without first being seen from a considerable distance – and that was over the summit of the snow-capped peak below which the village lay. This was a route of approach which would have made a fully equipped Everest expedition pause for thought before attempting it.

Mackenzie and the guerrillas, approaching from the south, arrived by a route that was only slightly less difficult. They could see the village and be seen from it while still a good hour's journey away, as they negotiated a rocky path barely eight feet wide. The mountain towered on one side and a precipitous drop lay below them on the other. In places, the path narrowed to no more than a ledge, where single file was necessary.

When the column came to a complete standstill some distance from the village and showed no sign of moving, Mackenzie led his mule forward through the snake of troops straggled along nearly a mile and a half of mountain path. They were not enthusiastic to let him pass but he refused to be intimidated and kept pushing through them.

The hold-up had occurred at the head of the column. Here, the path widened slightly and curved in towards the heart of the mountain and away from the precipice, so that the route was dominated on the right by the mountain itself and on the left by an upcurled lip of rock which obscured the valley below.

On each side of this defile, men with rifles were covering any further advance by the column. On the path itself, a burly figure in an army great-coat was standing pistol in hand and blocking the way of Kirkos and Petrea. Angry words were being exchanged.

Mackenzie pushed to the front.

'What's the trouble?' he asked. 'Why have we stopped?'

'Because this goat here has ordered us to stop,' said Kirkos. 'He says his men will open fire if we advance another step.'

The man in the great-coat was a handsome giant with alert eyes and a slightly hawkish nose which did not detract from his good looks. There was something very business-like about the man which commanded Kirkos's caution.

'Who are you?' asked Mackenzie in Greek.

'Orestes,' Kirkos replied for him. 'Captain Orestes, a mercenary of the Fascist King George, and a collaborationist spy.'

Captain Orestes gazed at Kirkos with calm contempt.

'Take your Communist rabble and go back the way you came,' he said quietly. 'I do not want to shed any

Greek blood – even if in this instance it would be doing my country a considerable service'

'Will someone please tell me what the hell's going on?' said Mackenzie.

'My apologies, Captain,' said Orestes. 'You must be *Claymore?* You are expected and will be made welcome, but I cannot allow these ELAS murderers any further into our territory. The Germans and the Italians are quite enough to contend with.'

Mackenzie privately shared the Greek captain's misgivings. He was equally aware that one of the prime aims of his mission was to help unify the rival guerrilla factions.

'Colonel Cephalus and his battalion will be engaged in operations asked for by the Allied Command,' he said. 'My orders are to co-ordinate these operations, using your unit and another commanded by a Captain Ionidas. How do you propose I do my job if you're all going to let domestic political arguments get in the way?'

'We are quite prepared to forget politics until the Germans are defeated, Captain.' Orestes spoke in the same quiet voice. 'It's the Communists who need your lecture. They're the ones who have been committing atrocities all over Greece against our people. We can't fight the Germans and watch our backs at the same time.'

'Lies!' shouted Kirkos. 'Propagandist lies!'

Petrea shouldered past him and faced Orestes from inches away. Her face was contorted with a passion of righteous fury.

'If killing Greeks will serve your country, Orestes, then the first you will have to kill will be a woman. Look, I am unarmed. That should give you courage. I am going to walk towards the village. The only way you will be able to stop me will be by shooting me in the back.'

She thrust past him and walked without a turn of her head through the defile. The Greek captain made no effort to stop her.

When she had walked about twenty yards, she turned with a triumphant smile.

'Well, Captain Orestes? Do you have no stomach for killing Greek patriots? That's what I am! And that's what all those men you are so afraid of are!'

The men at the head of the Communist column, who had been watching silently, fingers on triggers, gave a great cheer.

Petrea taunted Orestes some more.

'Call your dogs off!' she called, waving a mocking arm at the men on the heights above the path. 'You need have no fear, Captain. The *Anglos* will guarantee your safety. He has the whole British Empire to back him up. Isn't that so, *Anglos?*'

'I hate to say it, but she's right,' Mackenzie murmured to Orestes. 'Save your bullets for the Germans. We'll work this out.'

Captain Orestes did not reply. With a shrug of defeat, he turned away. He signalled to his men to let the column through.

A roar went up from the ELAS guerrillas. One of them started up a revolutionary hymn. Four abreast, the column marched into Methravioplos, the mountains echoing to the singing of the Internationale.

Orestes had fifty men camped in and around the village. They watched sullenly as Kirkos and his men streamed through and made camp on a patch of steeply sloping meadowland beyond.

Searching for a friendly face, Mackenzie's spirits lifted at the sight of a British Army uniform coming towards him. Corporal Wild of the Royal Corps of Signals seemed equally pleased to catch sight of him.

'Are you Captain Mackenzie, sir?' he enquired. 'The Yankee lieutenant has been on the lookout for you for

109

the past two days. He and Colonel Garrow thought you must have been captured.'

The Corporal led Mackenzie to a sprawling white house which seemed to have been chiselled from the contour of the mountain. The back of the house was built of solid rock, with windows only at the front.

Mackenzie followed the Corporal through a kitchen into a small bedroom. It contained only a black-painted chest of drawers and a rickety brass bedstead. Peering up from above grey blankets draping the bed was the emaciated face of Colonel William Garrow, alias *Broadsword*.

'Captain Mackenzie's arrived, sir,' said Corporal Wild. 'Brought half the Red Army from Karpenisi with him.'

He made to withdraw.

'The Colonel's been very ill,' he whispered to Mackenzie. 'I'll leave you to talk to him. I'll get all your stuff off the mule and put it in with the American lieutenant's gear. You'll have to share with him.'

'That's OK, Corporal. Thank you. You'll need a hand. There's one rather heavy piece on the mule.'

'I'll get my oppo to give me a hand. We're the radio operators, by the way. In case you were wondering.'

Mackenzie turned his attention to the man in the bed. Colonel Garrow looked as if he didn't have long for this world. His cheeks were sunken, his eyes dark hollows. His arms were thin spindles of bone covered by grey skin.

'Glad you made it, Mackenzie.'

The words came in a whisper from the thin blue-tinged lips. 'Lieutenant Preston has gone on a recce with Captain Ionidas. He should be back soon. He told me you had a little accident when you left the submarine.'

'One of the dinghies capsized and its cargo went in the drink. I stayed behind to do a little salvage work.'

'What about the gold?'

110

'That's what was in the sea. It's outside. The Signals Corporal is bringing it in. Look, sir, have you seen a doctor? You don't look in very good shape.'

'I'm weak as a kitten. Captain Orestes brought a civvie doctor to see me – but there was nothing he could do.' The Colonel laughed weakly. 'The fella told me I needed rest and a nourishing diet. Fat bloody chance! I had dysentry, now pneumonia. I was on my way to meet you in Karpenisi – wanted to meet that ruffian, Spiro, too – but I didn't have the strength. Two of Orestes's men carried me fifteen miles to this village to lay up. I wanted you to make your headquarters here anyway.'

He lay back, gasping for breath. Mackenzie wanted to leave him to sleep, but a scrawny arm reached out and clutched his sleeve.

'You can't just piss off and leave me, Mackenzie. Damnit, I've been lying here keeping myself alive with the prospect of getting all your news from Cairo. That Yank's a nice fella but couldn't tell me much. Why the hell didn't they drop you from the air? You could have been here a couple of weeks ago instead of traipsing all over the Med in a sub and then hoofing it from the coast.'

'The big brass wouldn't risk dropping the gold by parachute in case it missed the Dee-zed and got lost or stolen. They insisted it go by sea.'

'Ten times as risky by sea,' said Garrow. 'What about that chap Cephalus, who landed with you? Used to be one of Spiro's lieutenants. What the hell was he doing in Egypt?'

'Spiro, or EAM, sent him over for talks with the Greek Government-in-Exile.'

'What were they talking about?'

Mackenzie frowned.

'EAM wants to be recognised at home and abroad as the one and only political authority for Greece. As far as I can gather, they sent Cephalus over to tell the Greek politicians in Egypt to get stuffed.'

'He had to go to Egypt to tell them that?'

'Who knows why the Communists do anything they do?' said Mackenzie glumly. 'Did you hear about the trouble with the Greek Brigade?'

'What trouble?'

Someone was spreading EAM propaganda amongst the Greek troops in Egypt. Have you seen any signs that there's a campaign going on to set Greek against Greek? Here, I mean, as well as what's going on in Egypt?'

'I have stayed well clear of their politics. I don't understand them and I have absolutely no intention of getting involved. You will do the same.'

'We won't be able to sit on the fence indefinitely. I arrived here with Kirkos . . .Cephalus . . .He's a colonel in the ELAS now, by the way – and he insisted on bringing his whole ruddy battalion with him. Captain Orestes wasn't going to let them into the village. He was all for a showdown.'

Garrow gave a hoarse little laugh.

'All talk, my boy. They're always making growling noises, at each other but it never comes to anything. This is Orestes's territory. He'd be jealous as hell. I hope you sorted it out.'

'Orestes let us through eventually – but it's not Orestes I'm worried about. I have a nasty feeling it's not going to be easy to keep the peace.'

Garrow leaned out of the bed, breathing in wheezy gasps as he sought support by holding Mackenzie's arm. He was alarmed and anxious.

'You must never take sides. Never! Whatever you do, you must never get involved.'

'And what do we do if they start shooting at each other and we're in the middle?' asked Mackenzie.

'We duck!' said Garrow. 'Look, Mackenzie, you're

going to have to find a safe place to put the gold until a war council has been called. We're going to call all the guerrilla leaders to meet with the Allied Military Mission, possibly at Pertouli, and get them to sign a treaty of co-operation with us and with each other. They're going to have to forget their silly little feuds and play their parts in an overall military strategy.'

'And the gold?'

'The gold you brought over is ear-marked for Spiro and his cut-throats. But they are not going to get it unless they toe the line and sign the treaty.'

At Colonel Garrow's suggestion, Mackenzie enlisted the aid of the two wireless operators and they carried the chest of gold sovereigns into a cellar hewn out of the rock below the house. This windowless tomb had once been used to store dried goatmeat. Now it was the repository of old and crudely-made pieces of furniture in a sorry state of disrepair. The air was foul and dank.

Mackenzie had the chest stowed under a dilapidated wooden bedstead, which had a stained and tattered goatswool mattress rolled on its top. Mackenzie draped the mattress – which had lost most of its stuffing – over the end of the bed, so that it concealed the chest.

'Dare I ask what's in that box, Captain?' said Corporal Wild. He and the other operator were breathless from carrying it.

'A couple of hundredweight of trouble,' said Mackenzie. 'You've never seen that box, Corporal, and that goes for your mate, too. As far as the pair of you are concerned, that box doesn't even exist. Understood?'

'Understood,' confirmed the Corporal. He turned to his companion. 'You get the message, Bert? We've just given ourselves hernias lifting sweet-eff-all!'

Mackenzie prepared some signals for transmission to Cairo and had just finished when Preston returned with Captain Ionidas and his unit. Ionidas was a small, wiry man with a droopy moustache and lugubrious expression. He was a former Greek Army regular whose sad face, Mackenzie soon discovered, belied the keen sense of humour of its owner.

Preston's initial job in Greece was to join up with an active guerrilla unit and gain experience in their kind of warfare. Later, as more and more Americans were dropped into Greece as members of the Allied Military Mission, his role would be to train and organise the new arrivals.

At Garrow's suggestion, the American was to spend two or three months working closely with Ionidas, whom he reckoned a professional soldier of the highest calibre.

When Mackenzie had brought the American up to date on most of his adventures since the pair had parted company, he called a conference with the two Greek captains. Like Orestes, Ionidas was of Royalist sympathies and most uneasy about the presence of Kirkos and his men in Methravioplos. The Communist guerrillas outnumbered the joint forces of Ionidas and Orestes by two to one. A concern, too, was the feeding of Kirkos and his men, who were used to requisitioning any supplies they needed from the villages through which they passed. They had no hope of victualling such an army from the desperately poor area round Methravioplos which, in any case, the Royalist Greeks considered 'their' territory.

Both Ionidas and Orestes urged Mackenzie to send Kirkos and his guerrillas back to Karpenisi until such time as they were needed for the attack on German communications of which Mackenzie had spoken.

Happy as Mackenzie would have been to comply, his own inclination was to get the guerrillas into action against the Germans as quickly as possible in the hope of welding the rival factions into a fighting force. The shared dangers of battle might prove to be a far stronger unifying force than a thousand reasoned arguments.

The two Royalists reluctantly accepted to do things his way on his promise to radio Cairo with a request for an immediate air drop of field rations.

Cairo responded quickly. The drop was made the following night.

While Orestes and his men lit decoy beacon fires – which the Germans saw from their coastal bases and promptly bombed – Ionidas and his men collected the much-needed food supplies from the real Drop Zone some thirty miles away.

CHAPTER EIGHT

The Baited Hook

Christina Kirkos sat in the waiting-room of the dentist's surgery, flicking over the pages of a tattered magazine. The magazine was four years old.

She put it aside and stared at the green walls. The paint was peeling. The place, like so many shops, offices and similar establishments in Greece, was looking decidedly run-down. But there was no money these days to buy paint. And there was no paint to be bought, anyway.

A man shuffled out of the surgery holding a handkerchief to his mouth. He was so preoccupied at the loss of a tooth – removed without pain-killer or anaesthetic – that he did not even glance in Christina's direction.

A man in a short white jacket appeared at the surgery door. He had a moon face and his hair was plastered down with grease. There was something unctuous about Bernardini which Christina disliked. It had nothing to do with the fact that the man was half-Italian. He had been a regular contact of hers ever since she had taken on courier work for the mountain guerrillas. This was her fourth visit to the town of Agrinion to buy information from him.

'Come in, my dear,' said Bernardini. 'Is it that wisdom tooth troubling you again?'

Christina followed the white jacket into the narrow surgery and seated herself in the adjustable chair with its spittoon fitted to one arm. Bernardini plugged the lead from a dental drill into a wall socket and switched it on. It buzzed with a high-pitched metallic drone.

'Just in case someone comes into the waiting-room, my dear,' he said.

He allowed the drill to drone away in his hand and bent his face to Christina's. For a man versed in oral hygiene, he had very foul breath.

'I have news for you,' he whispered, 'but there have been the usual expenses.'

Christina fished in the pocket of her coat and produced a roll of money. The dentist took it from her and slipped it into a pocket of his white jacket.

'The Germans are moving in troops from France. There will be two convoys coming south from Ioannina within the next ten days. My friend, the Italian major, talked of nothing else when he came to dinner the other night.'

'What details do you have?'

'They are moving the First Panzer Division from France. This will be the advance guard. The Germans have been talking much of a British invasion of Greece being expected. They will be bringing in many reinforcements because they think the invasion will come in late spring or early summer.'

'Is that all your news?'

'You wanted details,' said Bernardini, 'I can give you details. A week tonight there is a convoy due here in Agrinion at daybreak - a thousand infantrymen. My friend, the Italian major, has to see that there is food waiting for them before they move on to Patras the same day. The following day, he has to organise breakfasts for a hundred personnel arriving at first light with a supply convoy. These men are mainly drivers and the like. This convoy will be carrying many supplies but it will be guarded by only a single platoon from the garrison at Ioannina. Can you remember all that?'

'I'll remember. You are quite sure of this information? And you have the days right?'

'I would stake my life on it,' said Bernardini.

'You may have to,' said Christina grimly.

A few moments later, she was walking briskly towards an undertaker's premises in another part of the town. A villager from near Blasios had died in Agrinion only the previous day and she had arranged a lift in the hearse taking the body home for burial. The ride would save her a day's march.

An hour after Christina had left the dentist's, a man in a grey polo-neck sweater and black trousers entered Bernardini's waiting-room. The man sat down opposite a woman and small boy. He waited with a bored expression until woman and boy had seen the dentist. Then he went in and sat down in the adjustable chair as Bernardini closed the outer door.

'Is it your wisdom tooth that has been troubling you, Herr Hoffman?' Bernardini asked in his ingratiating way. He started the electric drill.

'Forget that nonsense,' said Hoffman brusquely. 'You said you had news but you would not say anything over the phone. What has happened? Has the woman been to see you?'

'The same one as before. I told her exactly what you told me to say.'

'Good,' said Hoffman. 'You have done very well. Where did you tell her you got the information?'

'She thinks I am on very friendly terms with an Italian major. I take it, Herr Hoffman, that there will be some expenses due to me for my trouble?'

Hoffman sighed and took out a leather wallet. He counted off several bills and handed them to the dentist.

'Buy yourself a new drill,' he said. 'That one you have there sounds clapped out!'

Half an hour later, from a small room at the rear of

118

German Military HQ, Agrinion, Hoffman was speaking to HQ, Ioannina.

'This is Keller,' came a voice over the line. 'Has there been a development, Hoffman?'

'Yes, a young lady from the mountains called for dental treatment today – just as you said she would.'

'Good. Good,' said Keller. 'And did she get the filling which was prepared for her?'

'She swallowed it whole,' said Hoffman, smiling to himself. 'So, it looks good for a week tomorrow.'

'Excellent,' said Keller. 'Von Harzer will be pleased. Oh, and you'll never guess, Hoffman. One of these crazy things has happened which you'll never believe. Remember we fed our dentist friend all that nonsense about the First Panzer Division being transferred to France?'

'Yes.'

'Well, it isn't nonsense after all. We have just received word here from Berlin. The First Panzer is being moved to Greece immediately. Would you believe it? We shall have to be very careful about inventing fairy-stories in the future. We no sooner dream up something than Berlin makes it an official order!'

CHAPTER NINE

Intelligence Received

Corporal Wild's announcement that there was a visitor outside did not prepare Mackenzie for the shock of seeing Christina Kirkos for the first time since the after-dinner scene at Karpenisi. He stood embarrassed and tongue-tied when Wild showed her into the kitchen of the house at Methravioplos. Wild then retired unobtrusively, leaving the pair alone.

I care, Christina. I really care. It's important to me ... now ... what happens to you ... and I won't be able to stop caring ... because there's no going back.'

How empty those words of his sounded now. They had been uttered in that mountain-top *kaliva* down near the coast – and he had meant them when he said them. But, from the moment he had risen from her arms, what had his promise of caring amounted to? Strangely, she had exacted no demands – as if she had been prepared to accept full responsibility for what had happened between them.

'This is a surprise, Christina,' he said lamely.

'Not an embarrassing one, I hope.'

'No ... Look, what happened between us ... I'm sorry. It has only made things unpleasant for you. I didn't mean ...'

'You wish you hadn't got involved?'

'That's not what I said.'

'But it's what you feel,' she said. 'Ok, so forget it. It

wasn't your blame. Nothing happened that I didn't want to happen.'

He rested his hands on her shoulders and looked down at her gravely.

'There have been times when I wished that nothing had happened between us, Christina. But something did and I'm not going to forget it. It's just that . . . well, right now, I haven't much time to do or say the right things as far as you are concerned. God, that sounds bloody trite!'

She smiled at his struggle to find the words to say those things which were understood unspoken and better left that way. There was a look of such worldly wisdom in her eyes, and a tolerance that he felt like a gauche and inadequate schoolboy before her.

'I have been trying to understand,' he said. 'You . . . me . . .'

She put her forefinger across his lips in admonition to silence, to say no more.

'Remember what you said about selling yourself, about having nothing left of yourself to give? I gave myself to you Mac . . . To prove to myself that nobody owned me, I don't want anything in return – your thanks or your conscience or anything else.'

She kissed him lightly on the lips and then ducked out of range in case it gave him ideas.

'Christina – let me try to get you out of Greece. Away from Kirkos, away from all this bloody misery and the danger that goes with it,'

She laughed.

'How do you propose to do that?'

'There are ways. If you could get to the Thessaly coast, there are fishing boats that do the run to Turkey. We have people there.'

She was touched by the genuine concern in his face.

'It's sweet of you, Mac. But it's no go. I wouldn't stand a chance. I wouldn't get half way to the east coast. You're forgetting that I'm a signed-up soldier in the National Army of Liberation. They shoot deserters. A short trial to impress the troops ... Then, bang! A bullet in the back of the head.'

'But you're an American citizen, a woman. They might be willing to release you. The Allied Military Mission might help. I could speak to the British Colonel here in Methravioplos ... You could meet him, get him on your side.'

She turned to face him, sadness and affection in her expression.

'It really is nice to have you care Mac, but just stop and think for a minute. Do you go to your Colonel and say: "Look old buddy, I slept with an ELAS officer's wife and I'd like to do her a good turn. I want to slip her out of the country. Her husband will probably make an international incident out of it but we can worry about that later." '

Christina shook her head.

'Thank's Mac, but forget it.'

Mackenzie's shoulders dropped defeatedly.

'I just wish there was something I could do.'

'You could offer me something to eat. Or some tea or coffee. I've come a long way.'

Apologising for his lack of thoughtfulness, Mackenzie rescued some tea, which was stewing in a pot on the stove, and warmed up a tin of beef stew in a pan of water. He emptied the can of stew onto an aluminium plate and set it before her with some *babota*, the heavy corn bread which a farmer down the valley had sold to Corporal Wild.

She watched his culinary activities with an air of amusement.

'You're letting the side down,' she observed. 'A Greek male would never had done this for me. He would have told me where everything was and told me to get on with it.'

'I don't often have a chance to entertain socially,' Mackenzie said.

'I should have told you,' she said. 'This isn't really a social visit. I'm here to report to my commanding officer.'

'Kirkos?'

'Yes. He says he's finished with me, by the way, that our marriage is all washed up. But I haven't exactly been given my freedom. He has dispensed with my services as his wife but I have been retained as intelligence courier for his battalion and general errand-girl.'

Mackenzie was astonished by the casualness of her revelation.

'But this changes everything!' he said. 'Don't you see . . . ?'

'It changes nothing,' she broke in sharply. 'George put it to me very clearly. He has released me from the discipline of marriage – which he says I did not take seriously – but not from the discipline of the Liberation Army, which he says I had better take seriously. The clause in my marriage to ELAS about "until death do us part" is one which is rigorously enforced – even if they have to do the terminating part themselves.'

'It's grotesque,' said Mackenzie.

'The Greeks have a genius for drama and tragedy,' said Christina. 'I've lived here long enough to see the elements of comedy in it all. George doesn't want me any more but he wants to go on punishing me for being a lousy wife to him. And he's got the perfect answer – he's going to walk me to death. He has a network of spies and informers all over Greece and he'll keep me running to and fro between them until I get caught and shot or fall off a mountain and break my neck.'

'Kirkos said I hadn't begun to find out what a bastard he was. Hell, Christina, I can't let him get away with it. I'm the one who landed you in this. You've got to let me do something.'

'It's my problem,' she said evenly. 'There's nothing you can do. It would only make things worse. Where is my loving husband, anyway?'

'He's away on a scouting trip towards Arta. Nothing desperate. Just sizing up bridges which we might blow. He hasn't exactly been co-operative since we got here, but he and his men haven't been quite the headache I expected at first. The local boys resent them like hell. If I don't get them into action soon, they'll be at each other's throats.'

'Don't ever trust him, Mac.' There was an urgent, almost pleading note in Christina's voice. 'He hates you. Not just because of me. There's more to it – something deeper. For some reason, he is afraid of you. There's something basically honest about you which scares him.'

'I don't know about me scaring him,' said Mackenzie 'He scares me. I just can't figure him out. Why didn't he just blow his top when he found out about us? He never seems to react to anything the way most people would react. When he should be angry, he acts friendly. And just when you're beginning to think he's human after all, he spits like a cobra. He is never exactly what he seems to be. Every time I think I have him taped, I find that he has *me* taped and he's ten jumps ahead of me. It's not me he's scared of, Christina – it's something else. Something I haven't been able even to guess at.'

They were sitting in the kitchen, sipping second mugs of unsweetened tea, when Corporal Wild came in, two paces ahead of George Kirkos.

'He insisted on just barging in, sir,' said Wild apologetically.

'That's alright Corporal,' said Mackenzie. 'The Colonel is just in time for tea.'

Wild, with an eloquent expression of disbelief, retired from the scene.

'Sit down, Colonel,' invited Mackenzie. 'Your wife

124

and I have just been discussing . . . affairs of mutual interest.'

Kirkos had a look like thunder. It changed through degrees to bewilderment, to genuine amusement. It was the first time Mackenzie had seen the Greek laugh with merriment. But he did so now, unreservedly.

'Obviously I said something funny,' said Mackenzie.

'It is the beauty, the audacity of your insolence,' Kirkos roared, still trying to contain his laughter. 'You once said I had no sense of humour, Captain – but you were wrong. *Affairs* of mutual interest! Ha! That is very good. You see what makes me laugh? If the joke is barbed enough and delivered with sheer effrontery, it delights me. Even if I am the victim.'

'I find that a great comfort,' said Mackenzie.

Kirkos was almost affable.

'Come now, Captain. Don't look so glum. You are not still thinking about Karpenisi and our . . . well, exchange of words. Surely you did not expect me to jump for joy when I found out you had been taking your pleasures with my wife?'

'I would have understood it if you had tried to beat the hell out of me,' said Mackenzie. 'I just don't read you at all, Colonel. I have decided it would be easier to understand Einstein's theory of relativity than the way your mind works.'

'Surely Christina has told you that we came to an agreement in Karpenisi?' Kirkos looked questioningly from one to the other. 'The matter is over. Has Christina not told you that she made me see what I was reluctant to accept? That I have lost my wife? Our marriage is finished. It pains me . . . But perhaps I should have recognised the truth long ago.'

'So, we are forgiven?' said Mackenzie wryly.

Kirkos frowned.

'I didn't say that, Captain. Forgiveness does not come easily to me. But as you have been at pains to remind us all so frequently, we are in the middle of a war. Until Greece has been liberated, personal quarrels and enmities must be forgotten or put aside. If there are any reckonings to be settled, they must wait.'

Christina Kirkos was staring at her husband with scarcely concealed disbelief.

'That's a tune I haven't heard before,' she said. 'Does that mean that you will let me leave? That I can really have my freedom?'

Kirkos returned her stare coldly.

'You have always had your freedom, Christina. Unlike me, you have no idea what it is to lose that precious commodity. I just do not want you in my life any more. All you have ever been is an embarrassment.'

'You haven't answered my question, George. Are you saying that the National Army of Liberation is going to give me an honourable discharge? Or even a dishonourable one?'

Kirkos smiled.

'That I'm afraid, is something out of my power and which might be rather difficult to arrange. But you are a woman – and General Spiro might be persuaded to give you work more suited to your obvious talents.'

Kirkos contrived to fill the last remark with a dirty innuendo which escaped neither Christina nor Mackenzie. Christina flushed angrily.

'I thought you'd become all noble a moment ago. I knew it was too good to be true.'

He ignored the anger in her eyes.

'Dear Christina, I can overlook the fact that as your husband, I never quite commanded the respect which was my due – but as your superior officer and battalion commander, I am still entitled to it. And I intend to have it. In Karpenisi you were given orders to go to Agrinion because one of our agents there had information of some value to pass on. Your presence here suggests that you are now in possession of that intelligence. I suggest that, like me, you forget personal considerations for the time being and attend to the business that brought you to Methravioplos.'

Mackenzie stood up. Kirkos was now more of a puzzle to him than ever before. There seemed to be no predictable pattern to the man's behaviour. Only one thing was sure. No matter how that unpredictability manifested itself, there was underlying it and embodied in it a conscious stream of menace.

Mackenzie could feel this menace now. It emanated from Kirkos in currents, reaching a peak of intensity when the man spoke and acted – as he was doing now – in a cold and unemotional manner.

The cold eyes were on Mackenzie.

'Well, Captain, don't you agree? Wouldn't you say the intelligence from Agrinion is more worthy of our attention than other things?'

'And not really my business? It's all right. You'll want to hear what Christina has to report in privacy. I'll see you are not disturbed. I'll take a walk.'

'But there is no need for you to leave,' said Kirkos smoothly. 'I am sure that Christina's news from Agrinion will be of interest to everyone here in Methravioplos. I was about to suggest that you might like to summon Orestes and his Royalist friend, Ionidas, and your American friend, Preston.'

This kind of co-operative goodwill was the last thing Mackenzie expected from Kirkos. He wasn't going to argue with it.

'I'll give the others a shout,' he said. 'I'm sure they'll be as impressed as I am at your willingness to share your intelligence secrets.'

When the others were all present, Kirkos nodded to Christina.

'We're waiting, my dear. What did you find out in Agrinion from our paid collaborator?'

Without giving details of the identity of her

informant, but telling briefly how the contact in Agrinion had cultivated the friendship of an Italian officer, Christina recounted the information about the German convoys expected in Agrinion from Ioannina by way of Arta and the coast road.

'How sure can you be of this man in Agrinion?' asked Ionidas, tugging thoughtfully at his flowing moustache.

'He has not failed us up to now,' said Kirkos. 'We could check on the information quite easily,' said Orestes. The others looked at him expectantly, waiting for him to elaborate.

'If we watch the coast road next Tuesday night and a convoy goes south, then we'll know the information is correct and that a second convoy will travel down on Wednesday.'

'That makes sense to me,' said Mackenzie. 'A couple of men could do the watching. If they see the first convoy go down on schedule, we hit the second.'

'We could hit both convoys,' said Kirkos.

'Three hundred men against a thousand?' said Ionidas. 'I like these odds. But risking such an engagement could cost more casualties than we can afford. It would be more prudent to go for the supplies on the second night.'

'Are you afraid of a thousand Germans?' scoffed Kirkos.

Ionidas fixed his questioner with a steely look.

'I have faced a thousand Germans with thirty men,' he said quietly, 'and I carry the wounds to prove it. What battle experience do you have, Colonel?'

Kirkos waved an arm and laughed with forced bonhomie.

'I was making a joke, Captain. I, too, believe it would be unwise to tackle the first convoy. You were all looking so solemn! I just had to say something, eh?'

From the looks he got from Orestes and Ionidas, the

Royalist Greeks made it plain to Kirkos that they would have preferred his silence.

CHAPTER TEN

Ambush

A fitful moon peered from behind high clouds. In those moments when its pale silvery light was not diffused by scurrying clouds, it glinted on the sea beyond the road and made the grey ribbon of road itself starkly visible.

Mackenzie had a feeling of elation. A high pitch of excitement had tingled in him since sunset, when he had given the order to march. The three hundred men from Methravioplos had made the journey from their base in two stages. Their last halting place before the road had been a forested slope some twelve miles from their destination.

The location of the ambush had been carefully chosen. Ionidas had insisted that they pick a spot as far as possible from villages or habitation. Past experience had shown that the Germans had a nasty habit, after an ambush, of making reprisals on the nearest village; usually by taking a dozen or more hostages and shooting them.

No one had quarrelled with the location Ionidas had finally suggested himself. It was an isolated area of coast with terrain which lent itself admirably to the enterprise. The road, after hugging the coast along a straight stretch, swung inland across the neck of a peninsula and twisted for two or three kilometres before rejoining the sea. Ionidas marked the peninsula on the map.

'Here,' he said 'where the road bends, there is high ground to three sides. The road runs straight towards this high ground here for nearly a kilometre and it passes between high ground on both sides for almost the whole way. If we can allow the enemy to advance almost to the bend in the road, we can rain fire on him from above the bend and stop him in his tracks. This will be the sign for our men above the road on the seaward side to rake him with enfilade fire and possibly drive him towards our third force on his landward flank.'

The plan outlined by Ionidas was accepted with only some squabbling about the deployment of the three forces. In the end, the Greek Royalists had given in to Kirkos's insistence that his larger body of men be given the landward position above the convoy's left flank. Orestes would take the position which lay front-on to the enemy's approach while Ionidas would hold the high ground between the sea and the road.

Two scouts from Kirkos's battalion had been despatched twenty-four hours ahead of the main force. They had returned to confirm that a large convoy of Germans had moved south on the Tuesday night. The men had counted more than seventy vehicles.

The attack was on.

Before the road came in sight, the marching songs and the murmur of excited talk – which had risen in the night between-times – had long since stopped. Now, the only the sounds were the steady footfalls of the marching men and the clank of weapons.

From a hill, high above the road, Mackenzie marshalled the final development. Ionidas and his men moved off first, to cross the road and site their three machine-guns and sundry rifles on the high ground beyond. Preston, bright with eagerness, went with him; pleased that this detachment had drawn the most vulnerable of all the ambush positions. In the event of things going wrong, they would have to fight their way back across the road towards the safety of the hills.

Orestes went next, to mount his three machine-guns in the rocks which looked straight down the road towards the enemy's approach.

Finally, Kirkos extended his column along the landward ridges which looked down from a line almost parallel to the road and gazed beyond it to the sea.

Mackenzie, having waited until Kirkos had positioned his men, decided to take up his own station with Orestes, where he would get the first view of any approaching column. He found the Greek officer stretched flat on his stomach on a rock which leaned out above the middle of his three machine-gun sites. He was watching the road with binoculars.

'Mind if I keep you company?' asked Mackenzie.

Orestes was deep into an account of a love affair he'd had with a Cretan beauty when there was a shout from nearby: '*Prosehete!*'

At the warning to look out, Orestes focused his binoculars on the road.

'There's something moving on the road!' he said in a whisper to Mackenzie. 'Coming this way!'

He peered into the binoculars.

'Vehicles of some kind. They're running without headlights. Can't be much fun for the drivers.'

'Probably using tail lights only,' said Mackenzie. 'Can I have a look?'

He squinted into the night-glasses which Orestes passed to him, adjusting them to suit his own eyes.

'No sign of motor-cycle outriders. Is that usual?'

'No. They usually have cycles or a fast scout car well in front. Do you hear something?'

Mackenzie already had his head tilted to one side, listening.

'Tanks,' he said. 'It sounds like bloody tanks!'

The noise grew steadily. Mackenzie felt a cold shiver run from the base of his spine to his neck. The convoy was crawling towards them at what seemed an agonisingly slow pace but, as it approached, the metallic clatter of caterpillar tracks on the surface of the road became louder and louder.

Mackenzie's mouth had gone quite dry. Every instinct, all his experience of battle and long days of training, seemed to be shouting that something was wrong. Terribly wrong. Don't give the signal to fire, his brain was screaming. There's something not right. He waited, making no sound, making no movement.

The leading vehicle in the convoy was now less than half a mile away. Mackenzie could feel the night-glasses tremble in his hands as he refocused on it. There was something odd about its shape. What the hell was it?

The shape gradually took on a recognisable outline. Mackenzie sucked in his breath so sharply that Orestes peered anxiously at him and muttered: 'What's wrong?'

'There's an armoured personnel carrier right at the front – and there are more behind.' His voice was a hoarse whisper. 'I couldn't make out what the hell it was at first. There's something like an upside-down snow plough on the leader. They've built two bloody great shields on top of the thing. They stick out nearly the width of the road.'

Orestes was studying the specially armoured vehicles.

'I have never seen anything like them before. The other carriers are the same. I bet there's twenty or thirty men behind the shields. It doesn't look like any supply column to me. Maybe we should let them through.'

This was the thought that was buzzing like a hornet in Mackenzie's brain. But other thoughts fought it. Hell, he had three hundred men grouped around the hills in selected firing points. His force was ten times the size of any ambush party the Germans had ever seen on this road. He could imagine what Kirkos would say later if they didn't open fire. It would look as if he'd lost his nerve. He could foresee a fresh outbreak of quarrelling amongst the guerrilla factions if they returned to base without firing a shot.

The possibilities flashed through his mind. He could feel Orestes's eyes boring into him from the shadows. The noise of the half-tracks on the road was now a high-pitched screaming in his ears.

'Fire now!' he shouted to Orestes. 'Tell your men to open fire now!'

The night was suddenly filled with the thundering bark of the machine-gun immediately below their look-out position. It was joined immediately by the guns to right and left. Three more machine-guns poured fire on the convoy from the high ground on the seaward side of the road. Rifle shots joined the chorus of chattering guns.

The convoy halted abruptly at the first burst. But there was no sign of panic down on the road. Scuttle-helmeted soldiers leapt from the line of carriers but precision rather than frenzy characterised their movements. Some fell beneath the hail of bullets but the Germans side-stepped their fallen comrades and fanned out amongst the rocks beside the road in orderly groups. Even as he watched the enemy, Mackenzie marvelled at their discipline and apparent disregard for the bullets which filled the air in a murderous crossfire. All along the convoy, soldiers were spilling from their transports. Spandau fire from the middle of the convoy began to rake the hillside. The first bursts were too high and bullets sang against rock well above the Greek positions and ricocheted into the night.

A series of strange popping explosions, audible above the barking machine-guns, preceded bursts of fiery light which hung against the slopes and bathed the crags in an eerie orange glow. Flares!

Now came a fresh sound to the cacophony of battle. And Mackenzie at once realised the significance of those orderly groups of the enemy moving like drill teams.

The unmistakable whine of mortars sent fear grating over raw nerve ends like a joiner's rasp across the grain of virgin wood.

The shells exploded towards the end of their arcs of flight, filling the air with a random fury of burning metal. Mackenzie heard a scream from the gun position below him. A shape pitched outward and plummetted twenty or more feet before thudding against rock and pirouetting down the hill in slow-motion cartwheel and sliding to a halt. The machine-gun below was silent.

Mackenzie was aware of Orestes moving to his right and disappearing below the level of their ridge. A moment later, the machine-gun was firing again and Mackenzie knew that Orestes had sponged all images of desirable women from his mind and the hand that had caressed a Cretan girl was now squeezing an orgasm of death from the barrel of a Bren.

At the distant end of the convoy, vehicles were moving off the road. This left room for the leading carriers to reverse along the way they had come. And this they did, impervious to the fire being directed at them. Simultaneously, the German troops skirting the road began to fall back in an orderly fashion, narrowing the angle of crossfire aimed at them.

This was the moment when the guns of Kirkos's men should have opened up on the Germans. The effect of fresh enfilade fire along the convoy's left flank would have been devastating. But the ridges to the east of the road were silent. The two guns of Kirkos did not fire.

The terrible thought took seed in Mackenzie's mind that Kirkos might never give the order to fire. He would sit up there smiling as the Germans and the Royalist Greeks fought to the death. Mackenzie was filled with an urgency to warn Ionidas and the men to the west of the road of the fears which by the minute were becoming a dread certainty.

He left the ridge with its panoramic view of the battle,

intending to circle down to the right as Orestes had done. Orestes would now have to cover his Royalist friends' escape across the road and he would need to be told. Breasting a boulder towards the machine-gun position, Mackenzie suddenly found himself hurled sideways in a shattering blast of red-hot air. Flying metal gouged itself into the rock against which his body had been pressed. Half-stunned but with no injuries other than bruising from his fall, he picked himself up and limped along the ledge of rock leading to the machine-gun site. He halted, vomit rising to his throat, at the sight which met his eyes.

Orestes lay on his back on the rocky platform, his face and chest a mass of blood and pulverised flesh. The twisted bodies of three other men lay close by in the postures of their deaths.

Mackenzie hurried on, seeking a way down to the road. Mortar shells continued to rain down on the hillside. Only one machine-gun was now firing in reply.

There was no cover at the foot of the hill. Mackenzie crouched behind the last outcrop of protective rock, surveying the open ground before him. Thirty yards away lay the slope he wanted to reach. Less than half this distance away was the road, where it began its lazy curve away to his left across flat treeless ground.

He gritted his teeth and broke cover. He ran in long leaping strides. The air was alive with singing bullets and shrapnel from mortar shells but the Germans were concentrating their fire high, raking the hill behind him and not aiming at targets which they could not see. Although his breakneck dash was at a level below the solid sheets of ordnance being hurled against the hillside, the terror of feeling exposed to its fury took on an extra nightmare dimension for the running man. On the hard metal of the road, the world seemed to be exploding around his ears in a cataclysm of blinding light and monstrous sound. He felt a total nakedness to every screaming bullet and, with it, almost a resigned certainty that his flesh and bone would be shredded to fragments with an uncountable multiplicity of hits. Every fraction of a second with passed with the knowledge of his continued survival astounded him with almost galvanic shock because survival seemed beyond all possibility. Ten yards . . . seven yards . . . two great paces now . . . He flung himself to the ground as it banked slowly upwards and cover offered itself in the rocks which studded the hem of the hill. There seemed no reality in the knowledge that he had made it to the other side. He had to force disbelief from his mind as he lay panting, his chest rising and falling like a bellows. Slowly, with more normal breathing, feelings of triumph and thanksgiving warmed him like a flush. For a moment, he lay where he was, his eyes searching out the hill above him. He noted the features: every visible outcrop, cleft and ridge. Taking a circular route not directly exposed to the unabating German fire he began to work his way upwards towards the positions held by Ionidas and his men.

He greeted each manned position through which he passed, warning the men to be ready to withdraw when he passed the word. But there was no sign of Ionidas. He passed a machine-gun crewed by two Greeks. It was a .50 calibre Browning mounted on a tripod and it had jammed. The men were furiously dismantling it and cursing volubly as each directed the other what should be done. They seemed oblivious to the bullets pitting the rock-face above them.

'Mac, what the hell?'

Preston's voice seemed to come from nowhere. Startled, Mackenzie looked all around him until, finally, he located the source of the voice about six feet above his head. The American was lying flat on his stomach with only his head protruding over the ridge he occupied.

Mackenzie clambered up beside him. The American

had chosen an excellent observation point. It commanded a good view of the road and across it to the east. It also had an uninterrupted view of the north, across the narrow strip of ground which lay between the road and the sea.

'We're running low on ammo,' said the American.

'We've got other things to worry about,' said Mackenzie. 'Where's Ionidas?'

'He took a dozen men over towards the beach and he was going to have a go at the nearest mortar positions from the side. He reckoned they wouldn't be expecting an attack from the sea at road level. The Krauts have just been throwing everything they have at the ridges.'

Mackenzie swore.

'The silly bastard will get himself killed. Jerry must have three or four hundred men down there and they're not bloody novices. I was going to tell Ionidas to pull out.

'But the Krauts have been pulling back,' said Preston.

'Only because they were far too exposed at the front. Right now they're re-grouping and getting themselves organised to come at us. They'll probably try to outflank us from two sides and maybe try to take us head-on too. They also probably have reinforcements belting up from Agrinion to catch us right in the middle.

'They can't outflank us from the far side of the road, Mac. They'll walk right into Kirkos and his red army. When are you going to bring them into the ball game anyway?'

'Don't you realise Kirkos is sitting up there without any intention of lifting a finger?' snapped Mackenzie. 'They're not going to bloody help!'

The American was incredulous.

'Come off it, Mac. Heck, I know he doesn't go much on Ionidas, him being Academy trained and all that, but even Kirkos wouldn't just stand by. Where would that leave us?'

'Up to our necks in it, that's where!' said Mackenzie. 'So, how the hell do I stop Ionidas from committing suicide? Orestes is dead already — and half his men.'

'You're not going to stop Ionidas. Christ Almighty! There he goes!' The American was pointing down. 'Look at that, will you?'

Ionidas had indeed gone into action. Although the detail could not be seen from their observation point, Mackenzie and the American were able to observe the devastating efficiency with which Ionidas struck the German positions from the direction of the sea.

The Greeks must have crawled unseen along the sea shore and come in from the beach with such stealth that they got to within yards of the leading German vehicle and the mortar crews in their vicinity.

Attacking with grenades, the Greeks took the Germans completely by surprise and wreaked such havoc that it was impossible to believe that only a dozen men were responsible. Three of the troop carriers burst into flames and a trough of mortar shells exploded with a spectacular pyrotechnical eruption. German soldiers, unaware of the direction or exact nature of the attack, were stampeding in all directions.

Ionidas and his men caused such confusion at the head of the column that, after forcing home their attack, they were able to cross the road in front of the convoy and successfully gain the cover to the east.

Mackenzie wanted to stand up and cheer. He followed the action by spotting the flashes of exploding grenades as they pin-pointed the progress of the guerrillas from west to east. He realised too, that Ionidas had injected his own brand of genius in the tactical plan agreed beforehand.

If the Germans now pursued the small band of guerrillas, they would be led right into the waiting guns of

Kirkos. And this was what appeared to be happening. For the first time, muzzle flashes lit up the ridges occupied by the ELAS battalion.

Mackenzie breathed a sigh of relief.

'Looks like you were wrong about Kirkos,' said Preston.

'He certainly waited long enough,' Mackenzie replied. He was now scanning the German positions illuminated by the blazing trucks.

Men were moving towards the sea on one side of the road and running at the crouch towards the high ground on the far side of the road.

'Here they come,' said Mackenzie. 'Time we were getting out of here, Leo.'

They made their way back along the highest ridge, shouting orders to the men of Ionidas's unit to evacuate all the ground between the road and the sea. Individually and in small groups, carrying their wounded, the men headed towards the bend in the road which separated them from the hill occupied by Orestes's small force, or what was left of it.

For the moment there was a lull in the firing from the Germans but Mackenzie knew the respite was only temporary. Crossing the road from west to east was not the terrifying proposition it had been only a short time before in the other direction.

The two officers urged the guerrillas across quickly and signalled to the survivors of Orestes's band to abandon their positions and make for the ridges occupied by Kirkos and his Reds.

The Germans were now advancing along the road, and a new hurricane of machine-gun fire and mortar fire blasted the hillside occupied only minutes before by the Orestes unit. The guerrillas circled towards the high ridges and were half way up the hillside to the east of the road before the Germans realised the Greeks were escaping. They immediately began to plaster the middle

140

ground of the slopes east of the road with mortar shells and sustained Spandau fire. More flares were fired and the hill was bathed in orange light.

Mackenzie and the American were at the very tail of the groups of men retreating from the road. Ahead of them, the guerrillas were strung out in a curving line, with those at the rear on a level little more than forty feet above the road, although some distance from it.

Mackenzie was crouched momentarily in cover a few yards behind his companion when he was aware that the American was screaming frenziedly at the top of his voice. His attention was on the heights, not the road. Horror churned in Mackenzie when he scanned upwards and ahead and saw the cause of Preston's anguished but useless protest.

The men ahead of them were falling like ninepins as they neared the high ridges and came under a murderous fire from above. Kirkos and his ELAS guerrillas were plainly intent on doing what the Germans had failed to accomplish – and that was wipe out the Royalist guerrillas to a man. The reason why Kirkos had first opened fire was now clear to Mackenzie. He, too, had observed the grenade attack which Ionidas and his handful of men had made on the German column – but he had not ordered his barrage of fire to cover the gallant little band's escape . . . Ionidas and his twelve had been mercilessly cut down from the heights where they believed their safety had lain.

The carnage on the hillside continued. Many of the Royalist guerrillas had been working their way upwards along a natural track which wound across the breast of the hill in a deep gouge. This ditch-like indentation afforded the escapers concealment from below but none from above. When the Royalists came under the withering fire of the ELAS guns, those who could scattered from this escape channel which nature had provided. Some scrambled out of it and went streaming down the slope towards the advancing Germans, only to run into an equal intensity of lethal fire. They were caught like wingless partridges between two lines of guns. Some, guns blazing, tried to storm the ridges above. None got to within thirty feet of the Communist guns. They were chopped down as if by an invisible sickle.

The American ahead of Mackenzie stood up. He waved his arms at the high ridges above.

'Stop firing, you bastards!' he screamed. 'Stop firing!'

His answer was a machine-gun burst which dug chunks from the rocks all around and peppered the ground at his feet. Miraculously, not one found the target at which it was aimed. Mackenzie pulled the American to the ground.

'Over there!' he pointed. 'It's our only chance!'

A ditch-like furrow, not unlike the one in which most of the Greeks had been trapped, ran from their position towards the south end of the hillside. It roughly followed the contour of the level they had reached and provided cover from above and below. It was overhung by rock and was protected from below by a bulging outcrop which resembled an upturned swollen lip.

The two men had passed immediately below the outcrop on their way upwards moments before. Now, they crawled towards the natural corridor formed by its upper side. They reached it safely.

Now, they were able to move quickly at a half-crouched position along its entire length. It extended for seventy yards and then, to their dismay, they found it petered out into open hillside. The bald ground was bereft of cover and stretched for a good hundred yards.

Beyond the open ground, a ridge ran at right angles to the east-facing slope. It offered Mackenzie a glimmer of hope. If they could reach that ridge and get over the top, escape to the south was a possibility. For beyond, the ground dropped away behind the hill on which Orestes had sited his guns. If they could clear the ridge, they would not be seen from the ELAS positions and would be well obscured from the Germans below.

'There's only one way,' said the American. 'We'll have to make a dash for it.' He had obviously been making the same calculations.

'I'll give you a ten-yard start,' said Mackenzie, 'and I've got a month's pay says I'll beat you to the top.'

'You're on,' said Preston. 'Here goes!'

He broke cover and sprinted over the uneven ground. Mackenzie let him get more than half way to the top before making his break. The American was almost at the ridge before the first bullets began to fly from the ELAS positions. Preston flung himself over the ridge as he reached it and found himself slithering face-down over rain-smoothed boulder. His legs slewed sideways and he tumbled in a twisting arc to fall several feet before thudding on to a flat rock.

He hauled himself back to the ridge to peer over it down the way he had come. Mackenzie was thirty yards away, sprinting like a deer. Bullets were ricocheting crazily in all directions, whining off the smooth stone.

Mackenzie could see Preston's eyes, round with fear for him, as he neared the ridge. He had only paces to go when his feet went from under him. In the same instant, he felt as if a giant fish-hook had caught him by the shoulder and he had been jerked in the air. Then he was falling and a murderous punch seemed to materialise from nowhere and his right eye was enveloped in pain. The ground came up to hit him.

Through a mist of blood he tried to crawl. He could hear Preston shouting at him but he could see nothing. Preston's voice again penetrated his fuddled brain.

'I'm coming for you, Mac. For Christ's sake, hold on. I'm coming for you!'

Mackenzie was aware of a flurry of stone and then the American was dragging him to the ridge. They reached the top and then the American lost his footing and they were both falling. Mackenzie could feel himself slipping over smooth rock, his legs entangled with his rescuer's. There was a final thud as his body battered against solid stone.

He swam back to consciousness. His chest and back were gripped in a heavy numbness of pain. He could see nothing. The inside of his head seemed to be on fire. If only he could sleep – just lie there and surrender to blessed sleep. Then the pain would go away.

Preston was speaking to him. The American's voice seemed to be coming from a great distance away. He was saying something about a field dressing. Mackenzie could feel hands thrusting inside his jacket in the area of his shoulder. Pain flared and all was dark again.

He opened his eyes. Where was he? Water dripped on his face. He could still see nothing. His right eye was on fire. He closed it tight shut. He squinted with the other one. It seemed wet, as if covered in water. It was better when he kept both eyes closed. Someone was sponging his face.

He kept his right eye shut but opened the left. There was a shape there. The shape was murmuring to him. It was Preston.

Mackenzie recognised the clank of the water-bottle top striking against the neck of the bottle. Preston was bathing his face. What was he saying? He concentrated on the voice.

'Mac, Mac. You're going to make it, boy. Come on. I'm going to have to carry you.'

The words roused Mackenzie. Memory came flooding back. He stared up with his better eye at the shadow that was Preston's face. His mind was lucid now. He tried to speak. His voice was a croak.

'Leo . . . Leo . . . You've got to get the hell out of here . . . Just leave me . . . Go, you silly bastard . . . You've got to . . .'

'I'm not leaving you!'

An almost desperate anger forced its way through Mackenzie's pain. There was near hysteria in his urgency.

'I'm ordering you . . . I'm giving you a direct order . . . Can't you see that this is as far as I'm going? I'm ordering you to save yourself.'

'I'm not leaving you here, Mac.'

'You bloody well are!' The effort of the words was almost too much for him. His head sagged back helplessly. He fought for strength to say more. He found it.

'One of us has to get out and tell what happened.' He gasped out the words.'It isn't going to be me. For God's sake go when I tell you!'

'Not without you, Mac.'

Mackenzie tried to sit up but pain forced him back again. He closed his eyes. He spoke from the prone position in the clipped tones of a schoolboy reciting a poem.

'I'm ordering you for the last time, Lieutenant . . . You will go . . . You will not try to go to Methravioplos . . . You will make for Giannopouli . . . Now, go!'

He was right, Preston knew, but everything in him rebelled at leaving his comrade there to bleed his life away. He stood up. Fury and anguish were tearing at his insides.

'I'll get Kirkos for you, Mac. That's the only thing that's making me leave. Somebody has to get that bastard. I'll get that stinking bastard for you!'

'Go, Leo! Now!'

The American gripped Mackenzie's forearm and gave it a gentle squeeze in a silent gesture of farewell. He started down the slope towards the south at a steady run. He could scarcely see the boulders strewing the path before him. Tears were streaming down his face. He was crying like a child.

Keller watched the battle from behind the armoured radio truck. The truck had been well to the rear of the convoy but had run off the road to allow the forward personnel carriers to reverse to a better position. Except for some nasty moments when the front of the convoy had been attacked by grenade-throwing guerrillas, the operation had gone smoothly.

'You can recall your men now, I think,' he said to Colonel von Harzer.

The Colonel was studying the hills to the east of the road through binoculars.

'There are terrorists right along the top ridges. Did you see it, Colonel-General Keller? They shot down their own men. It is incredible!'

'There is no treachery more distasteful than Greek treachery,' said Keller. 'I hope you will agree that there has been enough butchery for one night?'

'My men could storm those ridges,' said von Harzer. 'I don't like leaving a job half done.'

'The losses would not be worth it. Perhaps if you had a few eighty-eights to soften the way for you? I cannot, of course, tell you what to do – but as far as my end of the operation is concerned, I am quite happy with the night's work. There is no point in incurring senseless losses when our main objectives have been attained.'

'You are right, of course,' said von Harzer. 'A frontal attack against those heights would be playing the terrorists' game for them. We could lose half our men getting to the top and then find when we got there that the enemy had vanished into the night.'

He turned to face a young lieutenant, who had been hovering nearby.

'Schreiber, make the recall signal.'

The Lieutenant fired three green Very signals in quick succession. The troops strung out on the hillside, and those who had advanced a mile along and to the west of the road, began an orderly withdrawal. One platoon

146

would withdraw while another covered their retreat, and so on: this leap-frogging of positions continued until the convoy was flanked in a close defensive perimeter. The wounded were already being lifted into ambulances which had been manoeuvred up through the two lanes of armoured personnel carriers. Within half an hour, the convoy was ready to move off.

Warm sunlight beating on Mackenzie's face told him that he was alive. He could not open his right eye. He tried to open his left but congealed blood had frozen the eyelashes to the skin above his cheek-bone. When he finally did work the eye open, there seemed to be a skin over it which reduced his vision. He was aware of bright light striking his eyeball through a haze of pink.

He found he could move his toes and his legs. Any other movement sent a pain searing across his chest and across his back. So he lay still.

A long way away, he heard voices. Two voices. Two men talking to each other across a distance. Their conversation was sporadic. There was another sound – the steady scrabble of mules' hooves on stony hillside.

Privates Petrani and Borello were conscripts into Mussolini's army. They did not particularly care for occupation duty in Greece but agreed it was preferable to Libya. They had a string of six mules and had been systematically covering the most southerly slope of the hillside collecting corpses from the battle of the night before. Other soldiers with similar teams of mules were strung out along the hillside to the north engaged in the same gruesome task. The men had white handkerchiefs knotted over nose and mouth. The warm spring morning had brought out hundreds of flies. More than anything else in their work, Privates Petrani and Borello hated flies.

Second on Angelo Petrani's list of hates were the bossy Tedeschi, the Germans.

147

'We get all the dirty work to do,' he complained to Borello. 'If they are going to massacre Greeks, then they should clear up the mess afterwards.'

'Quiet a moment, Angelo,' said Borello. 'Did you not hear a cry?'

'What kind of cry? I heard nothing.'

'It was like an animal in pain. There it is again.'

This time both men heard it. It came from over the ridge above them to the right.

'I'll take a look,' said Petrani.

He clambered up to the ridge and looked over.

'*Che vada*, Angelo?' called Borello.

'*Un Inglesi!*' exclaimed Petrani. 'An officer! And he is not dead.'

CHAPTER ELEVEN

Wars Within Wars

Sir Neil Maitland, otherwise 'Commander Six', paced impatiently beside a french window. It overlooked a garden which displayed the first colours of spring. But the English garden held no interest for him this sunny morning in February.

'The Prime Minister will see you now, sir.'

Maitland turned with a start at the woman's voice. He followed her along a carpeted corridor.

Winston Churchill was sitting up in bed, smoking a cigar. A sheaf of papers was spread across the eiderdown in front of him.

'I was sorry to hear about your illness, sir,' said Maitland.

'Just a chill. I was in Tripoli earlier in the month – watched the victory parade . . . Did this old warrior's heart good. Unfortunately, Maitland, London's climate is less benign to these old bones than Libya's.'

The Prime Minister's illness had, in fact, been rather more than a chill. He had been severely ill with pneumonia.

He glowered over the top of his glasses at Maitland.

'You have bad news from Greece?'

'Yes. A major civil war seems to have broken out right under the noses of the Germans. ELAS guerrillas are systematically wiping out every other guerrilla organisation refusing to hand over their arms and accept ELAS command.'

149

Churchill listened with an expression of great weariness on his face as Maitland detailed the known instances of Communist treachery. His expression changed to one of anger as the catalogue continued. The muscles in his jaw quivered.

Maitland remained silent as the Prime Minister launched himself into a bitter denunciation of Communist perfidy and thundered at him that 'the bloody hand of Bolshevism' must not be allowed to prevail.

Catching the look on Maitland's face, Churchill's mood suddenly changed. He peered at Maitland impishly over the top of his glasses.

'I am only telling you what you already know. You are thinking that I should reserve my rhetoric for the House?'

'Not at all, sir,' said Maitland, who had been thinking precisely that.

'No matter,' said Churchill. 'What about our men in Greece? Have they not tried to intervene to put a stop to this senseless bloodshed?'

'They have tried – but I fear it may have cost some of them their lives. In most instances, their attempts to keep the peace were just brushed aside by the Communists. In others – where we fear the worst – there has just been silence. We don't know what has happened.'

'What started it? Why start a revolution *now*?'

'The Germans are sending reinforcements to Greece . . . from France and from Russia. They seem to think – and the Greek Communists seem to have the same idea – that we'll be invading Greece any day . . . Especially now that we have kicked Rommel out of Egypt and Libya.'

'But the Combined Chiefs of Staff haven't made any decision yet on the next stage of the war!' said Churchill. 'It's far from definite what we'll do next in the Mediterranean.'

'I realise that, sir. But the Greek Communists are not

150

taking any chances. They're convinced Greece is next on the cards for us and they're determined that when Liberation does take place, they are going to be the boys in full political control.'

Churchill looked thoughtful.

'What about the troubles with the Greek Brigade?'

'All quiet on that particular front for the moment.'

'You know that there has been a cabinet reshuffle? Prime Minister Tsouderos is bringing some more Republicans into his Government to keep the troops happy. Not that that will appease the EAM in Athens.'

'Only one thing will appease the EAM in Athens, sir,' said Maitland, 'and that is Greece with a Communist Government.'

'Over my dead body,' growled Churchill. 'Heaven forbid that I live to see the day when the red flag of Communism flies over Athens!'

Manfried Keller looked out across the roof-tops of Athens. From where he stood, he could see the red flag of National Socialist Germany – with its swastika emblem – as it fluttered from the mast above German headquarters.

His own HQ was less well advertised. He and his staff occupied the top floors of the Hotel Artemis. Keller was waiting for a telephone call from Franz von Harzer in Ioannina. It was being relayed via Athens Military HQ and Keller's direct line to the switchboard there.

The telephone gave a long ring. Keller picked up the instrument.

'Is that you, Colonel-General Keller? Von Harzer here. I thought you might like to know the final tally for Operation Wolf the other night. Berlin have already cabled their congratulations. Naturally, I told them that it would have been impossible without the Abwehr's magnificent intelligence work.'

'Your men did well,' said Keller. 'I would have stayed

151

on with you for a day or two if Hoffmann and I hadn't been needed urgently here in Athens. The Greek guerrillas have gone to war with each other up in the mountains on a much bigger scale than even I thought was possible. But you were to tell me the final score for our little battle. How did it go?'

'Our own losses were light,' said von Harzer. 'Nine dead and seventeen wounded. The Italians from Agrinion collected what was left of the terrorists on Thursday. One has to bring them in or they accuse us of hogging the limelight. Anyway, they collected one hundred and three dead, five serviceable machine-guns and seven dozen rifles. It was the most successful engagement we've had against the terrorists since the start of the occupation. Oh, and the Italians took three prisoners, all badly wounded. Two of them died on the way to Agrinion — which makes our count a hundred and five — and the other survivor was in pretty bad shape. He had the uniform of a British captain and was carrying English cigarettes. Benodetto has him under guard in some hospital or other. No doubt your people will want to interrogate him?'

'An English prisoner, eh?' said Keller. 'I should like to interrogate him myself.'

'You had better hurry then,' said von Harzer. 'They didn't expect him to last. Lost too much blood. Poor devil was blinded, too.'

After Keller had rung off, he placed a call to Benodetto, the Italian commander at Agrinion. The Italian was effusive in his desire to co-operate. There was much haranguing of switchboard operators in voluble Italian. Finally, Keller was told that he had a direct line to the hospital to which the English Captain had been taken.

An Italian sergeant was on the other end of the line. He was in charge of the guard placed on the prisoner and he started to explain in elaborate detail why, in the interests of security, all inquiries concerning the prisoner had to be referred to him. To whom was he talking?

Keller could visualise the self-important buffoon coming to awed attention when he informed him that he was talking to the Chief of German Intelligence for the Eastern Mediterranean Sector. The Sergeant bumbled something about finding the doctor in charge of the prisoner.

There was a further delay while the call was transferred to the office of a Dr Kurt Jansen. To Keller's great relief, the doctor answered the call in impeccable German and asked in what way he could be of service to the German officer in Athens.

'Thank goodness I've found one German in Agrinion,' said Keller, whose Italian was limited. 'It makes conversation much easier. Especially on this very bad line. This is Colonel-General Keller of Military Intelligence, Doctor. I want to come and interrogate the English prisoner as soon as possible. Is he well enough to answer questions?'

Dr Kurt Jansen was Swedish, not German, but he did not correct Keller about his nationality. Jansen paused a long time before speaking. Then, with deliberation, he said:

'I am sorry to disappoint you, Colonel-General, but it will not be possible to question the English officer.'

'Is he too far gone?' asked Keller. 'Can't he be given some drugs or stimulants which will pep him up long enough to answer one or two questions?'

'It is not that, Colonel-General. You are just too late. I have to tell you that the Englishman died only twenty minutes ago.'

Dr Kurt Jansen put the telephone back in its cradle. He drew the back of his hand across a forehead damp with sweat. What devil of madness had prompted him to tell the Abwehr general that the Englishman had died?

153

Certainly, one of his patients had died only twenty minutes ago – but the Englishman was still holding his own. Jansen told himself he was a fool. He had allowed those Greek nurses to pressurise him into jeopardising not only his work here at the Foundation but possibly his life. If the Germans found out about his stupid lie – as surely they would – Jansen had no doubt they would conclude that he was working hand in glove with the Greek resistance.

Head Nurse Marina Stavrides found Jansen seated in his office staring morosely at the telephone.

'You look ill, Doctor,' she said worriedly. And, indeed, his pallor was ghostly. 'Doctor, is something wrong?'

Jansen did not answer. He seemed mesmerised by that telephone, the instrument which had somehow provoked his folly.

'Doctor, you were up all last night with that English boy and there's no more we can do now for poor Mr Binas. Why don't you go home now and get some rest?'

Jansen looked at the Head Nurse as if wondering where she had come from.

'I have just told the Germans that the English officer died twenty minutes ago.'

'But it was Mr Binas who died. The *Anglos* is a little better. His pulse is stronger. I've just come from him. Doctor, you must be overtired.'

Jansen shook his head sadly.

'I'm mad, not overtired. You and your nursing staff are to blame. You and your talk of what the Germans would do to the Englishman. They wanted to interrogate him. That's why I told them he was dead – so that they would leave him alone.'

Comprehension dawned on the nurse's face.

'You . . . you did it to save him! Oh, Doctor, how wonderful! Now, we can help him to escape!'

Jansen looked at the woman sourly.

154

'In his condition? It is impossible. Soon, the Germans will arrive to make sure he *is* beyond questioning. They'll get their hands on him in spite of my stupid lie. And they'll arrest me, too!'

Head Nurse Stavrides was not so easily defeated.

'We must think of something!' she urged. 'We must think of a way out.'

Jansen was utterly pessimistic. There was no way out. He could only shake his head is disbelief, a few moments later, when Nurse Stavrides – with uncontained excitement – began to outline a possible solution.

'It will never work!' Jansen said when he had heard her out. 'It is too preposterous for words. There are far too many people involved to keep such a thing secret.'

'We shall see,' said Nurse Stavrides. 'No Greek would ever betray you, Doctor. I'm going to get the others in here right away to talk about it.'

The Italian sergeant and one of his men were playing cards at a small table a few feet away from the prisoner's bed. They both looked up when Head Nurse Stavrides breezed into the small single ward.

'I'll have to borrow the patient for five minutes,' she said, in moderately good Italian. 'Doctor wants to take some X-rays.'

The Sergeant eyed the nurse's plumpish frame appreciatively.

'You could borrow me for five minutes,' he said waggishly. 'There's more life in me than there is in that one on the bed there!'

Nurse Stavrides made a coquettish little frown.

'Surely you're good for more than five minutes, *Sergente*,' she said, and dodged the hand that came out to pinch her bottom. The door swung open and a younger nurse pushed a stretcher trolley into the room.

'I have a winning hand here,' the Sergeant complained

without rancour. 'Why do you nurses never interrupt when I'm losing?'

'Don't let us disturb your game,' said Nurse Stavrides. 'We're just taking the Tommy here to the radiography room. We'll bring him straight back.'

'I hope he survives the journey. He doesn't look too good to me,' said the Sergeant. He stood up and looked down at the pathetic figure on the bed. The head was swathed in bandages with only mouth and nostrils exposed. A drip feed was attached to the man's left hand, which protruded from a striped pyjama sleeve. The right shoulder and chest had been heavily bandaged and the pyjama jacket had been drawn round the right shoulder and fastened with a safety pin to the bandaging.

The two nurses lifted the injured man gently on to the trolley. Then one detached the drip bottle from its stand and carried it alongside the trolley. The Sergeant watched the women guide the trolley along the corridor and through the swing doors of the radiography room. Then he returned to his game of cards.

Inside the radiography room, the nurses went speedily into action as soon as the doors swung shut behind them. They lifted the stretcher down to the floor, placing it alongside another stretcher, on which lay the body covered by a sheet.

Nurse Stavrides pulled back the sheet. The man who lay there had already been bandaged around the head and chest in a fashion identical to the wounded British officer. While the other nurse held the drip, Nurse Stavrides eased off the officer's pyjama jacket and transferred it to the dead man. She pinned it into place and then replaced the drip feed. Her companion, meantime, had attached the drip bottle to a stand, exchanging it with a bottle which Nurse Stavrides now wired to the corpse.

They lifted the dead man on to the trolley. For a

moment the leads from the two drip bottles became entangled but, after some manoeuvring, the exchange was complete. Leaving Mackenzie on his stretcher on the floor, the two nurses pushed the trolley out through the swing doors.

'That was quick work,' said the Italian sergeant, as the nurses wheeled the trolley back into the small ward. The women lifted the inert body on to the bed.

Nurse Stavrides looked anxious.

'The Doctor hasn't seen the patient yet. He took a turn in the radio room,' she said to the Sergeant. 'Nurse, hurry and find the Doctor.'

The Italians looked on with curiosity as Jansen appeared at the younger nurse's heels and busied himself over the patient on the bed. Taking the left wrist in his hand, he felt for a non-existent pulse. Then he bent low over the mouth aperture in the mummified face. With a stethoscope he listened for a heart which had stopped beating some fifty minutes before. Jansen straightened with a gesture of despair.

'*Morto?*' asked the Sergeant.

'*Si Sergente,*' said Jansen. '*Il capitano Inglese e morto.*'

Jansen covered the dead man with the sheet. He faced the Sergeant.

'What about the burial? I had better let the *Commandante* know, I suppose.'

'*Si, Dottore.* There will be papers, regulations . . . the usual stuff.'

'The Tommy had no identification bracelet,' said Jansen. 'We called him Captain Unknown. I'll ring Benodetto and find out what has to be done.'

'Doctor?'

'Yes, Nurse Stavrides.'

'Perhaps the Tommy could be buried at my village, by my people? If the *Commandante* would permit it. Somewhere, perhaps, a wife and a mother grieve for this unknown man. He died for Greece as well as his own flag. We could not save him, but we can honour him in his final journey as one of our own.'

The Italian sergeant, moved by the nurse's words – she had spoken in Italian for his benefit – drew himself to attention.

'I am a soldier, *Dottore*. We Italians respect the fallen. I, Sergente Guido Sciama, salute a brave enemy.'

He faced the bed and saluted briskly. Then he crossed himself. He turned to Jansen.

'Only *il Commandante* can decide about the funeral,' he said.

Jansen promised to telephone Benodetto immediately from his office. Instructing the nurses to remove the body to the hospital mortuary, he went out to the corridor. There, he paused for a moment and leaned back against the wall. His hands were trembling. How he had been able to go through with the charade in there he had no idea. But the deception had been carried a stage further now. There was no going back.

He went on to his office and picked up the telephone. Benodetto was his usual agreeable self until Jansen mentioned the nurse's request about the burial.

'We do not want the Greeks staging a spectacle which mobs could turn into a demonstration against the forces of occupation,' he declared. 'I could never permit such a thing.'

'It will not be that at all,' said Jansen, trying to keep the voice even. 'You must understand that the nurse fought to save this man's life. He awakened in them all the mercy of their calling – because he could not see, because he was alone and wounded in a foreign country, without friends. Now, they are saddened beyond measure because they lost the battle for his life . . . And still no one even knows his name. They just want to give him a Christian farewell – not more than half a dozen people present. They see themselves as representing the wife or mother who waits somewhere for a loved one who will never come home.'

Like the Sergeant before him, Benodetto was moved.

'Poor fellow. I feel we should bury him with full military honours – but our allies, the Germans, frown on any such show for enemy soldiers who consort with terrorists. Perhaps, in the circumstances, I could allow the English captain to be buried as you suggest. Indeed, I shall not only permit it, I shall attend in person as official representative of the Occupying Forces.'

'My nurses will be honoured, I'm sure,' said Jansen. 'And they will respect you more, *Commandante*, for the honour you accord to a fallen enemy.'

In the meantime, Mackenzie – still deep in the drug-induced coma of post-operative shock – had been quietly installed in the private room formerly occupied by the late Ion Binas. Head Nurse Stavrides was going about her duties but taking care to be never far from a window which gave her a view of the main gate. She was anxious not to miss the arrival of the widow of Ion Binas.

The woman did not yet know of the death of her husband. Jansen had telephoned her at her home some thirty miles away to inform her of the death – but she had already left home for the hospital in response to an earlier call which had expressed concern about his condition.

Nurse Stavrides had unshakeable faith in the staff of the Bernadotte Foundation Clinic to guard with their lives the secret of the English soldier's supposed death. The unknown quantity in the elaborate deception was Eleni Binas, the widow of the man who had died. Marina Stavrides had never quite known what to make of Mrs Binas. She had always found her a rather haughty person, seemingly pre-occupied by some private sadness or misery.

On the occasions she had visited her ailing husband,

none of the staff of the Clinic had ever got much more than cool formality out of Eleni Binas. There was an aloofness in her manner which did not invite idle conversation. Hoity-toity was how Nurse Stavrides thought of the woman – but she hoped that underneath that cool unapproachable façade, Eleni Binas was a true and patriotic Greek.

There was no way of telling in advance just how the Binas woman was going to react to the twin shocks of her husband's death and the invitation to surrender his body for burial under a nameless cross.

CHAPTER TWELVE

A Grave near Agrinion

Preston knew something was wrong. His suspicions had
been vaguely stirred on the first night's trek from Giannopouli. Enough to make him uneasy but not enough
to make him do anything about it. He had simply come
to the conclusion that he had been saddled with two of
the surliest guards in Greece and let it go at that.

Now, two days' march from Giannopouli, Preston's
assessment of the two Greek guerrillas was that they
were more than perversely uncommunicative, they were
down-right evasive.

The nightmare of the battle on the coast road had
not receded from his mind. He had blundered away
from the battlefield in such a state of numbed shock
and self-recrimination for abandoning Mackenzie that
he had paid little heed at first to where he was going.
When he suddenly found himself on the Arta-Agrinion
highway some miles south of the scene of the ambush,
he had pulled himself together and considered the
options open to him.

Mackenzie had told him to head for Giannopouli,
probably with the idea that Preston might find someone
there who would help him make contact with the BLO
known to be operating in Western Roumelia. Preston
knew there would be no percentage in trying to reach
Garrow in Methravioplos. He had no chance of
reaching the village ahead of Kirkos and his killers who,
he reckoned, would take over there after murdering

Garrow and the two radio men. A lust to revenge himself on Kirkos was strong in Preston, but he was realistic enough to reject thoughts of embarkation on a one-man campaign of such futility. His number one duty was survival, perhaps escape from Greece altogether, so that the Allied leadership could be made aware of the Communist treachery he had witnessed. He was sure in his mind that Kirkos's callous betrayal of the Greek Royalist units was not simply the whim of a political maverick. It was part of something much more sinister, and the sooner the world knew about it the better.

It astonished Preston to realise that he had come to Greece only a matter of weeks ago with a report for Communist military achievement which bordered on admiration. Admittedly, this had been gained from afar and perhaps in reaction to some of the materialistic excesses of his native United States of America. Also, Communism exerted – with its reforming ideals – a particular appeal to a young man fired with visions of curing the world's ills.

Now, with the massacre of the Greek patriots so fresh in his mind, Preston had lost forever the rose-coloured view of Communism. He had thought Mackenzie to be cynical in his outlook. Now it all made terrifying sense. And he was determined to let the British Military Command know just what kind of fire they were playing with. If the British didn't stop supplying the ELAS with guns and ammunition, then the mountains of Greece would run red with blood before long. Greek blood.

The blood of his Greek mother ran strong in Preston. There was a vigorous strain of *philotimo* in him: that spirit of honour which preserves as inviolable man's right to freedom as an individual. It sang in him now as he strode south along the road towards Agrinion. Like the messenger from Marathon, there was a steely resolve powering his tired body. He would accomplish his task, one way or another, if it meant battling to the last breath.

He had continued south along the road until he saw ahead a river bridge guarded by Italian soldiers. Keeping well out of sight, he had circled inland and then followed the river upstream, looking for a narrow point to cross. Tying his clothes in a bundle, he had swum the icy river and continued south across the road which ran parallel with the bank on the far side.

The first streaks of daylight were pale grey in the eastern sky before he had stopped to rest. In a tiny valley, through which a hill stream gurgled, he bedded down amid some dwarf cypresses struggling for existence in an otherwise barren landscape. He had awakened with the sun warm on his face and to the sound of a dozen goats bleating a chorus as they foraged around the trees. About ten feet away, a boy of fourteen was sitting on a rock gazing at him with unafraid curiosity.

The boy's home was nearby and less than a kilometre from Giannopouli. His mother – a thin pinch-faced widow in ankle-length black – had been kindness itself; taking him into her home and offering hospitality that was stinted only by the desperate poverty of her lot. Neither woman nor boy knew of any British soldiers in the surrounding hills but there was a man in Giannopouli who knew of these things. If he couldn't help . . . then he would know someone. There wasn't a Greek between here and Agrinion who wouldn't help the *Anglos* find his comrades.

The mother had sent the boy off immediately to Giannopouli while she had insisted on feeding Preston some white goat cheese and coarse bread and a glass of vinegary wine. The boy had returned with the news that the man they knew was holding a council with his acquaintances and help would be forthcoming. In the meantime, Preston was to stay where he was because

163

an Italian patrol had spent part of the morning hanging around the crossroads below the town and questioning anyone heading for Amphilochia.

Preston had spent the night curled on a black horse-hair couch which accommodated about three-quarters of his body. Because the Greeks were the least security-conscious people he had ever encountered, he tried not to worry about news of his presence being broadcast too far and wide. Although Greece had possibly the poorest roads and communications system in Europe, the speed at which news travelled was bewildering. Often, of course, a story at the end of its travels bore not too close a resemblance to the original. It was said that one could not cough in Athens without it being notified in Salonika as pneumonia.

Next day, an elderly man turned up at the widow's house and was brought in to meet Preston. The man had heard of a great battle on the coast road. There were rumours of hundreds of dead. He wished to shake the hand of the young soldier who had fought in the battle. He also had a message for him. Two men from Agrinion would come the following night and guide him to a place in the mountains where a British major was thought to be operating.

According to the man, word of Preston's plight had gone out along the grapevine and there wasn't a Greek between Agrinion and Empesos who hadn't offered to help. The two from Agrinion, however, were 'official'.

It was no comfort to Preston that so many people knew of his whereabouts, but the man from Gianno-pouli laughed at his fears. 'You are one of us,' he had said. 'We would never betray you.'

An hour after dark on the second evening, Preston had taken his leave of the widow – her blessings and good wishes ringing in his ears – and had set out in company of a small swarthy man called Zotos and a

164

surly, seemingly nameless giant, whose only communication was an occasional grunt.

Zotos was spokesman for both but he was so vague and offhand that Preston soon became exasperated with him. Yes, he would take the *Anglos* to a British group but, no, he couldn't say exactly where the group was. Yes, it was possible they would contact the group next day . . . On the other hand, it might take several days to find them.

Extracting solid information from the man was like trying to wring juice out of a billiard ball. Now, after marching for thirty-six hours out of the last forty-eight – in which they had crossed two rivers, circled a large lake and covered many miles of mountain track – Preston was growing more and more impatient at the absence of contact with the British group of which Zotos had spoken. But the more he questioned Zotos, the more evasive were the Greek's replies. At last his patience was exhausted.

Zotos was a few yards ahead of him on the trail with the giant taking up the rear. Preston called out to Zotos:

'Hold it right there, *Kirie*. This is as far as I go.'

The guerrilla looked back at him questioningly.

'This is as far as I go,' Preston repeated.

'Only a few miles more now,' said Zotos. 'Soon we find the English major.'

Preston had taken a map from his pocket and was unfolding it. He pointed to a stretch of water far below them.

'That water over there – it's part of Lake Kremaston, isn't it?'

Zotos came back to peer at the map over Preston's shoulder.

'I do not need maps,' he hedged. 'What does it matter what the lake is called?'

'These two peaks to the south and east . . . They must be Kaliskouda and Tymfrestos,' said Preston.

'What if they are?'

'Tymfrestos sits right at the back of Karpenisi. If we keep going in the direction we're heading, we're going to hit the road that runs from Karpenisi to the big lake. If you were to lay me a dollar for every ten I'd put beside it, I'd bet you were taking me straight to Karpenisi.'

Zotos shuffled uneasily.

'So, maybe we find the English major in Karpenisi. What does it matter?'

'This little piggy ain't going to Karpenisi,' said Preston firmly. 'You guys go right ahead but I know for a fact there are no British military in Karpenisi. It's Spiro's town and hoatching with ELAS men – and for reasons I needn't go into, I'm not going anywhere near it.'

The big Greek, whom Preston had mentally nick-named Cyclops, had overtaken them and stood astride the trail at Preston's back. Preston intercepted a meaningful look which Zotos flashed at the man behind him. Now the suspicions which the American had been nursing over the past two days began to solidify into terrible certainties.

'There is too much talk,' said Zotos. 'We waste time and it will soon be too dark to see the trail.'

'You boys go on,' replied Preston. 'I'll catch you up.'

Again a look passed between Zotos and Cyclops. Zotos gave a slight nod of his head. The giant raised his rifle and brought the butt crashing down on Preston's head. The American fell face down across the trail. Blood oozed through his woollen cap.

Cyclops raised the rifle again to repeat the treatment but Zotos waved him away.

'We are to take him to Spiro alive. Take his gun.'

Preston came to with blinding lances of pain bayoneting his brain. He forced his eyes open.

Zotos was rifling the pack which had been on the American's back. Cyclops was toying with the Elgin watch which had been issued to Preston in Egypt. Preston found that his wrists had been tied in front of him but that his legs were free.

Cyclops grinned down at Preston. He held out the American's watch.

'It is a very good watch. I keep it.'

'You bastards! Cut me loose.'

Zotos strolled over and spat. The spittle landed inches from Preston's face.

'Silence, you son of a pox-ridden whore. We go now to Karpenisi. On your feet!'

Preston tried to move but his head spun. He didn't make it. Zotos aimed a kick at his haunch.

'On your feet!'

Preston struggled to his feet. The pain in his head was blinding him but he stared hate at Zotos.

'What am I – a prisoner of war? Or are you just going to finish off the dirty work that your Communist buddies didn't quite complete on the Agrinion road?'

Zotos studied him with contempt. Now that he had the American at his mercy, he seemed prepared to be a lot more communicative.

'We know all about you, *Americanos*. You were with that traitor filth, Ionidas, at Methravioplos. We were told you would run like rabbits while soldiers of the Revolution fought the German guns. And that is what happened on the coast, eh? While our comrades died you and the King-loving scum took to your heels like cowards.'

Preston returned the man's contemptuous stare.

'You got it the wrong way round, buddy boy. Where do you get your information? Radio Moscow or Tokyo Rose?'

Zotos ignored him. The reference to Tokyo Rose was completely lost on him.

'We have known for some weeks that Ionidas and his collaborationists pigs were planning to betray the

Liberation Army to the Fascists. In every village we have been ready. Now we are at war with all collaborationists. They will all be liquidated.'

He stared at Zotos, wondering if the man had any comprehension of the evil for which he seemed to be such a willing tool and mouthpiece. Was there any ability to reason behind those gloating, confident eyes? Or was he completely mindless?

'Look, Zotos,' said Preston. 'Maybe I'm not too bright – and a lot of what has happened to me will probably substantiate that – but there's an awful lot going on that just doesn't make any sense to me. Somebody has been conning you blind about Ionidas. He and a dozen men – the people you call scum – took on about four hundred Germans with grenades. They just went straight at them . . . And they would have got away with it if your ELAS friends had given them the covering fire to get away. Instead, your ELAS chums shot them down like it was a turkey-shoot. You can take my word for it. I was there. I saw it.'

Zotos was unmoved.

'The word of a coward is worth nothing.'

'All right, tell me this then,' said Preston. 'How could you, wherever you were, know beforehand what was going to happen on the Agrinion road? Before the operation was even planned? I helped to plan that attack just over a week ago and, until then, no target nor time nor location had even been selected. If you knew beforehand what was going to happen, it was because either the ELAS set the whole thing up or the Germans did . . . Or they did it together. If the Germans and the Liberation Army had planned the whole thing as a way of getting rid of a hundred real Greek patriots, it couldn't have worked better. Whose side are you on, Zotos? Has EAM done a deal with the Germans?'

Zotos sneered.

'Your lies will not save you. You and the collbor-

168

ationists deserted – just as we had been warned you would. We were expecting you, *Americanos*. Although why your life should be spared, I do not know. Our orders were to find and kill all traitors and deserters who reached our area, but not the officers in British uniform – not unless they interfered. The *Americanos* in particular was not to be harmed. General Spiro himself ordered that you were to be brought to Karpenisi, by force if you did not go willingly, so that you could tell him personally of the treachery of Ionidas and the other renegade, Orestes.'

'You knew about *me* – an American in British uniform? When?'

'Within hours of you running from the Germans. No matter where you had run we would have known – to Amphilochia, to Arta, to Empesos, to Agrinion. If the Germans had caught you first and taken you prisoner, we would have known. Even in places where we are not welcome, we have eyes and ears. That is why the Revolution will be victorious in Greece.'

The Greek's eyes gleamed fanatically as he boasted. Preston realised with despair that there was no way any words of his would sway him one way or another.

'There was another British officer, Zotos – a captain. No doubt you heard about him on this marvellous grapevine of yours?'

'He was taken prisoner and is held by the Italians in Agrinion,' said Zotos.

'Then he's alive!' Preston's heart lifted. Amid all that happened, no single piece of information could have raised his spirits more. Mackenzie was alive!

'Do not be too happy for your friend,' said Zotos, enjoying the cruelty of his words. 'You will never see him again. They said he would not live for more than a day, two days at the most. Pray that he is already dead, *Americanos* . . . that he died before the Germans started asking him questions. Now, move yourself. *Grighora!* Quickly! Come on, march!'

Cyclops, openly impatient at the talkativeness of his comrade and their prisoner, prodded Preston roughly with his rifle. The American lurched forward, despair now heavier in him than ever before. He thought of his last emotional promise to Mackenzie, his vow to take revenge on Kirkos. He was conscious of a total emptiness now in his passionate declaration. He had messed things up, good. Mackenzie would never have been suckered by Zotos and his moronic pal the way he had allowed himself to be. He would have been wise to Zotos right from the start.

Preston's one glimmer of hope lay with Spiro. The fact that the General had wanted him brought to Karpenisi alive suggested the possiblity that Kirkos's treachery might have been unofficial, that he had allowed his hatred of the Royalists to indulge in excesses which not even ELAS could sanction.

Even now, Preston could not bring himself to believe that what had happened back there on the Agrinion road could possibly be part of a calculated plan in which a nation practised genocide against itself.

Eleni Binas lingered by the open grave into which the coffin had been lowered some minutes earlier. The handful of other mourners were already making their way slowly towards the gates of the tiny cemetery and, nearby, the grave-digger waited patiently to complete his task.

The funeral party included the Italian *Commandante* – resplendent in uniform and medals – three nurses from the hospital, Dr Jansen, and the two aged parents of Head Nurse Stavrides. The priest who had conducted the brief burial ceremony was talking solemnly with the driver of the ambulance which had brought the body on its last journey. Three elderly men from the village,

170

who had helped to carry the coffin to the grave, stood in a self-conscious little group away from the others.

Eleni Binas took a final look at the grave.

'Goodbye, Ion,' she whispered.

She turned and walked slowly after the others.

There had been no storm from Eleni. She had accepted the news of her husband's death and the proposed deception with astonishing calm. She had listened quietly as Nurse Stavrides, in a state of great agitation, had poured out the whole story and supplemented it with pleas for forgiveness and co-operation. When the nurse had finished, Eleni had sat deep in thought, letting it all sink in. Then she had said:

'Poor Ion. Very little he did in his short life had any point or purpose. It is ironic that death should give him the opportunity to achieve something.'

Eleni Binas had introduced a much-needed element of calm authority to the off-the-cuff conspiracy initiated by Jansen and the nurses at the Clinic.

'Do you propose to keep the wounded man here for the duration of the Occupation?' she had asked pointedly. 'Do any of you have a single thought in your heads about how he can be helped to escape?'

Jansen and Nurse Stavrides had had to admit that they had given no thought to the situation beyond the point of soliciting her agreement to the burial of her husband in a grave that would not even carry his name.

'It must be obvious to you,' Eleni had said, 'that every day you keep this man here in the hospital you run a constant risk of discovery. Therefore, for his safety and your own, you must get him out of the hospital and as far away from it as possible at the earliest opportunity.'

Jansen and Nurse Stavrides agreed – but neither had any idea of how this was to be accomplished. The man needed constant care and attention. If his condition improved, he could perhaps be moved in three or four days. But he was going to need months of convalescence. On top of that, it would be three weeks or more before it could be ascertained whether or not his sight had been damaged beyond repair. The chances were one in three that he would be permanently blind in his right eye and one in twenty that he would be blind in the left.

'It seems to me,' Eleni Binas had said, 'that you have all rushed into this with more hope than intelligence. However, I grant that you were motivated by compassion, with little or no thought of the risk or possible consequences to yourselves, so your folly is pardonable.'

'What are we to do now?' Jansen had asked miserably.

'You will get on with the job of making that English soldier fit to travel,' Eleni Binas has replied firmly. 'Keep him in Ion's room at the hospital and do not allow anyone into that room who is not directly involved in nursing him. When he is well enough to be moved, you will have him brought to my home on the island, where everything will be in readiness for him.'

Jansen's delight at the proposal was more than a little tinged by the thought of transferring responsibility for the helpless fugitive to someone else's shoulders.

'That is wonderful, Mrs Binas. But it means you will be running a great risk. What of your husband's friends and the people who live near you? Who can be trusted? How are you going to hide this man?'

'Dr Jansen,' came the withering reply. 'If I didn't feel a great deal more competent than you or anyone here at the hospital to handle this situation, I would not have suggested it. You may not know it, but my husband and I have lived a very isolated existence for these past few years. I know what I'm doing.'

Christina Kirkos stared her husband straight in the eye. She had been cooped up in an attic room of the house in Karpenisi for two months, with no explanation of why she had been made a prisoner. Her only visitor during all that time had been the crippled peasant girl who brought her food twice a day.

Now, after making repeated demands of the girl to see Kirkos or anyone else who could explain why she had been locked up, George Kirkos had finally come.

'Why? Why? Why?' she had screamed at her husband. 'Is this the freedom you promised?'

Kirkos seemed genuinely surprised at her unkempt and dishevelled appearance.

'I didn't know you were being held like this,' he said. 'It was Spiro's doing, not mine.'

'You must have known something.'

'Only what Petrea told me.'

'Her! So, she's at the back of it!'

Kirkos seemed unable to bear looking at her. He turned his head away and stared out of the tiny window.

'I swear I knew nothing about it, Christina. I've been constantly on the move for the past six weeks. When I sent you back here from Methravioplos, I honestly thought I was doing you a good turn. Spiro was wanting someone who could do decoding. I thought you would be happier doing that than courier work.'

'There was only one snag. I don't know any Russian. I spent two days with that creep Karolov up in that radio shack on the top of the mountain – then Kosta marched in here one morning and had me locked in this room. What is going on, George? Why are they doing this to me?'

'You are going to stand trial,' said Kirkos hoarsely.

'Trial? Why? What for? George, what are they going to do with me?'

'Nothing will happen to you, Christina. It will be a formality. You will be acquitted. It is a case of putting the record straight.'

'For heaven's sake, what is that supposed to mean?'

Kirkos faced her.

'You remember the dentist in Agrinion? The man you paid for information?'

'Bernardini? What about him?'

'He tipped off the Germans that we were going to attack one of the convoys on the Arta-Agrinion road. They were ready for us. We walked right into a trap.'

A chill of fear tip-toed up Christina's spine. The fear was not only for herself.

'What happened?' she whispered.

'We lost more than a hundred men. It was a shambles. The British are trying to put the blame on ELAS for what happened. Spiro promised a full inquiry. That is why you will be tried, so that what really happened can all go on record. I know you were not involved with Bernardini, that you simply carried out orders from me. But only by accusing you and clearing you with the evidence which can be produced will we convince the British that Bernardini was the real traitor.'

Christina slumped on the mattress that served as her bed. The whole thing was like a crazy nightmare which seemed to go on and on. If, somewhere, there was a crumb of comfort, it was in George's new attitude to her. He seemed strangely chastened and sympathetic, as if – for once – she was the victim of events which he did not control, and he regretted it. She stole a glance at him and all her mistrust of him returned. She caught a flicker of smiling triumph in his eyes.

'I'm glad you can find something to smile about,' she said.

'I'm not smiling,' he lied. 'I was wondering how to break a certain piece of news to you.'

She looked at him anxiously.

'What?'

'The British captain – the one who was your lover . . . He was killed.'

Christina's face crumpled. A flood of emotiion welled

in her, unbidden. She choked on a grief which wept not just for a lover but for more than that, for something he had brought briefly into her life — a dream of honest hope and reason and good intention in a sick world.

Kirkos watched her tears impassively.

'Did he mean so much to you?' he asked.

'I liked him,' she sobbed. 'Can you understand that I liked him because he was kind to me? Just like you were once kind to me, George. Before you became eaten up with hate.'

She stared at him through her tears.

'Who is going to be kind to me now, George? Who is there now who's going to care one little bit what becomes of me?'

'It's too late for tears, Christina. It's too late now for self-pity.'

'My pity isn't all for myself, George.'

'What do you mean?'

'I mean that I have more to think about than just me. I've got to think about what is going to happen when my baby is born.'

BOOK TWO

CHAPTER THIRTEEN

The Seeds of Artemis

A breeze from the south-west was gusting up from Phaleron Bay across the city of Athens. The German flag on top of the Acropolis was straining away from its halyard.

Manfried Keller looked out from his window in the Hotel Artemis. In his right hand he held a letter which had arrived from Berlin in the Top Secret bag less than an hour ago. Keller's arm hung by his side, the letter limp against his trouser leg. He raised the letter now and read it for a third time. It was addressed to Keller personally and, at the top, was dated: 27th February 1944. It read:

Dear Keller.

On the 18th of this month, our illustrious Führer signed a decreee, from which I quote: 'I order the creation of a unified German Secret Service.'

I shall not burden you with all the details, other than to acquaint you with the facts that I have been appointed overall chief of the new service. It will incorporate the SS Intelligence Service, of which I was formerly the head, and the Abwehr.

It was my wish that the resources of the two services be integrated as smoothly and as expeditiously as possible. It is imperative that, during the transitional period, all departments continue to function with maximum efficiency. I am depending on the complete co-operation of all heads of departments. As from 1st March 1944, you will assume control of the Central Mediterranean and Eastern Mediterranean Departments. I suggest you make immediate arrangements for transfer of your headquarters and staff to a suitable location in Italy.

It is not my intention to effect wholesale changes in the staffing and running of what was formerly the Abwehr, simply for the sake of change. Changes *will* be made, but I am anxious to impress on all Abwehr personnel – particularly those who looked upon the SS Intelligence Service as a rival rather than a companion organisation – that their positions and past records will be respected.

Changes will be necessary. Your own position, and that of every member of your staff, will be subject to review. No member of the Service, however, need fear the outcome if his efficiency is proven and his loyalty to the Führer found to be beyond question.

I note that previously, in your capacity as Controller of the Eastern Mediterranean Department, you worked directly with Admiral Wilhelm Canaris. In future, you will deal directly with me and I trust that our association will be a happy and fruitful one.

My old friend, Wilhelm, sends you his warmest regards. You may be interested to know that he has been given a new appointment at the Ministry of Economic Affairs.

Strictly between ourselves, Wilhelm confided in me that he had to keep you on a very tight rein because some of your ideas were not only unorthodox but downright unethical. I am encouraged by this to believe that you may find me a more progressive and sympathetic chief. We are engaged in a war to the death and ethical considerations cut little ice with me.

Wilhelm said that you had an obsession about assassinating Churchill. Frankly, I cannot understand what he found to be so reprehensible in an enterprise which would render such an outstanding service to the Reich. Indeed, his inhibitions may partly explain the wretched failure of the expedition to eliminate Churchill last November. As it took place in England, I doubt if Canaris even mentioned it to you. He is not noted for broadcasting news of the Abwehr's more disastrous failures.

In spite of the débâcle, the Führer has by no means lost interest in the idea of eliminating Churchill. So, I shall be interested to hear more from you on the subject. Any sound plan would not only get my backing but such special resources as may be required would receive priority availability.

Heil Hitler.

Walther Schellenberg,
Chief of Joint Intelligence Services

Keller read the letter for a third time with strangely mixed feelings. What a hypocrite Schellenberg was! The way he talked about 'his old friend, Wilhelm' as if the pair were great buddies.

It was true that Canaris and Schellenberg met nearly every day of the week – but they were like rival stags after the same hind: each weighing the other up all the time, testing for the other's strength and probing for his weaknesses. It was anything but friendship.

Poor old Wilhelm,. The Blacks had got him out of the Abwehr at last. It was a wonder that an SS man hadn't already appeared in Athens to tell Keller how to run his department. But maybe that was only a matter of time – in spite of Schellenberg's extension of the Keller empire to Italy and all the talk about no whole-sale changes being made. Unless . . .

Keller was touched that Canaris had gone out of his way to protect him. Wilhelm must have known that by

181

hinting to Schellenberg that he was a fanatic who needed a tight rein, he was saying precisely the things which would endear Keller to the SS.

Canaris had even mentioned the Churchill obsession, knowing damned well that it wasn't an obsession at all. Schellenberg had reacted exactly as Canaris had intended. He had come to the conclusion that Keller was a nasty unscrupulous bastard with all the makings of a good SS man.

The mention of some kind of attempt on Churchill surprised Keller. It was news to him, and he wondered what had gone wrong.

Keller paced up and down the room. What was he to do? Canaris had given him the chance, however slender, of saving his position and his skin. It would be almost disloyal to Canaris not to accept the opportunity.

Keller crossed to a desk and took out some sheets of notepaper. He selected a plain sheet, and put to one side some old stationery which had belonged to the hotel.

Taking a fountain pen from his pocket, he wrote in block capitals on the blank sheet: OPERATION HUNTER. Then he thought for a few moments and decided he didn't like his first choice of codename. He scored the words out. His eye fell on the old hotel notepaper. He smiled and started to write again.

This time, he wrote: OPERATION ARTEMIS.

In a neat script, he wrote underneath: 'The object of the above operation is the assassination of Winston Churchill . . .'

He wrote continuously for an hour. At the end of that time, he felt quite pleased with his efforts. What he had written was not quite a blueprint for Churchill's assassination, more a first chapter of a thesis which would ensure the survival of Manfried Keller.

Into it had gone all his theories on political assassination, the wide variety of techniques which could be employed, the necessity to place responsibility for the outrage where the greatest political embarrassment would result, the desirability even of tricking non-German agencies into committing the deed.

Schellenberg could not help but be impressed.

Preston was glad to put the squalor of Naples behind him. The devastation, the begging children, the general lack of sanitation - the very sights and sounds of a city ravaged by war – depressed him.

'Where is it you have to take me?' he asked the driver of the jeep. He glanced at the man beside him as he spoke. He had the poker-faced detachment which seemed to be the hallmark of all military policemen.

'It's a villa a few miles out the coast road. Nice place with a view of Capri and the bay. Won't be long now.'

A winding drive led from the main road through lime trees already rich with spring foliage. The villa nestled in a rocky cove with profuse shrub gardens stepping in narrow terraces to a sandy beach.

A military policeman in white helmet and gaiters sunned himself on the terrace facing the drive. He ambled across to the jeep.

'They're waiting for you, sir. Colonel Radmeyer said I was to take you right up the moment you arrived. Mr Cassidy is with him and some British guy. Will you follow me, sir?'

As Preston followed the MP into the house, he braced himself for what he knew was ahead.

'They're upstairs – in the Vista Room,' volunteered the MP. 'Don't know if I should be warning you, sir, but that Mr Cassidy seems to be one hell of an angry man.'

'That makes two of us, soldier,' said Preston. He had been waiting for this showdown since just before

Christmas, when he had been put under virtual house arrest in Cairo.

The Vista Room was a magnificent long room with a breath-taking view of the sea. It had french windows along its entire length which opened to a broad balcony with a wrought-iron rail. All but one of the french windows were closed. Three men sat at one end of a marble-topped table which had seating around it for twelve.

Two of the men were in civilian cloths. One, a bull-like figure in a Panama suit, reminded Preston of the movie actor, Edward Arnold. The other civilian was more casually dressed in slacks, open yellow shirt and blue pullover. He had a paisley-patterned silk kerchief knotted at his neck and tucked into the shirt.

The third man was in US Army uniform. Preston recognised Colonel Vincent Radmeyer of the OSS. Radmeyer rose.

'Find yourself a seat, Lieutenant. This get-together is official but it's informal. The gentleman on my right is Mr Cassidy of the State Department and the gentleman on my left is Sir Neil Maitland, who is a British Government expert on Greek affairs.'

Radmeyer sat down and looked questioningly at Cassidy.

'Anything you want to say at this stage, sir?'

'There's a lot I'd like to say,' said Cassidy, and he was glaring at Preston. 'I've been wanting to do some plain speaking to this young man ever since the Cairo Embassy cabled Washington about the threats he had been making to our officials there.'

Preston's lips tightened with anger but he kept his temper in check.

'Young man,' Cassidy went on, 'you have made waves all the way up to the President and caused me more trouble than a barrowload of monkeys, but I have promised the Secretary to give you a fair hearing. What

184

you say for yourself had better be good or, goddamn me, I am going to make it my personal business to have you put safely behind bars for the rest of the goddamned war!'

Preston was ice cool in his anger now. He returned Cassidy's stare without a waver of his eyes.

'You work in diplomacy, Mr Cassidy. I always believed that the essence of diplomacy was the temperate discussion of thorny subjects in a dispassionate and courteous manner. If you are going to begin by threatening me, what hope can I hold out that you are interested in reaching a conclusion that has anything to do with truth or justice?'

Cassidy's bull neck seemed to swell visibly and take on a purplish hue. Radmeyer's eyes were popping, but there was a glint in Maitland's which might have been merriment.

'You insolent whipper-snapper!' snarled Cassidy. 'Don't you talk to me like some ten-cent lawyer. Don't you realise that this could, and maybe should have been, settled by a court-martial? And that there's enough evidence against you to put you in a penitentiary for twenty years?'

'By evidence, I take it you mean the bullshit which the Greek Communists have been feeding the starry-eyed wonder who negotiated my release from General Spiro?'

'Now wait a minute,' put in Radmeyer. 'Harvey is one of our best men and you owe him quite a lot.'

'With all respect, sir, Harvey is a jerk. He seems to think that Spiro is some kind of Robin Hood. Spiro has him eating out of his hand. As for the negotiating he did on my behalf, oh boy, can he bargain! All h e did was agree with everything the Communists said about the treacherous Royalists and Republicans and sold me down the river. He signed documents which said I was a deserter, mentally unstable, a coward and God knows

185

what all else. Oh, he really set me up. These bastards held me prisoner for five goddamned months and all Harvey did was pat them on the head and tell them that if he had been in command up there he would probably have had me shot!'

It was Cassidy's turn to weigh in.

'I don't know much about this guy Harvey,' he said, 'but from the information I do have, Lieutenant, I can't understand why you're making this Spiro out to be such a bogeyman. Wasn't he the guy who provided you with guides to get you down from the mountains to the east coast and out of Greece on a fisherman's boat?'

'Yes, he did. But only because he thought I was completely discredited and nobody would believe a word I said.'

'He helped you get out and the first thing you did when you got to Turkey was shout blue murder about him to one of our consular staff?'

Preston groaned his despair.

'Can't you see, Mr Cassidy, why I wanted to tell the world about Spiro and the other Communist bands in Greece? They are conning the Allied Governments into supplying them with vast quantities of guns – but they are not using them against the Germans. They are using them to wipe out every Greek who stands between them and a Communist state.'

Preston turned to Maitland.

'The British know what's going on. Surely, sir, your Intelligence people can confirm what I'm saying.'

'We do know that the Communists want to run the show,' said Maitland. 'And they certainly cut up pretty rough in February of last year – but my Government is as reluctant as the American to get its fingers burnt politically. We got all the guerrilla leaders to meet our Military Mission last July and sign a treaty of co-operation. They were all there . . . ELAS, EDES and EKKA.

186

We insisted that if they didn't stop feuding between themselves, they would get no more guns and no more money. They all promised to toe the line.'

'And have they toed the line, sir?' asked Preston. 'Have the ELAS people kept their word?'

'No,' said Maitland. 'There have been flare-ups. There's no doubt ELAS were the instigators of trouble in October and November. They have far more men under arms than the other factions, Royalist or Republican, and they tried to muscle in on the others' territories. It's a delicate situation.'

'Isn't this getting away from the point?' said Cassidy. 'Both the British and American Governments are acutely aware of the delicacy of the political situation in occupied Greece, but that is not what is at issue here. The only people who can solve the political problems of Greece are the Greeks. Neither the American nor the British Government has any right to interfere with the internal affairs of that country.'

Preston threw his hands up in disgust.

'Thus spake Pontius Pilate,' he said.

'Watch your tongue, young man,' growled Cassidy. 'Let me remind you that the reason I am here is to settle what is going to be done about that loud mouth of yours. At the end of the day, what actually happened to you in Greece is of very little importance because it's not going to make the slightest difference to the conduct of our foreign policy or our war strategy. Whatever the rights or wrongs of your case, you committed a grave misdemeanour in Cairo, and the sole purpose of my mission to Italy is to gauge the extent of any future embarrassment you are likely to cause the United States Government and recommend any course of further action.'

'So I am really on trial? And you are the judge and jury?'

'That's about the size of it,' said Cassidy.

'And what exactly am I charged with?'

'You could be nailed on a whole string of charges under the Military Discipline Act, but we are prepared to let these pass for the moment. The most serious of the offences you committed was ... that while still bound by an oath of secrecy and engaged in confidential work relating to the external security of the United States, you threatened before witnesses to disclose to the Press certain matters of a highly inflammatory character and of a nature – because of their doubtful veracity – damaging to the United States.'

'You are referring to the slanging match I had in the Cairo Embassy with that pompous little jack-in-office who told me I was suspended from duty pending an inquiry?'

'That little jack-in-office, as you well know, is a former Colonel in the US Marines and one of the Ambassador's senior advisers.'

'He kept giving me the same old story day after day. I could see no one, I was to speak to no one, and nothing could be done until the OSS sent somebody from Naples. When I said I should maybe go and spill my story to the Press, I was only trying to get him off his backside and do something.'

'You should not have made that threat,' said Radmeyer. 'The Cairo authorities were perfectly correct to take from it that you were a high security risk and take the action they did in restricting your movements. You must realise, if nothing else, that it has greatly jeopardised any chances you had of staying in the Service.'

'That figures,' said Preston with a sorrowful shake of his head. 'I get shot at by the Germans, I get shot at by the Greeks ... Now I'm getting shot at by Uncle Sam. Maybe it would have been tidier all round if Cephalus and his Reds had got me back there on the Agrinion road and it had been Captain Mackenzie who got away.

He knew the score all right. And to think I didn't really believe him when he tried to put me wise to the ways the Communists worked.'

Cassidy was drumming impatiently on the table-top with his finger. His attitude conveyed plainly that his time and everyone else's was being unnecessarily wasted by this impossibly obstinate man. Maitland had reacted with a sharp straightening of his head at the mention of Mackenzie's name, but if it had been his intention to speak, he had had second thoughts about it and said nothing. It was Radmeyer who latched on to Preston's mention of the action on the Agrinion road.

'Tell us about the ambush on the German convoy,' said Radmeyer. 'You have claimed that only the two Royalist groups engaged the enemy and that the ELAS irregulars under Cephalus shot the Royalists down instead of covering their withdrawal.'

'That is exactly what happened, sir. The Germans were advancing up the hill from the road and the ELAS battalion were spread out all along the high ridges. We were caught right in the middle. Mac and I were the last to leave the road, otherwise we wouldn't have had the chance we did to escape. Mac, Captain Mackenzie, was fatally wounded only a few yards from safety. I went back and got him but he ordered me to leave him and get word out about what happened.'

Radmeyer frowned.

'But, General Spiro's account of the incident is quite different. He says that a collaborator tipped the Germans off about the attack and that while his guerrillas were taking on twice their number in Germans, the Royalist units scattered and ran, you among them.'

'That is a lie – a bloody obscene lie!' Preston's hands were trembling with anger. 'That's the story they dinned into me a hundred times a day when they held me prisoner in Karpenisi. That's what was on the document they tried to get me to sign every day for nearly a hundred and fifty days — but I didn't sign it. Harvey signed it for me, the bastard! But I *know* what happened on the Agrinion road, for Christ's sake, I was *there!* Harvey wasn't there, Spiro wasn't there, you weren't there . . . But I *was*. I was the only one who got out alive!'

'Just moderate your language, son,' said Radmeyer. 'It won't help to lose your temper.'

'Isn't it simply the case,' put in Cassidy, 'that you are paranoiac about Communists and that you are determined to accuse them of every conceivable crime you can think of as a smoke-screen for your own cowardice? Isn't the truth of the matter, Lieutenant, that you'll say anything to draw attention away from the fact that you have a yellow streak up your back a mile wide?'

Preston leapt from his chair and, before any of the others could move, he had hammered a right fist then a left into the face of Cassidy. The man went over backwards, chair with him. He scrambled away from the chair and cowered like a whipped dog. The skin around one cheek-bone was broken and blood trickled down on to his jacket. He held a hand to his face. Preston stood over him, shouting:

'You fat bastard! What do you know of yellow streaks sitting in an armchair in Washington? You call me a coward, you fat slob! Get up, you bastard, and I'll separate your pig head from the rest of you so fast that you'll . . .'

Preston never completed his threat. A shout from Radmeyer had brought two military policemen running into the room and he found himself seized and pinioned by the arms.

'Get him out of here!' roared Radmeyer.

Preston was being bundled from the room as Cassidy got shakily to his feet.

'Obviously the man is a maniac,' he stuttered. 'He should be locked up!'

Radmeyer turned to Cassidy with a look of unconcealed disgust on his face.

'There is no excuse for what happened just now, Mr Cassidy. I'm sorry Preston attacked you like that – but you did say a very provocative thing. Are you all right?'

'I guess I'll live. Maybe I did push him too far.'

'There will have to be a court-martial now. At least it solves the problem of what we are going to do about Preston. That little contretemps will cost him two years in the slammer. He won't rock the boat there. Pity, I hate to see a young man crack up like that.'

Maitland, who had been a silent watcher, suddenly spoke up.

'Gentlemen, has it occurred to either of you that that young man could be telling the truth?'

Cassidy and Radmeyer looked at Maitland with expressions which questioned his naïvety.

'Harvey's report was very complete.' said Radmeyer. 'He went into the case very thoroughly at Karpenisi. General Spiro gave him access to witnesses who fought at the ambush on the Agrinion road ... He let him study his private reports to Athens ... Showed him documents of an inquiry he himself had carried out. They were so upset about the Germans apparently having prior knowledge of the ambush that they put one of their own agents on trial – a woman who was the wife of one of their big-shots, Colonel Cephalus. She and her husband didn't get on and Spiro suspected, or somebody did, that she had tipped off the Germans in the hope that Cephalus would get bumped off in the attack.'

It was Maitland who now looked at Radmeyer as if the American were the naïve one.

'Rather an elaborate way to settle a domestic problem,' he observed. 'The girl was found not guilty,' said Radmeyer. 'What impressed Harvey was the picture the evidence gave him of what really happened at that ambush and how determined the ELAS people were to get at the truth. Spiro was quite blunt about the reasons for their concern. He said they could possibly afford a hundred casualties in a battle but they could not afford the loss of the guns which these men carried.'

'Yes, that's what he has constantly told us,' said Maitland. 'He has the men if we can give him the guns. What reason did Spiro give Harvey for keeping Preston a prisoner?'

'They said it was a form of protective custody. It seems that the guerrillas looked on Preston as a traitor, someone who had deserted them in the heat of battle. Spiro put Preston under wraps because he was afraid he would get a bullet in the back. Their own treatment of deserters is very harsh.'

'I wonder why Spiro never mentioned Preston's existence until after the treaty was signed in July,' said Maitland. 'Don't you think he was very dilatory in letting us know that he had an Allied officer locked up?'

'Does it make any difference now?'

'No, but it would have made a great deal of difference then. A few of our officers in Greece wanted us to break completely with the ELAS guerrillas. If Preston had not fallen into Spiro's hands and reached some of our other units . . . and if he had told his story then . . . and if it had been believed . . . I think we might have been much less accommodating to the Communists than we were.'

'An awful lot of ifs, Sir Neil. Look, it was Harvey's opinion – and Spiro's too, for that matter – that Preston cracked under the strain of guerrilla life and the horrors of his first night battle. He was surrounded by panicky troops and may even have tried to stop them running, who knows? The fact remains he crapped out. And after what happened a few moments ago, his goose is now cooked. We're going to have to put him away.'

'Is a court-martial necessary?' asked Cassidy.

'Hell sir, you're the one he assaulted,' protested Radmeyer. 'We can't pretend it just didn't happen.'

The man from Washington obviously had been having a lot of second thoughts.

'It doesn't need to go outside these four walls,' he said. 'My job was to get the whole thing sorted out quietly and informally. If there was a court-martial I would have to appear as a witness. A good defender could make me look pretty small ... Make out I provoked the attack. I'm not sure I want to get mixed up in a court-martial.'

'Then what the hell do we do with him?' asked Radmeyer.

'I was hoping you would have some bright ideas. Hell, Radmeyer, I'm not a vindictive man. I don't want to crucify that young man. Can't you just transfer him to the Aleutians of the South Pacific and I'll go home and say the whole mess is tidied up and no one will hear another word about it?'

'All I can do is send him back to the Army,' said Radmeyer, 'but that's no guarantee he'll keep his mouth shut. He's certainly finished as far as the OSS is concerned. We'd never use him again, that's for sure.'

'I think the guy needs treatment,' said Cassidy. 'Did you see the way he flew at me? Did you see his eyes? I want to do the humane thing, Radmeyer. And I want to do it quietly. No fuss. No Federal cases.'

'I could have him shipped home to a Rehabilitation Centre for psychologically disturbed soldiers, with a recommendation for a long cure. The fact that he has exhibited violence is enough to get him a long ticket. I could do that – although I can't say I would like doing it.'

'Maybe I can help,' said Maitland.

'How?' asked Cassidy.

'I'm willing to take him off your hands. I would like to put him back in British uniform and put him gainfully

193

to work amid the desert sand of Egypt. I can guarantee to keep him occupied for the duration of hostilities. I know you immediately, reclaimed him when he got out of Greece, but his temporary commission in the British Army has never been revoked. Technically he is still on our strength, and we desperately need officers who are fluent in Greek – as Preston is. His mother was Greek.'

'Just what kind of work would you give him to do?' asked Radmeyer.

'Oh, translating Greek to English, and vice versa. General communications work.'

Maitland spoke airily, wanting to sound helpful rather than anxious.

Radmeyer and Cassidy leapt at the idea like two drowning men reaching for the same straw. But there were technicalities. Preston still had rights as an American officer. He could not be compelled to accept Maitland's offer. The alternative, of course, was extended treatment in a Rehabilitation Centre. Maitland suggested that the choice should be put to Preston. Cassidy agreed, but reckoned that Preston would probably opt like a flash for a return to the United States.

Preston had been locked in the basement of the house. He looked up in surprise to see Colonel Radmeyer being admitted. The Colonel was closely followed by the Britisher, Maitland.

Radmeyer was looking at him in a rather worried, fatherly sort of way.

'You know you're all washed up with the OSS, son? And that you could face a court-martial for what happened upstairs?'

'OK Colonel, so I blew it, but good.'

'We won't make a case of it. Mr Cassidy has been very understanding about it. He thinks – and one or two others think – that you've been under a lot of strain. It can cause psychological disturbance without the guy it's happening to knowing an awful lot about it. We could ship you back to the States — but it would mean spending some time in a Rehabilitation Centre. Maybe a long time.'

'You think I've flipped my lid?' said Preston.

'I didn't say that, son. It's largely up to you what happens now. No action will be taken against you if you accept repatriation and a spell of treatment as an honourable casualty of war — but there is an alternative. The British still think you can be of use to them back in Egypt. It's a desk job but the work is important.'

Preston was on the point of telling Radmeyer what he could do with the desk job when he caught Maitland's eye. The British Government man was straining forward, every muscle tense, willing Preston with every concentrated thought-wave to read the message in his eyes.

Preston could not understand precisely what the Briton was trying to convey. Intuitively, however, he divined that Maitland was offering him an avenue of escape which he should take: that there was more to the 'desk job' than Radmeyer needed to know and he should not question it.

He looked levelly at Radmeyer.

'I would prefer to remain on active service sir. If the British will have me I'd be pleased to go back.'

Preston saw Maitland relax his intense pose. His eyes confirmed in silent message to Preston that he had made the correct decision.

Maitland pushed the bottle of whisky across the table to Preston.

'Help yourself. You look as though you need it and I've got a lot to tell you.'

Maitland had driven with Preston from Naples to Caserta, studiously avoiding any conversation about the events at the villa. Instead, the British Government man had talked at length about Italian cultivation of the vine and what kind of wines were produced in various parts of the country. He seemed to be quite an expert. Preston found his talk entertaining, but couldn't rid himself of the feeling that he was in the position of a young delinquent who had been relaxed into the custody of a fatherly-like probation officer.

Their destination in Caserta had been a small hotel, which had been taken over by the British Army. It seemed to Preston that it was being used as some kind of intelligence operations centre. Maitland had dispossessed a major of a small office room and invited Preston to make himself comfortable in a hide armchair at one side of the Major's vacated desk. He had left the American briefly, returning with a bottle of White Horse whisky and two glasses.

'I don't get it, sir,' said Preston as he poured himself a good shot of the Scotch. 'My own people were ready to throw me out with the garbage and you come along and bail me out. Why?'

'Because I think you're a very courageous man and a truthful one,' said Maitland. 'I believe your story. You have been telling the truth right from the start and no amount of pressure is going to make you change it.'

'Couldn't you have spoken up a bit louder back at the villa, if that's what you think?'

'It wouldn't have done any good,' said Maitland. 'I'm sorry to say it, but your Government doesn't want to know the truth about what is going on in Greece. The same can be said about some people in the British Government. Accepting a disagreeable truth is not easy. It invariably means that you have to do something about it – when it's easier to hold on to long-cherished illusions.'

'Colonel Radmeyer said you wanted me for a desk job.' said Preston.

'Radmeyer may have said it was a desk job. I didn't. I said the work was in general communications and would involve translating Greek into English and vice versa.'

'You want me as an interpreter?'

'In a way, yes. I want to make you Liaison Officer to a Greek infantry battalion. It's stationed in Egypt and is part of the Greek Brigade. You liked Captain Mackenzie, didn't you?'

'Yes, I did. But what has that go to do with it?'

'Mackenzie was engaged on special work for me. His role as a BLO was a cover. Unfortunately, he was killed before he even got to first base. That's an American expression, isn't it? The RAF would put it another way – they would say that he never got off the ground. The point is this . . . I want you to finish the job that Mackenzie started.'

Preston stared wide-eyed at Maitland.

'You mean Mac was some kind of spy? A spy in uniform?'

'That's one way of putting it. There's no law says a spy has to wear dark glasses and a false beard.'

'And that's what you want me to be, a spy? A British spy?'

'Yes.'

'But spying on the Greeks? Hell, I'm half-Greek myself. I'd only do it if it meant I had half a chance of getting back at the bastards who killed Mac.'

Maitland frowned.

'Revenge wouldn't be part of your brief. I want you to unmask our enemies, Lieutenant, and supply proof of their guilt. You probably got some satisfaction today from punching Cassidy on the nose – that was a kind of revenge. But it didn't strengthen your efforts to establish the truth – it weakened them. Our job, Lieutenant, is to identify and expose the killers who pretend to be our friends, so that they can be seen in the open for what they are. More than that, we want to know who aids and comforts them and why.'

Maitland grinned.

'In your own vernacular, Yank – I'm offering you a chance to get back in the ball game.'

A broad grin lit up Preston's face.

'Now, that's language I can understand. You've got yourself a man. When do I start?'

'With a bit of luck, you'll be on a plane for Egypt tomorrow.' Maitland permitted himself a sly smile. 'I told Major Williams to make the necessary arrangements when I borrowed his office.'

'There's just one thing I don't understand,' said Preston. 'What is the connection between the Greek Army in Egypt and the ELAS in Greece?'

'That's what I'm hoping you'll find out,' said Maitland. 'The Greek Brigade is going to be our starting-point this time. I may have made a mistake with Mackenzie by putting him on to the wrong quarry.'

'Would you care to explain? You are still talking in riddles as far as I'm concerned.'

'I thought George Kirkos was the man to watch,' said Maitland. 'You know him only too well, don't you? The illustrious Colonel Cephalus. He is at the heart of the puzzle somewhere. He holds a key – but maybe he was too clever for Mackenzie. It's possible that he even used the ambush on the Agrinion road as a way of getting rid of Mackenzie as well as a hundred Royalists. I just don't know.'

'What exactly are you trying to find out?'

'I want to know who is dealing the cards,' said Maitland, 'and I want to know where the cards are. The sleepers as well as those that are face up, the jokers as well as the aces. I want to know if it's Berlin that's calling the shots or if it's Moscow. At times it seems as if the Nazis and the Communists had formed an unholy alliance because, between them, they keep taking the pot. The game seems rigged against Britain and Greece because we're the ones who never win.'

'I still don't get the connection with the Greek Army,' said Preston.

'There has been a lot of trouble with the Greek Brigade – threats of mutiny, demands to have the King deposed. Most of it seems Communist inspired, some of it is genuine discontent, but the only people it helps are those we're supposed to be fighting – the Nazis. It's the same in Greece. The Communists have never made any serious attempt to fight the Germans and they are seriously hampering the efforts of those who are fighting men. They seem more intent on preserving their army and squashing any Greek opposition to Communism. Heaven knows the political waters of Greece are muddy enough as things are – but somebody or some group is going to an awful lot of trouble to stir them up and make them muddier still. I want to find out who is doing the stirring and why. Somebody somewhere has a foot in two camps and is playing a very nasty double game. Of that I'm almost certain. Somebody somewhere is working for both the Communists and the Nazis.'

Preston toyed with his glass thoughtfully.

'You suspected that Kirkos was this somebody?' he asked.

'He was a possible. The last trouble we had with the Greek Brigade flared up a year ago – just after he had been in Egypt. There was some rattling of swords but the whole thing fizzled out. But there's trouble brewing again in the Brigade and Kirkos has never been out of Greece. I want you to be installed with the Brigade before this fresh trouble comes to a head. Because you can bet your boots that it will come to a head.'

Maitland took the bottle from the table and filled Preston's glass.

'Drink up, Lieutenant,' he said. 'I'm coming to the part which you may not like.'

Preston raised the glass in salute. He took a sip of the whisky and grinned at Maitland.

'OK, sir. Break it gently. The job carries the rank of acting private in the Greek Army and is unpaid.'

On the contrary, You'll get special pay,' said Maitland. 'You see there are special risks involved. I have to tell you that you will be the second agent I've wangled into this job. The first man, whose place you'll be taking, had a rather unfortunate accident on the gunnery range. A grenade blew up in his face. He was killed instantly.'

'Accidents do happen,' said Preston lightly.

'Yes,' agreed Maitland. 'That was the verdict of the official inquiry. Only it wasn't an accident. He was murdered.'

CHAPTER FOURTEEN

The Hostage

From an upstairs window, Eleni Binas watched the figure on the terrace. He got out of the cane chair and began his parade. His paces were slow and deliberate at first, then he stepped up to a brisk walk. Forty-seven paces exactly from one end of the terrace to the other. Up and down he went like a sentry.

He made a parade ten times, five times in each direction, then he stopped near the centre of the terrace at the stone steps which led down to the lakeside garden. There were twelve stone steps. The man walked down the steps, turned sharply and climbed them again. Up and down the steps he went. Six times up, six times down.

After the sixth ascent, he leaned against the stone balustrade. His head sagged wearily forward. In the still evening air, Eleni could hear the wheezing labour of his breathing. She closed the window and went down through the house to the terrace.

Mackenzie pushed himself up from the balustrade at the sound of her footsteps clicking towards him over the stone slabs. Like a schoolboy caught red-handed in a misdemeanour, he shuffled guiltily towards the cane chair.

'It's a lovely evening,' he greeted her, trying to conceal his shortage of breath.

Eleni Binas stood over him sternly.

'Are you trying to kill yourself? I was watching you

201

from the window – ten times across the terrace, six times up and down the steps . . .'

'Dr Jansen said I was to exercise.'

'He said gentle exercise – not train for the Olympics!'

'I've got to get myself fit!'

'You are perfectly safe here,' said Eleni. 'There is no hurry for you to leave. I have told you a hundred times.'

'It has been a year . . . More than a year,' said Mackenzie testily. 'I came to Greece to do a job. I can't do it sitting around here on my backside.'

'You think only of revenge for what happened to you. You are obsessed with it. You are not fit to do any job. Dr Jansen has risked his life coming out here to try to make your body whole but he should have been working on the damage to your mind. Or is it beyond repair?'

Mackenzie's hand went up involuntarily to his face, to the black leather patch which covered his sightless right eye.

'It was my eye that was beyond repair. My mind is in good working order,' he said. He stared with his other eye at the haughty, erect woman, at the angry tilt of her head and the way her, reddish-brown hair framed the perfect oval of her face. Not for the first time, he felt his breath catch in admiration at her carelessly arrogant beauty. Not even the angry pout of her lips detracted from the perfection of her features. She railed on at him:

'If your mind was in good working order, you would thank God that you have one good eye left to see the beauty that surrounds you here. Do I not feed you well? Haven't I nursed and cared for you – even when Dr Jansen said your life was hanging by a thread and there was no hope for you? Have you not had enough of war and killing that you still want more?'

Her breasts rose and fell with the passion of her words. Mackenzie was astonished to see a large pearl-

202

like tear roll down her cheek. He had never before seen Eleni Binas even mildly flustered. It was the first sign she had given that her emotions were not thermostatically controlled. The effect on him was to hoarsen his own voice almost to a whisper.

'You know I can never repay you, Eleni. You don't need to list the things I ought to be thankful for. I owe my life to you. You've protected me. You've looked after me. You have taken me into your home and given me everything, without any thought for yourself or the price you've had to pay. Can't you see that I can't go on getting deeper and deeper into your debt? You have given up more than a year of your life for me.'

She brushed the tear away with an angry gesture.

'I only did what any other woman in my position would have done. You owe me nothing.'

He shook his head.

'Don't you realise that with every day that passes and I remain here, I owe you more and more? I have been utterly dependent on you. Apart from old Agarista and her husband, you are the only person I ever see. I have forgotten what life was like without you being here morning, noon and night. Can't you see what is going to happen? If I don't force myself to go soon, I'll never want to leave. I'll start inventing reasons why I should stay.'

'Then stay,' said Eleni, her eyes suddenly bright. 'Here, we want for little. All we need is here on this island. Here, the war does not touch us. Having you here has given a purpose to my life. If you were to go away, my life would be empty and unbearable. I wouldn't know what to do with myself. I want you to stay.'

'As a substitute for the invalid husband you lost?' asked Mackenzie, and could have bitten his tongue out as soon as he had said it.

Her face went pale. If he had struck her, he could

not have hurt her more. She held herself erect, trying to conceal the very real womanly vulnerability that lurked behind the summoned mask of her dignity. She said:

'All you know about Ion is what I have told you. Maybe nursing a dying husband becomes a habit, so that when he goes you need someone or something to take his place. But it's also a way of showing love.'

She turned on her heel and walked into the house.

Mackenzie let his head fall forward. He sat there, slumped, hating himself and what he had become. He saw himself only as a bitter, useless shell of the man he had once been.

Rage had kept him alive in the weeks immediately after his return to conscious thought in Jansen's hospital. Rage at Kirkos and the treachery which had maimed him.

The sight of that right eye had completely gone in spite of Jansen's efforts to save it. The damage to the left eye was less severe. A chip of stone – no bigger than a pin-head and probably raised by a bullet gouging into solid rock – had lodged in the cornea. Jansen had removed the particle and the scar had remained free from infection and healed well. It had been several months, however, before Mackenzie had been able to enjoy full use of the eye without distortion of vision.

The chest would have been his most serious injury, necessitating removal of part of Mackenzie's right lung. It was this wound, and its complication with pneumonia, that had kept him here on the beautiful lake island where Ion and Eleni Binas had made their home.

In the first stages of his convalescence, a few faltering footsteps had been enough to make Mackenzie weak and exhausted. There had been setbacks, with Dr Jansen only able to make the journey from Agrinion to see him occasionally.

With the coming of spring, however, Mackenzie had turned the corner. Each day had seen him grow a little stronger. Physical effort of any kind exhausted him quickly but he was determined to force his body back to fitness. Always before him, taunting him, was the image of George Kirkos, the architect of all his misfortunes. Hatred of that face forced Mackenzie on, compelling him to walk strength into his wasted leg muscles and rhythm into the faltering bellows of his respiratory system.

Sitting on the terrace now, he didn't need Eleni Binas to remind him of the place's beauty. The evening sun glinted on the mountains to the east. They had a timeless majesty which invested the lake and its cypress-clad shores with a great tranquillity and timelessness.

It was true that the island in its land-locked lagoon was self-sufficient. It was only half a mile long and a little less than that broad but it had everything to sustain life. The only other inhabitants were old Petros and his wife, Agarista. The couple had grown up in service to the Binas family and had stayed on with Ion and Eleni when Ion had sold the Binas tobacco estates around Agrinion and the family's other interests in Athens and had retreated from the world to the island.

Petros and Agarista tended the goats and hens which roamed at will on the low open parts of the island. Petros also worked the walled vegetable garden with its rich variety of produce, while Agarista doubled as cook and caretaker at the Binas house.

If Mackenzie had searched the whole of Greece for a more comfortable, more isolated, more secure hideaway in which to recover from his wounds, he could not have found it. The occupation soldiers seldom ventured near the island. Once, a boatload of Italians had landed and requisitioned the few hens they were able to catch and a quantity of eggs and vegetables but, for the most part, they were left on their own.

Ion Binas had chosen his retreat well when he had turned his back on the world. There had been murmurs of surprise at the time only because Eleni – his socialite wife and daughter of one of the country's top families – had accepted to share his hermit-like existence without a word of dissent.

Eleni, however, had known of the wasting disease which would cripple and finally kill her husband before his thirty-fifth birthday. The world had not known. Now, he lay in a grave over which Eleni Binas had erected a small stone and for which she had chosen the simple inscription: 'His name is known to God.'

Mackenzie walked from the terrace into the house. He looked around him and knew he must take himself away from this place. More than a hatred of Kirkos motivated him now. More than a compelling lust for revenge spurred his need for flight. More than a sense of duty or mission. There was on him now a burdening awareness of the mantle of Ion Binas which fitted so comfortably and which, daily, became harder to shrug off.

Oh, yes, he owed Eleni Binas so very very much. But, more than that, he was falling in love with her more and more completely. Every day the emotion grew stronger and more difficult to deny. It obliterated all other thought from his mind – except perhaps for the thought that demanded the total denial of his love: the fear that it was his infirmity, his dependence on her, which inspired her devotion for him. If she had any love for him, was it centred on the very weakness in him that he despised?

Christina Kirkos turned back the woollen coverlet and looked down at her sleeping son. A warmth of feeling enveloped her; a wave of such tenderness that she wanted to smile and cry at the same time.

My beautiful Nikki, she thought. What a world of grief I've brought you into.

The hollow emptiness of her stomach was a physical

pain. In two days, her only food had been two bowls of watery fish soup. She left the baby and crossed to the window. The tiny flat was one floor up, over a ship chandler's shop, and looked over rooftops to the docks of the Piraeus. After the farce of her trial in Karpenisi, George Kirkos had sent her back to Athens to await the birth of her baby.

There had been no question of her going back to the Kirkos villa in Kalamaki. It had been taken over by the Germans and a number of officers were billeted there. Instead, Kirkos had given her the address in Piraeus – the home of Nanna Vlakhos, who had been nurse and retainer to the Kirkos family from the days of George's infancy.

She was a wizened old crone with a nose like an eagle's beak, and she worshipped the ground under George Kirkos's feet. Hadn't she nursed and reared him almost as her own from the moment he had first seen the light of day?

Nanna Vlakhos did not extend her regard for George to the American girl he had married. She had never been able to understand what he had seen in this tarty foreigner to make her his bride. For George's sake, however, Nanna Vlakhos was prepared to follow his instructions about giving shelter to Christina and seeing her over the birth of her baby.

Indeed, Nikki's arrival had complicated the uneasy relationship between Christina and the older woman. Nanna Vlakhos had claimed the child with proprietorial authority from the moment on the nurse's old double bed when the child had been safely delivered from his mother's body. She had so jealously guarded her right to be the baby's sole custodian that Christina was made to feel superfluous.

It was as if she had been made the vehicle for producing a property belonging exclusively to Nanna Vlakhos and George Kirkos. Christina's role ended with the conclusion of the gestation period. She was of no further use.

George had behaved with uncharacteristic gentleness and concern towards Christina after the bombshell news of her pregnancy, especially as the child's father was almost certainly Mackenzie. Kirkos had made it clear that he had no wish to resume a husband-wife relationship with Christina, but he was as anxious about the child as if it had been his own. He had given Christina a handsome amount of money to last her in Piraeus and entrusted her with a letter to Nanna Vlakhos.

Unfortunately, monetary inflation was at such a peak in the Athens area that the money had melted away like snow off a wall. Now, with the baby four months old, the last of the money had gone.

The April sun was warm through the glass of the window. Christina was about to move back when she saw the black-clad figure of Nanna Vlakhos in the street below. She was standing on the corner in earnest conversation with a short dumpy man with a shock of black hair and a droopy moustache. Christina saw the man take a large envelope from inside his jacket and hand it to the old woman. It disappeared into the depths of her voluminous shopping bag.

A few moments later, she heard the old woman's footsteps on the stairs. For once, when she came in, there were not the usual complaints about the shortage of food and the prices demanded for what little there was.

She ignored Christina and disappeared with her shopping bag into the little back bedroom. When she emerged, she acted slyly. There was not the usual cool hostility which she usually reserved for Christina. Instead, she displayed a false solicitude which puzzled the younger woman and made her wonder what the old bat was up to.

Nanna Vlakhos did not seem unduly perturbed by the lack of money.

'Unless I can get some money soon, we are going to starve,' said Christina. 'Did you have any luck at the market?'

'I got some fish. The stuff we would have thrown away in the old days, or given to the cat – but it will make soup and a bite to eat, too.'

The old woman seemed to be hugging some happy secret to herself.

'What are you so pleased about?' asked Christina.

'Me, pleased? You are imagining things. What have I got to feel pleased about? Are you going to try the cigarette factory for a job today?'

'Looks like I'll have to – but I don't like leaving Nikki.'

The old nurse bridled.

'The little angel will be safe with me. You should be out working, so that we can eat . . . Instead of living off an old woman.'

Christina's belly ached with hunger. The old woman was, of course, right. She would need to find work.

'You say they took some girls on at the factory yesterday?'

'So I was told. I don't know if it's true. Why don't you go and find out? Nikki has no need of you now he is off the breast. Fat lot he got out of you anyway.'

Christina slipped on her one pair of serviceable shoes. They had been soled with wood to last through the winter.

'I'll go, then. I'll see if I can get a job.'

She left the flat and walked down towards the harbour. The cigarette factory was on the edge of the dock area, its approach flanked by the grimy brick walls of warehouses.

A queue of women stood at the big iron gates.

'Here's another hopeful,' said a woman at the end of

the queue. Several heads turned to appraise the newcomer.

'Looking for a job, dearie?' said the woman who had announced Christina's arrival.

'Yes.' said Christina. 'What are the chances?'

'Not much for us,' said the woman. 'The ones up front have been here since just after curfew. Me, I had to walk all the way from Peristeri.'

'Is it worth waiting?'

The woman shrugged.

'They took on six yesterday . . . Said they would be wanting more today.'

Christina stood in the queue for three hours. At midday, some of the women at the front were admitted through the big gates. An hour later, a man in a white coat came out.

'You lot might as well go home,' he announced. 'We won't be taking any more workers now until the end of the month. Come back again then.'

The women turned away, talking bitterly among themselves. Some were in tears.

'How can I feed my children?' one of them wailed. It was a question that women were asking all over Athens. Christina had no reply.

She walked back slowly towards the flat.

The moment she opened the door, she knew that something was wrong. The place was eerily silent. Usually the old woman clattered about, talking to Nikki if he was awake.

The front room was empty. Nikki's bed had been the big bottom drawer of a chest of drawers, pulled out and set on the floor. The drawer had been replaced in the chest of drawers and closed. There was no sign of the bedding from it. Worse, there was no sign of Nikki.

She looked around, panic-stricken. His feeding bottle had gone. All his nappies – which she had washed that morning and left to dry on the wooden clothes-horse near the window – had gone.

Christina rushed into the back bedroom and threw open the doors of the closet. There was no sign of the coat which Nanna Vlakhos regarded as her Sunday best. And the battered suitcase which the old woman usually kept in the closet was no longer there.

Nanna Vlakhos had gone! And she had taken baby Nikki with her!

Scarcely knowing what she was doing, Christina ran from the flat and down into the street. She ran first one way, then another. She stopped passers-by, asking hysterically if they had seen an old woman and a baby. They stared in bewilderment at her and shook their heads.

She was running up the middle of the road now, and her nightmare took on a new quality. People seemed to vanish at her approach. Where before there had seemed to be hundreds of people in the street, there now seemed to be hardly any. The street was emptying for no apparent reason.

A man grabbed Christina roughly by the shoulders.

'Get off the street! Get off the street!' he yelled. 'The Germans are coming! They're picking up hostages!'

His words had no meaning for Christina. Her only thought was for Nikki. All that mattered was that she had to find Nikki.

The man ran off. She was alone now and the street had a deserted look. She watched without comprehension the approach of the big military truck. It braked to a stop in front of her but it could have run her over for all the significance it had for her.

It didn't even make sense to her when two German soldiers waved rifles in her face and ordered her round the back of the truck and told her to board.

They blinked at her in amazement when she screamed at them:

'My baby! Have you seen an old woman with my baby?'

One of the soldiers spoke to her in German. He was not unkindly, almost apologetic.

'I am sorry, Fraülein. We are only obeying orders. You must get on the truck.'

She did not understand his words. She found herself being led by the shoulder. Then she was hoisted up over the tail-gate where two more soldiers caught her by the arms and propelled her into the interior.

There were six civilians already in the truck; four youths and two women. One of the women – aged about forty and with a light in her eyes like fire gleaming on water – put an arm around Christina.

'Do not be afraid, my child. I will stay with you.'

Christina sobbed against her shoulder.

'My baby! My baby!'

'I know, I know,' crooned the woman softly. 'Trust him now to the hand of God . . . As I must do.'

The words somehow got through to Christina. Or perhaps it was the solace of the other woman's arms. Through the mist of her own tears, Christina looked up into the woman's face.

'You . . . You have lost your baby?'

'Here is my baby,' she said proudly.

She reached out with her left arm and drew one of the youths closer, so that Christina was staring up into his face. He was about sixteen years old. He had the same bright-eyed look as his mother. There was an extraordinary innocence and sensitivity in the face.

'He is my baby, my youngest,' the woman was saying. 'But I wrong him to call him a baby. He is a man. Isn't that so, Stephanos? You are a man and you are not afraid?'

The boy gripped his mother's hand and a look of communion and understanding passed between them.

'I am only afraid for you, Mother. Not for myself.'

'You are a good boy, Stephanos. No mother could have asked for a better son. I have been well blessed.'

'What is happening?' cried Christina. 'Where are we being taken?'

It was the boy who answered.

'A German soldier was stabbed near the docks last night. The Germans are giving until noon tomorrow for the man who did it to give himself up. We ... all of us have been taken as hostages.'

'They will shoot us?' Christina's voice was barely more than an agonised whisper. The desperate reality of where she was and what was happening slowly impinged itself upon her mind.

The woman gave her arm a gentle squeeze.

'If it is God's will that we must die, then we must die,' she said. 'But let us die like Greeks.'

CHAPTER FIFTEEN

Mutiny

Preston towelled the sweat from his neck and chest and lay back on the camp bed. The only clothing he wore was a pair of regulation army shorts but, even at that, he found the heat inside the tent almost unbearable. The leaders of the mutineers had ordered that all officers not prepared to join them were to remain in their tents with the side flaps down.

The trouble in the First Greek Brigade – which Maitland had forecast would come to a head – had erupted within two weeks of Preston taking up duty as Liaison Officer with the 7th Mountain Infantry.

The mutiny had been triggered by a leaflet circulating among the troops. This announced the formation in the Greek mountains, on the 26th March 1944, of the Political Committee of National Liberation. In the familiar heavy jargon of the Communists, the pamphlet denounced the Greek Government-in-Exile and its Prime Minister, Tsouderos. The new Political Committee – it said – was the one true voice of the Greek people. It urged Greeks everywhere to demand the immediate abolition of the Monarchy and the dissolution of the Tsouderos Government. Soldiers of the Greek Army were exhorted to show solidarity with the people of Greece by demanding immediate recognition of the Political Committee of National Liberation and by rejecting all officers and authorities maintaining allegiance to the Crown.

Led by officers with Republican sympathies, deputations of soldiers had promptly supported these demands. These deputations had been told that the King had already promised a national plebiscite about the future of the Monarchy after Liberation, but that he could not abdicate his authority in advance of such a plebiscite.

The statement had not quelled the angry rumblings. Instead, the Brigade had risen. Some officers were roughly handled. Those who declared for the mutineers were invited to help organise a defence perimeter against the British troops which were already cordoning off the entire area.

When news filtered into the camp that Tsouderos had resigned as Prime Minister, the mutineers interpreted this as an endorsement of their cause and encouragement that their other demands would be met.

Lieutenant Nikos Stratou, who shared a tent with Preston, was one of the officers who had tried to resist the mutineers. He had been badly bruised for his pains.

Stratou puzzled Preston. Usually he identified with the men in any arguments that were going. When the officers talked politics in the Mess – and they talked of little else – Stratou was the arch cynic and devil's advocate, deriding all shades of opinion with equal volubility. Yet, his reaction to the mutineers had been the most reactionary and outspoken. Whereas most of the Monarchy-aligned officers had tried to reason with the men, Stratou had waded into his own platoon with threats of firing squads and bloody murder. His unexpected attitude had had the effect of antagonising the waverers and moderates among the mutinous troops.

Preston looked across at Stratou now. He was stretched on the other camp bed. He held a rolled newspaper in his hand and he was amusing himself by waiting until a fly landed on the canvas above him and swatting it with the paper. As there was no shortage of obliging flies, the pastime was one which promised to last indefinitely.

Stratou was a handsome man. Tall – with the physique of a heavy-weight boxer – his weight was beautifully distributed throughout his long frame. He had gone out of his way to welcome Preston to the Battalion and it had been at the Greek's suggestion that they now shared the same tent. Apparently, Stratou had shared a tent with Fothergill – Preston's predecessor as liaison officer – and because of his close friendship with the Englishman, he had hoped he and Preston could get on equally good terms.

Swatting flies suddenly seemed to lose its appeal for Stratou. He pushed himself off the bed, curled the newspaper in a ball and threw it at the wall of the tent.

'Damn this bloody waiting!' Stratou suddenly snapped.

'It does get a bit monotonous,' agreed Preston. 'How long has it been now? I've lost track of the days.'

'It started on April second and today's the twenty-third. That's three whole weeks! Why don't the British just march in and shoot the bastards?'

Preston sat up and threw his scowling companion a cigarette.

'The last thing Middle East Command want to do is start another war. Have you got a match?' He paused while Stratou offered him a light. 'I certainly wouldn't like to be in the British commander's boots. If he tries to put troops in, some mad-hat is bound to fire off one of those fifty artillery pieces that the Brigade has pointing at the British lines.'

'That's likely to happen anyway,' said Stratou. 'The British obviously think they can starve us out, but hungry men do desperate things. The British should have moved in ten days ago when their last ultimatum ran out.'

'The men said their terms hadn't been met,' said

216

Preston. 'They obviously don't want Venizelos as Prime Minister any more than they wanted Tsouderos.'

'By Christ, Metaxas would have sorted the bastards out!' growled Stratou.

Preston made a face.

'The iron fist, eh? I didn't know you were a fan of Metaxas.'

Stratou became suddenly guarded.

'You know me, Leonidas. All politicians are shit. I was no fan of Metaxas. But, by God, he got things done for Greece.'

'A lot of Germans said the same thing about Hitler. I suppose it depends how fussy you are about the way things get done.'

Stratou gave Preston a long look.

'I wouldn't say that kind of thing too loudly around here if I were you. We Greeks are very touchy about our politics and, in spite of your Greek mother, you're an outsider.'

Preston threw up his hands in a gesture of grinning innocence.

'After three weeks cooped up in this tent, *you're telling me!* Heck, Nikos, I'm a neutral!'

'It was just a friendly warning.'

'I know, I know. I keep forgetting that outsiders don't last long with this outfit.'

'What in hell is that supposed to mean?'

'Oh, nothing,' shrugged Preston, 'but don't you think it was bloody odd that a guy of Fothergill's experience should pull the pin out of a grenade and stick around to see what happened?'

Stratou tensed and seemed to hold his breath. It was an age before he spoke:

'Fothergill was my good friend. What do you know about his death?'

'Nothing really. Only what I was told. That he got careless with a grenade.'

'It was an accident. I was there when it happened.'
Preston tried not to let his own tension show.

'What *did* happen?' he asked off-handedly.

Stratou relaxed.

'It was on the range. He was an expert with explosives. He was showing me how to rig a trip-wire booby trap with grenades buried in sand. He was going to fire it with a thirty-metre length of twine attached to the trip-wire – but he thought the loop of the trip-wire was set too close to the ground . . . Said it should be high enough to catch a man's boot. He went back to raise it. Next thing I knew there was an almighty bang. It was ghastly, I can tell you.'

Preston took a deep breath. He tried to make his voice sound jocular.

'A likely story,' he said. 'Are you sure you didn't accidentally pull the cord?'

Stratou seemed to wince. Just an instantaneous reaction that could have been surprise, alarm or even guilt. He eyed Preston uncertainly, seeking answers which were not offered in the American's broad friendly smile. He gave a snort of disbelief, a brief mirthless sound that might have been a stillborn laugh.

'You make a joke with me, Leonidas?'

Preston did not reply. Stratou continued to stare at him.

'Your joke is not funny, my friend. Why should you say such a thing to me, Leo? You know that I liked the Englishman very much . . . That his death grieved me?'

Preston spread his hands in a gesture of apology.

'I'm sorry, Nikos. It was a pretty sick thing to say. I guess the war has given me a pretty warped sense of humour. Can you forget I ever opened my big mouth? I apologise.'

The expression in Stratou's eyes did not immediately change. Suspicion lingered. But it died, disarmed by the lack of guile on the American's face. Stratou smiled.

218

'It is the heat and being cooped up in this damned tent . . . It has made us both edgy, eh?'

A moment later, the confrontation was forgotten. The sharp rattle of rifle fire startled both men. Preston gauged the distance at about a mile way. From beyond the tent came the sounds of shouting and running feet.

There was a renewed outbreak of firing. Stratou was already buttoning on his uniform shirt as Preston reached for his.

The Greek stuck his head out of the tent door.

'Our guards have gone,' he reported.

The two men emerged into bright sunlight. The occupants of other tents were also appearing tentatively.

A dozen British soldiers, wearing white armbands and with rifles at the ready, were advancing cautiously towards them along the avenue of tents.

'What's happening?' Preston asked one of them.

The man seemed surprised at being addressed in English.

'You American, sir?'

'I'm a British officer. Can you tell me what is happening? We've been held prisoner here for three weeks.'

'It's all over now, sir,' said the soldier. 'They've given up.'

'What was the firing?'

'Some of them tried to stop us coming in. They killed one of our blokes. But they don't really want to scrap with us. I reckon the sight of one of our chaps lying dead up there made 'em realise just what they were getting into.'

There was not just one person lying dead in the dream which woke Leandros. There were twelve. The clarity with which he could see the twelve bullet-ridden bodies brought him out in a cold sweat.

He sat up in bed and blinked at the blue enamel

alarm clock which sat on the cabinet a few feet away. It said five o'clock. The clock's loud tick echoed in the room. It had been an empty, joyless room these past two years, ever since the death of his beloved Panarista.

Leandros got up and drew the curtains. Piraeus was still asleep. The port seemed absurdly peaceful in the half-light of early morning. Soon it would be echoing to the sounds of a new day.

It was going to be a special day for Leandros. It was fitting, he thought, that today was his sixty-ninth birthday. Sixty-nine turbulent years had passed since he had come into the world a bundle of squawking innocence.

Well, he couldn't squawk at his departure from it, but perhaps the nature of his going could restore to him some of the innocence of his arrival. It was sad how the years of a man's life corrupted the flesh and the mind – but the Good Lord knew these things. Hadn't He walked on the earth and seen for Himself how man was born into sin? And hadn't He shown with His holy blood how the sins of man could be washed away?

On the bedroom dresser was a photo of Leandros and his wife on their wedding day. He picked it up and smiled, remembering the joy of that day and the years of his marriage. God knew how hard things had been at times, but he and Panarista had known great joy, too. Hadn't they been blessed with three fine sons who, in turn, had provided them with eleven grandchildren?

Life had not all been bad. Not by any means.

Leandros washed and shaved with great care. Proudly, he laid out his black serge suit, the one he kept for special occasions. Today was a special occasion.

He put on a fresh white shirt and looked out his cleanest collar. He studded the collar into the shirt and carefully knotted his square-ended black tie.

When he was dressed, it was still early. He sat down on the bed and waited.

The sun was rimming up over the islands of the Saronic Gulf before he moved. The rest of the house was coming to life.

He could hear young Leandros – his third son, who had been named for him – moving about downstairs and talking loudly to his wife, Ianessa. He could hear the three grandchildren, too, hungry as always and not quite realising why their bellies were always empty.

Old Leandros made his way downstairs.

His arrival created surprise. Why was he all dressed up as if for a wedding? Why was he up so early?

'Today, I'm sixty-nine,' he said. 'Can't a man get dressed up to celebrate the start of his seventieth year?'

Young Leandros and Ianessa kissed him. Then the old man took each child on his knee and kissed each of them, too. He felt his heart overflowing with a great tenderness.

His son had to leave for his work on the docks. Before he went, he took the old man aside.

'There is something about you today that worries me, Father.'

'You always were imaginative, even as a child.'

'I may be late tonight. After curfew.'

'Do not take unnecessary risks, my son. Your children need a father. You were lucky the night before last.'

'You know then that it was me the Germans were looking for?'

The old man signed.

'I know much more than you think. Your friends talk too much. You must take much care.'

The younger man looked at his father.

'I did not like killing the German. It was not how I thought it would be. He was old, with grey hair and a kind face. But he took us by surprise. I had no choice.'

'I know, my son.'

On an impulse, the younger man hugged his father.

'Have a good birthday, Father.'

'I shall make it a day to remember,' Leandros promised.

The old man left the house at eight. He walked to the low road skirting Phaleron Bay, his footsteps brisk for his age. Ten o'clock found him in the Plaka, the old city of Athens. He walked more slowly now, savouring the sights and sounds of the ancient street which crowded the foot of the Acropolis.

He paused at a poster, recently stuck on the wall at the entry of a discreetly located taverna. It told of the murder of a German soldier in Piraeus and said that if the perpetrator of the crime had not surrendered to the authorities by noon, twelve hostages would be shot in reprisal.

Thirty minutes later, Leandros tried to walk past the two sentries carrying sub-machine guns who patrolled the entry to German Military Headquarters.

'What do you want, old man?' said one of the sentries. 'Civilians are not allowed in here.' His German tongue was lost on Leandros, who gathered only that he was not being allowed to enter.

A German major, who was passing, demanded to know what was happening. He spoke to Leandros in laboured Greek.

'*Apaghorevete! Apaghorevete!*' he repeated. 'It is forbidden to enter.'

'Forbidden?' said Leandros. 'Are these the gates of paradise then? I want to surrender to the officer in charge. I am the man who killed one of your soldiers down in Piraeus the night before last. Do I have to kill this donkey of a sentry, too, before I can give myself up?'

From inside his jacket, he produced a First World War bayonet, a fearsome blade more than eighteen inches long.

The two sentries quickly covered him with their guns

222

and the Major took a quick step back, his eyebrows arched in alarm.

Ten minutes later, Leandros was standing, his wrists manacled, before the SS officer in charge of Civil Security. SS Oberführer Johann Albrecht stared grimly across his desk at the old man. A civilian interpreter hovered at his elbow and a young SS corporal clutching a pile of papers waited nearby. Two guards flanked Leandros.

Albrecht turned to the interpreter.

'Tell the old man his noble gesture to save the hostages is wasted. I do not believe he had anything to do with the murder of Driver Stein.'

The interpreter translated.

Leandros regarded the SS officer calmly.

'Tell the officer that the German soldier had nearly as many grey hairs as I had and that he was no match for me.'

His words were relayed to Albrecht, who spoke abruptly at the Corporal with the papers:

'How old was Driver Stein? Have we a description of him?'

The Corporal, wrestled with the papers. Finally he extracted a sheet.

'Stein was fifty-five. Blue eyes, grey hair . . .'

'How can this man have known about the grey hair?' snapped Albrecht.

'I don't know, sir.'

Albrecht turned to the interpreter.

'Ask him what more he can tell us?'

After a series of questions and answers between the interpreter and the old Greek, the former summarised the conversation for Albrecht.

'He says that he killed Driver Stein with that bayonet he was carrying. He says that surely our medical people studied the fatal wound and can confirm that he is telling the truth. They will find that the injury will

223

correspond exactly with a thrust from that weapon and from no other weapon.'

Albrecht turned to the Corporal.

'Do you think the old buzzard can possibly be telling the truth?'

'The pathologist could soon tell us. What he says about the bayonet is very convincing. It tallies with what the medical report says about the murder weapon.'

Albrecht waved a hand to the two guards.

'Put the homicidal old devil in a cell. We shall want to ask him some questions later about who his friends are who put him up to this.'

He turned to the Corporal again as Leandros was led away.

'Get Muller of Criminal Investigations to check up on the old man's background, family and so on. I doubt if he'll find anything. We have a better chance of making the old man talk. Oh, and let the pathologist have a look at the bayonet. If he's satisfied that it's the murder weapon, that's good enough for me. It looks like we may have to let the hostages go for a change – but the firing squad will at least have Stein's murderer . . . And possibly a crop of terrorists, too, if we can loosen the old man's tongue.'

Leandros did not give the firing squad the satisfaction of more than a single target. In spite of a brutal beating, he maintained stoutly that his killing of the German soldier, Driver Stein, had been accomplished unaided and was no more than the last defiant act of an old man protesting against the occupation of his country. Unable to break the old man's story, Albrecht signed the order for immediate execution.

The pen was still in his hand when the Corporal brought him the release forms for the twelve hostages for signature.

'This will show the Greeks that we keep our word,'

he confided to the Corporal. He had signed several of the forms when he looked up.

'Wasn't there a woman prisoner who had no identification papers?'

'Yes, sir – the very last form. Nobody's been able to get a word of sense out of her. She just stares in front of her as if she's been hypnotised. The doctor had a look at her and said that she's in a state of deep trauma.'

'Did he now? And what did the doctor say had caused this trauma – the prospect of being shot?'

'No, sir. One of the other women said that she had lost her baby. The doctor said that the death of a child was probably the cause of the shock. He thought she should be in hospital.'

'Typical of the medical profession,' said Albrecht. 'For all we know, the woman is a terrorist. We can't just let her go. What about all those other women we rounded up? The ones the Civil Authority didn't want to know about? None of them had papers.'

'They are being deported for factory labour. Most of them are whores the Italians left behind.'

'That's the answer, then. Send the crazed woman with them. It's one way of getting her off our hands. She's no damned use to us. You get all the forms filled in and I'll sign them first thing in the morning.'

Some weeks were to pass before a copy of the deportation documents relating to 'Prisoner (Female) – No. 7531' was drawn to the attention of Manfried Keller. Several months were to pass before its significance was to excite him. These events, however, were still some way in the future.

On the same day as the separate fates of old Leandros and Christina Kirkos were being decided in Albrecht's office, Keller was more than forty miles away.

At precisely five minutes before two on that day, Keller was walking up a winding path towards a Doric ruin, whose crumbling pillars could be seen ahead through a screen of trees.

And there was the Temple of Artemis, desolate now but not totally stripped of the glory it had once known. It had seen the passage of fifteen centuries. Keller surveyed it with unsentimental eyes. To him it was rather a sad ruin, decaying and neglected. Grass grew from the great stone slabs of the steps. Keller sat on one of these steps and ran a handkerchief over the sweating dome of his head. That climb from where he had left his car down on the road had been warm work.

He heard footsteps on the hill above the temple before he saw the approaching man. Or, rather, he heard the stones dislodged by the other's approach. His visitor had no beaten path to aid his arrival.

Keller detected an arrogant swagger in the man as he reached level ground and walked towards him through the trees. The man was dressed from head to foot in black – a close-fitting turtle-necked sweater and trousers which hugged his limbs. He moved with the easy grace of a panther and, Keller had no illusions, was probably just as dangerous.

The man stopped a few feet from Keller and surveyed the German with a smile that contained more insolence than felicity.

'So you came?'

'I had to see you. Did you think I wouldn't come?'

'There are not many live Germans to be seen in these parts. You took a risk in coming to the place I suggested.'

'So did you,' said Keller.

'Everything I do is one great risk. I have become used to it. Why did you want to see me? Considering the trouble we have taken to build up a sophisticated variety of communication methods, meeting in person like this is asking for trouble. Was it to award me the Iron Cross?'

'Which would you prefer: the Iron Cross or the Order of Lenin?'

'Wouldn't you like to know?' sneered the other. 'Surely our . . . well, unusual . . . working arrangement has proved satisfactory to all concerned?'

Keller acknowledged this with a slight bow of his head.

'I am leaving Greece,' he announced. 'We are moving lock, stock and barrel to Italy.'

'Some would say good riddance.'

'Are these the sentiments of George Kirkos?' asked Keller.

George Kirkos did not immediately reply. When he did, he chose his words with care:

'In the beginning, I worked for you because I was afraid of you and what you could do to me. I continued to work with you because it suited me to do so. Now, things are different. I don't see many benefits coming my way from continuing our, er, association. Unless you would care to point them out . . . ?'

Keller's lip curled.

'You are probably the most despicable bastard I've ever come across, Kirkos – and I specialise in them,' he said. 'But don't be too cocksure. You weren't so confident the first time we met. Do you remember it?'

The scowl which darkened Kirkos's face showed that he was unlikely to forget. Keller smiled. He said:

'I seem to remember a very terrified young man begging for his life to be spared. I have never seen such a frightened jelly of a human being. Do you remember? He promised to do anything. *Anything!* If only I would save him. And I did save him, didn't I?'

'I have kept my part of the bargain,' snapped Kirkos.

'Because – and I quote you – it suited you to do so. I could still make you the most hated and hunted man in Greece, Kirkos. Although I shall be leaving Greece, don't think that it lets you off the hook. There's

227

nowhere in the world where you would be safe from your Communist friends if they knew the whole truth about you. All I have to do is leave some documents where they will be found by the right people.'

'I could claim they were forgeries.'

Keller laughed.

'Ah, yes. That would appeal to your Communist friends. They are masters of forged evidence. They would really appreciate that. But they're not complete fools, Kirkos. They would work out how you have been playing my game to suit them and their game because it suited me and how, whatever you did, it suited George Kirkos best of all. You can only play both ends against the middle for so long.'

Keller was silent for a moment. Then he asked:

'What did you tell them when you joined up with them? That you had become a Metaxas informer within a week of your going to prison and that I simply inherited you? I bet you didn't. No, I bet you stuck pretty closely to the story I gave you . . . that you had been forced to work for the Abwehr as a condition of your release from prison, and that the only reason you agreed was to get a foot for them in the enemy camp. I bet you made no mention at all of all the Communists you fingered for instant execution.'

The playful smile vanished from Keller's face.

'What makes you think you don't have to be afraid of me any more, Kirkos? I hand-picked you from the scum in that prison because I knew that you were more than a survivor. You were someone ready to survive at any price — a Judas without the conscience of Judas. You would crucify your own mother and be able to justify it afterwards. I was looking for a double agent, Kirkos, and you make the best kind. But there's one thing you have to remember about double agents. Everybody uses them — but nobody ever, ever trusts them.'

Kirkos was tense and angry but there was no arrogance in him now. The palms of his hands were sticky with sweat. He was afraid. The fingers of his right hand were inches from the revolver holstered on his hip.

'My Communist friends think I have come here to kill you,' he said.

'But you have more sense,' said Keller. 'You still want to survive. And you still don't know why I wanted to see you. Maybe the Communists think I can be of no more use to them, Kirkos. But maybe your usefulness ends with mine. The moment you stop being of use to the Communists, Kirkos, you are dead. That's the trouble with double agents. They never outlive their usefulness.'

'I may yet outlive *you*. You may be just underestimating the power I have now. Soon, it won't matter in Greece what Berlin says or what Moscow says or what London says – it will be what Kirkos says.'

Keller grinned.

'Bravo! If I hadn't glimpsed something of your latent megalomania in the snivelling wretch I rescued from an Athens jail back in 1941, you would have still been rotting there. We can still be of use to each other, Kirkos. The difference between me and your Communist chums is that I have no intention of pursuing you after your usefulness ends. It will be a matter of complete indifference to me whether you live or die.'

'So, you do have a proposition?'

'Not in hard detail. All I have at the moment is the framework. The bricks and cement will come later. I can see you are hungry for power, Kirkos. Perhaps I can help you become the most powerful man in Greece. That's what you really want, isn't it? Power. Power to thumb your nose at me and the Russians.'

'Suppose I was interested in power. What could you possibly give me?'

'The key,' said Keller. 'I can give you the key.'

229

The men talked for two more hours. When Keller finally departed in order to drive back to Athens before dark, Kirkos made no move to leave. He watched the anonymous black car make its way along the snaking valley road and disappear beyond the brow of a distant hill. Kirkos gazed towards the spot and beyond it to the blue glimmer of the sea, then he turned and began to climb the slope behind the Temple of Artemis.

Just over the top, four men sunned themselves lazily in a grassy hollow. Rifles and packs lay beside them. One of the men jerked up on his elbows at the sound of Kirkos's approach.

'It's Cephalus,' he told the others. He got to his feet and walked to meet Kirkos.

'Well, Comrade, what did the German pig want?'

'He's leaving Athens to set up shop in Italy,' replied Kirkos. 'He didn't like to leave without saying goodbye.'

He would have walked on past the man but a heavy, thick-fingered hand closed on his upper arm.

'Do not be funny with me, Comrade. I have been waiting to hear a shot. I have heard nothing. You did not kill him?'

'Of course I didn't kill him!' flared Kirkos. He shook his arm free from the other's grip. 'Do you mind, Karolov?'

There were moments when Kirkos found it hard to contain his dislike for the Russian. This was one of them.

'The trouble with you, Comrade Karolov, is that you have only one solution for every problem – put a bullet in it! One would not think you came from a nation of chess-players. Your answer to every move you did not understand would be to burn the board!'

'If the German is leaving Greece, he will be of no further use to us. You should have killed him.'

'That kind of thinking could get you a very quick recall to Moscow,' said Kirkos. 'Your job is to advise.

230

Mine is to make the decisions. I shall decide who gets killed and when.'

'You only have the girl, Petrea, to thank for the trust that Moscow places in you. I do not place my trust so easily as Moscow. I have never liked this dealing with the Nazis, nor your part in it.'

'Then you won't be interested in what the German told me?'

Karolov's rage and frustration showed plainly on his face. His distrust of Kirkos was an instinctive thing but he had been proved wrong time after time about the value of the intelligence which the Greek had obtained through his Abwehr connections. Consequently, Moscow had looked on Kirkos as some kind of blue-eyed boy. His star had steadily been in the ascendant — and Karolov's had sunk lower and lower.

'What kind of deal have you made with the Nazis this time?' asked the Russian, reining his anger so that only a thin coating of contempt edged his words.

Kirkos savoured the other's slightly less hostile attitude.

'The Germans are drawing up plans for leaving Greece. Their engineers are already working on plans for demolishing docks and blocking ports ... Destroying anything they can't take with them.'

Karolov was suitably chastened.

'If this is true, then I must let Moscow know immediately.' In spite of himself, he was impressed by the import of Kirkos's news. But he looked questioningly at the Greek. 'Why has the German told you this?'

'Because he thought we might like to get our hands on some of the explosives they are shipping into Greece. He thought we might like to do a little demolition work ourselves.'

'But what is he getting out of it?' Karolov persisted. 'He is not passing on this kind of information out of the goodness of his heart. What does *he* want?'

231

'He wants me to help him have somebody killed.'

'Who?'

'He wouldn't say. Just that it was somebody important and not noted for his love of Communists. He thinks the opportunity may occur in Greece but he cannot be sure without definite information. He just wants us to be prepared to act quickly.'

'It sounds very airy-fairy to me. It smells to high heaven. What did you say?'

'I agreed,' said Kirkos. 'We have absolutely nothing to lose.'

CHAPTER SIXTEEN

The Sixth of June

The sixth of June was a notable day in Europe, where the attention of the world was focused on the Allied assault on Normandy. Elsewhere, events pursued a less spectacular course.

In Egypt, units of the First Greek Brigade were preparing to embark for Italy. A weeding out of trouble-makers had followed the abortive mutiny, which had ended after three weeks of siege and the death of one British officer. Now, after an intensive fortnight of training, the Brigade was moving out and anxious to prove its worth in battle.

The sixth of June held little real significance for Manfried Keller and his staff at Abwehr Headquarters in the Hotel Artemis - except that it was the last day but one they would spend in Athens. And except perhaps for a tiny discovery which, in due course, was to influence the still ephemeral plan called *Operation Artemis*.

It was Hoffmann who made the discovery. Most of the office's secret files and papers had already been packed into steel trunks for the journey to Italy. Only those documents accumulated in the past two months remained to be packed.

It was while sorting through the more routine of these that Hoffmann came across a Deportation Order relating to 'Prisoner (Female) – No. 7531'. The photograph attached to the Order caught his eye. He picked it up and studied it. Still holding it in his hand, he climbed the stairs to Keller's domain on the top floor.

He presented it to Keller, who stared at it in mystification.

'Am I supposed to know this woman?' he asked.

'Don't you know who it is?' replied Hoffmann. 'The last time I saw her was in Agrinion. She's the girl the mountain guerrillas used to send to the dentist. She is a member of ELAS.'

Keller held up the paper to which the photograph was clipped.

'This is a Deportation Order. She was arrested here in Athens . . . When?' He studied the sheet. 'Six weeks ago! And the fools deported her!'

Keller read the signature at the foot of the document.

'I might have known,' he groaned. 'Albrecht's department. The man is a complete incompetent. Do you know what he was before the war? A typewriter mechanic. So, the Blacks put him in charge of Civil Security in a place the size of Athens. He wouldn't have got a job with us as a clerk!'

'Is this worth following-up now? The woman, I mean.'

Keller considered.

'Better leave it until we get to Italy. If this woman is the one who used to call on our dentist friend in Agrinion, she might have the answers to a few things I'd like to know. I can't say I was ever satisfied with the official pronouncement on that dentist fellow's death . . . What was his name?'

'Bernardini,' supplied Hoffmann. 'They found him hanging from his own lavatory cistern. Suicide. Not that I've ever believed it either. Bernardini was the last man on earth to have hanged himself. I thought at the time that it was murder and I still do. If you ask me, he was bumped off by his friends from the mountains after that ambush we set up on the Agrinion road. He was the

234

one we got to feed the girl with the phoney information, remember?'

'I remember,' said Keller. 'That's why this woman is interesting. My own contact in the mountains must have used her as his go-between. It's a wonder he didn't bump her off, too. He is very adept at covering his tracks. I wonder why he didn't have her killed.'

'You've never told anyone who this contact of yours is,' said Hoffmann. 'Not that I'm prying. He sounds like he could be rather dangerous to know.'

'He is,' agreed Keller. 'I'll tell you about him one of these days, Hoffmann, perhaps when we get to Italy. Don't think I am writing him off because we are leaving Greece. Something in my bones tells me he is going to play a vital part in a little mischief I'm dreaming up.'

'Perhaps I should know better than ask you what that mischief might be?'

'You should, Hoffmann, you should. Let me just say that I am working on the Big One – the masterstroke – but all my ideas are like the myriad pieces of a jigsaw. I have no idea what the final picture will be or even if all the pieces tumbling through my hands belong to the picture I want to make. All I know is that one day soon, some of the pieces will connect and the beginnings of a picture will emerge. Then things will begin to happen.'

He mused for a moment in silence. Then he went on:

'Time for the BBC news,' he said. 'I want to hear what they say about the landings in France.'

Less than two hundred miles to the east – in the lagooned lowlands near Agrinion – Mackenzie, too, heard about the Normandy landings on the BBC Overseas Service. He was listening to the big cabinet radio which adorned the smaller of the two public rooms fronting the terrace of the Binas home.

The news exhilarated him. He wanted to share it. He went running to tell Eleni Binas.

'Up here,' she answered him. 'What is it?'

He found her in the dressing-room which adjoined her bedroom on the first floor. She sat before a mirror brushing her long lustrous hair. It was the first time he had seen her with her hair let down and he halted in surprise.

'What is it, Jamie?' She had lately insisted on calling him this. Not James or Jim or Jimmy or the more accustomed Mac, but Jamie – because of its Scottishness.

'France has been invaded. We've landed in Normandy.' The words came out flatly, the excitement gone from his voice. He was staring at her. She was intent on her own image in the mirror, brushing methodically from the centre of her scalp to the extremities of the gleaming red tresses.

She turned now and smiled at him.

'Did you have a swim?'

'Yes. Right round the island and back to where I started from.'

'No shortage of breath?'

'I rested a couple of times. Just lay floating in the water until I got my breath back. I feel good now. Strong enough for anything.'

He said the last aggressively, as if challenging her to deny it.

'You look the picture of health,' she said. And he did. He was wearing a white sports shirt over blue shorts – both garments had been Ion's – and his long muscled legs were brown from the sun. His arms and face, too, were brown – with the black patch over his eye adding a dramatic, buccaneering touch to his appearance.

'Eleni, I've got to leave here.'

'I know.'

'No arguments?'

'No arguments.'

'It's not revenge any more. That's not why I'm going.

236

I'm not going to fight a personal war. I still have a lot of hate left, but that's not why I'm going.'

'I know it's not hate,' she said. 'I know that now. No more than my wanting you to stay was because I'd be like a little girl without her favourite doll. I was suffocating you, Jamie, wasn't I?'

'No, you weren't suffocating me. You gave me back my life.'

'You gave me something to live for. Are you afraid to be truthful with me, Jamie? Are you afraid to tell me the real reason why you must go?'

'Its not a matter of being truthful, Eleni. But maybe it has something to do with being afraid . . . Afraid that the truth will offend, or that it will cause pain.'

'You said that hate wasn't making you go. Is it love?'

Mackenzie's breath caught in his throat. He did not reply. She got up from the stool and came towards him. Her chin was up in that regal way. Her high-necked housecoat fell against the graceful lines of her body as she moved. The hem brushed against the floor with each liquid nuance of her hips.

'Is it love that's driving you away, Jamie?' she said. 'I'm not afraid to be truthful, even if it offends or causes pain – because in my case, speaking the truth is more likely to invite pain. I'm a proud woman, Jamie, but I'm not too proud to tell you that I love you. And it's because I love you that I will not stop you walking out of my life.'

His eyes were wide with bewilderment.

'You . . . You love me?'

'Is it so strange? At first, all I wanted to do was make you well. And maybe you did fill some psychological gap in my life by taking Ion's place. But ever since that day on the terrace a couple of months ago, I've known that there was more to it than that. I've wanted to feel your arms about me. I've longed for you to hold me

237

and comfort me and say you cared for me and desired me.'

She stood, eyes cast down. She had thrown away her pride in order to say what she felt but there was still dignity in every line of her humility.

Mackenzie was like a man carved from stone. He had lain awake at nights dreaming of Eleni, desiring her, aching for her. But it had been fantasy, nocturnal self-indulgence – because he could not bring himself to believe that this wheezing, half-blind man he had become was desirable to any woman, especially the one who had endured with him the most piteous stages of his weakness.

'You can't love me, Eleni. What you feel is pity.'

Her eyes flashed.

'Do I have to throw myself at your feet? You have had so much pity for yourself, Jamie, that even now you can't spare the smallest drop for me. I'm the one who needs pity! If you can't give me your love, for God's sake feel some pity for me!'

His arms reached out for her and he held her close against his chest. His hand cupped the back of her head.

'Oh, Eleni. All I've ever had to give you was my love. I've never had the right to expect yours on top of everything else you've given me. I'm not . . . I don't think I can ever be . . . the man you deserve. I can't allow you to waste yourself on me.'

She looked up at him, eyes glistening.

'You'll come back? You *will* come back?'

'Yes, I'll come back. By the time I do, you'll know if what you feel for me is real or was just a kind of madness. Then, if you'll still have me . . .'

He held her face in his hands and looked down into her eyes. They were wide with anxiety for him.

'Have you thought what you're going to do? When you leave?'

'I'll make for Kandela. Old Petros told me that they

238

were talking after Mass on Sunday of a guerrilla group up near there. It has a British officer.'

'When will you leave?'

'Tomorrow.'

'So soon? Must it be so soon?' she asked.

'Every minute with you here makes it more difficult. I'm already thinking it's madness to leave you. Why didn't you scream at me and shout at me and tell me you never wanted to see me again? It would have been easier. Instead, you've told me you love me and it's tearing me in two. I was boasting how strong I was, Eleni, but now I realise just how weak I am.'

She snuggled closely against him.

'Do you want to make love to me?'

'More than anything else in the world. But I want things to be right for us, Eleni. I want you to come to me of your own free will, knowing that what you feel for me is not just a passing madness you're going to regret. I want you to know what kind of man I am and the kind of man I've been. I want you to come to me knowing all the things I know about myself and without it making any difference to your wanting me.'

His arms tightened around her and they kissed. Into their embrace went all the longings and secret hopes which each had tightly bottled up for so long. The mild flush of that first emotional contact became a raging fever of eager possession.

She pressed her body into his. He folded her to him, their bodies mutually seeking to adhere in a totality of tactile possibility. They broke apart, still desperate with longing.

'Oh, Eleni . . . Eleni, my love. I never want to let you go.'

'Will you go tomorrow . . . as you intended?'

'Yes.'

'Then we have only today.'

She pulled herself away from him. Then she held out a hand.

'Come.'

She led him through the connecting door of the dressing-room into the bedroom. He allowed himself to be led, not quite sure of her intentions. She sat him down on the big double divan bed.

'Wait here,' she said. 'I just want to go downstairs and have a word with Agarista. I won't be long.'

She was gone for nearly five minutes. Mackenzie leaned back on the bed, luxuriating in the knowledge that this was where she slept. Here, she had actually lain at nights thinking of him with desire. The thought warmed him.

'I've told Agarista that we'll find ourselves something to eat when we feel like it,' she said. She had silently returned to the room. 'Agarista cried when I told her you were leaving us.'

He sat up on an elbow and looked at her.

'You are very beautiful,' he said.

She started to undo the buttons of her kaftan house-coat. There were about twenty buttons between neck and ankle. She was naked underneath. She stepped out of the housecoat, letting it fall to the floor.

Her body was a tawny brown and perfect in shape. Her full breasts had a slightly upward tilt and her stomach was flat. Her legs were straight and met in an exciting confluence of flesh and wisp of reddish hair.

She faced him, aware of the effect her nakedness had on him, excited by his admiration.

He rose from the bed and stood with open arms. She stepped inside them and his kiss burned down on her mouth. He kissed her mouth, her neck, her breasts.

She eased his shirt away from his shoulders and pressed the soft, wet sweetness of her lips on to his flesh. His hand swept away the button at the top of his shorts. They slid over his hips and dropped to the floor.

She arched away from him and lay back on the sheep-skin rug which covered the floor beside the bed. He followed her down, his body seeking hers. He shuddered as her cool hands found him and drew his manhood into her. A cry of ecstasy burst from her as her body welcomed the urgent thrust of his flesh.

Their bodies joined, contorting in unison, tumbling in an accelerating frenzy of passion towards a cataclysmic climax which left them trembling in recurring shock-waves of joy.

Far away, on the beaches of Normandy, armies were pouring ashore on what survivors were to call the longest day. For Mackenzie and the woman he loved, it was a day that neither wanted to end. It sped past and was gone in what seemed no more than the twinkling of an eye.

CHAPTER SEVENTEEN

Appointments in Italy

Sir Neil Maitland was admitted to the Villa Rivalta at just after six in the morning. In spite of the earliness of the hour, he was shown immediately to the Prime Minister's room. He found Churchill poring over a huge map of Europe.

The great man acknowledged Maitland's arrival and bade him find a seat, but did not abandon his study of the map. When he did turn away from it eventually, there was a look of thunder on his face.

For the next hour Maitland had to listen to a tirade from the great man on the monstrous way the Russians were behaving about the Poles, who had risen against the Germans in Warsaw. When this ceased he added, as if a sop to Cerberus: 'I'm glad that our problems with the Greek Brigade were sorted out without a bloodbath.'

'They're here in Italy now, sir. Probably already in the line. We managed to weed out all the trouble-makers but I've still got a man with the Brigade keeping an eye on things. He's certain there isn't a Communist sympathiser left . . .' Maitland paused. 'But there is one Nazi.'

Churchill's expression was fierce.

'A what!'

'A Nazi, sir – a Greek infantry officer. We're fairly certain he's an Abwehr plant and has been in constant touch with the other side for nearly two years.'

'But this is preposterous! How can such a thing happen?'

'There was no way of checking up on all the people who escaped from Greece to Egypt in 1941. He was like a thousand others ... Said he got out by the skin of his teeth and all he was interested in was getting another crack at the Germans. We had to take a lot of these volunteers at face value. It was a case of beggars not being able to be choosers. Things were pretty desperate.'

'And what have you done about this traitor, or enemy agent, or whatever he is?' demanded Churchill. 'The Greek Brigade is now part of our Eighth Army and the thought of having a viper in the bosom of such an illustrious fighting force is offensive even to contemplate.

Maitland's face reddened.

'I can assure you, sir, that this man will not be allowed to remain at liberty any longer than is necessary.'

'You mean he hasn't been arrested!'

'We can lift him any time we feel like it, sir,' said Maitland. 'It has suited us to let him believe he's safe. He has no idea we are on to him and he has been leading us to German agents all over the place. Now, we're hoping our Greek friend will lead us to any agents Jerry may have left behind our advance in Italy. With luck, we'll turn them and keep German Intelligence fed with false information.'

Some of the steam went from the Prime Minister's outrage.

'I suppose you cloak-and-dagger experts know your own job best,' he said grudgingly. 'But God help you if anything goes wrong. What about the situation in Greece? There seems no doubt that the Germans are pulling out.'

'I've had lots of contradictory reports,' said Maitland. 'One of my agents says that the Communists have plans to seize the Parliament Buildings, the Police Stations and all the Public Utilities in Athens the moment the Germans leave. It could be very tricky, sir, if our troops don't go in fast. It would pay us to send in an expeditionary force now — before the Germans leave.'

'We would if we could,' said Churchill. 'The great tragedy is that we shall have to weaken Wilson's forces to provide a force for Greece. It's doubtful if we can spare a Division. We shall be lucky if we can muster ten thousand men for a Greek expedition.'

Maitland frowned.

'A Division won't be nearly enough, sir. The force we send will be met by a Communist army of a hundred thousand men.'

For a moment, Churchill's face had a stricken look. His voice, when he spoke, quivered with deep emotion.

'May God forbid that our men are not welcomed in friendship and rejoicing,' he said. 'The people of Greece have suffered enough.'

A shell had left a great hole in the dome of the Ancona Opera House. In the warm August evening, this unwanted source of ventilation caused no discomfort to the tightly packed audience of servicemen nor to the ENSA players who, on stage, were presenting the Rattigan comedy, 'While the Sun Shines.'

Preston stood at the rear of a side gallery. He was not watching the stage. His gaze seldom strayed from an officer who was sitting in the stalls, three rows from the front. At the end of the First Act, the officer rose and made his way up the aisle to the exit. Preston pressed through a squash of servicemen who, unable to obtain seats, thronged the rear of the gallery where he had his vantage point.

On the stair which led down to the foyer, Preston caught a glimpse of Nikos Stratou pushing through the glass doors to the street. He followed quickly. The street was crowded with uniformed men but it took only a moment to locate the tall figure of Stratou. With a quick glance over his shoulder, the Greek paused for a moment opposite the Opera House and then began to walk quickly through the unhurrying crowds.

Keeping a discreet distance, Preston followed. The town sloped down towards the harbour and it was this general direction which Stratou took. His course was steadily downhill across several intersections.

Rounding one corner, Preston thought he had lost him by letting him get too far ahead. He ducked back quickly into a shop doorway when he realised that the Greek was sitting at a pavement café but thirty yards away. Only the fact that Stratou was intent on giving an order to a waiter allowed the American to reach the doorway unseen.

A woman came up to Stratou's table. They exchanged a greeting and Stratou stood politely and held a chair for her to sit. He made a signal to the waiter who, moments later, arrived with two glasses of wine.

Preston remained in the doorway, his back to the café. A plate-glass window mirrored the street for him. His view of Stratou and the woman was maintained in snatches as passers-by momentarily obscured the reflected scene of café frontage. The pair were deep in conversation. A note passed from Stratou's hand. Preston saw the woman quickly place it in her handbag.

A moment later, Stratou stood up and shook hands with the woman. Then he walked straight towards the shop from which Preston was watching. The American sought the deepest shadows of the doorway and bent as if peering into the interior of the shop. The Greek walked past the doorway without a glance inside.

There was no sign of Stratou when Preston straightened and dared to look both ways along the street. His interest now, however, was all on the woman.

She was vacating her seat at the pavement table. She

walked away in the direction opposite to that taken by her recent companion. Preston moved out into the street and followed her.

She took a series of right turns until their path was uphill, away from the roads leading to the harbour and back towards the area of the Opera House. They reached a neighbourhood where few people were in the street. There were fewer cafés here, mainly shops and business premises which had long since closed for the day.

The woman stopped before blue-fronted premises with the name 'Annabella' on a sign which protruded from the wall. Across a frosted glass window was the shadow-scripted word, 'Coiffures'. The woman opened the front door with a key which she took from her bag. Then she went inside.

Preston walked past the hairdressing salon, noting the street number. At the end of the street was a spaghetti house. He went in and asked the proprietor if he could use the telephone.

Five minutes later, two jeeps with helmeted soldiers roared past the spaghetti house. The jeeps halted outside the hairdressing salon and the soldiers spilled out. Without ceremony, they broke down the front door of the salon and burst inside.

Some time later, the woman was led out and driven away in one of the jeeps. Inside the salon, a captain from Military Intelligence was examining a short-wave transmitter and the codebook which had been found open beside it. In his hand he held some sheets of paper which had been torn from a pad. On one was written a message detailing the disposition of tank squadrons of the New Zealand Armoured Corps in the vicinity of Pesaro. The message had been partially coded. But it had not been transmitted.

The Palazzo Emiliano was roughly midway between the

towns of Faenza and Forli, some miles off the Rimini-Bologna highway. To the west, the peak of Monte Cimone stood dark against the sky and, on a clear day, Keller could see the Adriatic, nearly thirty miles away to the east.

His new headquarters were the most luxurious he had ever experienced. When he had moved in during the month of June, the armies battling for Italy had been far to the south. Now, with autumn nearly upon them, the sounds of war rolled along the southern horizon like distant thunder. Each day, the sounds drew nearer.

Keller was worried. Schellenberg had been throwing his weight around, insinuating SS men into every function of the Abwehr. The Blacks would soon be running the whole show. Keller had been shaken when word had filtered back from Berlin that Wilhelm Canaris had been arrested. He wondered if it would only be a matter of time before he, too, was led away by the Blacks.

More than ever, Keller became aware that *Operation Artemis* was the one thing that could save him. Schellenberg had mentioned it to Hitler and the Führer had been interested, demanding more details. Now, Schellenberg was pressing Keller hard for a definite plan – and only Keller knew how far away that plan was from operational reality. He was no further forward with it than he had been in February when he had sent his treatise to Berlin.

There were other things to worry about. One of his best agents had been sending information which, in the event, had proved to be totally misleading.

Keller lifted the telephone and rang Hoffman's office on the ground floor.

'Look up and see me, will you, Hoffman? And bring all your notes on the stuff we were discussing yesterday.'

Hoffman arrived clutching a thick file of papers. He

had the worried, strained look of someone working too long hours for too little reward.

'Well, have you dug up any answers for me?' asked Keller.

'One definite thing. Our communications people are ninety-nine per cent certain that the Fugacci woman in Ancona didn't send that item about the New Zealand armour being taken out of the Eighth Army line and being moved south. It wasn't her key. Our operators swear that it's somebody else at the other end.'

Keller frowned.

'Which means that the British have Fugacci and they are now feeding us a load of codswallop.'

'It looks very like it. Tenth Army reconnaissance say the New Zealanders' tanks are still where they've been for the past week. Near Pesaro.'

'I think the British are on to Stratou,' said Keller. 'Ever since he got to Italy, the stuff he has been passing on has never been quite right. In fact, it has stunk.'

'What are you going to do?'

'Tell him it's time to bale out. We've got to get a message to him and tell him he's blown. Perhaps he can get across to our lines. He's near enough. We could tip off our forward troops if we had any idea where he might try to get across. Have a word with the area commander at Rimini and see if they have any bright ideas.'

'Right, I'll just make a note of that,' said Hoffmann. 'What do you want next? There's a long signal from Naples about Churchill's meeting with Tito. But it's all wind and waffle — not a line of hard information or anything we don't already know.'

'Leave that until last then. What else do you have?'

'This should interest you, sir,' said Hoffmann. He placed a closely typed report in front of Keller. It ran to four pages. 'It's from the SS in Milan. They've picked up our Greek runaway.'

'Have they, by God!' said Keller, perking up. 'Not before time. What's the story?'

'Well, you remember Albrecht had her deported to Germany for factory labour and she jumped the train in Milan during an air raid?'

'Yes, yes, but that's old history. She got away before we'd left Greece. Where did they get her? And how has she managed to stay out of sight for nearly six months?'

Hoffman enjoyed revealing what he believed to be shocking incompetence on the part of the SS.

'They picked her up only a mile from where she jumped the train. She had been living with a railway-worker and his family. The Blacks had people watching buses and trains and God knows what else and all the time she was only a stone's throw from where she disappeared.'

'For five months!' exclaimed Keller. 'She's been in the same place for five months!'

'That's not all,' said Hoffmann. 'They only found her by accident. The Blacks were looking for some Communist trouble-maker in some café or other and just happened to question everyone in the café at the time of their raid. Our woman had no papers and was taken in as a matter of routine.'

'Have you been in touch with Milan?'

'Yes. I told them we wanted to question her. They said we wouldn't have any difficulty. She has been talking her head off already.'

Keller tapped the report with a finger.

'Is it all in here?'

'Yes. Her name, incidentally, is Christina Kirkos and she says she is American by birth. A lot of what she says didn't make much sense to the Blacks, nor to me for that matter. A lot about her husband kidnapping her baby. I hope you can make something out of it.'

Keller, however, was scarcely paying attention. He had straightened bolt upright at the mention of the name of Kirkos. His mind had immediately taken him back to a room in an Athens prison in 1941, where he had scanned through a sheaf of dossiers on political prisoners. There had been an item on the dossier of George Kirkos. In particular, an entry opposite 'Next of kin'. Keller could remember the exact words: 'Wife – Christina Margaret Price, born Plattsburgh, New York, USA, 3rd November 1914.'

Hoffman was eyeing him curiously.

'What is it, sir? Are you feeling all right?'

Keller came back to the present. A slow smile lit his face.

CHAPTER EIGHTEEN

Assault on Rimini

Shells had been pumping into Rimini since dusk the evening before. Three batteries had made sure that the German occupants of the town would have had to be very heavy sleepers indeed to get more than five minutes' sleep at a time.

At precisely 4 a.m., the main barrage started. Three hundred guns were ranged against the town and, now, they came into action as if triggered by a single hand. The night sky was made almost as bright as noon as flashes lit the landscape with such speed and continuity that the natural order of night and day seemed to have been reversed. The intervals without blazing light were so brief that it was as if day were being transformed by transitory shafts of darkness.

At first light, the Greek Brigade began to move forward. Some units moved through the exhausted British and Canadian infantry astride the dominating heights of Fortunata Hill. The weary Tommies and Canucks gave thumbs-up signs to the grim-faced Greeks who advanced, bayonets fixed, towards the town below.

The 7th Mountain Infantry had been detailed to clear strong-points east of the coast road and enter Citta Vecchia, the old town. As Liaison Officer, Preston could have taken a back seat at Brigade Command HQ. Instead, he had asked for and been given the job of artillery observer and co-ordinator for two companies spear-heading the attack east of the road. His immediate

251

objective was the establishment of a forward observation-post where a radio link could be maintained with a Royal Artillery battery dug in almost on the sea shore south of the town.

Nikos Stratou's platoon was on the right of the attack. Preston knew he was perhaps taking unnecessary risks in trying to keep fairly close to Stratou. But somehow he had to try. Maitland had made that very clear at his meeting with him in Ancona.

After the arrest of the agent Donata Fugacci in Ancona, Maitland had wanted to take Stratou out of circulation. Apart from his spying activities, the man was almost certainly responsible for Fothergill's murder back in Egypt, and there were incalculable risks in allowing a spy to operate in and around the Eighth Army's front line. There were limitless opportunities for sabotage, and there was no saying what harm he could bring down on the Greek Brigade in particular if he had the slightest opportunity to communicate with the enemy.

Preston, however, had asked Maitland not to take Stratou out of circulation just yet. The Greek had been visibly on edge since about a week after the arrest of the Fugacci woman and Preston was sure that it was because he was planning something. Either that or he was cracking up. Stratou was jumping at his own shadow. And there had to be a reason.

'Does he suspect you?' Maitland had asked.

'No. I'll stake my life on it,' Preston had replied, drawing from Maitland the reminder that Fothergill had unsuccessfully done precisely that.

It annoyed Preston, however, that he had been unable to break one important secret of Stratou's operation: how the enemy communicated with him. Stratou relayed his information in the same way every time, by contacting other agents who were in radio communication with the Germans. But it was still a mystery how

Stratou received his instructions on when and where to locate these other agents. It was impossible that he carried all the necessary information in his head. The enemy had some way of getting messages to the Greek – and Preston had wanted just a little more time to find out how.

Maitland had finally relented. The credit side for allowing Stratou more rope showed a healthy balance. Through him, four enemy agents were now in the bag. Preston had been given until the end of September to bring the tally up to five. After that, it was curtains for Stratou.

Now, as he moved forward into a curtain of cloud thrown up by smoke grenades, Preston realised that the time-limit set by Maitland was fast running out. Three weeks had passed since he had spoken to Maitland. Now, only nine days remained in September - and Stratou still hadn't made a move.

With Stratou so much on his mind, Preston had had little time to indulge in nervous anticipation of the 7th's first major action since reaching the front. Until now, they had served only in a reserve role. Today was different. For many of the Greeks, 21st September was the day they had waited for – the day when at last they could strike back at the hated Germans. For many of the Greeks, 21st September was to have another significance. It was to be the day they died.

The reality of where he was burst on Preston like a thunderclap. But the shattering explosion which threw him off his feet was no natural phenomenon. Dazed, he crawled blindly forward until his left hand sank wrist-deep into what he thought was a pool of mud.

He withdrew it in horror, nausea washing over him in waves as he realised he had sunk his hand into the bloody remains of the man ahead of him who, seconds before, had trod on a land-mine.

Corporal Pattakos and Private Sakis – who between

253

them were carrying the radio equipment with which Preston was to set up his Op – ran forward to assist him. Preston vomited over the Corporal's assisting arm, his eyes wide with apology in the very act.

Pattakos seemed able to ignore the horror of the corpse and the mess on his sleeve. He helped Preston to his feet. Twenty-year-old Private Sakis turned away and gagged.

They were on cleared open ground, a stretch of land which may once have been pleasant gardens or parkland but was now as barren as the moon. It was pitted with shell-holes and the black stumps of trees.

Ahead, the Germans had razed a row of houses to the ground and cleared away the rubble so that only the flat top of the foundations remained. Metal stakes had been driven into the ground and festooned with barbed wire. Beyond the wire, the land dipped gently, then inclined upwards again towards buildings which marked the outside perimeter of the town. This ring had been fortified with defensive positions which enjoyed a clear arc of fire across the open ground to the wire.

Preston glimpsed this forbidding scene when he and his two companions were forced to a halt by a press of men ahead who found their way barred by the wire. The three crouched on the rim of a shell crater, peering into the smoke which writhed along the surface of the land.

There was a shout for Bangalore torpedoes, and groups of men carrying these long tubes moved through the leaders and began the task of insinuating them into the folds of barbed wire. Their arrival signalled a murderous concentration of sustained Spandau fire from the German line. A young Greek officer – supervising the laying of the Bangalore torpedoes – strode about, disregarding the fire, roaring at those not engaged in the operation to stay well back and keep their heads down. Suddenly, his waistline was an eruption of scarlet and he sprawled on the wire and hung there as if crucified.

As bullets continued to rake the wire, they tore at the ragdoll of a body, spewing pieces of his torn flesh over the men closest to the wire. Their faces and uniforms were spattered with bloody fragments. Within seconds, there was little left clinging to the wire that was recognisable as a human being.

Even the strong-stomached Corporal Pattakos buried his face in the earth and did not look. Preston forced himself to watch the horror, determined to endure his revulsion without surrendering a second time to the heaving nausea he felt.

It was a relief and a mercy when the first string of torpedoes was detonated and the earth and wire erupted in a cloud of earth and smoke. Here and there, passages had been carved through the entanglements.

A grizzled sergeant with a moustache like a wire brush was quickly on his feet, urging men through the gaps. He, himself, went through like a bull, forcing the pace of others ahead of him who were picking their way carefully through the obstructions.

The first wave of infantry got no nearer the German positions than half way across the dip of land. The second, under cover of a barrage of smoke shells fired from mortars, stormed the German positions, clearing them at bayonet point. Preston and his two men went forward with the second wave. They had already selected their objective – a barn-like building of ochre-coloured stone with a tall square tower at one end. It housed German soldiers who were firing down from narrow vertical windows just below the red pantiled roof.

A light artillery piece firing away on the right – possibly a 25-pounder – took care of the German occupants. The red roof of the tower suddenly disintegrated in a shower of falling brick and masonry.

A squad of infantry, more than a hundred yards ahead of Preston and the two Greeks, rushed the main building with grenades and then occupied the rubble to engage enemy soldiers falling back to houses beyond.

When Preston reached the tower, it was to find the main door blocked solid with rubble on the inside. Two walls were almost intact. The other two had fallen inwards to form a mountain of brick and stone. Signalling to Pattakos and Sakis to follow him, Preston began to climb this mountain of rubble. At the top, a reasonably secure platform had survived. It was the top landing of a stone staircase built solidly against one of the standing gables.

Preston dislodged a few loose bricks and looked out over Rimini – or what was left of it. The town had been rich with handsome Renaissance buildings. Now, only one or two seemed to be left standing in a sea of devastation. Less than a mile away, a calculated act of devastation was taking place. A self-propelled German eighty-eight was reversing into a two-storeyed house. The house collapsed on top of the leviathan, leaving little visible but the sinister barrel of the artillery piece. The rubble made effective camouflage.

Two streets away, a German mortar squad moved into full view. Even as Preston watched, the weapon was set up and began firing over his own position on to the open ground across which Greek soldiers were still streaming.

Corporal Pattakos was already setting up the two American-made transmitter-receivers and motioning to Sakis to rig the umbrella aerial so that it couldn't be seen over the top of the tower. Preston crawled down beside them. 'Foxtrot Charlie Bravo Five' was almost ready to go on the air.

It was the job of Pattakos to keep open links with Company Command and Battalion Command while Preston talked direct to Artillery Control.

The battle raged all day, house by house, street by street. Late in the afternoon, rain-clouds – which had been building up over the Adriatic – rolled in from the east. With darkness only an hour away, huge raindrops began to splatter the scorched earth. The dust, which had permeated the town in gusting clouds, subsided and the streets became rivers of trackless mud.

Corpses, which had stiffened beneath layers of rubble dust and baked in the sun, now ran grey with slime and became grotesque islands in gathering pools of water. The dead were everywhere, down payment on every hectare of land won.

By nightfall, the Germans had been driven across the Marrechio River into the northern half of the town. The Greeks had crossed the river at several points and were repelling determined counter-attacks on their bridge-heads. Rimini, however, was to all intents and purposes in the hands of the Eighth Army. And the Greek Brigade had won back its honour.

A relieving company of Polish infantrymen, in capes, moved up through the ruins of the town and the six hundred Greek dead who lay in the streets as Preston made his way to Battalion Command. His work for the day was done. He was lucky to be alive. The tower had come under intense fire throughout the whole of the afternoon but he had continued to relay target information to the artillery in the rear. Finally, a shell-hit near the base of the building had undermined the whole shaky structure. The tower had started to crumble underneath them.

Private Sakis had broken a leg as the three men had scrambled down and jumped for their lives. Corporal Pattakos had not made it. He had been caught by an avalanche of falling masonry and carried by it through the gaping roof of the adjacent building.

Preston walked dreamlike through the battered town. He was tired. His legs were lead weights. His mouth and throat were parched. The rain against his face was refreshing. He ran his tongue around his cracked lips, tasting the saltiness as the rivulets mingled with the grime and dried sweat on his face.

A burning German truck hissed and spluttered in the rain. Here and there, huddles of Greek soldiers sheltered in ruins, eating from mess tins. There were no civilians to be seen. Most of the local population had fled inland, days before, to San Marino.

Preston wanted just to lie down somewhere and sleep. The sight of a familiar figure limping towards him made him suddenly revive. For the first time since early morning, Preston was reminded of Stratou. The man limping towards him was Pyros Partsalides, Stratou's veteran platoon sergeant.

The Sergeant had one trouser-leg stripped away and he was sporting a field-dressing taped round the calf of his right leg. Preston greeted the Sergeant. Where were his men? How had they got on?

'I am all that is left of the platoon,' said the Sergeant. Tears mingled with rain on the man's face. 'Because of this!' he muttered angrily, indicating his injured leg.

'What happened?'

'We lost half our men in the first assault. When we got through the enemy line, the Lieutenant wouldn't wait for the support platoon to catch up. He went charging on like a madman. We could hardly keep up with him. We were in a maze of back alleys and we could hear the Germans shouting to each other on the roofs of the houses above us but he still kept going . . .'

'How were you hit?'

'I wasn't hit! That's what's so damnable. I fell down a flight of steps and spiked myself on my own bayonet. I couldn't walk. The others just kept going without me.'

'Did you see what happened to them?'

'No, but they must have been completely cut off. I was lying there half stupid from the knock I took when a squad of Germans came along – the same way as we had come! They wanted to know how the hell I had got past them. I didn't tell them there had been about twenty of us and that the others must have been about half way to Venice by then.'

Preston had a sinking feeling in the pit of his stomach.

'Then the others could still be alive?' he said.

The other man looked at him with a pigs-might-fly kind of expression.

'If they are alive, then they're in the bag. Half the German Army must have been between them and our own line.'

'What happened to you?'

The Sergeant displayed his injured leg.

'A German medic put this dressing on and they just left me propped up against a wall. He had a long harangue with an officer about it but I couldn't understand a word they were saying. I thought they were going to shoot me. But more likely, the officer was saying he wasn't going to be lumbered by a prisoner who couldn't walk. I don't know. They just took my rifle and left me there.'

'You were lucky.'

'Lucky!' snorted the Sergeant. 'I am dishonoured. I have lost a whole platoon. should have preferred to die with them than be the only one left.

Preston put a comforting arm on the Sergeant's shoulder.

'There's no dishonour. You did all you could.'

He was conscious of the lameness of his words. He wanted to tell the man that if anyone was to blame for the loss of his platoon then the guilty party was staring him in the face. It would never have happened if Stratou had been arrested when Maitland had suggested it.

There was no doubt in Preston's mind that Stratou had taken a desperate gamble with his own life and the lives of those with him by seeking to infiltrate the

259

German positions with the intention of being cut off. It was the act of a very desperate man. Had he realised that retribution had been about to catch up with him, with the almost certain outcome of death on a prison scaffold? Perhaps that was what made such a suicidal dash as Stratou had made an attractive possibility, because the odds against success were considerable. The chances of his getting killed long before he was in any position to give himself up were infinitely greater than any other option.

At the Battalion Command Post, the cost of the battle was being tallied. The news – that his devotion to duty in manning the observation-point under continuous fire had earned a commendation for a decoration – meant nothing to Preston. Confirmation of another item of news weighed much too heavily on his mind.

Lieutenant Nikos Stratou had been posted missing in action, presumed killed.

Nikos Stratou was very much alive.

He sat in a truck, a blanket over his naked shoulders, counting the number of times he had escaped death by inches in that one day. The truck was one of many heading north on the main coast road out of Rimini. Units decimated by the long day's fighting were falling back beyond the river north of the town to regroup.

The traffic slowed at a bridge crossing. Engineers had lowered cradles over the parapets and men were at work wiring up explosive charges under the main span. The work above the black waters of the already swollen river continued despite the torrential rain.

Across the bridge, the truck left the road and drove over open ground. Several scout cars and a big motor caravan were parked among trees. Stratou's truck halted beside the caravan and the guard sitting with Stratou motioned him with his gun to get out.

The Greek was led into the lighted interior of the caravan.

Major Kurt Kassel surveyed the newcomer from behind steel-rimmed glasses.

'Ah, so this is Lieutenant Stratou. Sit down, Lieutenant. Shall I send for some clothes for you?'

'I'm not cold. It doesn't matter,' Stratou replied in German.

The Major decided anyway that Stratou should have clothes. He turned to a soldier sitting beside a radio tranmitter and ordered him to see what could be found for the Lieutenant.

'I have been in touch with Colonel-General Keller's headquarters,' said Kassel. He spread his arms. 'The Colonel-General is not there. He had to make an unexpected trip to Greece. And his assistant is in Milan. So, we have not been able to confirm your story.'

Stratou frowned.

'You don't think I've been making it up?'

'Of course not,' smiled Kassel. 'You might say we've been expecting you. A couple of weeks ago, the Area Commander was asked to alert our forward units about an Abwehr agent possibly trying to get across the line. I regret to say that he was unable to comply with the request – such a thing is quite impractical in a war zone where there is enough to do coping with a determined enemy – but, at least, it warned us that someone like you might turn up. I must say we did not expect an officer from an enemy infantry unit.'

Stratou gave a humourless laugh.

'There must be easier ways of getting across the line alive than by leading an infantry attack. It isn't an experience I hope to repeat.'

'What happened to your clothes?' asked Kassel.

'I left them with my platoon.' He shook his head. 'Poor bastards - they would have followed me to hell. When we were surrounded, I was just going to put out

261

a white flag and surrender – but I didn't even suggest it. They would have thought I was delirious.'

'What did you do?'

'We were holed up in what I think was a lemonade factory . . . a rather odd place built over mineral springs and underground canals. I took off my clothes to explore one of the water courses. I told the men I would try to find a way out and that if I wasn't back in half an hour, they would just have to fight their way out of the place.'

'And did you enjoy your subterranean swim?'

'It got me out.'

'I was told one of our men took a shot at you when he saw you crawling out of a sewer at the river.'

'He damned near got me!'

Stratou took the blanket off and exhibited a purple-red weal across his upper arm.

'You should have something on that,' said Kassel. 'After what you've been through, it would be a great pity if you were to die of blood poisoning.'

CHAPTER NINETEEN

Gifts for an Assassin

It all began to happen at once. Keller hummed snatches of Beethoven's Fifth Symphony as he finished sorting through a tray of fifty or more reports and signals. They had accumulated during his week-long absence from the Palazzo Emiliano.

Outside, the weather was bleak. It was now raining for the third successive day, and the superb views from the Palazzo were lost in the dripping low clouds which shrouded mountains and lowlands alike.

Keller was glad he had made the trip to Athens for another meeting with Kirkos. They had met in a small flat above a ship's chandler's in Piraeus. It had not been the most discreet of meeting-places for either man – but the meeting had gone far better than Keller had dared to hope. For reasons which Kirkos hadn't revealed, the Greek had been shopping for artillery and had even been prepared to pay for it with British gold.

Now, since his return to the Palazzo, the various pieces of a jigsaw which had haunted Keller's mind for months were beginning to fall into place. *Operation Artemis* was no longer an ephemeral fancy. It now had a shape.

Keller rang for Hoffmann.

'Close the door, Hoffmann, and lock it,' he instructed the younger man on his arrival. 'You and I are going to have a long session and I don't want anyone barging in here and disturbing us. We may be here until this time tomorrow.'

Hoffmann arched his eyebrows.

'Something special, sir?'

'Something very special. We are going to arrange a funeral.'

'Anyone I know, sir?'

'I don't think you've ever met the individual in question. His name is Churchill. Winston Churchill.'

Hoffmann's jaw dropped.

'Are you serious, sir?'

'I've never been more serious about anything in my life,' said Keller. 'It's the Big One I mentioned to you, Hoffmann – the master-stroke! *Operation Artemis!*'

Hoffmann listened intently as Keller first outlined his general views on political assassination. It was some time later that he indicated a small pile of papers on his desk.

'These are all items which were waiting for me when I got back from Athens. They may seem unconnected to you, Hoffmann, but they are all links in a chain. You and I are going to join all the links together and make *Operation Artemis.*'

First, he picked up a rather dog-eared envelope and extracted the letter it contained.

'Do you know what this is, Hoffmann? It's a letter which has taken seven months to reach me. It gives the strongest indication I've had yet that Churchill intends to make an official visit to Athens in the not-too-distant future. But I'll come back to that later. Let's take a look at the next link in the chain.'

He selected three type-written sheets from the bundle in front of him.

'This came from Walther Schellenberg, our illustrious new chief,' he announced.

'What is it, sir?'

'Just a note devoid of subtlety telling me what to

expect if I don't get ahead at once with *Operation Artemis*. The interesting thing is the enclosure – a list of secret experimental weapons, any one of which can be put at our disposal. Most of them are radio-controlled rocket weapons which were built at an experimental station on the Baltic coast but which won't be going into production.'

'You mean, like the stuff we're dropping on London just now – the V-bombs?'

'The big stuff we are dropping on London evolved from the same experimental weaponry. The gadgets on this list are mainly those that, for one reason or another, didn't make the grade. They didn't go into production because they didn't have the range or they weren't accurate enough . . . They're the prototypes of the failures, if you like. But they are working prototypes. If we can find a use for one of them, we can have it. I have already asked Schellenberg to send us the X24 – the one called the Javelin.'

He put the papers in his hand to one side.

'We'll come back to the Javelin later. Here's item number three.'

He handed Hoffmann a signal message.

'That's from Major Kassel at Tenth Army Intelligence. Nikos Stratou got safely through our lines at Rimini. He's none the worse . . . and temporarily unemployed.'

'Ah, yes,' said Hoffmann, 'I spoke to Kassel on the phone before you got back from Athens. They were holding Stratou for security clearance.'

'That has now been taken care of,' said Keller. He extracted yet another signal from the pile in front of him. 'Here perhaps is the most interesting of all my little items. Number four. This also was provided by Tenth Army Intelligence. Have a look at it.'

Hoffmann took the paper. It was a report from an Intelligence Captain attached to a Panzer-Grenadier

Division facing the Eighth Army near the tiny republic of San Marino. It told of the capture by an engineer company of an unusual heavy vehicle and trailer.

The German engineers – who had been dismantling a pontoon bridge as part of a planned withdrawal – had been astonished when a huge pantechnicon with an equally big trailer in tow had lumbered across the bridge they were dismantling. It had stopped on the north side of the river and the driver had got out and asked the German engineers for directions.

Hoffmann looked up from the report to see that Keller was sitting with a broad grin on his face.

'This is unbelievable, sir.'

'Read on,' said Keller. 'It is like grand farce. Don't believe it if anyone tells you that war is all tragedy.'

Hoffmann continued to read.

The report described the driver of the huge vehicle as a strangely spoken Eurasian youth of eighteen. He wore a British-style khaki uniform, devoid of insignia apart from a shoulder tap with the letters, WIMPA. The young driver imagined the German sappers to be French or Poles or some of the other nationalities making up the Eighth Army because he did not recognise their uniforms. The Germans had promptly informed him of their nationality, adding that the young man should now consider himself their prisoner.

Apparently, the young man had refused to accept this. He said he couldn't be made a prisoner (a) because he was a civilian and a non-combatant and (b) because he had to get to Taranto before 25th October or he would miss the ship which was to take him and the vehicles to Greece. He said that Mr Nicholson would confirm that he was telling the truth.

'Who is Mr Nicholson?' asked the engineers. And where was he?

'In the van,' was the reply. And it was true enough. Snoring his head off in the driving cab was an Englishman in the same style of uniform. Mr Nicholson was promptly awakened and told he was a prisoner. The Englishman – who reeked strongly of whisky and was found to have several cases of it stored in the van – was as surprised as the driver had been to find himself anywhere near the German lines.

His surprise was justified because the vehicles should have been a hundred miles to the south of Ancona and not – as was the case - nearly a hundred miles north of the seaport.

The explanation of their presence there was an extra-ordinary tale of incompetence and ignorance. The vehicles were a gift by an Indian potentate to the 4th Indian Division of the Eighth Army and had been unloaded from a ship in Ancona only the day before.

Nicholson had reported to a Transit Officer in Ancona, only to be told that the 4th Indian Division was in the process of being withdrawn from the line for transfer to Greece. Shipping space had already been fully allocated for the Division. Unless something could be done quickly, it looked as if Nicholson and his two vehicles would be stranded in Italy while the troops for whom they were intended would be miles away across the Ionian Sea.

The Transit Officer had gone to a great deal of trouble to contact Divisional Headquarters first and then Sea Transport HQ in Taranto in an effort to solve Nicholson's problem. The outcome was that a place had been found for the vehicles on a ship scheduled for a convoy leaving Taranto for Greece on 25th October. It was a small ship, not designated for military use because it was Swedish and neutral, but chartered by UNRRA to carry food and medical supplies. As Nicholson and his driver were civilians and the nature of their work was health-oriented rather than strictly military, there was no prohibition on their transport by a neutral ship. The vessel had a heavy-lift derrick and could take the two vehicles as deck cargo. The one proviso was that men and vehicles make their own way to Taranto, arriving not later than 24th October.

The appropriate embarkation papers, plus petrol requisition slips for the journey south, had all been supplied to Nicholson in great haste. All he had to do was find his way to Taranto – and he might have done if his driver had not turned north instead of south and, finally, had become hopelessly lost.

Adding a final touch of absurdity to the report was the revelation of the precise function of the magnificently appointed vehicles. In gilt lettering on the side of each van was the legend, MBADU. The initials stood for 'Mobile Baths and Deinfestation Unit'.

The vehicles were equipped with water-tanks, a generator, shower cubicles and all the mod cons for delousing verminous soldiers coming out of the line. Nicholson and his driver were not military personnel but civilians employed by an organisation called WIMPA – Welfare (Indian Military Personnel) Association. The troops called them 'Wimpies'.

When Hoffmann had finished reading the report, he laid it down on Keller's desk.

'This is all very amusing and it provides some interesting intelligence on enemy movements – but does it have any significance for *Artemis?*'

'Don't you see what it provides us with if we can act quickly enough?' said Keller.

'Frankly, no.'

Keller gave an impatient sigh and looked at Hoffmann as if he were a rather obtuse child.

'Free transport to Greece!' he exclaimed. 'I've been racking my brains trying to figure out how I could get a rather sophisticated weapon to Greece for my assassin – and here, the British have supplied me with the perfect means. It has been handed to me on a plate!'

Hoffmann was still more than a little mystified.

'You are going to let these two idiots go?' He shook his head. 'You don't really mean to let them go back across the line with something hidden in their vans?'

'No,' said Keller, exasperated that his assistant couldn't follow the working of his mind. 'I'm certainly going to send the vans back across the line – but in the hands of two people of my choosing. They will take the place of this Nicholson and his stupid driver, drive the vans to Taranto and deliver our surprise package safely to Greece.'

Hoffmann continued to look doubtful.

'What's wrong?' asked Keller. 'Don't you like the idea?'

'I can think of a lot of snags,' said Hoffmann with honesty.

'Of course, there are snags,' replied Keller testily. 'A thousand things can go wrong. That's why you and I are going to put our heads together and stay at it until we get all the details right.'

Six hours later, Keller's desk was covered with sheets of paper on which copious notes had been made. The air was thick with tobacco smoke. Both men were in shirt-sleeves.

Hoffmann still had reservations about *Operation Artemis*. He did not share Keller's almost obsessional belief in it. The plan was bold. It was imaginative, mind-boggling even in its sweep and calculated impudence. But it depended far too much on incalculables.

The biggest question-mark of all was over Christina Kirkos and the role Keller had envisaged for her. There would be nothing to stop her giving the whole show away to the British at the very first opportunity. Too much depended on her never learning the whole story.

Yes, thought Hoffmann, of all the links in the chain, Christina Kirkos was the weakest.

The cell door opened and Christina's stomach turned

over. Every time the key turned in the lock, dread gripped at her very bowels. Was this to be it? Was this to be the time they ripped out her fingernails or burned her with red-hot irons? Or was it to be quick? A volley of bullets and Christina Kirkos would be no more?

The Gestapo officer at the door was looking at her in the same way that he always did, with that loathsome leer of superiority which accented his power and her vulnerability. His eyes degraded her. He closed the door and took two steps into the cell. He was carrying a bundle wrapped in brown paper.

'Take your clothes off,' he said.

She hesitated. Her hands were trembling.

'Do I have to do it for you?' he snapped. 'Take your clothes off! Everything!'

She began to undress. It was not a big operation. Just a case of removing the shapeless grey prison dress they had given her and slipping off the rough bloomers of the same drab colour. She cowered in her nakedness.

The man came over and walked round her in a circle. She flinched as he ran his hands over her body.

'All right,' he said. 'You'll do.'

She looked at him, bewildered.

'Just going by the rule-book,' he said. 'Got to make sure you've no weapons concealed about the person, same as when you came in.'

He emptied the contents of the brown paper parcel on the floor. There was a blue blouse, a navy-coloured skirt, a cardigan, a pair of sandals and a pair of cotton panties.

'Put them on,' he said.

She dressed quickly, not knowing what it meant.

'Let's go,' he said.

She followed him out of the cell and along past a long row of others just like it. They went up a staircase, along a corridor and into an office full of bright sunlight. A man in a light grey civilian suit was standing staring out of the window.

Hoffmann turned to face her. She recognised him as the man who had interrogated her at length – when was it, a week ago? She could not remember. Time had lost all meaning for her.

'You are to come with me,' Hoffmann said. 'We have more questions to ask you.'

The Gestapo man took a sheet of paper from the desk.

'There's this to sign, Major Hoffmann. A receipt for the prisoner.'

'Of course,' said Hoffmann, and scrawled his signature on the paper.

The Gestapo man gave a smiling bow to Christina as she followed Hoffmann from the room.

'Au revoir,' he said.

They went out to a grey sedan which was parked in the courtyard of the prison. Hoffmann opened the passenger door and told her to get in. He climbed in the other side and took the wheel. In thirty minutes, they were away from the sprawl of Milan and speeding south-east towards Piacenza.

'Where are you taking me?' she asked.

'You'll find out. I told you we had more questions to ask you.'

'I've told you everything,' she said. 'I've held nothing back.'

'We'll see,' said Hoffmann. He managed to insinuate threat into his tone. It would do no harm, he thought, if he gave the impression that it was his intention to beat information out of her.

She was looking at him out of the corner of her eye. He wasn't bad-looking, this one. He had a clean, military appearance which the civilian suit did not entirely disguise. His temples were beginning to grey. Certainly, he was an improvement on that moron back at the prison. She said:

'You're not going to hurt me? I'll do anything you ask. *Anything!* But please don't hurt me.'

He threw her a look. Her skirt had ridden up on her brown thighs and she made no effort to pull it down. She looked at him now, kittenishly. There was no mistaking what she had meant with that *anything*.

Oh, woman – he thought – you're in a bad way! Somebody should have told you that I like busty women. There's hardly anything of you there to get hold of. He turned his attention back to the road.

The airfield near Forli was shut in by low cloud. The heavens continued to drain an unending torrent on the whole of the plain from the mountains to the Adriatic. In a well-guarded hangar at one edge of the airfield, work was going on with the aid of arc-lamps.

A team of Luftwaffe mechanics had been stripping the interior of a big pantechnicon-like vehicle. A cylindrical water tank and a generator had been removed and two carpenters were reinforcing the floor of the vehicle with stout timber beams. The vehicle had the letters MBADU printed in gilt letters on its side.

Close by was a second vehicle – an eight-wheeled caravan-type trailer almost the same size as its companion.

Beyond the trailer, two mechanics were riveting small metal plates to a strange-looking piece of apparatus. The metal plates had instructions on them, printed in the Russian language. These translated to warn would-be operators such things as: 'Check panel switch is at OFF position before loading circuit is connected.'

The base of the apparatus was about twelve feet long. This consisted of a heavy metal frame with rubber-rimmed wheels at each end. A hydraulic jacking arrangement allowed the base to rest flush with the ground – as it was now – or to be raised so that the wheels took the weight. The wheels had their own independent suspension system and were mounted on hinged wing-like legs.

In order to move the machine on its wheels, the centre was raised hydraulically, an operation which simultaneously lowered the wheeled legs.

A second web-like framework was mounted on the base frame and looked similar in shape to a navigator's sextant. This, in fact, housed launching rails which could be inclined through any angle from twenty degrees from the horizontal to ten degrees from the perpendicular. These launching rails were themselves ingeniously constructed to extend telescopically or retract to a fraction of their operational length.

Manfried Keller was fascinated by the machine. It was the first mobile rocket-launcher he had ever seen and he was impressed by the engineering architecture which had gone into its construction. The complexity of the hydraulics alone was a source of wonder in that so many moving parts, fulfilling a multiplicty of functions, could be contained in so compact a space. As someone without a strong mechanical bent, Keller felt that if he had sat down to design such a contraption, it would have finished up about the size of the Eiffel Tower in order to accommodate all the refinements.

The whole thing was operated electronically from a control panel of such simplicity that a child could have handled it. The control panel was mounted on a separate console unit which housed the power system and heavy-duty batteries. It had to be linked to the launcher by a long hose connection through which a multiplicity of cables ran. This allowed the operator to control firing of a missile at a distance which was safe from the ground blast accompanying a launch.

'Well, what do you think of it, Colonel-General?'

Keller turned. The speaker was Major Werner of

Weapons Research, who had accompanied the Javelin on its journey from the Baltic coast to Forli. He had a grey boiler-suit pulled over his uniform.

'Astonishing,' said Keller. 'Absolutely astonishing.'

'But not terribly practical as a weapon of war,' said Werner. 'Otherwise we would have been mass producing them by now.'

'It is still a marvellous engineering job,' insisted Keller. 'Why do you say it isn't practical?'

Werner pointed to three long narrow crates on the floor of the hangar.

'It can only fire the X24 missile – and we've come a long way since it was invented,' said Werner. 'The X24 depends on a homing transmitter being sited in the target area. Our latest missiles are not nearly so primitive. They have a navigational device which allows them to strike at the chosen point of longitude and latitude at which the target selector is set. And, give or take a few hundred metres, they hit right on the button.'

'The Javelin will be admirable for my purpose anyway,' said Keller. 'What do you think of our transporters?'

'Quite ingenious,' said Werner.

Keller smiled.

'By the time the men have finished, the Javelin will be well hidden. Everything will be boxed off inside the vans and looking very normal. I just hope nobody tries to take a shower!'

'Why are you having Russian markings put over everything? Or am I not allowed to ask?'

Keller spread his hands demonstratively.

'You know the Russians, Major. They claim to have invented everything, from the telephone to a vaccine for smallpox. It would be churlish of us not to allow them to have credit for the Javelin as well.'

The roads around Bologna were thick with military

traffic. South of the city, Hoffmann fumed at the delay caused by tank transporters rumbling towards the front. At Firenza, he left the Emilian Highway and took a narrow, poorly surfaced road leading to the mountains.

Christina Kirkos sat tight-lipped beside him as the car bumped and splashed along a series of back roads made dangerous by rain, which continued to fall heavily. They were skirting a high wooded valley, the windscreen wipers going furiously, when the meagre headlights picked out a screen of foliage across the road ahead.

The car slewed in the mud as Hoffmann braked. The car slithered to a halt only feet from the fallen tree which was blocking the road.

Ghostly figures materialised out of the shadows. The front doors of the car were pulled open simultaneously. Driver and passenger found themselves staring up into the menacing short barrels of machine-pistols.

'Get out!' they were ordered in Italian.

A tall figure in a wide-brimmed hat and rain cape spoke to Christina.

'Are you Christina Kirkos, wife of George Kirkos?'

'Yes – but what is happening? Who are you?'

'No questions,' said the man. 'We are friends. That is all that matters.'

He turned to a man who was holding a long coat over the top of his head as protection against the rain.

'You know what to do with the German?'

'Sì. Lasciate fare a me.'

Christina saw Hoffmann prodded and pushed by three men towards a cluster of trees. The group disappeared from view. There was a short burst of firing. The men returned without Hoffmann.

'It is done,' said the man with the coat over his head.

'Good,' said the one who seemed to be in charge. He turned to Christina. 'Come, Signora. You must be glad to be free. Food and drink are waiting for you.'

275

Bewildered, Christina allowed herself to be led around the tree blocking the road. A farm truck of uncertain age was parked at the far side. The man in the wide-brimmed hat helped her up into the cab, then climbed in the driver's side. He shouted to the man with the coat over his head.

'You know what to do, Ernesto?'

'Sure. We'll clear the road and take the German's car.'

The driver started the engine and switched on the windscreen wiper. The single blade clicked back and forth like a noisy grandfather clock's pendulum. The wheels of the truck raced in the mud before taking a grip. The big cone-shaped headlights stabbed out into the slanting rain and they moved off.

The journey took about an hour. Christina lapsed into silence when she realised that the driver was not going to answer any of her questions. They arrived at a muddy yard, flanked by steadings and a square-looking house with shutters on the windows.

Christina was led into a low-ceilinged kitchen. In the centre, a scrubbed wooden table had a place set for one. On the platter was part of a ham. Bread, cheese, butter, a jar of pickled vegetables and a big wooden bowl of fruit made appetising companions. A coffee pot bubbled on the stove.

'Help yourself,' said the man in the wide-brimmed hat, indicating the table. 'There's a towel on the shelf over there if you want to dry off a bit first. Someone is coming here to see you — but take your time with the food. He'll not be here for at least an hour. He will answer all your questions when he comes.'

Christina suddenly realised that she was ravenous. She approached the table.

'Aren't you eating?'

'I have eaten already. I will take some coffee with you.'

Doing justice to the food on the table did away with the immediate need for conversation. When Christina had done, the pair sat in a silence which she found uneasy. The man smiled at her often, as if to reassure her.

Two hours passed before the sound of a car's arrival in the yard broke the monotony.

'That'll be the boss now,' said the man.

There was a mutter of voices outside and the kitchen door opened to reveal a man of about fifty-five. He was wearing an oilskin coat and rubber boots and a wide-brimmed hat not dissimilar to that of Christina's companion.

He threw off the oilskin coat, shook it, and hung it on a peg behind the door. He placed his dripping hat on top. Christina saw that he was quite bald, with a shiny dome of a head.

'*Kalispera*,' he said to her in Greek. 'Good evening.' He mopped rain from his tanned face with a handkerchief.

'*Fenete pos tha vreksi*,' he murmured.

His smiling observation that it looked like rain drew the glimmer of a smile from Christina. She found his use of Greek strangely comforting. The man's eyes had a humorous glint to them and he had a kindly face.

There was strength, too. Christina guessed that this was a man who could be very persuasive if he set his mind to it.

A look passed between the man and Christina's erstwhile host. The latter went out, leaving her alone with the newcomer.

'I hope you enjoyed your meal, Madame Kirkos.'

'Thank you, I did,' She looked at him uncertainly. 'Are you going to tell me what is happening? Are you partisans? How does everyone know my name? Who are you?'

He held up a hand to staunch the flow of questions.

277

'Please, please. One thing at a time.' He produced a gold cigarette case and held it out to her. 'Let's make ourselves comfortable,' he suggested. 'And relax – you are among friends. Perhaps you will pour me a cup of that coffee?'

They sat near the stove.

'My name is not important,' he said. 'Let's just say it is Artemis.' Seeing her look, he added: 'I know I do not look like a Greek goddess, but perhaps you will forgive the seeming affectation of my choice.'

He grinned across at her.

'If your husband can adopt the name of Cephalus, who was a king, perhaps I can be forgiven for divine rather than monarchical aspirations?'

Christina smiled.

'You know my husband?'

'Yes, I do. If we hadn't been – er – associates, you would still be languishing in the hands of the Gestapo. We rescued you in the nick of time. You realise that it would only have been a matter of time before they shot you?'

Christina bowed her head in her hands. She nodded wordlessly.

'You shouldn't have told them about your activities in Greece,' Manfried Keller chided gently. 'It was signing your own death-warrant. You are lucky they let you live as long as they did.'

She took a deep breath and said:

'I'm grateful for what you . . . for what your men did . . . Thank you. I owe you my life.'

'You will get the chance to repay me,' said Keller. 'If anyone should be thanked it is your husband. He was most upset when he heard that the Gestapo had you in Milan. He felt he had treated you very badly. He was very ashamed. He asked me to try to rescue you.'

'But I don't understand. My husband? How could he have known?'

278

Keller smiled.

'As a matter of fact, I was the one who told him about you. I make it my business to know everything the Germans are doing in Italy . . . Just as Colonel Cephalus makes it his business to know what is going on in Greece. We have what you might call mutual interests.'

'You have seen George?'

'I was in Greece only a week ago. I had a most illuminating talk with your husband.' Keller paused. 'I was sorry to learn of the most unfortunate deterioration in your marriage relationship . . . And about what happened to your baby.'

Christina was on her feet, staring at Keller, open-mouthed with mystification. A thousand questions flooded her mind – but one was uppermost.

'*What do you know about my baby?*'

'Please don't become agitated, Madame Kirkos. Your baby is in excellent health and being well looked after. Please sit down.'

She stumbled back into her chair and sat down but she continued to look at Keller questioningly, unable to understand why this stranger should know so very much about her.

Keller laid a hand on her wrist. It was a gesture of reassurance.

'I want to give you the opportunity to get your son back,' he said.

'George had him stolen from me.'

'I know,' said Keller. 'And he was not very keen to give him up again. I had to overcome some reluctance on his part. However, I have something which he wants as badly as you want your son.'

She scarcely heard him.

'I *knew* George had Nikki! I knew it all the time! It's the only reason that old bitch would have run off with Nikki the way she did!'

Keller nodded.

'Ah, yes, the Vlakhos woman. She's the one who is looking after the boy.'

There was a wild-eyed desperation in Christina's face as she stared at Keller, searching for answers in his bland outward mask.

'George doesn't care what happens to me,' she cried. 'What do you want of me? Why are you pretending that I'm of any importance to him now? Why?'

'You're wrong about him not caring,' said Keller. 'He nearly broke up when I told him that the Gestapo had you. However much you think he may have hated you, that was one thing he didn't wish on you. I think it was because of his own time in prison in Athens. He knows what happens. He was almost sick at the thought that you might have been tortured.'

'The only torture I've had is wondering about Nikki – trying not to believe I would never see him again!'

'Whether or not you do depends on me, Madame Kirkos – and, of course, your own willingness to co-operate with me. How would you like to go back to Greece and your son, Nikki?'

Christina's heart was hammering with a hope that she thought had died inside her long ago. She could remember its death, pole-axed by dreadful reality . . . The cattle-truck full of women . . . The train pulling away from Athens . . . The moment when the numb mindless shock which had gripped her for days had suddenly exploded into screaming, fighting hysteria. They had been taking her away forever from her baby – her only treasure, her only joy, her only reason for living. Something in her had snapped. She had become maniacal in her need to protest, to fight with the fury of a tigress, to scream at cruel fate. A woman had pinned her to the floor, striking her face time and again, shouting at her to shut up and thank God she was alive.

Christina had emerged from shock, face to face with the reality that Nanna Vlakhos would ensure Nikki's

280

survival but that she alone could ensure her own. And so she had set about surviving, fortified by the thought that only by coming through the grim reality of her circumstances was there a tiny hope of ever seeing Nikki again.

Now, this man – this stranger – was offering fulfilment of the only dream that mattered to her: the chance to hold her baby in her arms once again.

'I'll do anything to get Nikki back,' she said. It was the second time that day she had offered herself unconditionally, but her memory of the first occasion had already faded from her mind.

'It will be dangerous. You won't be alone – but there will be great risk involved.'

'I will do anything,' Christina repeated, and Keller was heartened by the steely purpose in her voice.

It was two in the morning when Keller got back to the Palazzo Emiliano. It was not a long drive. The farmhouse to which Christina Kirkos had been taken was less than five miles from the Palazzo and, in former days, had been one of several within the ancient ducal estate of which the Palazzo was the ruling seat.

Hoffmann was waiting for Keller, not yet totally convinced that the charade in which he had taken part was worth the elaborate stage management which had gone into it.

'Well, well, if it isn't the late-lamented Major Hoffmann,' Keller greeted him cheerfully. 'How did you enjoy being dragged off by partisans and being shot?'

'I got soaking wet,' complained Hoffmann. 'Did you ever see such weather? How did it go with the girl?'

'She got the shock of her life when I told her what was involved, but she's ready to crawl across the Sahara Desert on her hands and knees if there's a chance of getting her child back. I think it's all going to work.'

'I still think it would be safer to use a man.'

Keller shook his head.

'No, the woman is ideal. I know there's a greater risk, but she's our guarantee to Kirkos that we'll supply the goods. He's a strange man. In a way that woman is his Achilles' heel. He has treated her abominably . . . He abandoned her, took her child away from her – but he all but disintegrated at the thought that he would be responsible for condemning her to a lingering death at the hands of the Blacks. He has little enough conscience but the last thing he wants on it is her death. Of course, I made it clear to him that if he didn't go along with my plan, I would make sure the whole of Greece knew that he not only worked for us but betrayed his own wife to the Gestapo.'

'Isn't that a rather low kind of blackmail?' said Hoffmann.

'My dear Hoffmann, surely you've been at this game long enough to know that when you are dealing with blackmailers, cheats and unprincipled rogues, you have to be better than they are at their own games. We are not dealing with Boy Scouts.'

'I suppose so,' said Hoffmann, somewhat crestfallen. 'I just don't understand what Kirkos hopes to gain from it all. Once he has the girl and the Javelin and the artillery you promised him, what's to stop him thumbing his nose at you?'

'His lust for power,' said Keller. 'I have shown him how he can become the master of Greece and he knows I'm right. He'll thumb his nose at me all right – but only when he has played all my cards exactly where I want them. I don't trust him to do anything he doesn't want to do, Hoffmann. The trick is in persuading him to believe that, no matter who came up with the idea first, carrying it out is going to leave him sitting on top of the castle.'

'When you first told me about him, you said that he played both sides – running with the Communists and yet playing our game at the same time. Will he let the Communists in on the plan to kill Churchill? They may just draw the line at that.'

'He may not tell them how it's to be done,' said Keller, 'but he will most certainly ask them for their backing to carry it out. He is as anxious as we are that the act is seen to have Communist blessing.'

'But why? Why should the Communists want Churchill dead?'

'Because he is totally opposed to a Communist Greece – and if his elimination would help in the slightest way to achieving a Communist Greece, they won't have the slightest hesitation in backing it, privately if not publicly.'

'And how can Kirkos come out of all that smelling of roses?' asked Hoffmann.

'Very easily,' said Keller. 'Simply by being the strongest man around when it comes to a trial of strength. By the end of this week, most of our troops will be out of Greece. What they will leave behind is a power vacuum. The Communists mean to seize power, Papandreou and his Government here in Italy hope to return in glory, the British will try to restore the Monarchy . . . They will all be at each others' throats – and Kirkos will be in the wings, waiting his chance. He will support the Communists against Papandreou and the British until he feels the moment is opportune to denounce Communist extremes. He will demand a Greek leadership which is not the puppet of either London or Moscow and he will offer himself as the man. And he will have the biggest single army. He is ready to depose Spiro as a lackey of the Russians and Spiro's men will follow him to a man. Spiro doesn't know it yet but history may remember him as the man who killed Churchill. It's ironic, isn't it, that Spiro may not live long enough to know about his fame?'

'I still have my doubts about Kirkos retaining any

sort of credibility with his own people. If he's the one who actually kills Churchill, how on earth is he going to shift the blame away from himself?' asked Hoffmann.

'The Communists taught him how to do that,' said Keller. 'They are masters of exploiting a power struggle for their own ends. Kirkos will commit the deed and then produce a body for the mob to howl at. He will throw them Spiro and say; "This is the monster I saved you from. Here is the assassin, the man who wanted to turn Greece into a province of Russia." '

Hoffmann sighed.

'There are times, sir, when the workings of your mind frighten me. I feel very much an innocent.'

'So you are, Hoffmann. So you are. You are really much too innocent a baby to be engaged on this sort of enterprise. Yet, there's a streak of realism in you, too. You're a practical fellow rather than wildly imaginative. That's why I have told you nothing about the other reason I have for using the Kirkos woman in *Operation Artemis*. I fear you will put it down to fairy-tale nonsense. Have you ever heard of the Gifts of Artemis, Hoffmann?'

'I'm sorry, sir. My education in that department is sadly neglected.'

'It's what makes the Kirkos woman's role fit so perfectly with the classic pattern,' enthused Keller. 'I remember the story only vaguely from my childhood, but what I do remember creates such an exciting parallel with the way things have been working out that I feel it would be tempting Fate to ignore the similarities . . . Or to depart from them.'

'What *were* the Gifts of Artemis?' asked Hoffmann.

Keller smiled, enjoying what he believed gave intrinsic classical beauty to the whole conception of *Operation Artemis*.

'The Gifts of Artemis, Hoffmann, were a spear and a hunting dog – a spear which never missed its target

284

and a hound which always got its quarry – the perfect hunting combination.'

Hoffmann's eyes widened.

'A magic spear, eh?' The significance had not eluded him. 'Like the Javelin? A missile which is guided to its target as if by magic – and should never miss. What about the hound?'

'In our case Stratou will have to fill that role, Hoffmann. His job will be watching over the young woman who is bearer of the Gifts.'

'Christina Kirkos?'

'Yes, but perhaps we should call her Procris.'

'Who on earth was Procris?'

'Unless my memory is playing tricks on me, Procris was the estranged wife of Cephalus. Artemis gave her the spear and the hound, which Cephalus coveted.'

'You're making this up,' said Hoffmann in disbelief.

'Not at all. It has all happened before. Procris returned to Greece disguised as a young man. Now you see why I had to use the woman. The very name Artemis was chosen for me by the gods. I kept encountering it at every turn, as if there was a special purpose in it. The same gods also provided me with a Cephalus and a marvellous weapon called the Javelin. It was as if all this was pre-ordained. Could I fly in the face of such omens and ignore the woman who was befriended by Artemis and given custody of the divine Gifts? Could I, Hoffmann? Could I?'

'I'm afraid I'm not superstitious, sir,' said Hoffmann. 'The parallels appeal to me in a romantic kind of way, but I would have preferred to improvise on the original theme as it suited me . . . Rather than slavishly try to duplicate the details of some ancient fairy-story.'

'You have no sense of destiny, Hoffmann,' said Keller sadly. 'No cosmic awareness of the pattern of things. There are times when I despair of you.'

CHAPTER TWENTY

The British are Coming

Mackenzie could see the rocky inlet where he had come ashore from HM Submarine *Seasnipe*. He was back almost at the spot where his Greek adventure had started. Was it only eighteen months ago? That stormy night seemed already light years away.

He was stretched flat on his belly on a limestone crag half way up Mount Varasovon. Before him was the magnificent panorama of the Gulf of Patras and the mountains of Achara.

The October sun glinted on the placid waters of the Gulf. They reached, like a great semi-circular mouth-bite, into the landmass of the Peloponnesus. Cape Papas bounded one end of the semi-circle. At the eastern extreme, the town of Patras gleamed white in the sunlight. Lazy curls of smoke drifted skyward from the port. From where he was, Mackenzie could discern the symmetrical grid system of streets and pick out the ancient Kastro overlooking the town from the south.

The rocky inlet where he had landed from the submarine was almost immediately below Mackenzie's vantage-point. Beyond was the marshy plain of Mesolongi and the shimmering green lagoons around Troulis.

The sound of an aircraft engine made Mackenzie look up. The lone Junkers 88 was at about three thousand feet and flying due west along the middle of the Gulf. It banked towards several specks on the ocean – ships, turning into the Gulf near Cape Papas.

Mackenzie watched the aircraft's flight. At first, he was unable to grasp the significance of what was happening when little black clouds appeared in angry puffs in the vicinity of the aircraft. Then he heard the distant pop-pop-pop of explosions and realised that the ships entering the Gulf were firing at the Junkers. At ocean level, gun-flashes belched from the ships. Crimson arcs of tracer shells climbed up towards the aeroplane as smaller guns on the ships opened fire. Silver plumes leaping from the water and a succession of heavy crumps told that the Junkers had dropped a stick of bombs.

The aircraft banked away to the north and then came streaking back almost directly over Mackenzie's watching-place. It was so close that he thought it must hit Mount Varasovon.

Mackenzie felt a pounding excitement as the line of ships came steadily up the Gulf. Preceded by two mine-sweepers, their progress was not speedy – but on they came. They made a magnificent sight – warships, speckled in dark and light grey camouflage colours and, Mackenzie had no doubt, flying the white ensign of the Royal Navy.

As they drew nearer, Mackenzie could see that the decks of the ships were thronged with men in khaki. The ships were heading straight for Patras.

He left his watching-place and began to make his way round the steep flank of the mountain, descending from barren limestone to where the skirt of the mountain was decked with olive groves.

Mackenzie had never made contact with the guerrillas at Kandela – for the simple reason that he had not been nearly as fit as he had believed when he left Eleni. Two nights sleeping in the open had brought about a recurrence of his pneumonia. He had stumbled into a small church near Astakos in a state of collapse and, there, he had been found by Pater Iskos, the seventy-year-old priest.

June and July had drifted away while Mackenzie had lain weak and feverish in an attic room, fed and nursed by the kindly old man. Scarcely strong enough to lift his head, he had despaired at the cruel fate which seemed to have marked him down always to be the recipient of mercy dispensed by strangers.

The hot sun of August had been therapeutic . . . Days by the sea looking out on the Ionian Islands . . . Days knowing that Eleni, his beloved Eleni, was only a short journey distant. What would she say if she knew that the man who had left her, so full of health and a sense of duty, had barely completed two days' marching before cracking up like a cheap watch?

Through Pater Iskos, efforts had been made to contact the guerrillas near Kandela. But no one came from the hills. No message was returned.

September had gone when Mackenzie announced himself fit to travel. Rumours that the Germans were evacuating the Peloponnesus made him decide to head south and east and try to get across the Gulf of Patras.

He had set out, avoiding roads and never trying to cover more than ten miles a day. Thus is was that on 3rd October he had reached the lower slopes of Mount Varasovon and camped for the night in an olive grove. On the morning of the following day, the last thing he had expected to see was a fleet of British ships in the Gulf.

In the five days since he had left Pater Iskos, Mackenzie had not shaved. His appearance was piratical. With his scrubby beard and the black patch over his right eye, he cut a fearsome figure – but a surging joy was in him as he made his way down the mountain.

He walked until he reached the metre-gauge railway which linked Agrinion and the tiny port of Kryoneri by thirty-eight miles of single track. Then he followed the railway.

Kryoneri was in a great state of excitement. The British ships could be seen at anchor off Patras across the Gulf. Every now and then, rumbling explosions boomed across the water from Patras. The entire population of Kryoneri seemed to be in the streets speculating on what was happening at the other side of the bay.

At the harbour, Mackenzie found that several boats were preparing to put to sea to greet the British. He found himself immediately surrounded when he revealed to one boat-owner that he was a British officer and wanted to get over to the Peloponnesus side of the Gulf.

Mackenzie was embraced and congratulated by excited Greeks. Two hours later, he was on the bridge of the British destroyer, HMS *Hostile*, in earnest conversation with her Captain.

That naval gentleman kept shaking his head with wonder as Mackenzie gave him a brief résumé of his adventures. In turn, he was able to tell Mackenzie that British troops ashore in Patras had already made contact with guerrillas who were part of an army led by a General Aris.

'Aris is the commanding general of ELAS but I've never met him,' said Mackenzie. 'He used to run with a bandit called Karalivanos, but he dumped him when he wouldn't toe the Communist line. Aris's real name is Athanasios Klaras and he's not noted for his love of the British. Our people will have to read very carefully with that gentleman. What are things like ashore?'

'Well, the Germans seem to have left only token forces. They're pulling back, blowing up everything as they go. It will take at least a week to clear the port of Patras for our shipping. But look, what can we do for you — personally that is? When did you last have a decent meal? How can we make you feel at home?'

Mackenzie gave a broad grin.

'If it's not too much trouble, I'd give a year's pay for a haircut, a shave and a hot bath – in that order.'

Having her hair cut short had been the thing that had troubled Christina Kirkos most. It had taken her only six hours' intensive tuition to master the thirteen-gear controls of the great pantechnicon-like van. She was apprehensive but not terrified at the prospect of driving the length of Italy and shipping secretly to Greece. She did not tremble with fright at the dangers outlined to her by Artemis – possibly because she was not fully able to comprehend these dangers – but she suffered horrors at the indignity of having her long hair cut off. It had been cropped short in the farmhouse kitchen, with the man who called himself Artemis looking on.

She had wanted to scream when the haircutter – who seemed more surgeon than barber – had, literally, welded a narrow strip of dark human hair to her upper lip. He had used a heat process which had left her with a blistering pain above her mouth.

'Be careful of it when you wash your face,' she had been instructed. 'It should hold all right for about six weeks. After that, it will begin to peel off.'

She could not believe her own reflection when she saw the result of the man's handiwork. The short boyish hair and the thin pencil of moustache had defeminised her in a way which she wouldn't have believed possible.

Christina recalled Mackenzie saying to her, eighteen long months before, that with her woollen cap over her ears she could pass for his brother. Well, she could now – with no difficulty at all. It was the face of a young man who stared back at her from the mirror, not that of a twenty-nine-year-old woman.

She had been fitted with a plain khaki battledress uniform in the British style. A blue shoulder-flash, with the letters WIMPA, was the only adornment. They had tailored the uniform to fit her and also provided a spare.

Her briefing had been intensive. Papers with which she had been provided gave her the male identity of one Emmanuel Herrera, born 1924 in Goa, of a French-Portuguese father and a Cochinese mother. The identity belonged to the former driver of the MBADU van, who was now safely under lock and key in Northern Italy.

Keller, himself, still acting a part for Christina's benefit, conducted most of her indoctrination into the role she had to play. He never fully defined for her who or what he was purporting to be. She in turn – because of her life as an ELAS courier and her encounters with many shadowy associates of George Kirkos – was in no way suspicious nor unduly curious about Keller. When Keller told her that in the past he had smuggled guns into Greece and hinted that his activities were commercial rather than political, Christina accepted it without question. She gathered that the vans probably contained guns for Kirkos, and she didn't question the need for the whole operation to be carried out without the British knowing a thing about it.

All that she really cared about was the successful conclusion of the operation. For her, it would end when the vans were driven into a garage in the Peristeri district of Athens and her son, Nikki, was restored to her. Nothing else mattered to her but that.

Nikos Stratou had simultaneously been undergoing intensive briefing only a few miles away at the Palazzo Emiliano. He was less than enthusiastic about the elaborate plan for his return to Greece under the alias of Edward Nicholson.

Hoffmann's Abwehr interrogators had had little difficulty in extracting the life history of the civilian who enjoyed the rank of Commissioner in the Welfare (Indian Military Personnel) Association. The man was an alcoholic and needed only a little priming with whisky to launch into the most intimate details of his life. Stratou was younger than Nicholson, but this did not seem to Keller to present a serious hazard.

Although Stratou had misgivings about *Operation Artemis* and returning to territory where he was 'blown', he warmed to it when he heard of the rewards. Keller was to lodge a hundred thousand Swiss francs in his account with the Bank of the Zurich-Beirut Corporation. In addition, George Kirkos was to pay Stratou one thousand British gold sovereigns for safe delivery of the Javelin. With this money he could effectively purchase his escape from Greece to the Lebanon.

Stratou's first meeting with Christina was not a happy one. She was dressed in the WIMPA uniform and Keller was anxious to gauge his reaction. Stratou had taken one look at Christina and said she would never do.

'Look at her chest, for God's sake!' he had complained loudly. 'She bulges!'

'You are making mountains out of molehills,' Keller had replied – a remark which had made Christina blush and Stratou roar with laughter. Keller, realising that his choice of words might have been made with more care, grinned sheepishly.

'We'll just have to iron out the bumps,' he said.

The outcome was that Christina had to suffer the mortificatiion of having bandage-strapping wound tightly across her breasts to flatten her modest thirty-two-inch bosom. Stratou admitted the result was satisfactory.

'Good,' said Keller. 'Everything is fixed for tomorrow night. That is when we get you through the lines.'

It was just after ten the following night when Christina and Stratou piled into the cab of the truck in which she had first arrived at the farmhouse. The driver was again the man in the wide-brimmed hat.

They drove in silence. Until now, all that had happened to Christina since the ambush had seemed unreal. Suddenly, as the first stage of *Operation Artemis* commenced in earnest, the reality – and the dangers – became vibrantly alive.

Three times during the drive, the truck went past encampments of German soliders. Christina could not hide her nervousness – a fact which troubled Stratou until he realised that she was the one person who had no idea that this was a German operation.

'It is all right,' said the driver, who had also detected her agitation, 'I drive this way every night. They are used to seeing the truck. They never stop me now.'

Soon they were in a heavily wooded valley. The narrow rutted road was deserted. Over the noise of the truck engine, they could hear a rolling thunder of sound.

'Try to get used to the guns,' the driver said to Christina. 'Both sides will be firing at each other all night long. The two main armies of the Germans and the British are some miles to the east of us. They face each other across the valley which runs inland from Rimini. We are making for a quiet part of the front.'

Progress was slow. No lights now. They had covered about three miles without headlights when dimly, ahead, they saw a figure in the road waving them down.

It was the man Christina knew only as Artemis.

'Wait here,' he told the driver of the truck. 'You two, come with me.'

Christina and Stratou followed Keller along a muddy track into the forest. A short distance into the wood, the big van and its trailer had been parked underneath a tunnel of pines from which the lower branches had been cut.

'They are well hidden, eh?' said Keller.

He faced Christina and Stratou.

'Well, this is it. From here you are on your own. You are now five miles from the nearest German defensive positions and about five hundred yards from the British.'

He saw the involuntary start which Christina gave.

'It's all right, my dear. You won't be caught up in any fighting. The British won't find out until daylight that the Germans have pulled out of these parts. And they'll pass right by this spot when they do find out.'

He outlined the exact situation.

If they had continued along the narrow road where the farm truck was now parked they would have come to a great ravine through which ran the Marecchia River. The British were on the other side of that impassable ravine and their engineers had been building a bridge across it for the past week. By next day, they would have the bridge complete and they would have vehicles streaming across it.

Christina and Stratou had only to bide their time, until they were sure that empty supply trucks were going back across the bridge, then they would emerge from their hiding-place and infiltrate into the traffic.

Keller shook hands with each of them in turn. He was in the grip of a deep emotion. *Operation Artemis* was his brainchild. It was the gamble on which he was staking not only his shirt but his skin as well. No longer was the operation a wisping fancy haunting the deep recesses of his mind, it was now a fact – an incontrovertible fact.

His work had been done. He had set the stage and written the script, improvising as he went along. He had furnished the props and chosen the players. Now, it was time for the curtain to rise and the drama to begin.

He stepped back into the shadows and then hurried along the track to the waiting farm truck.

The guns boomed all night long. Between the opposing armies – the Germans in the north and the Eighth Army in the south – there were eleven thousand artillery pieces along the two facing ranges of hills, which were separated by the ten-miles-broad flat of muddy valley floor.

The infantries of both armies were neck-deep in the mud of the valley floor, huddled only sixty yards from each other's lines in their stinking verminous holes. They drowned in the mud, while from the hills above them, ton after ton of exploding shells rained down.

'You had better get some sleep,' Stratou had advised Christina after Keller had gone. He, himself, had immediately retired to one of the two sleeping sections of the trailer. These were narrow single-berth compartments not unlike those of a sleeper train.

Christina could not face the claustrophobic gloom of her sleeping-berth. She had sat in the cab, listening to the unending thunder of the guns. Cold, seeping into her cramped legs, kept her awake. Hours later, she became aware that daylight was filtering through the trees. Steamy wisps of mist were dancing on the forest carpet. There was suddenly something strange about the morning.

Then she realised what it was. The guns were silent.

Stratou appeared half an hour later and persuaded her to rest in the trailer. He wakened her from a deep sleep at three in the afternoon. Her first conscious awareness after the sound of his voice was the noise of heavy trucks on the road.

'They've been coming north over the bridge since about ten this morning,' Stratou told her. 'The British must have established a supply point about two miles back along the road we came down last night. Empty trucks have been coming back since about noon. I think it's safe for us to go.'

Stratou offered to take first trick at the wheel of the big van. Christina did not argue.

He started the motor with an explosion of sound which sent birds into startled flight from the trees overhead. He nursed the van forward inches at a time until the massive tyres began to bite in the soft ground. He accelerated gently down the forest track to the road.

There was no traffic moving north now. Empty trucks were, however, returning at intervals of about two minutes from the forward supply point. All the traffic was south-bound to the bridge. Stratou noticed that most of the drivers were Indian.

As one vehicle rumbled past towards the bridge, Stratou nosed the van out from the trees and followed it. They rounded a bend between two great humps of rock and found themselves on the bridge. Christina gasped with alarm as she looked out from the passenger window of the cab. Only an eighteen-inches-high girder parapet stood between the big van and the white-foaming ribbon of river five hundred feet below. They seemed to be riding in space.

A red-capped military policeman was on the far side of the bridge.

'Keep that bloody great rattle-trap moving,' he bawled at Stratou. 'No stopping in the middle to admire the scenery! Keep that bloody thing moving!'

Stratou had no intention of stopping. Even he had paled at the unexpectedness of the yawning ravine and, momentarily, his foot had eased from the accelerator. Now, he gunned the van across in low gear and breathed an audible sigh of relief as they rounded a bend on the far side of the bridge and began a winding ascent up the slope which opened before them.

The engineers who had built the bridge were in bivouacs alongside the twisting road. They did not even look up as the van and trailer crawled by.

As they neared the end of the long climb from the bridge, the road forked left and joined up with a better-quality road running east and west.

'This is the main road from San Marino to Rimini,' Stratou said. 'We should be in Rimini in just over half an hour.'

The road hugged the face of the south range of hills looking out on the Rimini plain. It was busy with ammunition and fuel trucks engaged in a constant shuttle service. Now and again, a great eruption of earth and black smoke would explode from the hillside above or below the road as the big van and trailer lumbered along it. German artillerymen on the far side of the valley were simply making the Eighth Army aware of their existence. Occasionally, a British battery would reply from a position above the road.

Most of the gunners were asleep at this time of day, however. Their main activity was reserved for the hours of darkness, when search-lights would illuminate the valley floor and the artillery duelling began in earnest.

At a crossroads just outside Rimini, a redcap halted the big van.

'Where are you going, friend?' he shouted up to Stratou.

'South,' Stratou replied. 'With the Fourth Indian.'

'Another of that mob, eh? Where are you all going? It's a bloody long way to Bombay. Keep down to the right here and you're clear all the way to Ancona.'

The redcap waved the big van and trailer through.

'Taranto, here we come,' said Stratou, and smiled at Christina. She smiled back.

The first stage of *Operation Artemis* had gone without a hitch.

Nor was there any apparent impediment to the second stage.

A few days later, Keller received a signal from his agent in Taranto to say that Stratou and his companion had reached the port. He was exultant. He had arranged with Stratou to make a 'letter drop' in Taranto at the last possible moment before embarkation. The Taranto agent had collected the message on 23rd October and transmitted it immediately to the huge radio receivers at the Palazzo Emiliano.

The message said: 'PROCRIS ON HER WAY HOME WITH GIFTS.'

Trimming his sails to the winds of chance and exploiting them to the full was one of Keller's most highly developed characteristics. In the selection of Stratou, however, he miscalculated how fickle these winds could sometimes be.

When the Greek Prime Minister returned to Athens with his Government on Wednesday 18th October 1944, the situation impressed upon him the need for one thing – a Greek National Army into which the various guerrilla armies could be incorporated. This course was also urged upon George Papandreou by British Government ministers who accompanied him to Athens.

On 22nd October, a small team of officers from the Greek Brigade met staff from the British Sea Transport Officer's strength in Brindisi to discuss the shipping question. They moved on the following day for more discussions with the STO, Taranto. Acting for the team of Greek officers as interpreter was Lieutenant Leonidas Preston.

The winds of chance had brought, therefore, to Taranto on successive days: Niko Stratou and the one man above all others who knew him for what he was.

After the morning session of discussion with Sea Transport staff had broken up, Preston found himself paired with a grizzle-haired veteran of World War One. Lieutenant John Rankine, RNR, had been a Merchant Navy captain most of his life and had retired from the sea six months before Hitler's invasion of Poland. Now, in his sixtieth year and too old for sea-going with the Navy, he was an invaluable member of the administrative staff who organised the huge traffic into and out of Taranto.

He had invited Preston to lunch with him at the Naval

Base and, with an hour to spare before the afternoon discussions were scheduled to begin, had offered to show the American something of Old Taranto. Preston had happily accepted and the pair had set off on foot.

Taranto is built on a spit of land between two great expanses of water – the magnificent natural harbour of Taranto Bay and the land-locked lake which is known as the Mare Piccolo, the Little Sea. The great anchorage of the Bay is linked with the Mare Piccolo by a short canal, seventy feet wide. The canal bisects the spit of land on which Taranto is built. To the west of the canal is the Old City, rich with the history of centuries. To the east is the newer part of the seaport city.

Across the canal, a swing bridge connects new Taranto with the old. It opens to allow ships to pass in or out of the inner harbour, the Mare Piccolo. Preston and John Rankine, on their way to the Old City, were frustrated to find when they reached the bridge that it had been swung open. A ship was due out of the Mare Piccolo. The two men were forced to wait. They walked in the pleasant October sunshine to the seaward end of the canal in order to escape the crush of people and traffic queuing to cross the bridge.

Preston watched with interest as the ship in the Mare Piccolo lined its bows with the far end of the canal. He could hear the increased engine revolutions as the vessel changed from slow to half speed ahead and came at the narrow gap almost with a rush.

The SS *Mariestad* was a ship of about four thousand tons. She had loaded in Norfolk, Virginia with a cargo of foodstuffs and medical supplies. The vessel was under charter to the United Nations relief organisation, UNRRA, and had been ordered to Taranto for bunkers and direction to her final port of discharge.

The ship had taken on 750 tons of coal for its bunkers from the hulk, *Bengloe*, a torpedoed British freighter which had been towed into Taranto to end its days in the Mare Piccolo. The *Mariestad* had also taken on board in the inner harbour two large vehicles as deck cargo.

One was a pantechnicon-like van. It was now securely lashed and bottle-screwed to the starboard after-deck of the *Mariestad*. The other was a huge trailer, secured on the port after-deck. Both vehicles had the letters MBADU painted in gold lettering on their bottle-green sides.

Nikos Stratou and Christina Kirkos had come on deck to watch the departure from port. They leaned on the rail of the after-deck beside the trailer. Both were elated at the ease with which things had gone so far, although neither was complacent.

Christina could not shake off a constant self-consciousness in her absurd role of male impersonator. In the cab of the van it was never too bad, but when she had to move about in the open, exposed to other eyes, she felt sure she was being stared at and her guise penetrated.

Afraid, too, that her voice might at anytime give her away, she and Stratou and agreed that she should speak to no one. When on a couple of occasions, soldiers had engaged her in conversation with no more intent than passing the time of day, she had simply walked away, leaving behind an impression of a rude and surly disposition.

Since boarding the ship, she had become adept at sustaining this impression of unsociable surliness and had avoided communication with the friendly Swedish seamen. Stratou had helped by being as sociable with the Swedes as she was unsociable; indicating to the sailors that his driver was a strange introverted loner who should be given a wide berth.

The Swedish captain, a man called Jorgensen, had allotted the pair two boat-deck cabins and a small mess-room to which a jovial assistant cook delivered all their

300

meals. This meant that they not only had privacy, being the only passengers, but they did not need to have any more contact with the officers and crew than they chose.

Stratou, acutely aware that he might be recognised, had taken two precautions with his appearance. Keller had given him a pair of horn-rimmed glasses – fitted with plain glass – and these he now wore constantly. Also, he was allowing a moustache to grow. These were simple enough measures but – Stratou believed – effective ways of altering his appearance.

As the *Mariestad* steamed at five knots through the cutting between the Mare Piccolo and Taranto Bay, the vessel had about seven feet clearance on either side. As the ship passed the inswung span of the bridge in the middle of the cut, Stratou – leaning against the after-deck rail and far from sorry that this was his final contact with Italy – momentarily removed his horn-rimmed glasses and ran a hand against his forehead. The ship was level with the seaward end of the cut in the short space of time required to complete the simple movement of wiping his forehead and returning the glasses to the bridge of his nose.

This was the precise instant in which he found himself staring straight into the face of Leonidas Preston.

Preston was standing on the quayside beside a naval officer. He had a cigarette in his hand and he had one foot up on a bollard, leaning against his raised knee.

The two men were less than twelve feet away from each other. Briefly, their eyes met.

The man on the ship replaced the glasses which he had been holding in his hand and then casually turned his back. He was trembling.

The man on the quay experienced a shuddering thrill of recognition. But it died with the absence of any noticeable response from the figure on the ship.

'You look like you've just seen a ghost,' observed John Rankine.

'For a moment I thought I had,' said Preston. 'Someone on the deck of that ship. He looked the spitting image of an old friend . . . Or, rather, an old enemy.'

'That's the *Mariestad*, a Swede. She's going out with that convoy you can see forming up in the Bay.'

The *Mariestad* was now well clear of the cut and was turning so that the big blue and yellow flag of Sweden, painted on her light grey hull, could be clearly seen.

Preston was trying to recapture the image of a moment before: the tall figure on the deck and the big trucks with MB . . . something . . . on the sides. He shook his head. There was no way it could be Stratou. It was an impossibility.

He'd had Stratou on the brain ever since Rimini. He was seeing him in every shadow.

CHAPTER TWENTY-ONE

Conspiracy

The chairman of the meeting was a sallow-faced man in his middle fifties. Pancrates Natsinas had started political life as a Socialist but, dismayed by the Socialists' moderate approach to winning power in Greece, he had quickly switched allegiance to the KKE, the Greek Communist Party.

Two lengthy stays in the Soviet Union during the thirties had made him a devoted disciple of Stalin and a willing evangelist of World Revolution. But, carefully schooled by the Kremlin, he did not preach in the market square. He remained wholly in the background, planning and calculating, getting others to front his ideas. Others got the key appointments, the accolades, the public applause and, sometimes, the avenging bullets – but Natsinas had the power. It was something which he could retain indefinitely. The single governing factor was that he did exactly what Moscow told him to do.

He had to come into his own in Greece when KKE initiative had led to the establishment of EAM. He was a founding-father – but content to remain an *eminence grise*, working in the shadows, directing, manipulating. He knew that when he pulled the strings the members of EAM jumped and danced like well-trained puppets.

He looked around the faces of the men and women crowded into the basement meeting room of the International Labour Society. The seedy premises in downtown Athens had been closed by the Germans but had re-opened the day after Liberation. Only eighteen people were present but, from the hubbub, it seemed that a dozen different political meetings were taking place. Those present could be roughly divided into two categories; military commanders and political activists. All were proven supporters of Socialist Revolution.

There was only one man present about whom Natsinas had faint reservations, General Cephalus. Moscow regarded Cephalus highly, but Natsinas had misgivings about the way he had built a large personal following around himself and stolen the thunder of his seniors.

Spiro's nose had certainly been put out of joint when Cephalus had been given the rank of General only a month ago. Yet, Spiro had only himself to blame. He had been content to sit on his backside in Karpenisi while Cephalus had been recruiting new battalions all over Western Greece.

What impressed Moscow, of course, was the way Cephalus had got his hands on all the field-guns and ammunition of an Italian artillery company right under the noses of the departing Germans. It had been the result of a deal he had made with his Abwehr contacts, naturally. Natsinas had reservations about that, too, but Moscow seemed to think that Cephalus had tricked the Germans blind at every turn. Moscow was impressed by results and that was what Cephalus had given them – results.

Eighteen months before, Cephalus had had two hundred men under his command. By his own efforts, he had built that up to an army of twelve thousand. About a thousand of these men were German and Italian deserters – but even a revolutionary army needs a quota of mercenaries. Their recruitment had saved the necessity of training Greek peasants, many of whom were illiterate, to use the Italian 75 mm guns Cephalus now had.

Natsinas called the meeting to order.

'Comrades,' he addressed them, 'first of all, I want to thank you for the excellent demonstrations of solidarity which you organised in Athens on the eighteenth of October. We have shown our strength to Papandreou and the British. We have welcomed them and celebrated Liberation with them but we have also let them see that ours is the power. We have let them see that only at their peril can they ignore that power.'

A chorus of approval greeted Natsinas's remarks. There was one dissenting voice.

General Spiro pushed his great bulk from a bench at one side of the cellar and held up a hand for silence.

'I say we have missed a glorious chance!' he declared. 'We should have seized power the moment the Germans started to leave. Athens would have been ours now. We should have occupied every barracks and police station and government building, instead of letting the British stroll in and play the conquering heroes. Now, Papandreou wants us to lay down our arms and disband our armies so that the Royalist scum can take over.'

Spiro's point of view was not without support. Heads nodded in agreement and there were murmurs of approval. Natsinas was smiling as he now held up his hands, seeking to be heard.

'I admit we were slow to appreciate the situation, but the British moved very quickly. They flew their aircraft into Megara and Kalamaki far sooner than we expected. Without possession of these airfields, we would have been putting everything at risk.'

'Then, let us take the airfields,' shouted Spiro. 'That will achieve more than getting our men to stand in Constitution Square shouting "We want no king."'

Again Spiro got support. Natsinas appealed for silence.

'Comrades, comrades . . . Let me acquaint you with the facts of life. The British have only a small force in

305

Greece – in the Peloponnesus and here in Athens. We have more than ninety thousand men under arms and can throw the British into the sea whenever we feel like it.'

Natsinas ignored shouts of: 'Why don't we?' He continued speaking in a calm unflurried manner.

'We control nine-tenths of Greece. That is a reality. We have the civil and political power – and the military power to back it up. So, why should we resort to bloody means to win our ends when it can be done without a shot being fired? All that Papandreou can do is talk. All that the British can do is talk. We can talk with them – but we shall take with us to the conference table a big stick. They shall bargain with their tongues. We shall bargain with our big stick. We cannot lose.'

This drew applause from the small gathering. Spiro, however, was still scowling.

'We cannot feed our armies with words,' he protested.

Natsinas stared at him blandly.

'There is food coming into the country now,' he said. 'Haven't you seen all the ships out there in Phaleron Bay?'

'The British control the food. They guard it and ration it out. Am I to go cap in hand to them?'

'If your men need food, General Spiro, they must take it where they find it.'

'Even if it means killing a few British soliders?' asked Spiro.

Natsinas shrugged.

'If his men are starving, no general would be held responsible for any unfortunate lapses of discipline on their part in obtaining food for their bellies. Who could blame them for buying bread with bullets? Officially, of course, we would deprecate any such actions. Wouldn't we, General Spiro?'

'Yes, yes, of course,' said Spiro, but he was grinning

broadly, as were a number of other ELAS officers present.

When the meeting finally broke up, Natsinas found George Kirkos deep in conversation with his political officer, the woman Petrea.

'I was wanting a word with you, General Cephalus.'

Petrea, whose back was to Natsinas, whirled angrily at the interruption but her expression became deferential when she recognised Natsinas.

'You will excuse me then?' she said.

'Don't go,' said Natsinas. 'I just wanted to know more about this secret plan of the Comrade-General's which has got Karolov all so steamed up. I believe he has complained to Moscow about being frozen out. He says you are planning to assassinate someone but you won't tell him who or where or how.'

'Karolov is a fool,' said Petrea, but Kirkos held up a hand.

'Karolov is many things but he is not a fool. The truth, Comrade Natsinas, is that he is jealous of me. You must know it better than anyone, because he has opposed every operation I have planned. This time I'm not giving him the opportunity. The fewer people who know about it the better.'

'Am I to be taken into your confidence?' asked Natsinas. His tone of voice was mild but it still managed to convey an underlying suggestion of threat. 'The Party does not approve of unilateral operations . . . Even by its favourite generals.'

'I've no intention of acting unilaterally,' said Kirkos. 'What I have in mind is in the Party's interest . . . But it is an undertaking of such delicacy, politically, that I hesitate to say too much about it to anyone while the physical details of the plan are incomplete.'

'If it's a matter of political delicacy, then it's something which I should know about,' said Natsinas.

'Naturally,' replied Kirkos. 'Is there somewhere we could talk? Somewhere less public?'

They went to Natsinas's home, an unpretentious flat near Monastiraki Square. Natsinas offered ouzo to Kirkos and Petrea and then got right to the point without preamble.

'Whom do you intend to assassinate, General Cephalus?'

'You tell me,' said Kirkos evasively. 'Who would you say is the biggest single stumbling-block to the establishment of a Communist Government in Greece?'

'Do not play guessing games with me,' said Natsinas coldly.

'I'm not playing guessing games. I asked a serious question. I have someone in mind for elimination, but I confess there are difficulties. I am quite prepared to let you or the Party choose the target. Heaven knows, I've liquidated enough Class Enemies for you in the past two years. But this time I want an important enemy – not the head of some provincial Nome or a Monarchist nobody.'

Natsinas was silent.

'Can't you think of anyone?' taunted Kirkos.

'If you are serious . . . I, personally, would like to get rid of Papandreou and his British puppets of Ministers.'

'Have you no ambition, Comrade Natsinas? Do Papandreou and his lap-dogs really stand between you and a Communist Greece? We could kill them any time – and all at once.'

'How?'

'By demanding a meeting with them – the whole Cabinet. Our delegates, of course, would be delayed . . . So that none of them would be hurt when the building blew up.'

Natsinas stared at Kirkos in amazement.

'You're a cool one, aren't you, Cephalus? I do believe there is absolutely nothing you would stop at. You would kill your own grandmother if you saw an advantage to it.'

'So would you,' said Kirkos calmly. 'Do you think I don't know who draws up those lists of Class Enemies we've been systematically destroying since 1941? Do you think I don't know who said that the only kind of opposition which a Revolution can tolerate is dead opposition?'

Natsinas turned and squinted at Petrea with raised eyebrows.

'Have you been talking about me out of school, Comrade? Don't you know that what is said at meetings of the Political Commissariat should not be repeated outside its locked doors?'

'The business of the Commissariat may be secret but surely a revolutionary maxim is the property of the people,' said Petrea stiffly.

Natsinas made a face. What a pompous bitch. He smiled at Kirkos.

'So you think I lack ambition in my choice of enemies? All right then, how about liquidating the British Ambassador, Leeper? Or his political boss, Macmillan? Or how about the British military commander, General Scobie? It's the British who stand between us and control of our country, not Papandreou.'

'Now you're talking,' said Kirkos. 'But why not aim higher yet? How about the man who gives Leeper and Macmillan and Scobie their orders?'

'Churchill?'

There was a long silence. Natsinas was deep in thought.

'Churchill is at this minute in Moscow discussing war plans with Marshal Stalin. Do you wish us to invite him to Athens? Ask him to drop in here on his way home to London so that we can put a bullet in him?'

'He will come to Athens in the very near future.'

'What makes you so sure?'

'You must take my word for it. He will come.'

'So will Christmas.'

Natsinas shook his head.

'What could we hope to gain by killing Churchill? It would rouse world opinion against us. He is a hero to the Allies, to the Americans in particular. To many Greeks. The Americans would send huge armies against us.'

'That's what some loyal but misguided Marxists said when Lenin agreed to the killing of the Czar and his family. Look what happened – the Revolution survived it. And its enemies were denied a rallying-point.'

Petrea joined in.

'The Americans will not lift a finger. Already they have been loudly critical of Churchill. They have accused him of meddling in Greek affairs and foisting a King on us that nobody wants.'

Natsinas nodded.

'That makes more sense. Perhaps it would create a situation which we could exploit. We could begin right away with protests that the presence of British troops is offensive, a provocation to the Greek people . . . That they behave brutally, like an army of occupation . . . We should demand their immediate withdrawal. The British will not go, of course, but if something were to happen to Churchill . . . The whole thing could be blamed on the continued presence of British troops on our soil. The incident could be used as a lever to force their withdrawal.'

Natsinas smiled at Kirkos.

'Comrade, I think I may have underestimated you in the past. I thought that perhaps you were more interested in your own glory than in the Cause which we all serve. I apologise for misjudging you. You are someone after my own heart. You are not content simply to talk about Revolution, you want to make things happen.'

310

'Then you will support General Cephalus?' said Petrea. 'Karolov's slanders cannot be allowed to go on.'

'I have some weight with the Party, here and in Moscow. Leave Karolov to me.' He cocked an eye at Kirkos. 'Now perhaps you'll tell me what you have in mind, Comrade.'

Kirkos lit a cigarette before answering.

'There's not much to tell. I have several contingency plans rather than one hard and fast project. This is necessary because, one, we do not know exactly when Churchill intends to visit Athens and, two, what his movements will be. One thing is certain - I am not going to leave things to a sniper. A sniper could be spotted before he gets a bullet off. I am going to make certain of Churchill even if it means taking everybody in his vicinity with him. In one big bang.'

'So that's why, you have been hoarding dynamite?' said Natsinas. Kirkos looked at him in surprise.

'How do you know about the dynamite?'

'All Greece knows about your dynamite. It is already legend how your men occupied the power-station and saved the electric supply. And how your men beat off a German attack.' Natsinas shrugged. 'Perhaps not everyone knows what happened to the two or more tons of dynamite which the Germans left in the power-station with the intention of blowing it off the map . . . But I know you carried it off to some hiding-place, General. What do you intend to do with it?'

Kirkos smiled crookedly.

'It is under the Grande Bretagne Hotel, Comrade Natsinas. When it goes up, there will not be much left of Constitution Square.'

'You expect Churchill to stay there?'

'Why not? Papandreou and his gang are already installed there. Every distinguished visitor who comes to Athens stays there. It is only one of the contingencies I've catered for.'

311

'What are the others?'

'These depend on me receiving a rather sophisticated piece of artillery in time. It is on its way to Athens.'

'A gun? What kind of gun?'

'I can't describe it because I've never seen it. But if it lives up to the salesman's propaganda, it is quite a weapon. It never misses its target. It is radio-directed.'

Natsinas sat forward in his chair, his eyes wide.

'How could you get your hands on such a weapon?'

'The same way I have acquired most of my artillery.'

'You stole it from the Germans?'

Kirkos treated Natsinas to a reproachful look.

'Stole it, Comrade? Do you think I am a bandit like Spiro? No, this weapon is costing a lot of money. I have to pay for it with British gold.'

'And where will you get British gold?'

'Gold is where you find it,' said Kirkos. He was enjoying teasing Natsinas. 'The British lost some gold in the mountains a year or so back. I found it.'

There was unconcealed distrust in the look which Natsinas directed at Kirkos.

'If British gold fell into your hands, that would have made it the property of EAM. Why did you not report this . . . find?'

'Oh but I did,' smiled Kirkos. 'I sent some of it to Spiro. Didn't *he* report it? No, obviously not. That's partly why I didn't send it all. I had my suspicions about him. The other reason I kept it was quite legitimate – an order from EAM, no less, instructing me to acquire by levies and taxes within my operational area and, *by such means as were necessary*, all monies required for the subsistence of my command and its maintenance as an operational force.'

'So that's the secret of your impressive recruiting figures?' said Natsins. 'I've been told that your men were better fed and better equipped than any other band in Greece. We thought it was some magic in your personality, Comrade. No one guessed that it was gold.'

Petrea was devouring every word with a glow of rapt admiration on her face. Natsinas, too, was impressed by Kirkos's performance, but not prepared to show it. But a high compliment was in order.

'A letter I have from Marshal Stalin expressed much the same sentiments. Russia cannot support us too publicly if it comes to a shooting war with the British. They have warned us not to start anything we can't finish. Everything depends on how far the British are prepared to go in their support of Papandreou. If they back him to the hilt, then it will mean war. But our policy for the moment is to secure the political initiative we hold. We must let the British see that their policies are meaningless without our help. Then, they may give in and leave of their own accord. Your little scheme to kill Churchill could do the trick on its own – especially if, beforehand, we can accuse the British troops of atrocities against the civil population.'

'I am sure that can be arranged,' said Kirkos slyly.

'Just one word of warning, General,' said Natsinas. 'Events may demand that our strategy takes its own course, regardless of this enterprise of yours. And if things go wrong . . . If sacrifices have to be made . . . We would not hesitate to sacrifice you–' he fixed a baleful eye on Petrea '–and your close associates.'

'You, of course, will safeguard your own position, Comrade Natsinas?' Kirkos's voice was gently mocking. 'If we bring this off, you will modestly admit that you had a part in it. If we fail, you will cast the first stone . . . being without sin.'

The B29 swooped low over Phaleron Bay. More than a hundred ships lay at anchor below. There were freighters, gantry landing-ships, warships of every shape and size from small wooden mine-sweepers to the three-

313

funnelled Greek cruiser *Averof* with its heavy 9.2-inch guns.

Maitland was kneeling behind the pilot, who had invited him up front to see the spectacle of ships and get his first glimpse of Athens. The aircraft circled the Acropolis. The blue and white flag of Greece now fluttered proudly there in place of the hated Nazi emblem which had been hauled down and burned three weeks before.

'We'll be touching down in approximately one minute,' said the pilot. 'Maybe you'd better go back and take your seat now, sir. It could be a bumpy landing. The Germans left a lot of holes in the runway.'

Maitland returned to his seat in the bomber's interior. A moment later, the aircraft looped in low from seaward and over the coast road east of Kalamaki. Scorching tyres squealed on the pitted tarmac as it landed and then wheeled slowly towards a line of parked Spitfires.

The Army had laid on a jeep for Maitland. The 509th Military General Hospital had been established in a hotel a little way out from the city centre, on a pleasant avenue below Mount Lycabettos. The jeep took Maitland directly to the hospital.

He found Mackenzie pacing the small room in which he had been confined since his arrival from Patras. Maitland was shocked by the change in the younger man's appearance. He remembered him as rather chubby-cheeked and broad of back and hip; not disproportionately heavy but well-made. Now, his cheeks seemed hollow and he was as lean as a broomhandle; thinner by at least thirty pounds.

Mackenzie stared at Maitland with his good eye. The patch on the other magnified the ferocity of his expression. He was wearing a white towel robe over pyjamas. He did not at first recognise the neatly turned-out figure in the dark suit and regimental tie.

'Commander Six,' he said, as recognition dawned.

Maitland shook hands.

'Now I do believe in resurrection. Glad to see you, Mackenzie. Are they treating you all right?'

'Are they hell! I'm on the point of breaking out, sir.' A smile only slightly softened Mackenzie's vehemence as he went on: 'They've got a sergeant-major of a nursing sister who's bullying the bloody life out of me, sir. She comes in here every half hour and gives me dog's abuse because I won't stay in bed. There's not a damned thing wrong with me and they're treating me like a geriatric!'

'I spoke to the doctor on my way up,' said Maitland. 'You're missing a large chunk of lung. You've got yourself a ticket to Civvy Street, Captain.'

Mackenzie's face fell.

'They . . . You're not invaliding me out?'

'I'm not,' said Maitland, 'but the Army wants to. They've got a sanatorium in the wilds of Aberdeenshire where they want you to stay for a spell. They want a long look at that chest of yours. You'll get a pension at the end of it.'

Anger flamed in Mackenzie's face.

'I don't want their bloody pension – and I'm not going home to be invalided out. I want to stay in Greece – get my discharge here if it comes to that.'

Maitland frowned. Then his expression changed.

'Have you got anything to drink out of?' he asked. From inside his jacket he produced a silver flask in a leather casing. Mackenzie brightened. He crossed to the wash-hand bowl and rinsed a glass which had contained a toothbrush.

Maitland had poured whisky from his flask into the silver sheath from its base. He now poured some into Mackenzie's glass.

'Let's sit and talk about this.'

They settled themselves into the two cane armchairs

which were the room's only furniture in addition to the bed. They sat by the window, with its splendid view of Mount Lycabettos and the Temple of Jupiter.

'Why do you want to stay in Greece?' asked Maitland.

'I like it here. And I have personal reasons.'

'Do you, by God? These wouldn't include settling old scores?'

'They might.'

'Your old friend, Cephalus, is a general now. Did you know? I'm told he now has more than ten thousand men. They are squatting all over Piraeus and camped around the hills nearby. One way or another, the ELAS must have close on fifty thousand men in or around Athens.'

'They mean to take over,' said Mackenzie. 'You know that, don't you? You know what's going on outside Athens, too, I hope? They're combing every town and village rounding up everyone who won't sing "The Red Flag". They're butchering every known opponent of Communism and rounding up all the "don't-knows" and uncommitted – whole families . . . Herding them all up into the mountains.'

'I've heard rumours. It's hard to get an accurate picture of what's happening outside Athens. That's why I want you to go on working for me.'

'In spite of the cock-up I made?'

'I can pull a few strings if you don't want to go home. The one and only consideration is your physical fitness.'

Mackenzie played with the patch over his eye. 'I'm fit as a fiddle. I just didn't think you would want me to go on working for the Section. I'm no bloody good as a spy. I'm no good at pretending. I can't hide the way I feel . . . If I'm angry, it shows. If I hate somebody's guts, I tell them.'

Maitland did not reply immediately. He drained his whisky and looked at Mackenzie long and hard. He

didn't want to push Mackenzie. It was like chasing a
wounded man back into the trenches within minutes of
him being stretchered out of the line. Yet, it would be
a pity too if Mackenzie's knowledge of the Greek situation were to be wasted. He came to a decision.

'There's a friend of yours due in Athens this afternoon. He had a bad time of it here in Greece after you
and he parted company – and almost as bad a time
after he got out. I was hoping the pair of you would
team up.'

Mackenzie's expression was quizzical.

'Leo? Are you talking about Leo Preston?'

'Yes. He made such a fuss about what happened to
you that his own people, the OSS, disowned him. He
has been working for me ever since. I had hoped that
you and he would help me find the lady.'

Mackenzie's heart had warmed with joy at the
thought of seeing Preston again. But he said:

'What lady?'

Maitland pulled some papers from an inside pocket
and extracted a small photograph from among them.
He handed it to Mackenzie.

'Do you know her?'

He stared at it. He was unable to repress a stab of
guilt.

'It's Christina – Christina Kirkos. Where did you get
it?'

'From the Americans. They didn't know until your
friend, Preston, told them that she was American. It
didn't excite them much at the time but all of a sudden
she has become important. They have just worked out
that one of their nationals is the wife of a top ELAS
general and they've decided she would make a
wonderful recruit for the OSS.'

'They're crazy if they think that,' said Mackenzie.

'Why do you say that?'

'Because I know her. For a start, she's estranged from

317

her husband. Do the Yanks know that? Just by contacting her, they could put her life in danger. The Reds would put a bullet in her quicker than you could wink if they got so much as a whiff that she'd been approached.'

'She hasn't been approached yet,' said Maitland.

'What makes the Americans think she can be of any use to them?'

'They have a man, Harvey, who is very thick with Spiro. Harvey has reported jealousies in the ELAS leadership. Spiro has been hinting to him that Cephalus is angling to take over the whole show.'

'What is Spiro after?'

'Guarantees,' said Maitland. 'He wants the Americans to stop us – the British – from interfering in what he calls the legitimate self-determination of the Greek people. He says we want to impose a Monarchy which the Greek people do not want . . .'

'And?'

'And the Yanks have a strict policy of non-interference in the political affairs of liberated countries. Spiro knows this. He wants them to pressure us into adopting the same line. He has been telling them that if America allows EAM to set up a Greek Democratic Republic and stops us from interfering, they'll be upholding the noblest concepts in their own constitution!'

'And what does Spiro want for himself?'

'He wants them to acknowledge him as a patriot and freedom-fighter and to put the finger on Cephalus as a political opportunist. He hasn't said as much, naturally, but I get the impression that the people he is really trying to impress are his mates in EAM and the Kremlin. He wants Moscow to recognise him as the man who effectively neutralised America and Britain and cleared the way for a Communist take-over of Greece. He wants to be the blue-eyed boy instead of Cephalus. Unfortunately, the Americans think Spiro is genuine. He has even hinted to them that Cephalus collaborated with the Germans.'

'He could be right in that,' said Mackenzie. 'What happened on the Agrinion road eighteen months ago wasn't just an unhappy coincidence. The Germans were tipped off about our ambush, I'm sure. We walked into a trap.'

For the first time since that terrible night, Mackenzie learned of the subsequent events. Anger burned in him as Maitland recounted Preston's ordeal in captivity and how he had been branded as coward and liar. At the end of it – when Maitland had answered the questions with which Mackenzie bombarded him – Mackenzie said:

'What exactly do you want me to do, sir?'

'I want you and Preston to find Christina Kirkos before anyone else does. You both know her, so that gives us an advantage. According to Harvey, the American liaison officer at Karpenisi, she was in Karpenisi until just over a year ago. There's no way of confirming it, but Cephalus is supposed to have sent her back to Athens because she was expecting a child.'

The colour drained from Mackenzie's face.

'A child?'

'Does it surprise you? It happens, you know. Those long winter nights up in the mountains.'

Mackenzie stared out the window. There was no reason why – because he had spent one passionate night with Christina Kirkos – he should jump to the conclusion that he was the father of her child. And yet the certainty that he was, imposed itself on his mind and would not go away. Maitland, ignorant of the significance his words had held, was still talking on.

'My hunch is that Christina Kirkos is still in Athens,' he was saying. Mackenzie forced himself to pay attention.

'Why is it so important to you to find her?' he asked.

'Because of this,' replied Maitland. He took a slip of paper and passed it to Mackenzie. Seven words were written on the paper.

'I don't understand,' said Mackenzie.

'For some time now, we have been monitoring radio signals on a certain frequency – at our listening-station at Caserta in Italy. The Germans left a lot of agents behind as they retreated north in Italy. Thanks to your friend, Preston, we bagged quite a few of them and the codes they used – but a lot of them are still at large and sending stuff back. Most of the messages we have intercepted have made sense – but this one has had our experts baffled.'

Mackenzie read the message aloud:

'Procris on her way home with gifts.'

He shook his head. Maitland smiled grimly.

'It didn't make any kind of sense to me until one of our chaps in Caserta gave up on it. He said: "It's Greek to me!" '

'And to me,' said Mackenzie. 'I don't get it.'

'Greek!' emphasised Maitland. 'Greek! I was trying to make sense of it in an Italian context. But it has nothing to do with Italy. The connection is Greek!'

'I still don't get it.'

'Think of your Greek mythology, man,' prompted Maitland. 'Don't you know who Procris was?'

'There was a racehorse called Procris . . .'

'Procris was the wife of Cephalus!' exclaimed Maitland. 'Not only that, she was the *estranged* wife of Cephalus!'

Mackenzie cocked his good eye at Maitland.

'Christina Kirkos? You think this has something to do with Christina Kirkos?'

'I'm sure of it. It's all beginning to make a picture – and not a very pretty picture. You know better than anyone the kind of treachery that Cephalus is capable

320

of. Add to that, Spiro's hints and our own suspicions about him dealing with the Germans ... And the strange business of Christina Kirkos being tried by the Communists for collaboration and then being cleared ... Then her mysterious disappearance from Karpenisi — allegedly because she was expecting a child. And here's something else to ponder. Do you know where the German Secret Service had their offices in Athens? A place called the Hotel Artemis, at the back of Ermou Street. I believe the Greeks tried to burn it down recently.'

Mackenzie frowned.

'What has a hotel got to do with it?'

'Your Greek mythology again,' said Maitland. 'That message we intercepted ... It mentions Procris and the gifts. Procris became reconciled with Cephalus when she returned home with the gifts of Artemis — a legendary spear which always hit its target once it had been thrown and a hunting dog which always caught its quarry.'

Mackenzie grinned.

'Well, Christina shouldn't be too hard to find if she's walking around Athens with a spear in one hand and leading a bloody great dog with the other.'

There was no answering smile on Maitland's face.

'I don't pretend to know what significance the reference to the gifts has,' he said, an edge to his voice, 'but I have a gut feeling that tells me it's important. The message foxed me too long trying to place its meaning against events in Italy. Here in Greece, where we've got a political volcano, I have the feeling that it's vital. It almost certainly tells us that Christina Kirkos has been working for the Germans all along and probably still is. It's the only interpretation I can put on the message.'

'The names could just be coincidence,' said Mackenzie.

'I don't believe in coincidences,' said Maitland. 'I

321

want to find that woman and find out what she and Kirkos are up to.'

CHAPTER TWENTY-TWO

The Return

The *Mariestad* swung at anchor off the port of Piraeus. In Christina Kirkos the sight of the port and the sprawl of Athens on the slopes to the east evoked feelings of relief beyond description.

She came out on deck to watch the seamen rig the heavy derrick which was to lift the big van and trailer into the LCT moored alongside. Earlier, a launch had put a British soldier of the Royal Engineers aboard the *Mariestad*. The soldier had told Stratou how to find the Docks Transit Officer in Piraeus. They were to report to him immediately the vans were disembarked.

Christina sat up in the cab of the van with Stratou as the landing-craft nosed away from the *Mariestad* and threaded its way through the crowded anchorage towards Piraeus.

The port was open only to smaller craft. The masts and funnels of block ships sunk by the Germans jutted from the water across the harbour entrance and off the principal quays. The quays themselves had been almost totally destroyed. German engineers had dynamited every berthing space, and the quay wall was discernible only here and there between heaps of rubble tumbled into the water.

A slipway had been created by bulldozing rubble in an incline to the water's edge. The LCT slid towards this point and dropped its ramp with a resounding metallic clatter. Stratou started the motor of the big van and powered it at the slope of the primitive slipway. He manoeuvred the heavy vehicles along a road cleared through the debris of demolished cargo sheds, halting eventually before a newly erected timber hut with a big notice outside. The notice said: 'DOCKS TRANSIT OFFICER – All Drivers Must Report Inside.'

Stratou went in. A soldier was sitting at a desk, typing. Beyond him, a Royal Engineers lieutenant with a sandy-coloured moustache was sticking coloured pins into a huge map of Athens and its environs. The Lieutenant turned.

'What can I do for you?' he asked Stratou.

Stratou held out a sheaf of papers.

'I was told to drop these off here. They said you would tell me how to find the Fourth Indian Division.'

The Lieutenant consulted papers on his desk.

'What ship?' he asked.

'The *Mariestad*.'

'Ah yes. You must be the Mobile Baths Unit. The Indian Div. is guarding the airfield out past Kalamaki on the beach road. I'll show you how to get there on the map.'

Stratou emerged from the hut and rejoined Christina in the cab. The van was stopped a little farther on. Troops in battle kit were manning a barbed-wire barrier placed across the docks entrance.

A sergeant carefully examined a transit clearance document which Stratou had been given by the officer in the hut.

'Know how to get to the airfield, sir? Take the first right and stick to the coast road. It can't be more than three miles. Just follow the smell of the curry pots.'

'Thanks,' said Stratou.

He put the van into gear and drove past the barrier. The road looped round behind a go-down stacked with crates of empty olive oil bottles. Stratou kept glancing in the mirror until he was sure the road barrier was no longer in sight. When he was sure they were well clear of it, he breathed a sigh of relief. They were now approaching a three-way road intersection.

'The man said turn right for Kalamaki,' he said to Christina.

'I heard him. It's Peristeri we want.'

'I know the way,' said Stratou, and turned the van and trailer sharp left at the intersection. The big vehicle lumbered away uphill, away from the coast road.

'We're almost there,' said Stratou jubilantly. 'We're almost there.'

The fifteen-hundredweight truck was touching seventy on the short straight stretches of the road. Preston sat beside the driver, hoping fervently that he would reach Athens alive. The man beside him drove as if it were his last day on earth – and with such a reckless abandon that it was quite likely to be.

The truck took a sharp bend with a sideways screech of protesting tyres.

'Do we have to go so fast, Corporal?' Preston inquired softly.

'I've got a date at six,' said the Corporal.

'With an undertaker?'

The man laughed and eased his foot off the accelerator.

'I reckon we'll make it,' he said.

The original summons to Athens had come to Preston in Rimini, after his return north from Taranto. He had gathered from it that he was finally being relieved of his liaison duties with the Greek Brigade and being detached for special services of an upspecified nature. He had flown in a Dakota from Bari to Megara with a Greek infantry company. In Megara, he had received orders instructing him to report to Maitland at the Grande Bretagne Hotel in Athens.

There was a Victorian graciousness to the interior of

the Grande Bretagne which wasn't altogether to Preston's taste. He wasn't over-fond of hotels which made you feel like you were entering a cathedral. Carrying his gear, Preston ignored the desk to reconnoitre the public rooms.

He spotted Maitland almost immediately in the majestic public lounge. He was sitting at a table with a tall, lean man in uniform. The companion had a patch over one eye. Preston was only a few feet away from the table when he dropped his kit and gave such a shout that coversations stopped and every face in the lounge turned towards him.

'Mac!'

Mackenzie leapt from his chair. The two men embraced in a fierce bearhug. Preston could scarely speak.

'I don't believe it! I just don't believe it! Gosh, you old son-of-a-gun, is it really you?'

Maitland tolerantly let the two men babble on, exchanging breathless questions and answers punctuated by exclamations of spontaneous joy at their reunion.

'This calls for a celebration, sir,' Preston said to Maitland. 'Do we have your permission to get drunk?'

'Permission granted,' laughed Maitland, 'but on one condition.'

Mackenzie and Preston looked at him expectantly.

'The condition is that you don't mind an old stuffed shirt like me sharing the first bottle, before quietly fading away. And it's a bit public here. Upstairs in my room it just so happens that I've got a couple of bottles of Glenfiddich. Let's go and see if it tastes like I remember it.'

Maitland had, in fact, a small suite of rooms at his disposal. They were high-ceilinged and much less grand than the public rooms downstairs. They reminded Mackenzie vaguely of the Station Hotel in Bradford.

The three had made only short inroads into the Glen-fiddich when all the lights in the hotel went out. Mackenzie and Preston refused to let such a minor inconvenience interrupt their drinking, but Maitland stormed off to see what had caused the failure.

He returned fifteen minutes later with an aged retainer carrying a kerosene lantern.

'I'm not quite sure what the trouble is,' Maitland reported. 'I got three different stories in as many minutes. Somebody said the electricity workers have gone on strike as part of some EAM protest. Somebody else said the ELAS have sabotaged the power-station. Others think it's only a temporary failure.'

But the November darkness into which Athens was plunged was not to be temporary. Nor was it just a loss of artificial light. It was a blackness of mind and heart, the first lowering dark of a winter in which the flowers of amity and reason withered and died.

George Kirkos had established his Command Headquarters in the Paradissos Hotel. It was a quaint rambling building of considerable age, picturesquely situated above Piraeus and overlooking the Tourkolimani, the old Turkish Harbour. Its balconies and terraced garden walks had magnificent views to seaward.

Christina and Stratou were driven from the delivery destination of the vans – an old horse and wagon depot in Peristeri – to the Paradissos. They were taken in an ancient 1926 Chevrolet with Celluloid windows. It was fuelled with kerosene and would only start after being hand-primed with petrol. When the motor stalled, which it did frequently, the bonnet had to be lifted and the priming process laboriously repeated.

At the hotel, Stratou was whisked away by a guerrilla officer who introduced himself as Major Voutsas. Christina was delivered into the hands of a heavy-boned peasant woman with the build of a lumberjack and a laugh like a crawmill. She was a coarse but jolly woman who seemed to be housekeeper for the dozens of roughly clad gunmen camping all over the ground floor of the hotel.

The woman parried, or returned with interest, the ribald remarks flung at her by the guerrillas as she led Christina towards the stairs. Christina tried to ignore the curious scrutiny to which she was subjected by the men. She still wore the uncomfortably foreign garb of WIMPA driver and was more self-conscious than ever of the dark itch of hair above her mouth.

'They all call me the "Admiral",' said the woman. 'That's because I once had my own fish boat and know how to keep these whores' sons in order. The boss, General Cephalus, did not know when you were arriving, but everything has been ready for you for two weeks. You can make youself at home in his quarters until he comes.'

She led the way up the winding staircase to a gaily coloured room with red and white curtains over mullioned windows. It looked out across the bay, dotted with ships at anchor.

'I'd like a bath,' said Christina.

'Then you will have one. The tub's in there.' The woman waved a thumb in the direction of a door. 'We're short of water but the boss ... General Cephalus ... said you were to have everything you asked for. I'll boil up some kettles for you and bring them up.'

She stood, studying Christina and shaking her head.

'You *are* a woman?' Doubt lined her face.

'Unfortunately, yes. Do you have to stare at me like that?'

'It's amazing!' said the woman. 'You look like a nephew of mine. He was a bit pasty-faced, same as you. Died of tuberculosis when he was twenty-two. You look just like him. You'd never know you had nothing between your legs but hair. It's amazing!'

Christina spent a long time in the shallow bath. For the first time in weeks, she felt liberated in body. She spent a painful hour bathing her face, removing the absurd little moustache and its adhesive ribbon of skin-like material. Her mouth was raw and blotchy where it had been.

The 'Admiral' brought a selection of freshly laundered clothes for her. They had been 'liberated' from a 'collaborator's' store on Ermou Street. Donning a peach-coloured dress – it was slightly short for her and hugged her slim body – she felt like a woman again.

Some fluffiness returned to her hair after washing it. She back-brushed it so that it wisped up on the crown of her head and rose in a peak above the brow. Gone was the severe parting and oiled-down smoothness of the style she had effected in her role as Driver Herrera. The result was a gamin-like sauciness which was wholly feminine.

A nervous impatience filled her as she waited for Kirkos. She had done everything that had been asked of her. The van-load of guns - or whatever was secreted behind the panels of the Mobile Baths Unit – had been safely delivered to Athens. Now, the object of her participation in the strange and dangerous charade could be fulfilled. Nikki would be restored to her arms.

For long months in Italy, she had nursed and kept alive a bitter hatred for the man she had married. But its sharp edge had been eroded by what the man who called himself Artemis had told her: that Kirkos was the instigator of her escape. She found it puzzling that the author of so much of her misery should, in the end, be the architect of her salvation. It made her nervous about her imminent reunion with Kirkos. Was it possible that he wanted her back again? And, if he did, what were her own feelings? Could she force herself again into any kind of relationship with this cold, complex jigsaw puzzle of a man, whose unexpected moments of warmth could change in the flashing of an eye to bouts of domineering cruelty?

She did not hear Kirkos come into the room. He paused inside the doorway, startled at the change in her. He stood, motionless, watching her brushing the short wispy hair which so changed her appearance, making her almost child-like.

She sensed suddenly that she was no longer alone and jerked round with a cry of fear to look at the doorway. She had stored a lot of anger for this moment, but it flickered only briefly as she recognised him. It died before the look in his eyes. Of all the things she had expected to see there, the last thing she expected to see was penitence. She was totally unprepared for it.

George Kirkos's eyes were moist with tears. Christina was so changed that she was scarcely recognisable as the woman he had left in Piraeus a year before. It wasn't just the short hair. It was the liquid suffering in her eyes.

Ever since his last meeting with Keller, Kirkos had suffered torments that Christina might have been tortured by the Gestapo. This stemmed from his own days as a political prisoner and his near hysterical dread of being subjected to physical pain. During his marriage to Christina, he had not hesitated to inflict mental suffering on her – but he had done so out of what he considered was his moral right as a husband. He had never once – in spite of provocation – resorted to physical violence. It had come as a shock to him, therefore, when he realised that she might be the victim of the very kind of violence he dreaded, as a result, directly or indirectly, of his abandonment of her.

His need to compensate, to make things up to her, to redress the situation, was not inspired by love nor a capacity to be compassionate but a need to earn absolution for himself by doing enough to appease his own ego. There was no thought of seeking her forgiveness for any wrongs he had done her. He just wanted to show her sufficient kindness to be able to forgive himself for the distress he felt on her behalf.

'Where is Nikki?' said Christina.

'He is safe,' said Kirkos. 'Tomorrow, I shall take you to him. You look different, Christina.' He moved nearer her. She could not understand the look of tortured sadness on his face. Where was the strutting, arrogant leader of men?

'Did they hurt you? Did they, Christina?'

'Who?'

'The Gestapo.'

'Would you have given a damn if they had?' she snapped.

'Don't be angry with me, Christina. Please. A lot has happened to you that wasn't my blame. I've never wanted you hurt. I know what the Gestapo can do . . . I didn't want that for you.'

She snorted her disbelief.

'You have tortured me far more than the Gestapo ever could!' she flared. 'You took my baby away from me! Why did you do it, George? Why?'

He sighed and gave a forlorn shake of his head.

'I won't blame you if you don't believe me. But I wanted you to come back to me. I thought if I had the baby . . . I knew you wouldn't come back if I just asked you. My pride wouldn't have let me ask you anyway . . . I thought that if I took the boy, you would come back to me.'

'You can't make people love you by torturing them, George. It doesn't work that way. You have to show them that you really care. You've got it wrong the same way as your precious Liberation Army has got it wrong. You can't win people over to your side by putting the fear of God into them. It may get you obedience – but not love or respect . . . Only hate.'

'Do you hate me?'

'I don't feel anything, George. I'm beyond feeling. But don't think I'm not capable of hating you. There have been times in the last few months when I have lain awake at nights thinking of the ways I'd like to see you suffer for the ways you've made me suffer.'

'Is it too late, Christina?'

'For what?'

'For us.'

She stared at him.

'I think we both know it's too late, George. What do you want me for . . . a punch-bag? What makes you think I've got anything left for you?'

'I don't know what I want of you, Christina. Maybe I've lost the right to expect anything. But you're welcome to stay here . . . Big things are happening. You could be a part of them. The choice is yours . . .'

He reached out and rested his fingers on her wrist. It was a gentle gesture, an attempt to reassure. She started, as if his touch had been charged with electricity.

'Do I frighten you so much, Christina?'

Her wide eyes had the vulnerability of a fawn, the same startled innocence. It was not him she feared but herself. She could fight anything but kindness. She had encountered so little of it in recent times that she had no armament against it.

For months she had been crushed down by her own solitariness, by the absence in her life of a single being to whom she could turn in a totally hostile world.

Now she longed to reach out and cling to anything or anyone. Like any exhausted swimmer, she was ready to reach out for any floating spar, any support which would save her from sinking to the black depths.

Her eyes filled with tears. They were the tears of her own hopelessness. They were the tears, too, of her uncomprehending relief that a long dark night of misery and pain was giving way to a grey morning, bright with some kind of hope. Her limp arms trembled and reached out tentatively in a gesture which implied acceptance of an offered lifeline. She gave a strangled sob and clung to him, weeping. Surprised, and strangely disappointed that the wild and wayward spirit which had once sparked so vitally in her now seemed utterly crushed, he tried to comfort her.

CHAPTER TWENTY-THREE

Find The Lady

Searching Athens for clues to the whereabouts of Christina Kirkos proved to be a wearing and frustrating activity for Mackenzie and Preston. They had spent only one night at the Grande Bretagne. Next day, complete with identities and credentials supplied by Maitland, they had moved into a nearby hotel called the Alex.

It was a less pretentious establishment and housed an overflow of international newsmen from the Grande Bretagne, which was spilling over with correspondents of every nationality. While Preston masqueraded as correspondent of a Greek-language newspaper in New York, Mackenzie resumed, ostensibly, his peace-time role as representative of Fetter Lane News Services — a Fleet Street agency which syndicated material to subscribing provincial papers all over Britain. The only stories he filed were, however, the brief daily progress reports which went to Maitland. More correctly, they might have been called 'lack of progress' reports.

The most direct line of inquiry was, of course, prohibited to them. General Cephalus was known to have entrenched himself with part of his army in the Castella district of Piraeus and the obvious course would have been to seek him out — but it was a course which Preston and Mackenzie, for very good reasons, had no intention of taking. Indeed, they had to be extremely circumspect in their inquiries in order to avoid any possibility of their nature reaching the ears of any of the ELAS spies abounding in the city.

Already, ELAS guerrillas who had invaded Athens were establishing no-go areas in the city and exercising rigorous controls on citizens wishing to enter or leave these areas. The result was that Preston and Mackenzie had to restict their investigations to central Athens and the coastal residential areas east of Phaleron Bay.

Their starting-point was George Kirkos's villa in the Kalamaki district. It had been occupied by German officers for most of the war. Now, the empty house had been taken over by officers and men of a Signals unit based at the nearby airfield.

Their first break came from the revelation by one of the Signals officers that an old Greek came at regular intervals to tend the garden. The man had cared for the garden throughout the occupation and obviously knew the Kirkos family. He had told the officer that the owner of the villa had gone off to fight with the guerrillas in the mountains in 1941.

So, Preston and Mackenzie took it in turn to watch the villa for the old man's return. But days passed without sign of him, possibly – they reasoned – because of the dangerous situation in the streets.

It was on the tenth day – when they were ready to abandon their watch – that a shuffling figure in a shiny black overcoat let himself into the garden by a side gate and began sweeping fallen leaves from the terraced walls of the garden. It was the gardener.

At first, he would answer no questions. He said he was just a gardener/handyman who did his work and minded his own business. Athens, he reckoned, would be a happier place if everyone did the same. If you opened your mouth and said the wrong thing, you were likely to end up with a bullet in your back.

The gift of a pack of cigarettes made him more loquacious. He said he was risking his life tidying the garden in a house occupied by British troops. He had been warned by a gang of thugs camped in the block of flats where he lived that he would have his throat cut if he worked for the *Angloi*. He had tended the garden without pay all the time the Germans had been here, however, and he wasn't going to let the place go to ruin because some layabouts, drunk on gun powder, thought they could run the country.

It was not until Mackenzie revealed that he was a friend of Christina's that the old man grudgingly told all he knew. It was not much. He had not seen her since she had gone off to the mountains to join her husband. He did not know whether she was living or dead.

He did, however, know of one person who could help. Old Nanna Vlakhos, who had been nurse to the Kirkos family, had always kept in touch with young Mr Kirkos, even in the mountains. She was of mountain stock herself and young Mr George was like a son to her.

The old man had not seen Nanna Vlakhos for a long time but he believed she had a place in Piraeus. He knew the street but not the number. It was a small flat over a ship chandler's shop.

In the room they shared at the Alex, Mackenzie and Preston debated their next step. Quite clearly, the military khaki of their uniforms as war correspondents was a handicap in pursuing their investigations. There were too many places where they couldn't go for the simple reason that their clothes immediately identified them as foreigners. A complete change of tactics was necessary, especially if they were to venture into Piraeus.

Maitland, who was still insistent that the search for Christina Kirkos should continue, agreed. He wanted Mackenzie and Preston to follow up the slim Piraeus lead and remain undercover in the seaport, where ELAS and their sympathisers were particularly strong.

He introduced them to a Section Six man, Brady, who

controlled an intelligence-gathering network in Athens from a bolt-hole in the British Embassy. They left the Alex and, with Brady's help, rigged themselves out guerrilla-style in baggy trousers and sheepskin coats. They also obtained a battery of weapons to go with the part. Both had Mauser pistols inside their coats and carried Italian machine-carbines slung from their shoulders. The picture was made authentic with bandoliers draped about them in the manner so popular with the guerrillas.

An enclosed army truck called after dark to collect them. It dropped them an hour later in a deserted back street near Piraeus docks. They sat in a dark alley for half an hour, swigging from a bottle of retsina.

When they emerged from the alley, a casual observer might have imagined that they had consumed a couple of bottles each. Their slightly staggering progress was designed, however, to allay the suspicions of any observers, casual or otherwise, that they were anything other than what they seemed.

They halted at the ship chandler's to drink some more retsina. Although the front of the shop was in darkness, Preston could see a light shining in the interior beyond.

'Let's see if we can get a room here,' he slurred to Mackenzie. He began to hammer on the glass door. There was movement inside and they heard bolts being drawn.

A short fat man with a sweaty face peered out at them. He blanched at the sight of the eye-patched villain grinning drunkenly down at him.

'What is it? Why do you disturb me?' said the man.

'We need rooms,' said Mackenzie. 'We were told that the old woman upstairs rents rooms.'

'No one is living there just now. The old woman has gone away.'

He made to shut the door but Mackenzie placed a broad foot against it and the man nearly fell over as the door jerked against it.

'If the rooms are empty, we shall have them then,' said Mackenzie. 'How do we get in?'

'I do not know. I cannot help.'

Mackenzie grinned evilly at the man.

'The people who told us about the rooms – they said you had the key.'

It was a lucky shot in the dark. The fat man flustered.

'I do not have Mistress Vlakhos's permission to give the key to you.'

'Do you flaunt the authority of the Nation Army of Liberation?'

'No, no . . .'

'Then get the key,' said Mackenzie.

The man got the key. Mackenzie made him lead the way to the upstairs flat. There was no light. In spite of protests from the ship chandler about the shortage of kerosene, they made him fetch a lantern. The man then wanted to return to his own house but Preston pushed him into a chair.

'We want to know about the woman who lived here,' he said. 'Tell us about her.'

'Why do you want to know?' asked the man. The sweat streamed from him and his eyes were wide with fear.

'She knows where a friend of mine is living – a lady friend. A *young* lady friend,' said Preston.

'The one who had the baby?'

Preston and Mackenzie exchanged looks.

'What do you know about the baby?' asked Mackenzie.

'Only that the boy was born here. In this flat. Just about a year ago.' The fat man was terrified, eager now to tell them anything they wanted to know.

'Where did they go – the woman and the baby?' Preston flung the question.

'I don't know. I swear I don't know. She just vanished. One day they were all here – the old woman, the young one, and the baby . . . The next they were gone.'

'When was this?'

'I can't remember . . . Five, six months ago. They haven't been back since.'

'Are you trying to tell us they just disappeared into thin air?' rasped Mackenzie.

'I swear I never saw them again,' said the fat man.

'And no one has been near the flat?'

The sharp movement of the man's eyes told Mackenzie that another shot in the dark had registered.

'Has someone been to these rooms?' he asked menacingly.

'He was a friend of the Vlakhos woman. I never knew his name. I think he came from the mountains — although he was well-spoken. An educated man . . . But he was a guerrilla fighter like yourselves. He said he would have me killed if I spoke about him to anyone.'

'When was this?' asked Preston? 'What did he look like?'

The ship chandler described a man in his early thirties who dressed all in black. He had stayed two nights in the apartment. It had been before the Liberation, just before the Germans left Athens. He had entertained a visitor — a middle-aged man with a shiny bald dome of a head. The visitor was a foreigner. He spoke Greek fluently but with a definite accent. He could have been Polish or Russian, or even German.

'Did you meet this other man?' asked Mackenzie.

'He came to the shop. The friend of the Vlakhos woman had arranged it that way. He said that the man would come and ask if I stocked three-inch manila rope. He would give his name as Artemis. If the coast was clear I was to show him upstairs and then keep watch to see that they were not disturbed. He paid me in gold coins. Now he will kill me for telling you.'

'Not if you keep your mouth shut,' said Mackenzie.

339

'Tell no one you have spoken to us and you may live to a ripe old age. But breathe a word about this and I, personally, will cut you up in little pieces. That's a promise.'

They let him go. Then they searched the apartment from one end to the other. They found some clothing, including a sheepskin coat and a woollen hat which Mackenzie recognised. Christina Kirkos had been wearing them the last time he saw her. The two men sat down at the table to hold a council of war, the bottle of retsina between them. There was no point in wasting it.

'Well, what do you make of it, Mac?' asked Preston. 'Where do we go from here?'

Mackenzie screwed up his face.

'There's no doubt in my mind that Christina was here. And the guy who stayed here sounds a hell of a lot like George Kirkos. Who his visitor was, I don't know – but the name Artemis begins to make it every bit as sinister as Maitland seemed to think. Suppose the guy was a German – it was before the Jerries cleared out – what could Kirkos have been up to?'

'Some kind of deal? Maybe the squareheads left behind some kind of Trojan Horse. God, it makes my blood boil to know that Kirkos is holed up only a mile away, surrounded by his barbarian hordes. Why don't we just go in with a squad of armoured cars and take the bastard?'

'The Communists would just love that,' said Mackenzie sourly. 'Why do you think they've been ambushing our food convoys and shooting our lads in the back when they go for an off-duty drink? They want to get us angry. They're hoping some slap-happy company commander says to hell with it and wades into them with bazookas and bayonets. Then they'll shout bloody murder and accuse the British Army of waging war on innocent civilians.'

'We're still no nearer finding Christina Kirkos than we were at the start,' said Preston glumly. 'I think we should be looking for the mysterious Artemis.'

'All we know is that he's bald and speaks Greek with an accent,' said Mackenzie. 'That's not much to go on. but Maitland will be happy. He was dead right in not believing in coincidences.'

Preston grinned.

'Then he'd probably want my head on a silver salver for not telling him about a coincidence that happened to me.'

Mackenzie swallowed some retsina and grimaced as the raw liquor hit his throat.

'What coincidence?'

'It was nothing – probably imagination. I thought if I mentioned it to Maitland, he'd wheel me off to the nearest shrink and have my head examined. I was getting a fixation about a guy. I kept seeing him behind every bush.'

'So, tell me about it,' said Mackenzie. 'Astonish me with this coincidence.'

'Remember the guy I told you about? Stratou? The guy who gave us the slip in Rimini? Maitland nearly had kittens when he heard that he was missing.'

'I thought he was presumed killed,' said Mackenzie.

'That's what I wanted to believe and it's what Maitland wanted to believe and it's what went down in the record-book – but they never found his body. I think he got away.'

'And?' prompted Mackenzie.

'And I thought I saw him in Taranto – five weeks after he went missing.'

Mackenzie straightened bolt upright.

'You didn't tell Maitland?'

'No. Why the hell should I have done? It was too fantastic, too crazy. Like I said, I had this guy on my mind ... I probably just saw somebody who looked kind of like him.'

Preston related to Mackenzie the incident of seeing the tall figure on the deck of the *Mariestad* as the ship left the Mare Piccolo in Taranto.

'I can understand your doubts,' said Mackenzie thoughtfully, 'but I'm a bit like Maitland. I don't go a bundle on coincidences myself. I would have it checked out.'

'I did,' said Preston.

'Well, that's something.'

Preston shrugged.

'It didn't amount to much. The ship was Swedish and was loaded with food and medical supplies for Athens. At Taranto, they took on coal and a couple of civilian trucks – a de-infestation unit. The trucks were the gifts of some Indian Rajah to the Fourth Indian Division.'

'Gifts?' Mackenzie seized on the word. 'Gifts?'

'Yeah, gifts. Probably set the old guy back a hundred thousand rupees or so.'

'You used the word "gifts",' Mackenzie persisted. 'Maitland talked about "gifts" – the Gifts of Artemis. What was it that intercepted message said? Something about Procris being on her way home with gifts.'

'Jesus!' said Preston. His face was a study. 'Have I balled things up again? You don't honestly think there's a connection?'

'Maybe there isn't,' said Mackenzie, 'but we've got bloody little to go on as it is. It won't do any harm at all to find out what happened to that Swedish ship and her cargo. Brady or his contact will be at the "meets" we arranged every day, so we'll get them on to that. In the meantime, we'll stay put here and go on acting like a couple of trigger-happy yobbos from the mountains.'

'You mean stick around this dump?' Preston waved his arm at the room.

'It's better than sleeping rough,' grinned Mackenzie.

342

'Tomorrow, we'll drift round some of the tavernas where the ELAS boys congregate. If there's something in the wind, we may just get a hint of it if we keep our eyes and ears open.'

'We could also get our throats cut,' said Preston gloomily.

'That's a distinct possibility. Scared?'

'You bet your sweet life I am. I always faint at the sight of blood – especially my own!'

Two days of frequenting the tavernas of Piraeus provided Mackenzie and Preston with a greater tolerance of retsina and ouzo but little in the way of hard information. The ELAS guerrillas were obviously prepared for a major confrontation with the British troops in Athens, but had undoubtedly been told by their political commissars not to be too obstreperous in advance of a much-discussed general strike and mass demonstration.

Late on the second evening Preston and Mackenzie left a taverna off Karaiskaki Square for an arranged 'meet' with Brady. They made their way leisurely to the gardens which flanked Piraeus Cathedral. There, they were approached by a disreputable-looking character who seemed to have been avoiding contact with soap and water for several weeks. His striped jacket was stained with grease and reeked of stale fish. His equally greasy grey cap looked as if it had been bought pre-war and had never been off his head since its purchase. He was clutching a cigarette in one hand and he asked Mackenzie for a light.

As Mackenzie handed him a box of matches, the man whispered:

'You're right on time. I got the gen you asked for.'

Mackenzie drew his breath in sharply.

'Brady?'

'The suit isn't Savile Row – but this isn't St James's.

Keep walking through the gardens and act like you're telling me to piss off. I'll be trying to sell you a watch.'

He produced a wrist-watch from his pocket and showed it to them with a surreptitious air as they walked. He kept talking in a low voice.

'The Swedish ship *Mariestad* has sailed for Alex. She finished discharging her cargo on the eighth of November. The two trucks were a big van and trailer belonging to a civvy organisation called WIMPA. They run canteens and baths for Indian troops.'

Mackenzie swore loudly at Brady for the benefit of two men and a woman walking from the direction of the Cathedral. He told him rather rudely what to do with his tin watch.

Brady lurched back towards them and renewed his low-voiced monologue.

'There's something odd about the van and trailer from the *Mariestad*. They made up a Mobile Baths Unit . . . And were cleared by Docks Transit on November second. They only had to drive three miles to Indian div. HQ but they never arrived. Indian Div. didn't even know they were missing until I started asking questions.'

Mackenzie gave Brady a push and treated him to another flow of curses.

'Keep talking. This is interesting,' he muttered. 'Who was with the trucks?'

'A civilian called Nicholas and a driver called Herrera. They're missing, too. You've caused a real old stushy down at Indian Div. HQ. They think they'll be blamed for losing two welfare Johnnies they never even knew existed. They reckon ELAS must have nabbed them but they can't think why ELAS should want a delousing unit. What have you found out?'

Mackenzie pretended to take an interest in the watch. He took it from Brady and faced him, affecting to study it. It was his turn to recite in a low voice.

344

'You probably know all about the general strike EAM are threatening to call. It's timed for the third of December. We haven't been able to find out just what they intend but there's talk of a mass demonstration of EAM supporters in Constitution Square and at several police posts. I think they mean to use the mob as a cover and have a go at occupying Government buildings and police stations. If Scobie's headquarters crew haven't already guessed it, you can tell them that all hell is about to break loose. Especially here in Piraeus. The ELAS boys have been told to behave themselves until the day of the strike. After that, there's a promise that Athens will be open house. Does Maitland want us to stay on this side of the tracks?'

'He has gone back to Italy for a few days but he's up to high doh about ELAS. He's sure they'll fight sooner than turn in their guns to Scobie. He said you may have to forget all about finding the woman and concentrate on keeping the Embassy genned up on ELAS military moves. He wants you to have a radio so that you can keep in direct contact with the Embassy. He thinks EAM have just been playing for time, making political noises, but are really planning to take over by force.'

The morning after their 'meet' with Brady, Preston and Mackenzie made a sortie from their rooms above the ship chandler's, precisely following instructions given to them by Brady. Their destination was a derelict hut near the docks, just outside the defensive posts which British troops were setting up.

Inside the hut was a hand-cart, loaded with what appeared to be the household belongings of some refugee peasant: a couple of battered tin trunks, a brass bedstead, a straw mattress, and sundry cooking pots and pans.

The two men trundled the barrow through the streets without exciting undue interest and carried the contents up to the apartment above the ships chandler's. One of the trunks contained a short-wave radio, complete with instructions on call-signs and a manual showing how to rig an aerial with a coil of wire and the frame of the bedstead. The second trunk contained enough food for a month. Obviously, Brady thought they should be ready for a long siege. In this, he showed commendable foresight.

CHAPTER TWENTY-FOUR

Day of Revolution

A pale watery sun blinked through the high overcast. On this December Sunday, the biting breeze from the north promised early snow.

Preston and Mackenzie paid little attention to the chanting mob confronting the thin line of police in Constitution Square. Their interest was centred on two men, who had stayed at the rear of a contingent of demonstrators on the march up from Piraeus to central Athens.

Mackenzie had felt Preston's fingers dig into his arm in a fierce grip when the American had first spotted the two men. They had joined the marching demonstrators almost stealthily but remained on the fringe.

One of the men was short and swarthy. His companion was a shambling giant. Both carried rifles. Preston had felt a flush of anger and remembered hate when he had recognised Zotos and the man he had privately dubbed 'Cyclops'.

'Friends of yours?' Mackenzie had muttered.

'They're the bastards who took me to Karpenisi. They're a long way from home.'

'What do you think they're up to?'

'I don't know. They don't seem to be joining the parade — just tagging along behind. Let's follow them. If we get the chance to tag them in a nice quiet alley, there are some debts I'd like to repay.'

They might recognise you,' said Mackenzie. 'There's no point in risking our cover.'

'We can stay at a distance. Please, Mac.'

'OK. But if they twig us, I'll take the little guy. You can have Frankenstein for yourself!'

So Mackenzie and Preston had followed the procession.

Two days before, the Greek Government – on the advice of the British Military Commander – had declared a ban on public demonstrations in support of EAM's call for a general strike. As the man in charge of public security, General Scobie had decided that any big demonstration could lead to a total breakdown of law and order. Now, it seemed, the order was being defied. Large bodies of demonstrators, their ranks swelled by guerrillas, were converging on mid-Athens from all directions.

Following the Piraeus contingent, Mackenzie felt warning flutters of nervous excitement as the group reached Constitution Square. The Parliament Building had a line of police guarding it. Behind them was a sandbag wall with a machine-gun peeping from a gap.

Mackenzie took in the scene, as he and Preston jostled in the fringes of the crowd.

'I don't like this much,' he said quietly to Preston. 'I don't like the way they've got girls and youngsters out in front and the guys with guns bringing up the rear.'

Preston had not taken his eyes off Zotos. He plucked at Mackenzie's elbow.

'Look,' he said. Mackenzie turned in time to see Zotos and the giant disappear into an entry between a camera shop and the office of a shipping line.

'Shall we follow?' asked Preston.

'Not too fast,' cautioned Mackenzie. 'We don't want to walk into anything we can't get out of.'

They reached the entry next to the camera shop. An inside flight of stairs led to offices on the first floor.

There was no sign of the two guerrillas. Across the Square, the crowd was now dense in front of the Parliament Buildings. The slogan-chanting was reaching a crescendo.

Mackenzie stood back from the entry and looked at the building above, wondering what was housed there that could be of interest to the guerrillas. A cold shiver tickled down his spine as a narrow black rod poked its snout from an open window only twelve feet above his head.

He moved quickly into the entry, dragging Preston with him.

'Your friends are right overhead. One of them is pointing a rifle out a window.'

'What is he aiming at?' asked Preston tersely.

'I've no idea — but I don't like it. Let's go and find out.' He drew his Mauser from inside his coat and thumbed off the safety-catch. Preston did likewise. They moved stealthily towards the foot of the stairs. Mackenzie had a foot on the first step and was peering cautiously up the well when a single shot rang out. There was urgency now as they took the stairs two at a time. A second shot rang out.

On the first-floor landing, a window overlooking the Square was open. Zotos and the giant were kneeling side by side, rifles pointing across at the Parliament Buildings.

Zotos whirled at the sound of footsteps behind him. The shot he fired in the act of turning was misdirected as his rifle glanced upwards off his companion's shoulder. The bullet shattered into the plasterwork of the wall in the window alcove. Preston and Mackenzie fired almost simultaneously. Mackenzie's shot hit Zotos in the heart and the Greek slumped back against the window and slid to the floor. Preston's shot blew a hole in the side of the big guerrilla's head.

Retribution had come swiftly to the two guerrillas.

But they had already fired the shots which were to plunge Greece into Civil War.

Outside in the Square, bedlam had broken loose. In front of the Parliament Building, a policeman lay dead, a victim of the first rifle-shot. Nearby, another lay bleeding with a shattered shoulder.

An officer ordered the remaining police to take aim at the mob. It was pressing and heaving in waves before them. The officer screamed at the crowd to disperse or he would order his men to open fire. The youngsters at the front were trying to go back. They struggled and fought to retreat. Those at the rear were pushing the panicking front ranks forward.

The aiming policemen were nervous. Very nervous. Only they knew that, on instructions from above, their weapons had been loaded with blank cartridges. They knew they wouldn't stand a chance if bluff failed and the noise of the blank shells did not deter the mob.

The officer shouted the order to fire.

The crashing volley was followed by shrieks as the front rows of demonstrators panicked even more but found that their escape was made impossible by the surge of bodies behind. Screams rose as the struggling mass at the front realised that the men pushing them back now had guns in their hands and were trying in the mêlée to aim them at the police. Shots from the crowd whistled through the terrified front ranks. A number of demonstrators went down, victims of their own rear.

The police now saw that their blank cartridges had failed to disperse the crowd. They fell back before the advancing mob, screaming to the occupants of the sand-bagged machine-gun post to use the machine-gun. But the machine-gun remained silent.

Seeing the police waver and run, the mob now rolled forward with a hideous baying of sound. They threatened now to over-run the sandbag wall. When it seemed inevitable that they would, the machine-gun barked into life. A dozen bodies fell and the mob wavered. Then it began to stream back across to the west side of the Square. Another short burst and the Square began to empty at every corner as people fled in all directions.

Soon, but for the bodies left where they had fallen, the Square was empty. But sporadic firing continued as guerrillas sniped from surrounding buildings and their fire was returned by police who had reloaded their weapons with live bullets.

The shots fired in Constitution Square were to echo round the world. The EAM propaganda machine was working at full blast. They aroused violent criticism of Churchill both in the Press and Parliament in Britain. The British actions in Greece were widely condemned in America.

At this juncture, there appeared on the stage the powerful, bearded figure of Damaskinos, Archbishop of Athens. This man was much more than the spiritual leader of Greece. He was a patriot whose fearlessness had been proven by his outspoken defiance of the Nazis over the issue of deported labour. By sheer force of personality he had made the Germans back down.

This true patriot Churchill now persuaded a reluctant King of the Hellenes to appoint as his Regent in Athens and, to strengthen the Regent's authority, he decided himself to pay an immediate visit to Athens.

Many miles away, meanwhile in Berlin, Manfried Keller was being castigated by Walther Schellenberg for allowing a weapon of secret and advanced technology to be lost from German control. It was hypocrisy on Schellenberg's part to choose this particular device for removing Keller from his job, because he had personally sanctioned Keller's use of the Javelin and Hitler, himself, had endorsed the plan.

It was the apparent failure of *Operation Artemis*

which was the real cause of Keller's disgrace. Schellenberg, perhaps because of his own involvement, was unwilling to punish Keller as vindictively as was within his power. It sufficed him to strip Keller of his office in the Intelligence Service and have him transferred to a combat command in Poland.

Thus, the man who had written the scenario of *Operation Artemis* knew nothing of the impending fulfilment of the eventuality on which it had been conceived – Churchill's commitment to visit Athens. It was no consolation to the author that the stage had been lit, the props located and the cast assembled, because he did not know that all was now ready for the entry of the principal character – the figure on whom the entire play hinged.

CHAPTER TWENTY-FIVE

Spies

'What the hell is it, Mac?'

Preston's hoarse whisper received no immediate answer. He remained crouched behind the low stone wall peering into the darkness of the hillside. There was a rustle of movement as Mackenzie came slithering on his belly towards the wall. He clambered silently over the wall and sat down with his back to it. He was breathing heavily.

'I'm getting too old for this bloody game,' he gasped.

'What is it? What did you see?'

'I don't know. They're winching something up the hill. Some kind of machine. They've got guards posted all over the place. I nearly ran into one of them.'

From beyond the harbour, in the distance far below, came the chatter of machine-gun fire. Away to the east, in the direction of Athens, the crack of rifles echoed in the night air.

'I think we should get back,' said Mackenzie. 'In daylight, we may get a bettter chance to see what they've got up there on the hill. It's obviously something they're taking a lot of trouble to keep hidden. They could be piecing together a bloody great field-gun topside but if it is a gun, it's not like any I've ever seen. I wish I could have got closer.'

'There's no cover up there,' said Preston. 'I've looked up at that hill a hundred times in daylight and I don't think you could hide a water melon up there, never mind anything bigger. That bit of real estate is as barren as the bloody moon!'

'Hills from a distance can be deceptive. There could be rock gullies up on top where you could hide a double-decker bus.'

There were flutters of snow in the bitterly cold wind. Preston brushed melting flakes from his face.

'Maybe they're building a ski-lift,' he said with a grin.

Mackenzie smiled in the darkness.

'Well, it looks like we could have a white Christmas,' he said, 'Let's get out of here.'

The two men crept along behind the wall. The ground sloped steeply downwards to the white stucco gable of a house. Alongside the house, the rock and grass of the hillside gave way to a rough cobbled track which wound through a huddle of similar stucco-walled dwellings embroidering the apron of the hill's spreading lap.

No sound came from the houses and no flicker of light was visible as Preston and Mackenzie continued their descent into the alleys and high back streets of Piraeus. They kept about ten yards apart, Preston leading the way. He was walking quickly, keeping to the shadows, when a figure suddenly materialised from a doorway and barred his path.

The man wore a tattered, buttonless, Italian great-coat, held about him by a girdle of string. A tommy-gun was cradled in his arms. Mackenzie ducked into the shadows of an archway as Preston pushed roughly past the man ahead.

'Out of my way, Comrade,' he heard Preston say.

'Who are you?' said the man. 'What are you doing in this part? Don't you know this is Colonel Lougaris's district? He doesn't like people from other outfits sneaking around after dark.'

Preston eyed the tommy-gun. He had halted two paces beyond the man in the great-coat. The man had turned to face Preston, following him round so that the gun kept pointing straight at the American's chest.

'What is it to you who I am?' mocked Preston. 'What if I said I was a British Tommy? What would you do about it?'

'What I have a mind to do anyway – put a bullet in you. You talk pretty funny, Comrade. What kind of accent is that? Maybe you'd better come with me to the post and explain yourself. You don't sound like one of us.'

'I'm not going anywhere with you, Comrade,' said Preston. 'It's past my bedtime and my mother doesn't know I'm out.'

The conversation ended there. Mackenzie had crept silently forward from the archway where he had temporarily concealed himself. The man in the great-coat opened his mouth to speak but, before his tongue was able to form a word, Mackenzie's rifle butt clubbed into the back of his skull. The man pitched forward into Preston's arms, his jaw jerking open as if pulled down by a wire. His eyeballs rolled white and glassy like spinning marbles.

'Thanks,' said Preston, letting the body drop face down in the roadway, 'he was threatening to be rather awkward.' He slung his rifle over a shoulder and couched the fallen man's tommy-gun in his arms. 'I'll take this as a souvenir.'

Mackenzie helped him drag the man into the doorway from which he had originally sprung.

'He's going to have a very sore head when he wakes up,' muttered Preston.

'If he wakes up,' said Mackenzie.

Twice after that they encountered ELAS night patrols but evaded them without being seen. It was three in the morning before they reached the rooms over the ship chandler's shop.

Mackenzie immediately set up the radio. It was essential that Brady was told about the mysterious contraption which Kirko's guerrillas had been winching up the hill behind Piraeus under cover of darkness. Possibly, the RAF could take aerial photographs which would give a clue to what was going on.

Moments later, he was busy on the key, tapping out a message. The operator at the Embassy, less than eight miles away, acknowledged the signal and then told him to stand by to receive. Brady, it seemed, had a message for Mackenzie.

'What is it?' asked Preston, when Mackenzie had finished.

'Just a warning to keep well clear of some place or other at 0930 tomorrow. They've given the map co-ordinates.'

Preston glanced at the pad on which Mackenzie had decoded the signal.

'These are the co-ordinates we gave them this morning – the artillery position in Castella. Maybe they're going to bomb it.'

'I doubt that very much,' said Mackenzie. 'Scobie seems to be keeping the RAF for recce jobs. They haven't dropped a bomb on the opposition yet. Scared to, I suppose. Our people would get stick if we caused a lot of civilian casualties.'

Preston made a face.

'I bet there would be a far bigger stink if the odd bomb fell on some two-thousand-year-old ruin.'

'You're getting cynical in your old age, Leo.'

'You're goddamned right I am! With all respect to the British Government, Mac, they'll have to learn that they can't fight this little war with kid gloves on. The other side are playing for keeps and they're damned well winning. They're not going to stop until the hammer and sickle is flying up there on the Acropolis.'

The sunlight streaming into the flat did not wake them.

Instead, it was a series of sharp explosions, occurring so close together that the intervals between each could scarcely be detected.

Both men went flying to the window of the flat but it was impossible to see from there what was happening. Mackenzie looked at his watch.

'Damnation! It's half-past nine. We've slept in, Leo. That little lot must have been what Brady wanted us to keep out of Castella for.'

The explosions stopped as abruptly as they had begun. Less than two minutes had passed since the first crash of sound.

Preston held his head to one side, listening.

'I can't hear aircraft. Can you?'

'That was artillery,' said Mackenzie. 'Fairly big stuff by the sound of it – but not like anything I could identify. Our blokes don't have much heavier than twenty-five-pounders.'

Preston raised his eyebrows.

'The Navy?'

'That's it,' said Mackenzie. 'Naval guns. These boys can knock a bottle off a wall at fifteen miles. I bet that's what it was. I bet they've taken out those ELAS seventy-fives like coconuts at a fairground stall.'

Preston and Mackenzie were not given the immediate opportunity of confirming that the cause of their sudden awakening was short sharp naval bombardment. Both were startled into concern for their own security by a new and totally unexpected sound.

Someone was hammering on the door of the flat.

Mackenzie made a signal with his hand towards the tommy-gun taken from the ELAS guerrilla in the early hours of the morning. Preston acknowledged with a nod of the head. He picked it up and moved silently to one side of the door. Another nod of the head signalled his readiness.

Mackenzie padded on stockinged feet to the door and opened it.

The fat ship chandler from downstairs was standing there. He was nervously shifting his weight from one foot to the other like a small boy with a bladder problem.

'What do you want?' growled Mackenzie.

'She's come back,' the chandler blurted out. 'She wants the key.'

'Who wants the key?'

'The woman. The young one. The one who had the baby. She's downstairs now . . . Wanting the key.'

'Is she alone?'

'Yes.'

'Then let her have the key. Here, take it.'

There was a tremble of excitement in Mackenzie's hand as he took the key from the inside lock and handed it to the chandler.

'Lock the door and take the key down to her. She's an old friend - but I want to give her a surprise.'

An age seemed to tick away before they heard light footsteps on the stairs. Preston grinned across at Mackenzie and his thumbs-up signal expressed his own elation and excitement. Neither man had dreamed for an instant that Christina Kirkos would ever return to the apartment. Neither had entertained any strong expectation of ever seeing her again.

Now, in the middle of a city which had been ravaged for nearly three weeks by civil war, she had re-appeared as mysteriously as she had vanished.

A cry of shock was wrung from her throat as she stepped into the room. Her hand flew to her mouth as she saw the two men.

She stared at Mackenzie and he stared at her.

Recognition was a long time coming. She took in the rough clothes, the eye with the patch over it: trying to place a familiarity with the stance, the way he held his head. He, in turn, saw the short boyish crop of hair, not immediately associating the gamin face with his lover of a single night and the remembered sensation of his fingers running through the silky luxuriance of her hair.

He was the first to speak.

'It has been a long time, Christina.'

She was dumb before him. Because he was a ghost. A ghost who was not as she remembered him. How thin and gaunt he was! And what had happened to his eye?

She looked at the other man. The young American officer, of course. She tried to work out why they should be here in Piraeus, less than a mile from where Greeks and British soldiers faced each other across barricades of war. The sound of barking rifles and the chatter of machine-guns – which for days had been the background sounds to every waking thought – now seemed to be a deafening presence in the room. The sound seemed to wash over her, numbing her mind and negating her attempts to comprehend the bewildering puzzle of this encounter. Her mind sought escape from the need to comprehend and surrendered to the thundering pulse of her own heartbeat. She collapsed in a dead faint.

The explosions, which had wakened Preston and Mackenzie from exhausted sleep, roused raging feelings of dismay and fury in George Kirkos.

From the central tower of a cigarette factory in lower Piraeus, he had watched the destroyer sail close inshore and, in the space of little more than ninety seconds, wipe out his entire artillery force on the heights of Castella.

The Italian seventy-fives had been carefully positioned and camouflaged on a rocky terrace, screened above and below by trees. Kirkos had believed them immune to discovery and quite safe from the few light guns the British had. Yet the British destroyer had picked them off one at a time like clay pipes at a fair.

Kirkos was unaware that the cigarette factory – which was now the forward Command Post for the right wing of his Piraeus army – was the place where, earlier in the year, Christina Kirkos had tried to obtain work. The fact would have held little interest for him. Its significance to him was entirely military.

The factory was directly in the path of any bid the British might make to recapture the port of Piraeus from his victorious troops. Kirkos had fortified every gate-house and tower and had massed more than fifteen hundred man behind its citadel-like walls.

Its nerve-centre and principal observation-point was located in the main office tower which rose three storeys high from the heart of the factory complex. It stood in a central court, surrounded on all four sides by a closed square of long factory buildings. These in turn were surrounded by access yards and a larger square of outhouses and stout boundary walls.

From the central lookout point, Kirkos could see across the British lines on the east bank of the Ilissus and beyond to the coastal road below the Acropolis. Most of Piraeus lay above and behind him; all of it firmly in the control of his men, from the tip of the south peninsula to the summits of the two high hills behind the seaport.

He wondered why the expected British counter-attack did not come. For several days now, fresh troops had been arriving by ship and air from Italy and were concentrating on the far bank of the Ilissus. His intelligence agents had identified them as advance units of the 4th British Division.

Kirkos glanced at his watch. It was now ten minutes before ten. Natsinas had called a meeting with him for eleven. He would have to allow himself at least an hour to get back to the Paradissos.

Kirkos turned to Wolarski, the man he had appointed field commander in lower Piraeus.

'I'll have to leave shortly. I thought that when the warship bombarded our artillery positions that the British would attack.'

'The British won't attack in daylight, General. They are not fools. They know they would be massacred before they reach the outside wall. It would be suicidal for them to try.'

Wolarski was a Pole who had been drafted into the German Army but had deserted within two weeks of arriving in Greece. He had been with the guerrillas for over a year. His training as a German soldier had been an asset and Kirkos had promoted him quickly over the heads of longer-serving men on the strength of it. The Pole had repaid this trust by proving himself an able commander.

'What *did* you make of the naval attack? Kirkos asked the Pole.

'It made short work of our precious seventy-fives. Perhaps it was a warning. If the British used their warships against us, we would not stand much chance. That was deadly shooting – all our guns knocked out just like that!' He snapped his fingers. 'How did they know just where to fire?'

'Well, we made things rough, for the Tommies two days ago – those trucks we destroyed and that fuel dump fire we started. They could have plotted our guns positions then.'

The Pole was not convinced.

'They knew where to fire to the nearest centimetre. All those houses round about but they didn't as much as shake a tile off the roofs. I think the enemy have a spotter up there in Castella, General.'

'I think it much more likely their spotters are on those

361

ships out there in the bay,' said Kirkos. 'We have been fighting a land battle and it's easy to forget that every ship out there has a grandstand view, probably watching us through telescopes every minute. They may even have seen us move the guns into position. It's damnable anyway – losing these guns!'

Kirkos anger at the loss of the guns was only slightly allayed by the knowledge that, grievous as the loss was to his plans, it could have been worse. He still had one 75mm left and the launcher was intact.

He had selected the locations of both with mathematical care and had exercised the strictest of security during their installation. He allowed himself a satisfied smile that both weapons were now safely secreted on a hill which was plainly visible to the whole of Athens and Piraeus and every ship in the Bay – but only he and several of his most trusted men knew of their existence.

Petrea was waiting for him in the courtyard of the Paradissos Hotel.

'Natsinas has been here for fifteen minutes. I took him up to your rooms.'

'He's with Christina?'

Petrea's face soured at mention of the name.

'No, she went out. Is she giving you trouble again, General?'

Kirkos smiled.

'Still concerned about my love-life, Petrea? If you must know, Christina and I have both been disappointed by our re-union but we have come to terms with the situation. I don't want her and the child at the hotel any more – it's too much of a barracks anyway. There's an apartment in the town where she would be more comfortable. She said she might go and clean the place up. Did she take the child?'

'No, the "Admiral" is looking after the baby.'

Kirkos went into the hotel.

Thoughtfully, Petrea watched him go. Life had changed for her from the moment of Christina's return. Her zealot's ardour for the Cause which was meat and drink to her had undergone a strange deflation, at the very time when all her more exciting dreams seemed on the point of fulfilment. She knew that the emptiness was caused by her realisation that the man with whom she had found total identification of purpose might not, after all, need her as much as she needed him.

There was no other conclusion to be reached from Christina's return.

He needed more than a Party Comrade, more than a doctrinal fountain where he could refresh his faith, more than a talking text book. He appeared to need a woman whose only attributes were a sensuous body and a decadent mind.

It bewildered Petrea. It angered her. It gnawed away at the foundations of the certainties on which her entire attitude to life was built. Consequently, she had begun to wonder if it were possible that, somewhere along the line, she might have got things all wrong. And the more she thought about it, the more she began to believe that she had.

She saw it in a nutshell when she asked herself what she would do if the day ever came when she might have to choose between the Party and the man who occupied all her thoughts. It stunned her to realise that she would choose Kirkos without hesitation. Whatever the consequences. The blasphemy of her secret thoughts both appalled and exhilerated her.

Now, Kirkos's hint that he and Christina were not exactly compatible partners, that their re-union wasn't working out, filled Petra with new hope.

Upstairs in the hotel, Kirkos found Natsinas sipping a mug of coffee which the 'Admiral' had brought him.

'Sorry I'm late, Comrade Natsinas. I've been expecting the British to make a grab for the docks but they're still sitting on the other side of the river and not making a move. How are things elsewhere?'

'You know we took the airfield at Tatoi?'

'Yes, I'd heard. What about the field at Kephyssia?'

'It's only a matter of time before it falls to us, too. We've had it surrounded for ten days and the British won't be able to hold out much longer. They've got about eight hundred men on the base, mainly Air Force, and their ammunition must be nearly finished. According to our calculations, they ran out of food three days ago.'

Natsinas seemed extremely pleased with himself.

'You have done rather well yourself, General Cephalus. Especially when I remember how violently opposed you were to fighting the British before your own little private enterprise could take place. Didn't you find it awkward arguing against our offensive without being able to tell the Liberation Committee exactly what you planned for Churchill?'

'I still think it was a mistake to take on the British.'

'That surprises me,' said Natsinas. 'Driving them out of Piraeus the way you did was quite a feat. Do you know what they are calling your men? The Glory Brigade. I hear you made quite a haul in and around the docks.'

It was true. It had been a remarkable campaign in the seaport – and the booty had been considerable. EAM's signal to start a full-scale shooting war against the British had infuriated Kirkos almost as much as his subsequent success had pleased him. Once the war had started in earnest, he had been glad to demonstrate his muscle power to friend and foe alike.

Guerrilla groups to the north and east of Athens had achieved some success but none had equalled the spectacular achievements of Kirkos's army. Not only had he cleared the British out of Piraeus and forced them back on to their Phaleron Bay beach-head but he had captured, intact, large dumps of food, ammunition and fuel – much to the envy of other ELAS units.

Perhaps the engagement which had earned the 'Glory Brigade' tag more than any other single incident had been Wolarski's attack with a thousand men on British Armoured Brigade's headquarters. They had stormed and over-run the British base before eventually retiring with a hundred prisoners and a large quantity of automatic weapons.

'I suppose the High Command want me to hand over some of the captured supplies?' said Kirkos.

'Not that I know of,' said Natsinas. 'That isn't why I wanted to see you. You sound rather sore, Comrade. Is it because you think I took Spiro's advice and persuaded the Liberation Committee to argue with bullets instead of words?'

'If we had waited, there was a chance that the British might have withdrawn without a shot being fired.'

'Ah, yes, your Churchill plan. You are still sore about it. Surely, you realise that we couldn't wait indefinitely for the old man to come to Athens. Didn't you see the message from Stalin? Copies were sent to every command.'

Kirkos smiled.

'Yes, I saw it. I thought it was a masterpiece of ambiguity.'

'No one else did.'

'No one else wanted to.'

'Just what do you mean, Comrade-General?'

Kirkos stared unblinkingly at Natsinas.

'Stalin made it quite clear that the hour had come when we must repel foreign interference and smash the forces of imperialism once and for all. Oh, there was nothing ambiguous about that part, Comrade Natsinas. The language was quite unequivocal if a trifle clichéd. No, the sting was in the tail. Where it went on about

365

the Greeks and the Greeks alone commanding their own destiny and must fight for it or perish.

'I don't see anything ambiguous in that,' said Natsinas huffily.

'Don't you? Ambiguous is perhaps the wrong word,' said Kirkos. 'What I believe Stalin was making quite clear was that if we didn't beat the British then it would be our own bad luck. That whatever happened, he was not going to send the Red Army hotfoot across Macedonia to come to our rescue.'

Natsinas paled. He shook his head fiercely.

'No, no – you are wrong. The Generalissimo meant no such thing.' But, in spite of his vehemence, he did not convey the impression of a man who was convinced. The truth was that Kirkos's interpretation had not previously occurred to him. Now that it had, Natsinas was a worried man. The war against the British had only been started for one reason; the firmly held belief that it could not be lost. And no one on the Central Committee of EAM, including Natsinas, had believed it could be lost with the might of Russia four-square behind ELAS.

One man more than any other had led the clamour for all out war on the British. That man was Spiro. The message from Stalin had been the green light for everyone else, confirmation that Spiro was right and the more cautious EAM counsellors were wrong.

Spiro had forecast that ELAS would beat the British because America would tie British hands militarily and diplomatically. The meagre British forces would be like sitting ducks to ELAS because indecisive leadership and intense diplomatic pressure on their Government would prevent them from fighting back effectively.

The first week of the war had proved Spiro prophetic.

Britain and Churchill had been pilloried by world opinion and, in Athens, ELAS had enjoyed military success beyond expectation. The beleaguered British forces had been driven back inside four square miles of mid-Athens and a narrow strip of coast east of the mouth of the Ilissus.

But the picture was beginning to change. British reinforcements were arriving in increasing numbers. So far, they had not tried to break out of the ELAS stranglehold – but that could happen at any time.

All this went through Natsinas's head as he debated what he should do about the looming power battle in the ELAS leadership which was polarising into a straight fight between Spiro and Cephalus. Which horse should he back?

If Spiro had initially triumphed over Cephalus in the war councils, Cephalus had certainly made up for it by his spectacular success in the field. And now there were definite indications that perhaps Cephalus's more calculated strategy had been better all along.

Natsinas put down the coffee mug which he had been holding in his hand. He walked over to the window and stood there deep in thought.

'You look troubled, Comrade,' said Kirkos.

Natsinas turned and considered Kirkos with his pale, watery eyes.

'Do you think we could lose Athens? Do you think the British could drive us back into the mountains?'

Kirkos reflected before answering.

'Yes. I think they could. But it would mean destroying Athens, using their warship as artillery and supporting their ground troops with air strikes. I don't think they want to do that.'

'Why not?'

Kirkos shrugged his shoulders expressively.

'The whole world would condemn them. But that isn't what's stopping them. The fact is they don't want this war. They need every man they've got for the fight in Italy. I think we made a terrible mistake by trying to hurry things. If we had waited another month or two,

367

they would have been shipping their soldiers back to Italy – not pouring them in as fast as they can come. I think if they could find a face-saving way out, they would take it.'

Natsinas felt a glow of warmth at Kirkos's words. They were sufficient to make him decide which horse he was going to back.

'That's a very shrewd assessment,' he said. 'I think I told you before that I underestimated you. I say it again now. I'm sorry I didn't pay more attention to you three weeks ago and less to Spiro.'

'So am I.'

'Perhaps I can make amends. I came here to tell you that the British want to parley. Last night they got in touch with us to say that Field-Marshall Alexander is on his way here from Italy. He hopes to be in Athens on Christmas Eve. He wants to meet the ELAS command and discuss ways to end the war.'

'Alexander, eh? A bigger fish even than Scobie.'

'He is the Supreme Allied Commander for the Mediterranean. The fact he is coming suggests that your assessment of the situation was very close to the mark. I think, like you, that the British are looking for a way out. Do you think we should talk with them?'

'Yes. If they want off the hook, it can be on our terms. What do the others think?'

'Spiro is all for telling Alexander to go to hell. Others won't commit themselves until I nod my head. Quite a few were anxious to know what your reaction would be.'

'And which way will you nod your head?'

Natsinas put a bony hand on Kirkos's shoulder. 'I'm with you. Spiro thinks with his fists. I prefer men who use the small grey matter in their heads. I think it is time Spiro was taken down a peg or two. Between us, it shouldn't be too difficult.'

'So, we'll talk with the British?'

'Yes, General. And I want you to be one of our delegates.'

Kirkos felt an upsurge of triumph. As an ELAS delegate, the eyes of the world would be on him – and he had no doubt about the way he would play this new role. His brilliance as a soldier would precede him to the conference table and there, he would present himself as a moderate amongst hard-liners and extremists.

The fact that Natsinas had now put his weight behind him meant that this grey cardinal of Communism now saw him as a future leader of Communist Greece. That wasn't how Kirkos saw things but it fitted admirably with his long-term plans. Natsinas – who played no part in Kirkos's long-term plans – had also given him the opportunity to let the British and the non-Communists see that if Greece were to be united under one man, they could do worse than settle for him.

Natsinas had not been gone from the Paradissos two hours when an urgent despatch arrived from him by special messenger which had Kirkos revising all his plans in a fever of excitement.

The despatch was to let Kirkos know that a further communication had just reached him from British headquarters.

The text of this revealed that bad weather at sea had delayed Field-Marshal Alexander's arrival in Greece. He would not now arrive in Athens until Christmas Day. Also, the Field-Marshal hoped to bring with him to the proposed parley a distinguished personage. The presence of the second party was an illustration of the importance which the British Government and Mediterranean Command attached to the outcome of the talks.

The other person was Winston Churchill.

Kirkos let the surprise information sink in. He was aware as he read the despatch from Natsinas a second time that the hand holding the sheet of paper was trembling.

Today was 23rd December. In two days' time, on Christmas Day, Winston Churchill would be in Athens. The fact that he, George Kirkos, was likely to be one of the delegates to meet Churchill was still important in the light of the development but the talks, *per se*, no longer had the importance which he had attached to them two hours earlier. The development meant that he had to find another way of presenting himself to the British as a man of goodwill.

It also meant that the opportunity had come at last to put into execution Keller's strangely obsessional plan for the death of Churchill. Well, the plan to kill Churchill was no longer Keller's. It now belonged to George Kirkos and no one else. Kirkos was unaware that in the transfer of ownership, some of Keller's obsessional attachment to the plan had shifted to him. He was aware only that by carrying out Keller's intent, there could still be only one major beneficiary – and that was George Kirkos.

So Kirkos no longer thought of *Operation Artemis* as Keller's brain-child. Keller was no longer in the game. From the moment the Javelin launcher with its Russian markings had arrived in Greece, the operation had been Kirkos's.

Now, he had forty-eight hours to make the final refinements. There was no time to lose.

CHAPTER TWENTY-SIX

Fugitives

The only sound in the room was the sobbing of Christina Kirkos. She was slumped in a chair, her eyes red from weeping. Preston was standing at the window, staring stonily down at the road junction opposite the ship chandler's shop. Mackenzie was in the middle of the room, his balled fists pressed down on the table in front of him, all his attention focused on the girl in the chair. She kept her eyes averted from him.

Mackenzie straightened up with a sigh. He splashed some retsina into a glass from the bottle on the table. He walked round the table and put a hand gently on Christina's shoulder.

'Drink some of this,' he coaxed.

She looked up at him from a tear-stained face as she sipped the liquid. She made a face as the taste of the retsina got her. She shook her head, indicating she wanted no more.

'I'm not coming with you, Mac. Just count me out.'

She had said little else for the past hour.

'We don't want to fight with you, Christina. We can't let you go back to Kirkos. We want to save you.'

The look she gave him spoke her disbelief.

'You won't be able to save yourselves. You'll never get out of Piraeus alive. Any minute now, George is going to send somebody looking for me. Don't you realise that you are the ones in danger - not me! I just don't want to know.'

'Look, Christina, you can't just pull a blanket over your head and hope the world will go away. It won't. You're involved too deep. We can't let you just walk away from here any more than we can walk away and pretend we haven't seen you.'

'You can trust me,' she pleaded. 'I won't say a word about you. But, please, just let me go.'

Mackenzie turned away, weariness and despair etched on his face. He wanted to let her go. His heart told him that she would not deliberately betray their presence but his head refused to let him take such a risk. If she had been totally frank with them, it might have been different. Instead, she had told a tale so unlikely that they would be fools to let her out of their sight.

Preston turned from the window, his face unsmiling.

'It's not a question of Mac trusting you, sweetheart. I'm in this, too.' He moved towards her as he spoke, placing himself between her and Mackenzie and fixing her with hard eyes. 'Mac, for reasons of his own, doesn't want to say outright to you that you are a goddamned liar – but I don't have his reservations. I know for a fact that your rat of a husband worked with the Germans. We weren't sure about you. We just had suspicions . . . But not any more!'

He glared down at her. His voice was thick with anger as he went on:

'I don't buy any of that bullshit about you being caught by the Gestapo and being rescued by Italian partisans. I don't buy any of your goddamned story!'

'It's true! Everthing I told you was true!' She looked up at Preston with pleading in her eyes. 'You've got to believe me! I never worked for the Germans. Never!'

Preston regarded her pityingly.

'And this man who came with you on the Swedish ship? This Nikos Stratou you talked about? You want us to believe that he is a Greek patriot who just happened to be with the Italian partisans? Right?'

'I've told you the truth. I don't know if the Italians were partisans or bandits or smugglers or what. They told me nothing.'

'You're a goddamned liar!'

'Easy, Leo,' put in Mackenzie.

'No, Mac,' flared Preston. He whirled on Christina again. 'Look, baby, I've got news for you. We know Stratou. We flushed him for a Nazi months ago. So don't give us any more crap about Italian bandits. There is no way we are going to believe it!'

Christina put her head in her hands and started weeping again.

'Bawling your eyes out isn't going to make any difference,' said Preston. 'You might as well pack it up.'

Mackenzie gently drew him away. He made a sign, indicating that he would like to try his more sympathetic approach.

He put a hand on Christina's shoulder.

'Leo's right about Nikos Stratou, Christina. He's a known German agent. So, whatever you've been told about him is lies. Look, if it's any consolation, I don't disbelieve what you told us about the Gestapo and being a prisoner in Milan . . . It just didn't make sense to us and that's why Leo's so steamed up.'

She stole a grateful look at him. He tipped her chin up and gave her an encouraging smile.

'I didn't make that story up, Mac.'

'I know. If you'd been wanting to fool us, you would have dreamed up something a lot more plausible. I'm only guessing, Christina . . . But the way you escaped from the Germans . . . Isn't it possible that they tricked you? That the whole thing was staged for your benefit?'

She shook her head.

'But why? Why? It's all beyond me. I only wanted to

get back to Nikki. That was all I cared about. And it's all I care about now.'

'I didn't think you would ever go back to George Kirkos of your own accord,' said Mackenzie softly. 'Why did you, Christina?'

'Because of Nikki . . . And because there was no one else.' There was a soft light in her eyes and her gaze was directly at him as she added in a whisper: 'Not even Nikki's father.'

The slight quiver of Makenzie's fingers, still cupping her chin, told her that she did not need to elaborate. Mackenzie's face spoke his shame and agony.

'Nikki is my son?'

'Yes.'

The silence in the room seemed to throb. Preston looked from one to the other of them, mouth slightly open, aware that they were on territory he knew nothing about.

'Trust me for your son's sake,' breathed Christina. 'Let me go back to him. He's the only one in this world who needs me. That's all I ask – that you let me go back to him. I won't say anything about you being here, but it would be safer for you to leave. Please, please let me go back to Nikki.'

Mackenzie withdrew his hand from her face. He stood erect, staring straight ahead but seeing nothing. His whole being was focused inwards, concentrated on and seeing only the images in the frothing crucible of his mind.

The image of Eleni Binas was seldom far from his consciousness. Now, with pain searing his mind, he told himself that Eleni Binas was lost to him. He could never now claim Eleni with the love he felt for her. The mother of his son had a prior claim, even if obligation and not love was the foundation of that claim. It was like a bill presented for payment long after the liability had been fogotten. The late presentation made no difference.

Mackenzie knew he could no more shirk payment than he could deny incurring the liability.

'If we could get both you and Nikki out of Piraeus, would you come?' he asked her.

'I . . . I don't know,' Her voice was a breathless whisper.

'I would look after you. I . . . I would try to make you happy.'

Preston could keep silent no longer.

'Mac, you're crazy . . .'

'Stay out of this, Leo,' said Mackenzie. 'Well, Christina?'

She reached out a hand for his and gently squeezed the big spiky fingers. There was a current of extreme tenderness in the gesture and the look she gave him.

'Thank you, Captain Mac. You tempt me. But I made my decision seven weeks ago . . . When George took me back. It's not something I expect you to understand. I don't really understand it myself. But that's the way it is.'

'Are you happy with him?'

'Happy? It's not a question of being happy. I want very little from life now – only to be left in peace with Nikki. George knows this . . . and we've reached a kind of agreement. He hasn't been unkind.'

'Go to him then,' said Mackenzie. 'We won't stop you.'

'We can't let her go, Mac,' interrupted Preston. 'We've got orders, remember?'

'Our orders were to find her. Leo. Well, we have,'

'She knows more than she's saying about that contraption Kirkos has hidden up on the top of that hill.'

'I don't even know what you're talking about,' said Christina.

'Don't you?' Preston's voice was icy. 'Well, convince me you're as stupid as you make yourself out to be. We know for a fact that your husband has been in cahoots with the Germans for years . . . Probably since they sprung him from prison in forty-one. We also know that he and his German buddies went to a hell of a lot of trouble to bring a very big field-gun or something a damned sight more diabolical all the way from Italy – and that you helped him to bring it here. We also know for a fact that your playmate in this adventure is a German agent who is wanted, amongst other things, for murder. Now, if you know your husband like we know him, baby, you'll know that somewhere at the end of all this there's going to be bloody murder . . . We want to know who he has it in for this time because the last time it happened, a hundred good Greeks were massacred and Mac here escaped with one good eye and a hole in his chest. That ought to make you feel very happy.'

Christina looked at Mackenzie, her eyes wide.

'George did that . . . to you?'

'He sold us to the Germans . . . And then turned on us when we tried to escape. Leo and I were the only ones to get out alive.'

'George wouldn't . . . No!'

'He did,' said Preston.

Christna's face went white. She knew Mackenzie would not lie to her.

'I honestly don't know what was hidden in the big bath trucks from Italy. I never saw any guns. I wasn't interested. And nobody ever told me . . . Except . . .'

'Except what?' asked Preston.

She looked at the two men in bewilderment.

'Just something George said . . . It didn't make sense to me.'

'What did he say, Christina?' Mackenzie spoke softly.

She shook her head.

'It just didn't make sense. It was when he had Nikki brought to me at the Paradissos. I cried . . . I was so happy. I thanked him. He said he was the one who should be thanking me. Because I was the one who had put a spear in his hands.'

Preston and Mackenzie exchanged looks at the mention of 'spear'.

'What did he mean?' asked Preston.

'I don't know. I told you it didn't make sense to me. I didn't even connect it to whatever it was we brought from Italy until he had the three boxes brought to our room and I asked him what they were.'

'Boxes?' echoed Mackenzie. 'Boxes of what?'

'He didn't tell me. They were just plain grey metal boxes. About so big.' She indicated with spread hands. 'He put them under the bed and told me not to say a word about them to anyone. He said they would be at home under the bed because they'd been keeping me company all the way from Italy.'

'That's all he said?' queried Preston.

'No. He said he would tell me what they were when he took up javelin-throwing seriously.'

Preston frowned fiercely.

'Does he always talk in riddles? Didn't you ask him what he meant?'

'Of course I asked him, but he just laughed. And yes he does talk like that. He enjoys being mysterious.'

Mackenzie was thoughtful.

'Maybe it's not so mysterious,' he said. 'Spear . . . And javelin-throwing . . . One of the Gifts of Artemis was a spear.'

'Artemis? I've already told you about Artemis,' said Christina. 'He was a nice man. I liked him. But you're wrong about gifts. He wasn't giving anything to George. He was selling.'

'You may have been the one who was sold, Christina,' said Mackenzie. 'I think your nice Mr Artemis used you. But what it was all about, I don't know. Maybe if we could get our hands on one of those boxes . . .'

Christina stood up.

'No,' she said fiercely. 'I'm not getting involved any more. I don't give a damn for those boxes! And I don't give a damn for you men and your stupid war! I've had all the war I can take.'

'You'll have to make up your mind whose side you're on,' said Mackenzie.

'I'm on nobody's side but mine and Nikki's. I'm not on your side in this and I'm not on George's. You can fight it out between you.'

'We can't just let you walk away,' said Preston.

'Yes you can!' she flared. 'I came to this flat to tidy it up for Nikki and me – so we could live here. And that's what I'm going to do. Sit out your stupid war right her. I'm going back for Nikki now and you had better be gone by the time I get back!'

'Is that the way you want it?' asked Mackenzie.

'That's the way I want it!'

'Then that's the way it'll be,' said Mackenzie. He waved away the angry protest which was on Preston's lips. 'No, Leo. She won't blow the whistle on us. She means what she says. You could even say she's only following State Department policy like a good American citizen and staying strictly neutral.'

Preston glared at Mackenzie.

'For a crack like that I could bust you one on the jaw. I still don't buy her story.'

Mackenzie grinned and put his arm round Preston's shoulder.

'Leo, old friend, I seem to recall that the last time you got out of Greece, you had a story to tell that nobody wanted to buy. But the story was true, wasn't it? Why don't you give Christina the benefit of the doubt?'

Preston's angry scowl gave way to a sheepish grin.

'Touché,' he said. 'Touché,'

Christina's mind was in a turmoil as she hurried up the steeply sloping street to Castella. It had been a terrible shock to find Mackenzie and the American in Nanna Vlakhos's apartment, and her whole body was still trembling from the sapping emotional encounter which had taken place.

The events of the past year had battered her psyche to the edge of human toleration. She felt like a punctured football, left abandoned in the gutter to be kicked along the street of life by every passing rowdy.

She no longer felt capable of understanding her own actions. She longed only for peace, wanting only to follow the line of least resistance in the hope that it would eventually be given to her.

It had been ironic that Mackenzie had offered to take her away. She had been more than a little tempted. She knew that he would have stuck by her through thick and thin. Well, he would never know how close he was to being lumbered with her as a result of his sense of duty and doing the right thing. She had declined his invitation, not for her own sake but for his. It afforded her a small glow of warmth. She had done few selfless things in her life that she could remember about. Letting Mackenzie off the hook had made her feel good.

She knew she would probably soon be regretting it. It had not taken long to realise that going back to George Kirkos had been a mistake. But she was realistic about it. She had done it to be with Nikki again and because she was absolutely desperate. It had been too much to hope that they could have ever made a go of their marriage again after all that had happened. She knew he had taken her back in order to salve something in his own conscience. Having made the gesture, however, he seemed content to let it go at that. Her new and total submissiveness simply embarrassed him. There was a total absence of desire between them. He was trying to be kind and considerate and she was prepared to be acquiescent, without feigning an enthusiasm she did not feel. Both were playing roles which were totally false to their personalities.

The result was a relationship without a spark of vitality. Without a spark of anything. They had both realised it but neither had wanted to go back on the unwritten terms of their re-union.

Eventually, however, Christina had broached the possibility of her moving out with the baby from the Paradissos. Kirkos had leapt at the idea, providing reasons of his own why the move would be beneficial to all and yet keeping his side of the bargain by assuring her that she and the baby would want for nothing.

Christina still found herself incapable of wholly trusting him. Yet it was easier to pretend that the bed she had made for herself was not too uncomfortable than acknowledge the existence of burrs below the sheet.

Kirkos was not in their rooms at the Paradissos when Christina returned there. The 'Admiral' told her that ever since a despatch had arrived by special runner earlier in the day, there had been great comings and goings. The General had shut himself in the sitting-room at the far end of the first floor – which he used as a command office – and had given orders that he was on no account to be disturbed.

Christina bathed and fed Nikki and settled him in the big box-shaped baby carriage which doubled as a cot. She was impatient to return to the flat, to get away from the noisy barracks-like atmosphere of the Paradissos. At one time the first floor had been reasonably cut off from the guerrillas camped all over the ground floor, but they were now everywhere, sleeping in the first-floor corridors and lounging on the stair landings. It was almost impossible to move without falling over them.

She hesitated to burst in on the discussions which George Kirkos seemed to be having with all his most trusted officers but she was equally reluctant to go back to the Piraeus flat without telling him. Soon it would be dark. She decided to give him another fifteen minutes.

Nikki was asleep, so she spent the time packing clothes for herself and the baby in a pillow-slip provided by the 'Admiral'. The woman also loaded her up with food from the kitchen. There was no shortage of it. Crates of food – still with their Red Cross and relief organisation markings – had been stacked all over the kitchen and cellars. It had been plundered from stock-piles at the docks.

There was no sign of Kirkos emerging from the sitting-room at the far end of the building. Climbing over legs of guerrillas sprawled in the corridor outside her room Christina went out by a central door to the balcony which skirted the first floor and gave magnificent views of the Turkish Harbour and the Bay.

It was overcast with flurries of snow in the gusting north-east wind. Already, it was getting quite dark. Christina picked her way through broken flower-pots littering the balcony. It occurred to her that if she could attract George's attention throught the french window of his sitting-room office, he might spare a minute from his war discussions and come out to her.

The curtains across the french window were drawn, leaving slight chinks in the middle and at the side. The sliding doors were not fully closed. South-facing, the room was sheltered from the wind but draughts of air from outside gently lifted the curtains inside.

Christina drew back suddenly as she stole a glance through the crack.

Kirkos was sitting in an armchair with his back to the window. Standing facing him was the only other occupant of the room. It was Petrea.

The woman's attention was concentrated wholly on the man and she was talking in an agitated voice. Christina pressed close to the glass, straining to hear what

Petrea was saying. Her hatred and distrust of the other woman sharpened her need to know why she was closeted in such vehement conversation with her husband.

Petrea was not keeping her voice down.

'You are asking me to betray all I've lived for,' she was saying.

Kirkos's voice was low-pitched but audible.

'I am asking you to put your trust in me, Petrea, and not in Moscow. We are both Greeks, Petrea. The Russians do not understand Greece and have no intention of standing by EAM in the fight against the British. You know that I am dedicated to removing the old order and establishing a new. I want you to help me bring that about. I can do it without you but I want to do it with you.'

'Not while that woman sleeps in your bed.'

'Christina?

'Is her body any better than mine? I have never given myself to a man. Do you know why?'

'You have a lovely body . . . You must have had opportunities.'

'You could have had my body any time. You had only to take me. You are the only man to whom I would gladly give myself. Even now. Renounce your American woman once and for all and I will do anything you ask. I will kill for you . . . I will lie for you . . . I will betray the Party for you . . .'

George Kirkos made no immediate reply. Outside the window, Christina was tense with an anger that was tinged with surprise. She had believed that Kirkos was no stranger to Petrea's bed but, obviously, their devotion had been purely intellectual. No wonder that bitch in there was so eaten with frustration and jealousy! Kirkos was speaking again.

'So that's your price, Petrea? You want me to get rid of Christina?'

'Permanently.'

'How do you propose I do it? Just send her away?'

'It doesn't matter how, so long as it is done.'

'It matters to me. In a perverse way, I'm fond of her – in the way that one grows fond of a stray dog that one can never quite train to be obedient. Not that she's the same since the Germans had her. They did something that I never quite managed.They broke her spirit.'

Waves of humiliation washed over Christina as she heard herself discussed like a piece of furniture. Like a tentacle against her skin, she could also feel the clammy touch of fear.

'Perhaps it would save a lot of trouble if my wife were to meet with a fatal accident,' said Kirkos. 'I find the idea disagreeable but perhaps you don't have my inhibitions. No, I see it excites you. Is it something you would like to arrange?'

Christina could hear the gloat of triumph in the other woman's softly spoken reply. The words were indistinct but the sentiment was unmistakable. She stole a glance inside.

Kirkos had risen from his chair and was locked in a fierce embrace with Petrea. The woman was writhing voluptuously against him, almost slavering with desire as she pressed his hand against the quivering breast erupting from her open shirt.

Christina stumbled away from the window. Mingled with her shivering fear was a nausea which made her want to vomit.

She walked blindly along the corridor to the bedroom where Nikki was still sleeping. She ignored the cries of protest from the guerrillas on whose outstretched legs she trod in her headlong flight from what she had seen and heard.

Once in the room, she bundled the pillow-case of clothes on to the baby carriage. Then she had sudden thought and unloaded them again.

383

She lifted out the sleeping child and laid him carefully on the bed. Then she lifted out the mattress and the three padded leather seats which joined together to form the baby's bed inside the perambulator. Below was the trunk of space, designed to give leg-room to the young occupant in toddler years – when the middle bed section was removed and the child could sit on one of the two remaining seats.

Christina crawled under the big double bed and pulled out one of three identical metal boxes. It was about a foot square and quite heavy. She placed it in the recess in the baby carriage, packing some of her belongings round about it. Next, she replaced the three cushioned frames, laid the mattress on top and put the baby back in the carriage. She loaded the other things she was taking around the baby's feet and packed her supply of foodstuffs into a shopping pannier attached to the pram under the handle.

She pushed the baby carriage out of the room and into the corridor. Her way was barred by the inevitable sprawl of off-duty guerrillas. Two came to her aid. They carried the laden baby carriage down the stairs and across the crowded lobby lounge, depositing it for her in the cobbled courtyard.

She pushed the carriage past the guard squad with their cradled tommy-guns and wrappings of bandoliers. They grinned at her and told her that she would have snow for her Saint's Day. They knew she had been named for Christ and believed that, in Greek fashion, she would be celebrating her name day on Christ's traditional birthday.

She acknowledged their greetings and, once in the street, had to trot to keep the pram from running away from her down the steep hill. The baby carriage bumped and rattled on the uneven road as she made her way down from Castella. It had now grown quite dark.

Over and over, she told herself she must not give way

384

to panic. She knew exactly what she had to do. She had to keep moving quickly and remain calm. She could still escape and foil George and that murderous bitch. They were welcome to each other. Two rattlesnakes together – and that was a slander on rattlesnakes!

She prayed that Mackenzie and Preston would still be at the flat. She was almost certain that their intention was to abandon it but she reasoned that they would wait until an hour or two after dark before trying to infiltrate across the city to the British lines. Indeed she was banking on it. If they had already gone, she was lost.

Her heartbeats were echoing in her ears as she rounded the corner next to the ship chandler's shop. She pushed the perambulator into the narrow entry leading to the stairs and kicked on the foot-brake. Nikki was stirring restlessly. She rearranged his blanket more comfortably and, reassured by the happy little baby sigh he emitted in his sleep, she left him and moved towards the stairs.

The door of the flat was locked. She beat fiercely on the door. Nothing moved inside.

The sound of a footstep on the stairs behind her made her turn. Half way up the stairs was the shadowy bulk of the ship chandler.

'They went away,' he said. 'They said you wanted to come back and live here. But they wouldn't give me the key. They said you had one.'

Christina's heart sank.

'You're sure they've gone?'

'Of course I'm sure.'

He could have told her of the gold coins they had given him as 'rent', but he saw no need to do so.

'Are you going to stay?' asked the fat man.

She looked bleakly at him standing there in the shadows.

'No, I'm not staying.'

She pushed past him to the foot of the stairs and released the brake on the baby carriage with her foot.

'What will I do if someone else comes looking for you?' he called after her. 'Is the old woman coming back?'

'How should I know about the old woman?' she replied.'If anyone asks for me, tell them what you like. It won't make any difference.'

From beside the shop entrance, he watched her push the baby carriage along the empty street. One of the wheels was squeaking badly. The noise grated on the ear. She didn't appear even to notice it.

It had been quite dark for over an hour. Mackenzie nudged Preston with his elbow.

'I think we can chance it now.'

'I'm nearly frozen to this goddamned stone,' muttered Preston. 'I feel like Lot's wife.'

'I don't know if Lot's wife is available,' whispered Mackenzie. Preston began to explain that he had not meant that he desired Lot's wife but had been commenting on his own imminent petrification, when he caught the gleam of Mackenzie's teeth in a broad white grin. He grinned back ruefully.

'OK, OK – so you were making a joke and I fell flat on it,' acknowledged Preston. 'Forget it.'

The two men had been hiding in the rubble ruins of a dockside warehouse for more than two hours. They had not prolonged their stay in the flat over the ship chandler's after their encounter with Christina Kirkos earlier in the day. They had stayed only long enough to transmit a final message to Brady and then hide the radios in the roof space. They had decided to make their departure from Piraeus unencumbered by too much equipment.

During the remaining hours of daylight they had reconnoitred their escape route from behind the ELAS lines. It was an eventuality they had previously discussed at length.

During the early days of the fighting, it would not have been difficult to have reached mid-Athens by any of a dozen different routes. Now, every street bordering the British perimeter was sealed off and fortified by the guerrillas. The only way out was across water. There was no other way to circle round the ELAS strongpoints.

In the main dock area were several small craft, including an LCM, which Kirkos's men had captured when they over-ran the British positions in the docks. These, however, were heavily guarded by guerrillas.

Mackenzie and Preston had by-passed these craft and their guards and concentrated their search in the heavily devastated western area of the docks for anything else that would float. This area of the harbour would be doubly useful if anything could be found, they knew, because the harbour entrance was at this end and it offered access to the open waters stretching across to Salamis.

They were in luck. Grounded on the rubble slopes of a dynamited quay was a ship-painter's raft. Strips of its top planking had been torn out and what remained was slimed with black oil but Mackenzie had no doubt the tiny platform would float.

In the dark of the heavy overcast and no moon, his faith in the rafts seaworthiness — which was a degree stronger than Preston's - was now about to be put to the test.

The two men, with as little noise as possible, bumped the raft over the jagged slabs of the masonry which were all that remained of a wharf where ocean liners had berthed. Both were aware that the mole opposite them, only a quarter of a mile away across the black water of the harbour, housed an ELAS machine-gun post.

The grating of wood upon stone was deafening to their ears. Suddenly, with a gentle splash, the raft was afloat. Mackenzie was first aboard, flat on his belly. Preston choked back a cry of warning as one end of the raft sank with Mackenzie's weight. It threatened to tip right over.

Mackenzie inched forward, spreading his weight. The raft settled. Preston crawled after him, almost straddling him in his care to keep the raft stable. Again, one end tipped as Preston eased his body down in the narrow space alongside Mackenzie. He kicked the raft away from the rubble slope down which they had trundled it. It glided out into deep water.

Both men unslung their rifles to use as paddles. Every movement caused the raft to wobble dangerously. They remained flat on their bellies, facing the way they were heading and, making slow deliberate sweeps with their rifle butts, began to find a harmony of movement.

'We'll make for the wreck in the middle of the channel,' whispered Mackenzie. 'It'll hide us from those bandits on the mole.'

Preston grunted assent.

They passed close to the protruding mainmast of the sunken block-ship. Clear of it, they seemed perilously close to the machine-gun post on the mole. They could see the silhouettes of men and the glow from their cigarettes. The men's voices carried over the gently rippling waters of the harbour, raucous in the night.

Slowly, the raft glided out through the harbour neck. The water became choppy, breaking over the almost non-existent freeboard and washing over their outstretched legs.

They maintained a course directly away from the mole until it was only a dim shape behind them. Now, they executed a wide left turn which brought them more directly into the face of wind and sea.

Stealth was less important now. They struggled to

their knees so that they could paddle with the full weight of back and shoulders. The blackness was inky. Still, they kept the raft moving in the direction which would bring them eventually into the great anchorage of friendly ships.

Their concentration on keeping their craft afloat and staying on board it was so intense that the flood of light which suddenly bathed them almost startled them into capsizing the raft.

A voice hailed them in English from the darkness behind the blinding light.

'Put down your guns and raise your hands!"

Mackenzie was first to recover from the shock of the light.

'We'll fall in the bloody sea if we raise our hands!' he roared. 'For Christ's sake, move that light round a bit!'

There was a pause while the voice behind the light recovered from the unexpectedness of the admonition. Then the voice came again.

'Who are you? Oxford or Cambridge?'

This time it was Preston who replied.

'Neither — it's Christopher Columbus and friend looking for the Nantucket Light. Can we come aboard?'

The beam of light shifted and the dark hull of a destroyer became visible in its edge. The voice came again:

'We'll put a ladder down. Do you want a line for that piece of firewood or are you abandoning ship?'

'We're abandoning ship,' confirmed Preston.

Mackenzie was first to reach the destroyer's deck. An officer in a duffle-coat looked at him askance, taking in the rough wet clothes and the stern face with its eye-patch.

'Good God!' he said. 'It's Blackbeard the Pirate!'

CHAPTER TWENTY-SEVEN

Point of No Return

The sharp crack of sniper fire wakened the baby. He began to cry. Christina closed her ears to the sound and continued to trundle the baby carriage towards the road junction ahead.

A building on the corner had been damaged by shell-fire and the fallen masonry from the building had spilled half way across the road. She could see men on the near side of this rubble wall and guessed from the way they crouched when they moved that they must be close to British-held territory.

On her left, the corner was clear of obstruction and she could see the square beyond, across which was the continuation of the street she had been following. She was certain now she knew where she was. If she kept on across the intersection, the Ilissus River should be five or six hundred yards beyond. If she turned left, the road went up through western Athens to Peristeri. If she turned right, the road turned sharply back through about forty-five degrees and led straight back to Piraeus and the harbour. Peristeri and Piraeus were the last places she wanted to go. She had to get across the intersection ahead.

Suddenly the night was quiet. The firing, less than a street away, stopped. The only sounds now were the plaintive cries of Nikki and the tortured squeak which came from one slightly buckled wheel of the baby carriage.

She was very close to the wall of rubble blocking half the street when she became aware that the rifle-carrying men behind it were shouting to her.

'Go back!' a voice shouted in Greek. 'Do you want to be killed? Go back!'

Another voice said: 'It's a baby! A woman with a baby! Is she out of her head?'

One man made a move to leave the shelter of the barricade but a companion pulled him down. Christina heard his shout: 'Don't be a fool, Stephanos! You'll get yourself killed!'

'Somebody's got to stop her!' the man replied. 'Woman! Stay where you are!'

Christina ignored them. She hugged the left side of the road. She walked clear of the corner, right past them. The baby's crying was now like a banshee in the night. To Trooper Lawrie Peters in the turret of the 14-ton armoured car, just thirty yards north of the corner at which Christina and the baby carriage appeared, the sound of the baby's crying came as a paralysing surprise. His finger froze on the trigger.

The armoured car was tucked between two buildings, in a narrow alley leading to an enclosed court. The front of the vehicle was almost flush with the front of the buildings and its guns covered the broad expanse of square and the roads leading to it. The two tall buildings flanking the armoured car were occupied by British troops and, in fact, constituted the only British-held territory west of the highway from Piraeus to Peristeri.

Trooper Peters called out:

'Hold your fire! It's a woman and a baby.'

British soldiers occupied sandbag-fortified positions at every corner of the square except the one from which Christina had emerged. She kept going, walking right across the square, past a Bren emplacement facing the rubble barrier held by the ELAS.

A lieutenant moved from behind a wall of sandbags to intercept her. In laboured Greek, he tried to ask her who she was and where she was going? His relief was great when she answered in English.

'I'm an American citizen and this is my baby. Please let me pass.'

'How did you get here?'

'It's a long story. Can't you just let me pass?'

'Where do you think you're going?'

'The American Embassy.'

'That's a long way pushing a pram. Do you know where the Embassy is?'

'It's on Vasilissis Sophias Avenue. I know how to get there.'

'Do you have any identification papers?'

'No, they were destroyed.'

'It's not safe standing around here. You'd better come with me.'

He led the way to a truck parked off the road under cover of trees. The trees lined one side of the road beyond the square and extended into a grove off the road. The grove was sheltered by a high wall on its north side. A gate in the wall led to a Doric ruin. About thirty soldiers were resting in the lee of the wall.

The lieutenant spoke to a signaller manning a radio-telephone in the rear of the truck. Christina heard the man calling Battalion Headquarters. The signaller passed a phone-piece to the Lieutenant, who had a long conversation with HQ. He walked across to where Christina waited a little distance away.

'They're sending a vehicle for you from Battalion. Would you like a mug of tea? The boys have been brewing up.'

'Thank you,' said Christina. 'If you have hot water, maybe I could have some for the baby?'

The Lieutenant, who was anxious to return to his post, put her in the care of a corporal. He brought her

392

tea in an enamel mug and some hot water in a billy-can.

'I'll just go over there. It looks sheltered.' She pointed to the far end of the grove of trees.

The Corporal stared at her, slightly embarrassed. He could not be sure whether she intended to breast-feed the bawling infant or not.

'Of course, of course,' he said. 'I'll be over by the truck. If you want anything just give me a shout. Your transport should be here in half an hour.'

The tea made her feel better. She mixed some meal with the hot water and spooned it to Nikki, saving some of the hot water for him to sip. Then she changed him without moving him from the shelter of the peram-bulator. The wind was icy.

The soldiers, who had been resting, filed off towards the road junction while she was tending the baby. From the square came the sounds of renewed small-arms fire. She longed to be away from the spot. Fatigue and reac-tion were setting in now. She began to shiver. Crossing through the ELAS lines had been far easier than ever she had dreamed possible but the drain on her nervous energy had been considerable.

The thought of answering the questions which, she suspected, would be fired at her by British interrogators filled her with dread. When the Lieutenant told her about a truck being sent, she had guessed that it wasn't entirely kindness. They would want to know everything about her before they let her go anywhere.

It was just before midnight when a fifteen-hundred-weight truck, driving without lights, crossed the bridge half a mile east of the road intersection and accelerated up the slight incline towards the trees. It pulled in beside the radio truck. The driver jumped down and hailed the Corporal who had given Christina the tea.

The Corporal had a Bren gun stripped, and the

various pieces were set out on a poncho cape on the ground.

'Practising taking it to pieces and putting it together in the dark then?'

The Corporal looked up.

'I've done it before now with a blindfold on. Two minutes and twenty seconds is my record. Bloody thing's been jamming. What can I do you for, squire?'

'Intelligence Officer at Battalion told me to come down here and collect a woman and a kid.'

'She's just over there. Giving the nipper his supper, she was.'

The Corporal got to his feet.

'That's funny,' he said.

'What is?'

'She ain't there. Wonder where the hell she's wandered off to?'

'Maybe spending a penny,' said the driver. 'Want to give her a minute?'

The Corporal was suddenly uneasy.

'She wouldn't have just gone off, would she?'

'Search me,' said the driver. 'Were you supposed to be keeping an eye on her? Maybe she was spying for them Bolshevik bleeders up the road.'

They searched the grove of trees from one end to the other. The woman and the baby could not be found. They had vanished.

'She can't just have vanished into thin air!' raged George Kirkos.

He scowled at Major Voutsas, the man he had placed in charge of his private army's intelligence and security. 'How can a woman with a baby in a carriage just disappear?'

Voutsas shuffled uncomfortably.

'We just have these reports of her being seen at three different times.'

'Why wasn't she stopped and questioned?' bellowed Kirkos.

'A woman with a baby? No one thought it was important, General.'

'I'll tell you how important it is, Major Voutsas,' said Kirkos icily. 'She stole from here a very vital piece of equipment for the Javelin.'

Voutsas paled.

'I don't understand. I thought the weapon and the bombs were all taken up to the hill bunker. I have had a ring of men guarding the position night and day. No one has been allowed near the place. What is missing?'

Kirkos turned away self-consciously. He had taken care to enlighten as few people as possible about the workings of the Javelin. Perhaps he should have taken Voutsas more into his confidence. How could he now explain, without looking too great a fool, that his own wife had stolen one of three vital components of the Javelin from under his own bed?

'You were not to know about the part that has been stolen. I was going to put you fully in the picture tomorrow,' he said. 'Do you know what the Javelin is?'

'It seems to be some kind of mechanical catapult – a gun without a barrel. I don't really know. I have never seen a machine like it before.'

'No one in Greece has,' said Kirkos. 'It is a rocket-launcher. It fires rocket bombs into the air. When the rocket reaches the zenith of its flight and begins to fall, it is guided to its target, which it picks up on its aerial sensors.'

Voutsas looked at Kirkos blankly.

'You are wondering how the target sends out radio signals to attract the rocket?' said Kirkos. 'I'll tell you. The target sends out signals because we have hidden a small and ingenious transmitter in the target area. The transmitter sends out electro-magnetic vibrations of very high frequency and the guidance system of the rocket locks on to this beam and follows it to its source. Bang!'

'I think I understand,' said Voutsas.

'Do you? Then you will begin to appreciate the importance of what has been stolen. One of the three target-transmitters which I had locked in my room has been stolen.'

'We found some radio equipment in the roof of the house on top of the ship chandler's. American-made,' said Voutsas.

Kirkos's face crimsoned with anger.

'You what! Why didn't you tell me before?'

'With respect, General, you did not give me the chance,' protested Voutsas. 'You wanted to know only if we had found Madame Kirkos and the child.'

'You said there was no sign of her in the house but that she had been there just after dark. How did you find out?'

'We questioned the ship chandler – the fat one who lives downstairs. He said that two of our men were living in the apartment and that they met your wife earlier in the day and spent a long time with her.'

'Where is the chandler? Perhaps he is not telling all he knows.'

Voutsas looked apologetic.

'I'm afraid he is dead, General. We had to drag the answers out of him. Perhaps we were too rough with him.'

'Magnificent!' exclaimed Kirkos. 'We have one possible witness and my men beat him to death!'

'I think he told us all he knew,' said Voutsas. 'The men he talked about came to the flat three weeks ago. The chandler said they were our men, mountain men, but I think they were English spies. They had given the chandler gold. That is why we took the place apart. We found the radios hidden up under the roof.'

'Well, it explains one mystery,' said Kirkos. 'Wolarski

said only this morning that someone had spotted our gun positions for the British Navy. It seems he was right.'

'What are your orders now, General?'

'I want you to get every man available searching for my wife. I want her found . . . Dead or alive. I want that transmitter she stole returned here before morning.'

The time, when Voutsas went out to send men combing through Piraeus, was just ten minutes after midnight. He returned to the Paradissos in a highly agitated state at just before two in the morning. Kirkos was studying an ordnance map of Athens when the Major was shown into his room .

'Well, Voutsas, have you found her?'

The Major stood nervously searching for the right words.

'We are pretty sure we know where she is, General — but we can't reach her now.'

'What do you mean "can't" reach her?'

'A woman pushing a baby carriage went through our lines up on the Piraeus-Peristeri road. Our men tried to stop her but were pinned down by machine-gun fire from a British armoured car and couldn't get near her.'

'Was she killed?'

'No. Apparently, she just ignored the bullets.'

Kirkos sat for an hour after Voutsas had left, wrestling with the problem which Christina's defection had caused. Why had she suddenly gone like that? Who were the two men she had met at the Vlakhos flat? Was there a connection between that meeting and the theft of the target-transmitter? She was the only person who could have taken it. There was no other explanation.

Kirkos got down on his hands and knees and reached under the bed. He pulled the two remaining metal containers into the middle of the floor. He pressed his ear close to each of them in turn. He could hear nothing. Not the slightest vibration.

It was ironic that Christina had taken the box she undoubtedly had. Of the three, why had she taken that one? She couldn't have any idea of their function.

Nor could she have had any idea that Kirkos had removed the boxes from their hiding-place below the bed only twelve hours before, soon after he had received the message from Natsinas about Churchill arriving on Christmas Day.

There had been three boxes then, not two, and taking them out had been the prelude to an act of commitment. Like a Samurai warrior dedicating himself at his personal shrine before battle, Kirkos had knelt before the boxes and committed himself there and then to a path from which there could be no turning back. The lethal containers were the symbolic pivots on which his destiny was to turn and, conscious of a need to pass beyond the point of no return as far as their use was concerned, he had activated the mechanism inside one of them.

From the chain round his neck – where he had carried it ever since Nikos Stratou had delivered it to him personally – Kirkos had taken the four-inch cylindrical key. Then, selecting one of the boxes, he had inserted the key in a small aperture in the base and made one full turn.

There had been a loud click as the mechanism sealed inside had activated. A switch had set into operation a tiny motor with a gyroscopic movement boosted by power from a small electric cell. The motor would keep running for seven days before the electric cell gave out. Throughout this time, it would send into the atmosphere, via three small bell-shaped transmitting heads, the sonic vibrations which would act as homing signals for the Javelin's X24 missile.

By starting one of the pilot transmitters, Kirkos had given himself seven days to locate it at a chosen target and launch the first of the three rockets which, he was sure, would change the course of history.

Christina's theft of the activated pilot transmitter seriously complicated his plans. For a start, it had removed one of three chances of killing Churchill. He wondered if Christina had already handed the box over to the British. He could imagine their puzzlement if she had.

What would they make of a completely sealed metal box weighing about seven pounds? They might guess that the tiny aperture in the base was for some kind of key – but that alone would give little clue to the box's secret. If an ear were placed close to the surface of the box, they would hear a low humming noise – but what conclusions would they draw from that?

They would certainly think long and hard before cutting a way into the container. What if it were a time-bomb? That, surely, would be their first thought: that it was some kind of explosive device. Kirkos reasoned that if the British had that box in their hands they would treat it with the greatest of caution.

This realisation helped him reach a decision. The efficiency or otherwise of the Javelin had still to be proven to him. All that Christina had accomplished by stealing it was to provide him with a heaven-sent opportunity to put the weapon to the test.

Having made his decision, there was no time to lose. He would give the Javelin its test while it was still dark.

The snow, which had been threatening for two days without coming to anything, was still flurrying in the north-east wind as Kirkos climbed the hill. A few paces behind him, Nikos Stratou was hunched in a great-coat, still drowsy from the sleep from which he had been unceremoniously wakened half an hour previously.

Displeased as he was at being turned out of a warm bed at three in the morning of Christmas Eve, Stratou did not feel disposed to complain too loudly. Kirkos had treated him like a lord from the moment of his arrival. He had been quartered in a small but pleasant house in Castella so that he could rest after the trip from Italy. The owner of the house, a twenty-six-year-old widow, had not been mentioned as part of the amenities but had proved to be as compelling a reason as any for Stratou's decision to stay in Greece longer than he had intended.

Kirkos and Stratou had got on well together in the long sessions they'd had discussing the operation of the Javelin.

Stratou – who believed he had an intuitive gift for assessing life's winners and losers among his fellow-men – had immediately singled out Kirkos as a winner. Kirkos, on the other hand, had divined in Stratou a man who – if the price were right – would be totally loyal to his paymaster. More than that, he guessed that Stratou had an inbuilt need to earn his keep dangerously.

When Kirkos had invited Stratou to postpone his attempt to reach the Lebanon and throw in his lot with him, the former Abwehr agent accepted with surprising alacrity. It needed no more than Kirkos's promise that the thousand gold sovereigns which Stratou had already earned was only a trifle compared with the rewards which could eventually be his.

In the first instance, Stratou's immediate duties would be a major role in the operation for which the Javelin had been brought to Greece.

Kirkos's personal bodyguard – of half a dozen hand-picked men – straggled behind their leader and his companion as they neared the top of the hill. A voice rang out in challenge. Kirkos identified himself and led the way past a series of guard positions on the hill's south-eastern face: little more than pock-marks in the limestone of the hill, occupied by men with rifles.

Close to the summit, a hole had been blasted into the hill's brow and a gun platform had been hacked from the solid rock. The Germans had initially excavated the site, taking trouble to conceal it from seaward and the air. From below, the position was hidden by a natural rampart of smooth rock forming the lower jaw of the cavern mouth. A round bald overhang of rock canopied the cavern from above. A tunnel ran back through the hilltop from the site to a concealed opening on the other side of the high south- and east-facing ridge.

Once, the site had housed two eighty-eight mm guns. Now, its single artillery piece was the last of Kirkos's operable Italian seventy-fives. It had been pulled back inside the cavern so that its snout did not protrude beyond the rock overhang.

In daylight, the view from the position was breathtaking. The whole of Athens could be seen, with the 1000-feet-high carbuncle of Mount Lycabettos dominating the skyline to the east. In the nearer distance and slightly to the south of Lycabettos's cone top, the weathered pillars of the Parthenon and the Acropolis adorned the panorama. Further south glittered the waters of the Saronic Gulf and its pattern of islands.

Half an inch of snow powdered the pate of the hill above and beyond the gun position. The ground dipped in a hollow from the summit towards a ridge to the north-west. This far ridge faced Eleusis, half-way house on the road from Athens to Megara and gateway to the hinterland heights of Eleutherae.

A track led from the tunnel opening behind the high east ridge to a bunker sunk in the solid and imporous substrata of the skull-like hill's cranial area. This bunker had formerly been the sleeping quarters and storehouse of the German defence battery on the sea-facing brow of the hill.

Concrete and stone had been used cleverly to conceal the bunker system from the air and render it almost invisible against the stark terrain of the hilltop. The broad central well of the bunker had provided a ready-made platform for the Javelin launcher. The Germans had even left behind a roll-over canvas awning which both covered and camouflaged the central well. The catacomb-like quarters which spread out like burrows from the well had provided the bunker's custodians with shelter, if not comfort, at the bitter altitude.

Under the supervision of Kirkos and Stratou, the launcher's control console had been located thirty feet from the well on a rampart-like wall which skirted one end of the bunker. This elevated level of the structure had, because of its protective outer wall and view of the surrounding hilltop, been used by Kirkos's men for guard lookout. It doubled as an ideal control and observation platform, safe from the back-blast of the Javelin's missiles.

Kirkos now directed that the awning over the central well be rolled back and that the cable from the console be reeled out. The latter was led down a metal stairway, along an underground corridor to the well and connected to the launcher. When launcher and console were connected, the hydraulic arms of the launching cradle were extended and locked into position. Then the curved semi-circular frame which governed the angle of elevation was manually rotated through its cogs until the launching rails were within a few degrees of pointing vertically upwards.

The first of the torpedo-like X24 missiles was lifted from its crate by a chain block and tackle and laid tail-first into the waiting cradle. Then the clamps which would keep its flight true along the first few feet of its journey were slid into position. Stratou could not keep a slight tremble from his hand as he located and began to tighten a valve screw on the launching frame about one-third of the way up the positioned rocket. This pushed a copper probe out from the frame until it touched a copper band ringing the detonation chamber above the rocket's fuel supply. A surge of current passing from the probe to the copper band was all that was now required to send the missile powering into flight.

Stratou made final checks on the elevation and horizontal meters which were circuited to give readings to the nearest hundredth part of a second on the control console. Other dials showed the gyro-compass trajectory setting and the angular distance in tenths of a second between the zenith vertical of the launch position and the desired altitude of the missile.

Finally, he faced George Kirkos.

'It's all ready to go.'

Kirkos looked at his watch.

'I make the time four-seventeen. I want to watch from the gun position. Will you look after things here? Push the button at exactly four forty-five.'

Stratou synchronised his watch with Kirkos's.

'Don't you think we should go over those trajectory calculations again?'

'We went over them a hundred times when we bedded down the Javelin. There's no point in doing them again,' said Kirkos.

'The maps we used weren't exactly new and neither of us are engineers. It just needs a small error to botch the whole job.'

'Getting cold feet, Nikos?' There was an edge to Kirkos's voice. 'Yesterday afternoon, you had no doubts. You said the trajectory path was straight across Athens and the line cut the Parliament House in two. You said that even if the target pilot failed to function, we would still hit any target we wanted along that line.'

'Maybe I made a mistake.'

'There's one way to find out,' snapped Kirkos. 'We fire the rocket at four forty-five! Tell the men to clear the launch area.'

He climbed on to the low parapet of the observation-point and jumped down to the flinty ground of the hilltop. Tufts of withered spurge peeped from the thin covering of snow. The dark outline of trodden track, which wound across the hollow to behind the east ridge, stood out like a varicose vein on the hill's white, wintry skin. Kirkos followed the path to the overhung cave opening of the tunnel which ran under the ridge to the gun platform. A guard with a shaded flashlight escorted him through the tunnel to the larger chamber, where men were huddled round the seventy-five. The rocky balcony on to which it opened was exposed to the full bitterness of the north-east wind. The wind whistled into every recess of the cavern.

The men had blankets hooded over their heads and shoulders. They moved about constantly, stamping their feet for warmth.

Kirkos scarcely noticed the cold as he looked down on the lightless city of Athens. He was warmed by a glow of power. Athens had always been *his* city. He had only to walk its streets to feel the strength of his belonging. But there was more than just belonging in what he felt now. In the pre-dawn dark of this Christmas Eve morning, his feelings were proprietorial, of ownership. Before him was *his* kingdom.

Once, he had been a man without any sense of direction in life: not knowing where he was going or what he really wanted. His ambitions were without definition – and yet they had always been linked in an unspoken way with this historical city of his birth. Always, he had felt that his wandering steps – first this way and then another – were not unguided, not without purpose. He had been aware of it as a very young man facing the fearful maze of life, even when he had stumbled from one dead end to another. The diversions and blind alleys had not weakened his inner certainty that the way before him would ultimately become clear. He knew that, like Ulysses, he had to endure trials and tempests – learning from them – before his moment would come.

His excursions into politics, initially with a clandestine Republican movement, had led to his imprisonment and some disillusionment. He had come to despise those politicians with whom he aligned with a bitterness equal to that he had previously reserved for those he opposed. He had concluded that a political philosophy could always be a means but never an end. The real goal was power. And a man would be a fool to serve a philosophy in the pursuit of power when the only way of achieving it was to make the philosophy serve him. People tended to be the same in every party. Only the labels differed.

Kirkos had come to the conclusion that no extreme party could every hold sway in Greece for very long. He had recognised in himself a streak of individualism which was prevalent in most Greeks and decided that his countrymen would never accept regimentation under any philosophy which was narrow and rigid and allowed no outlet for individual expression. Most Greeks, he believed, would accept firm paternalistic leadership in the way they accepted the Orthodox religion – because of every Greek's sense of family. The only authority or structure of society to which the Greek could make his individualistic expression subservient was family. Class divisions in society meant nothing to him because the meanest Greek felt no inferiority as a result of personal poverty, and the most important man in any community - large or small, urban or rural – was not the wealthiest, the best-dressed, the best-educated or the most powerful, but the man deemed to be the wisest.

This, at any rate, was Kirkos's assessment and the reason why he believed that no party of the Extreme Right or Extreme Left would ever be accepted for long by the great majority of Greeks. This great majority belonged to a middle band of political opinion which was itself divided into two. These two middle groupings had much more in common with each other than with either of the extreme minorities of Right and Left. But, instead of merging their many common interests and aspirations, they tended to ally with the factions on their nearest fringe in the hope of marginally tipping the balance in their favour.

Thus, the Middle Right flirted with Fascism to gain ascendancy over the Middle Left and the Middle Left reciprocated by flirting with Communism. They were like two dogs who grew tails to wag at each other and then found that the tails could wag them.

It was a situation which Kirkos saw as fertile for exploitation. Circumstance rather than choice had made him the servant of the Fascist tail and the Communist tail. Now, he was ready to lop off the alien tails from the two great bodies of Greek opinion and unite them under his leadership.

Looking across benighted Athens, Kirkos could sense the closeness of his moment of destiny. He had endured much, suffered the will and the counsels of inferior men, as he had striven to find the path towards his own destiny. Now, the dead ends and blind alleys of the testing maze were far behind him and the mists had cleared to reveal his goal in sharp definition ahead.

He looked at his watch. It was four forty-five. He heard the rush of sound but did not see the bright flash of light as the rocket ignited.

In the bunker a quarter of a mile away, behind the hill summit, Nikos Stratou was gazing in awe at the vivid after-burn of orange light as the X24 missile lifted towards the heavens and disappeared into the low overcast.

Kirkos endured an agony of anti-climax as he waited to see the rocket curve a fiery path across the night sky - but there was nothing to be seen from his forward position. Low cloud completely obscured the rocket's pillaring flight. Then Kirkos saw what looked like a falling star about five miles distant. There was a white streak of light diving earthwards, followed by a lightning flash of red bouncing off the low cloud and momentarily illuminating the silhouettes of distant buildings. A cloud of orange fire flared briefly against the black velvet of the night. Seconds later, a low booming sound rolled from the heart of the city and echoed round the cavern walls of the gun-site.

The sound echoed and was gone, leaving the hilltop once more to the dark mantle of night and the eerie sighing of the wind.

The cruciform church was painted white and had a narrow arched doorway. A squat white tower with a red-pantiled dome roof, over the altar area, marked the head of the cross and the two arms were represented by short abutting buildings which were roofed like the dome with red pantiles.

As churches go, the church of St John Chrysostom in the Plaka district of Athens was a tiny one. It was tucked away high above the bustle of Adrianou Street and below the towering dominance of the Acropolis, built on a shelf of rock and surrounded by oleanders and aromatic shrubs, with fig trees growing wild from its enclosing walls.

Its peace seemed to reach out to Christina as she grew weary of her trek across Athens. She had been avoiding contact with the group of soldiers moving about the city and which she had seen as she had worked her way east from the Ilissus River bridge. By keeping off the bigger streets and following every side street and alley which seemed to bear east, she had worked her way across the city until she found herself in the Plaka and some distance off her original course.

Spatters of rain and biting cold wind made her long for any refuge in which she could shelter until daylight.

She wheeled the perambulator across the paved court-yard of the tiny church of St John Chrysostom.

The front door was unlocked. It creaked open at her touch. Candles, which had been lit at midnight, glowed with beckoning warmth from the altar area.

She hauled the baby carriage through the front door and pulled the door shut. The buckled wheel of the baby carriage squeaked shrilly as she made her way across the open tiled floor to the altar.

The peace of the tiny church enveloped her, warming her, or perhaps it just seemed so after the howl and bite of the wind outside. It was so still inside that the silence had the bliss of haven waters after an ocean crossing.

Nikki was awake but not crying. She lifted him and showed him the icons bathed in the flickering candle-light of the altar. On the right was the icon of Christ and, to the right of that, the icon of St John the Baptist. On the left was the icon of the Virgin and another for St John Chrysostom.

A low altar table had been decorated with figures of the Nativity. On another was a large round loaf, the *Christopsoma* – the Bread of Christ – with its cross made of dough in the middle, and decorated with four chestnuts on each side and a fifth in the centre.

With her own child in her arms, Christina felt an identifying compassion for the mother of the child born all those centuries before. Religion had played little part in her life but she sensed now a closeness to spiritual verities – as if a chink of light from a door had given a first hint of secrets to be revealed in the greater incan-descence beyond, from which the gleam of light sprang.

Feelings of sorrowing humility drenched through her, washing away guilt and anger and fatigue. She tried to remember a prayer but could not. Instead, the line of something she had sung as a little girl kept recurring in her mind. It was an anthem which had been part of a school Christmas concert when she was eight years old.

She remembered how the line had to be sung five or six times over by the small wavering treble voices while the deeper tones of the older boys punctuated the repeated line with plagal cadences of successive 'Amens'.

The line rang in her head and she heard herself saying it aloud.

'For I am washed clean in the blood of the Lamb.'

Nikki gurgled up at her, thinking she was speaking to him. She smiled and hugged the child happily to her breast.

She sat down on the steps of the altar, cradling him and soothing him to sleep. His eyes closed contentedly as she gently hummed him a lullaby.

High above the church, the sensors on the nose of the missile picked up the vibrations pulsing into the atmosphere and relayed the signals back to the sensitive receivers operating the rudder and fins controlling the rocket's flight.

The missile reared and bucked as the electronic guidance system searched for, held, and locked on to the beam from below. Then, its path ordained, the projectile hurtled in a steep dive towards the earth.

Its nose pierced the red-pantiled dome of the church with the ease of a needle through silk. The timber floor of the bell flat offered no more resistance than a muslin cloth. The missile struck a granite pillar at the side of the altar, snapping it cleanly in two before plummeting through the floor of the altar and exploding on contact with the rock of the hillside beneath.

The collapse of the pillar brought the dome crashing down on one side. The falling roof timbers were still cascading downwards when the floor of the church erupted upwards. The blast sought escape in every direction from the rocky wall of the hillside behind, below and flanking the two sides of the church. The walls of the building were literally torn apart as shockwaves of colliding air eddied from rock wall to rock wall with volcanic force.

The Church of St John Chrysostom had stood the ravages of ten centuries. Now, it was no more.

In the midst of the debris piled high across the transept, Christina Kirkos lay beneath the main crossbeam of the roof. Her baby lay beneath her, still clutched in her arms.

CHAPTER TWENTY-EIGHT

Christmas Eve

Mackenzie hummed 'Oh Come All Ye Faithful' as he strode along the paved walk towards the three dun-coloured caravan trailers which had been parked in a corner of the Royal Gardens.

It was a cold grey morning with sleet in the air, but Mackenzie's good spirits were equal to the bleak cheerlessness of the weather. Thanks to the Navy and an obliging RASC major at the Phaleron Bay beachhead, he and Preston had been speedily transported to the Hotel Grande Bretagne, had undergone a rigorous debriefing session with Maitland – who had returned from Italy three days before – and had been comfortably bedded just after midnight.

Now, in a crisp fresh battledress uniform and his skin still tingling from a cold-water shave, he felt renewed. Preston, a few paces behind him, was not at his sparkling best at this time of morning. He had been wakened some time before five by a thundering explosion from less than a mile away, in the direction of the Acropolis, and he had been unable to get back to sleep.

. 'Must you be so damned cheerful?' he complained to Mackenzie.

'It's Christmas Eve,' said Mackenzie, as if that explained it all. Preston was unimpressed.

'There isn't much peace on earth or goodwill around these parts,' he observed. The sharp crack of rifle fire could be heard to the west and to the north.

411

'Military Intelligence,' said Mackenzie as they passed two of the parked trailers, one of which was festooned with radio masts and antennae. 'Ours is the third van – the anonymous one.'

A guard at the door of the trailer asked them for the special ID cards with which Maitland had equipped them.

The Head of Section Six was already at work inside the trailer. He was bending over a huge map of Athens and talking to a captain wearing the red beret of the Parachute Regiment. A ceiling-high cabinet of radio equipment filled one wall of the trailer.

'Good afternoon, chaps,' said Maitland drily. 'None the worse from your raft expedition, I hope? this is Captain Drinkwater.'

The Captain nodded to the newcomers.

'Captain Drinkwater had to get out, too,' said Maitland. 'Wasn't as lucky as you though. he couldn't find a raft . . . Had to swim the Ilissus. He's been in Peristeri for the past three weeks. Tell 'em about it, Drinkwater.'

There was a fierce sullenness in the way Drinkwater eyed them.

'I was lucky to get out,' he said. 'those bloody butchers – the bastards who call themselves the EAM police – have been taking Peristeri apart house by house. I've been dodging them for a fortnight but yesterday I ran out of places to hide.'

'At least we had a comfortable funk-hole in Piraeus,' said Mackenzie. 'You sound a trifle bitter, Captain.'

'Bitter? If being filled up to the eyeballs with black burning hate is bitter, then I'm bitter! You'd feel the same if you'd seen what I've seen.'

'Bad?' asked Preston.

Drinkwater's lower lip trembled as he seemed to consider the inadequacy of Preston's laconic query. He bore all the signs of a man on the verge of a nervous crack-up. There was visible effort in his attempt to keep his voice under control.

'Bad?' he repeated. 'Bad? Do you know what these Communist bastards are doing over there? Do you?'

'Easy, Captain,' said Maitland. 'Preston and Mackenzie are not unacquainted with Communist brutality. Just tell them what you saw.'

Drinkwater drew a hand wearily over his eyes.

'I'm sorry. It's just that I haven't had much sleep lately and being hunted by these bastards has played hell with my sunny disposition.'

'You said that the EAM police were taking Peristeri apart?' prompted Mackenzie.

'Yes. House by house and street by street. Gangs of the thugs have been arresting everybody they had the slightest doubt about. Old men, women, whole families. The lucky ones were herded away.' He snorted: 'Prisoners of war, they said, for Christ's sake! Prisoners of war! God knows where they've taken them.'

'What about the unlucky ones?' asked Preston.

'They were shooting them by the hundred. I counted nearly two hundred bodies on two separate occasions. All ages – from old people to toddlers barely four years old. Hands tied behind their backs and tossed into trenches in the street like garbage.'

Drinkwater's listeners were silent, their horror and revulsion etched plainly on their faces. Drinkwater stared into space, seeing only the images which he would never erase from his mind. He spoke now, almost to himself.

'I want to go back. A hundred paras is all I need. I've memorised faces. I'd start with their top man, that butcher Spiro.'

'I'm afraid we've got other work to do,' said Maitland gruffly.

Drinkwater turned to face him, his eyes wide with passionate appeal.

'Whatever you want me to do, sir, remember I'm a fighting man. Give me work with a gun in my hand.'

Maitland put an understanding hand on Drinkwater's shoulder.

'If it's any consolation, you'll be in the field and you'll be armed. All three of you. But your job will be to use your brains and your knowledge of the enemy to sniff out his intentions. I am very much afraid that he may try a major piece of mischief in the next few days.'

Maitland dropped his bombshell quietly.

'Winston Churchill is arriving in Athens tomorrow,' he announced, his voice barely more than a whisper. His audience was suitably stunned. Maitland went on: 'Aginst the advice of myself and certain others, I must add. We are not burdened with the personal security of the Prime Minister – but his visit does create very considerable problems, in view of the situation here. It particularly will strain the resources of every branch of our intelligence and counter-intelligence services.

'But this is madness, sir,' said Mackenzie. 'Doesn't the Prime Minister know there's hardly a street in Athens that isn't under sniper fire from across the river?'

'If ELAS find out, there's no saying what they might try,' said Preston.

Maitland raised a silencing hand.

'I know the dangers – but the Prime Minister wouldn't be put off. Worse still, the other side know he's coming. An invitation was made yesterday to the ELAS leaders to meet the Prime Minister and Field-Marshall Alexander for talks.'

'You've got to be joking,' said Preston.

'I wish I were,' said Maitland. 'I don't need to tell any of you what a bargaining lever it would be for EAM if they had Churchill as a hostage as well as the ten thousand civilian hostages they're threatening to shoot unless we meet their demands.'

'You think they'll make a grab for Mr Churchill?' asked Preston.

Maitland's expression was bleak.

'I fear that very much. They've got the strength. They only need to knock one big hole in our perimeter and they could be swarming all over central Athens.'

'What exactly do you want us to do, sir?' asked Mackenzie.

'I'm going to give you roving commissions in western Athens. You all have a better knowledge of the political ramifications than the Intelligence chaps serving with the troops, and you all speak Greek. Now all Intelligence information will be fed back to HQ anyway, but I want you three to be near the action, to be on the spot to investigate any straw in the wind that bears any connection with Churchill's visit. If anything turns up, I may pull you all in to mount our own counter-operation – but your job will be to make sure the purely Army chaps don't let anything vital slip through their fingers.'

Maitland outlined what each man had to do: from interrogating newly captured prisoners to giving local commanders details of the ELAS-held territory they faced. They were to assess every item of Intelligence for its political as well as military significance.

'We are in a battle situation here,' he said. 'The city – what we have of it – is under siege . . . And with Churchill coming, we're putting a barrel of political dynamite right down in the middle of it. Scobie will have squads of troops guarding against stray bullets hitting the dynamite barrel. You will make damned sure that we get warning of any deliberate attempt to blow it sky-high.'

Drinkwater was allotted the Peristeri sector in the north, Mackenzie to the centre sector, while Preston would be in the most southerly sector at Phaleron Bay, facing Piraeus. Another team composed of both intelligence and counter-intelligence agents would undertake similar mobile roles on the extreme northern and eastern perimeters.

Mackenzie was asked to remain behind after Drinkwater and Preston had been dismissed to find their promised transport. Maitland glared at him when they were alone.

'I intended to tear you off a strip, young man, but I have more important things to worry about right now than your crass stupidity.'

'Sir?'

'Your revelations last night of your relationship with the Kirkos woman. I only spared you the rough edge of my tongue last night because I was a damned sight more concerned about Nikos Stratou turning up in Athens. You realise you were a bloody fool with that woman, Mackenzie?'

'I know, sir.' He returned Maitland's stare pugnaciously. 'But I did tell you I was a pretty lousy spy.'

'Yes, you did. You didn't tell me just how incompetent though! You should have been more frank with me in the first place, damnit! Instead of springing it on me at this late date that you're the father of her child. Christ Almighty, what a mess!'

Mackenzie remained silent.

'She refused your offer to get her out of Piraeus?' Maitland asked more calmly.

'Yes, sir.'

'Why do you think she's staying with Kirkos? From all accounts he treated her very badly before.'

'All she cares about now, sir, is the baby. I think she's had more than she can take. She just wants to be left in peace.'

'And you believed this story of hers about being deported and escaping in Italy and being rescued by a mysterious Italian called Artemis?'

'I know none of it makes much sense but I'm convinced she was telling me the truth. She has been used – by Artemis, whoever he is, and by her husband.'

'What makes you so sure?'

'You only need to see her, sir. What she has gone through is marked in every line of her face. There is a terrible change in her. The only thing that matters in this world to her is her baby. I don't think she questioned too closely any of the odd things that happened to her because all she was thinking about was the baby. She didn't think twice about Artemis or Stratou or what they put her up to . . . All she saw was a heaven-sent chance to get back here to her baby.'

'But that business of dressing up as a man. Why pick a woman for a job like that in the first place? It's the sort of crazy thing our own people would dream up, not the Abwehr. Why did they do it?'

'The point is that it worked,' said Mackenzie. 'Artemis got his precious gifts to Greece.'

'Yes,' mused Maitland. 'And they've followed the old legend almost to the letter. Did you know that Procris returned to Greece with the gifts, dressed as a youth?'

'No, sir, I didn't. Was that the end of the story? I mean, what happened to her?'

'It all ended rather unhappily for Procris, I'm afraid,' said Maitland. 'Don't you know what happened to her? She suspected that Cephalus was playing around with another woman and spied on him. He accidentally killed her with the hunting spear she had brought to him.'

'Poor Procris,' said Mackenzie. 'And so much for Greek legends! I'm happy to say that our Procris was very much alive at this time yesterday – and I hope she stays that way. What happened to Cephalus in the story? Did he live happily ever after?'

'I don't know what happened to Cephalus. Maybe we should consult the Oracle at Delphi. What bothers me in our present-day legend is the part played by one

Nikos Stratou. He must have had a good idea we were on to him in Italy. He must have known and the Germans must have known that he was "blown" – all washed up! Yet he sneaks back across our lines and gets all the way to Greece to deliver ... *what*? What was so important that would make a blown agent commit the cardinal sin of re-exposing himself again the way that he did?'

Maitland pounded a fist on the table.

'I'll tell you this, Mackenzie. He didn't do it for the sake of a few boxes of rifles! What the hell was in these baths wagons?'

'Just give me a couple of hundred of Drinkwater's paratroops and we can damned soon find out,' answered Mackenzie. 'It has to be that piece of ironmongery that they were hauling up the hill behind Piraeus the other night. Didn't the RAF get any pictures of that hill? I asked Brady to try to organise it.'

'He did,' said Maitland, and walked to a cabinet at the far end of the trailer. From a drawer, he took a pile of photographic prints. He laid these blow-ups in overlapping sequence on the table in front of Mackenzie.

'There you are! Every square inch of land between the Ilissus and Daphni. These are the heights there ... where you said all the activity was.'

Mackenzie studied the photgraphs with a puzzled frown.

'I can make out Castella. And this is the old Turkish harbour. But the hills behind the town haven't come out too well, have they?'

'Snow,' said Maitland. 'That bloody snow! If there's anything on these hills, it has been beautifully covered by the deep and crisp and even.'

'What's this dark line here?' Mackenzie pointed to what looked like a black hair on an expanse of white.

'I'm told it's a track. Apparently the Jerries had a

radar station or something of the sort up on the hill. That dark line is the track leading to what's left of their installations. Look, you can see tones of light grey at one end. The reconnaissance experts say it could be a bunker of some kind but there's nothing to suggest it's occupied.'

'It's worth finding out.'

'I agree,' said Maitland. 'You're not the only one to think it's worth a special raid. I even went so far as to suggest it to the GOC yesterday.'

'He vetoes it?'

'Categorically. He can't spare the troops. The priority is re-taking the docks and getting them operational. He thinks the evidence is too scanty for a special operation which could have absolutely nothing to show for it at the end but a load of casualties.'

'Does it need a big force? What about half a dozen picked men making a night drop on the east summit?'

'Are you volunteering?'

Mackenzie took his time about answering.

'Why not? I don't have anything planned for Christmas.'

Mackenzie drove the jeep down Ermou Street towards the Sacred Gates, site of the ancient wall of Athens and meeting-place of the roads from Piraeus, Eleusis and Boeotia. The whine of a rifle bullet caused the Signals Sergeant beside him to duck. Simultaneously, Mackenzie realised that he was being waved to the side of the road by a steel-helmeted soldier ahead.

He braked and brought the jeep to a halt in the lee of a high sandbag wall. The soldier from the road ducked smartly in beside them.

'Bit of sniper fire, sir. I wouldn't go any further for the moment unless you have to. Our lads are getting a line on the beggar's position. I'd give it five minutes.'

'Thanks,' said Mackenzie. 'Time we were calling in

anyway.' He turned to the Sergeant, who had pulled a pack of cigarettes from his pocket. 'Like to get HQ on the blower, Sergeant? Let them know where we are and ask them if they've got anything for us.'

The Sergeant put his cigarettes away with an air of resignation.

'Right, sir.'

Mackenzie unfolded a map.

'Tell 'em we're on Ermou Street and just west of the junction with Iphaistiou Street.'

'Will you say that last one again, sir?'

Mackenzie repeated the street name. He wondered how Preston was getting on. He tried to imagine what the American's reaction would be when he heard about the project night drop. He could guess:

'You actually volunteered to jump out of an aeroplane on to the top of a freezing mountain in the middle of the night? You are crazy out of your skull!' And he'd want to get in on the act.

The Sergeant interrupted his thoughts.

'There's a message from Leader Six. He wants you to go immediately to the Plaka district and contact a Captain Taylor of the Royal Engineers on Phlessa Street. He'll be on the lookout for you.'

Mackenzie consulted his map. He thought about making a U-turn but, remembering the sniper, he reversed the jeep for nearly a block, backed into an entry and then headed east along Ermou Stret. Turning into Monastiraki square, he swung left past the entrance to Hadrian's Library and powered the jeep towards Adrianou Street and the myriad lanes of the Plaka.

Captain Taylor of the Royal Engineers was leaning against the radiator grille of a fifteen-hundredweight truck parked half way along Phlessa Street. He stubbed out a cigarette under his heel and moved out into the middle of the road when he saw the approaching jeep.

'You the Johnnie from the Brains Department?' he asked Mackenzie cheerfully.

'Brains Department?'

'Intelligence. They said they were sending somebody for the box of tricks.'

Mackenzie looked at the man blankly. Captain Taylor, if this was him, seemed incapable of straightforward communication.

'I got a hurry signal to contact Captain Taylor, Royal Engineers. I wasn't given any details. Is your name Taylor?'

'In the flesh. Follow me, Captain. It's not far – three minutes' walk and all uphill.' He turned on his heel and took off at a brisk pace. Mackenzie ran to catch up with him.

'What exactly is the panic?' he asked.

'You must have heard the bang,' said Taylor. 'Hell of a clap at about five this morning. Damned shame, really . . . It was a pretty little church.'

'I don't know what the hell you're talking about, Captain,' said Mackenzie impatiently. 'Would you like to tell me exactly what happened?'

Taylor stopped and regarded Mackenzie with the weary look of one who has to go through life humouring his duller-witted brethren.

'The Church of St John Chrysostom was blown up at about five o'clock this morning. You'll see the shambles in a minute. Nobody knows what caused the explosion although some of the locals are trying to make out it was a bomb dropped from a British plane. Anyway, the priest and some helpers started clearing the wreckage at daylight to recover the holy icons from the altar. They found the bodies of a young woman and a baby. They also found what they thought was a time-bomb – and sent for me.'

'You're Bomb Disposal?'

'That's me – if it ticks we'll tackle it. It's a job with

421

never a dull moment but the life insurance premiums are exorbitant.'

Mackenzie smiled. He had always believed that Bomb Disposal volunteers had to be rather crazy. Taylor seemed to confirm it.

'I've had sabotage training and I know how to blow-things up. Dismantling bombs is something else again,' said Mackenzie. 'Why did they send for me?'

'Because it isn't a bomb,' said Taylor. 'The box was inside what was left of a baby's pram, somewhat battered but still more or less in one piece. I had to cut one side of the object away to get inside it.'

'Box?' said Mackenzie suddenly. 'A grey metal box about twelve to fifteen inches square?'

'Yeah. How did you know?'

Mackenzie felt an icy shiver raise the hairs on the back of his neck. The sensation of chill tickled down his spine. A woman, a baby, and a mysterious box!

Taylor was staring at him, unable to guess at the reasons for the draining of colour from Mackenzie's face and the look of horror he saw frozen there.

'I want to see the bodies,' Mackenzie said, his voice a whisper.

'They're up here.'

Taylor led they way up a lane to a narrow street. Directly facing them was the ruins of the Church of St John Chrysostom. Two groups of soldiers, their rifles cradled in their arms, were keeping a crowd of curious Greek civilians away from the scene. The street had been blocked off in both directions.

A bearded priest in black robes stood sentinel between two adjacent mounds covered by grey blankets. Mackenzie approached him. He knelt beside the bigger of the blanket-covered mounds.

'May I, Pater?' he said to the priest. 'I think I know them.'

The priest nodded.

Mackenzie turned down the corner of the blanket.

Christina's face had miraculously escaped injury. There was even a serenity about her in the repose of death. Not as much as a smudge of grime marred the smooth oval of her countenance beneath the short, wispy, raven hair.

Mackenzie looked up at the priest questioningly.

'I washed her face and head with wine, my son. Be content to look only at her face.'

'Thank you, Pater.'

He replaced the fold of blanket and stood up.

'Have you any idea how she came to be in the church, Pater?'

'She is not one of my flock. I do not know how she came to be here with the little one or what she sought in God's house in the middle of the night.'

'Peace,' murmured Mackenzie. 'I think she was looking for peace.'

'Then she has found it, my son. She has found it in the redeeming arms of our Saviour. Did you know her?'

'Yes.'

Mackenzie approached the smaller of the two covered mounds. He drew aside the blanket to look on the face of his son for the first time. An agony of emotion heaved up in him at the sight of the pathetic, lifeless bundle. He tried to choke back the sob but a pain-racked sound escaped from his throat. He knelt, covering his face with a hand as he tried to recover his composure.

The priest came behind him and placed a hand on his shoulder. Mackenzie could hear the quiet passion of the priest's softly spoken prayer.

'Lord, how long shall the wicked, how long shall the wicked triumph? They break in pieces thy people. They slay the widow and the stranger, and murder the fatherless. Who will rise up for me against the workers of iniquity? The wicked gather themselves together against the sound of the righteous and condemn the innocent blood. But the Lord is my defence and my God is the rock of my refuge . . .'

Mackenzie waited until he had finished. He stood and shook the priest's hand.

Taylor was standing some distance away, subdued and still mystified by the connection between the dead woman and the fierce-looking officer with the black eye-patch. No emotion showed on Mackenzie's face as he strode towards Taylor.

'Where's the box you were talking about, Captain Taylor?'

'Over there.' He pointed towards the rubble of the church. The battered box was sitting on top of a flat piece of stone.

Mackenzie walked over and studied it without touching it. Taylor removed a square of metal.

'I cut away one side to get into it,' he said.

'That was taking a risk, wasn't it?' said Mackenzie.

Taylor shrugged.

'Somebody had to do it. It wasn't like any booby-trap I've ever seen – and I've seen plenty.

'You said it wasn't a bomb?'

'No, I think it's an electronic signalling device, a radio. A very sophisticated one. Not that I'm an expert on radios. But it reminds me of a gadget I saw in Stuttgart before the war.'

'What kind of gadget?'

'It was on show at a science exhibition – a gadget for linking traffic signals. The idea was that in a long street with a whole series of traffic lights, you controlled all the lights from one master light. This contained a small transmitter which sent out a series of vibrations like a lighthouse beam. These were picked up by tiny receivers in all the other traffic lights. When the master light turned to red, all the other lights turned red. Or maybe it was green . . . I can't remember.'

'You think this is a transmitter?'

424

'Yes. See these bell-shaped things here?' He indicated with his forefinger. 'These are the transmitter heads. They rotate and are aligned to give out signals in any direction along a vertical line from the surface of the diaphragm.'

'I'll take your word for it. What's the significance?'

Taylor sighed. He took a notebook and pencil from his breast pocket.

'I'll draw you a picture,' he said. 'This little gadget, if placed on the ground, would transmit upwards . . . into the air. In a sweeping series of arcs. That's where it's different from the traffic-light gadget. It was set horizontally, sending out a beam which was more or less parallel with the earth.'

He drew furiously for a moment on his notebook, tore out the sheet of paper and passed it ot Mackenzie. He had drawn a square box at the foot of the page. From it radiated dotted lines in the shape of a fan.

Mackenzie studied it.

'This box sends out beams into the atmosphere like this?' he said. 'Like a curved ice-cream cone?'

Taylor beamed.

'Yes. And the only way of picking up the signals would be to fly into the ice-cream cone with a special electro-magnetic received and tuned to the same ultra-high frequency.'

Taylor's beam gave way to a frown.

'I had it all worked out what caused the explosion here, but there's an almighty flaw in my theory.'

'At least you have a theory,' said Mackenzie. 'My brain stopped coping with this five minutes ago. What was your theory?'

'Radio-controlled bombs. I reckoned that when the Jerries cleared out of Athens in October, they left dozens of these little transmitters lying about all over the city. They would wait until everything here was back to normal and then send over some bombers with radio-

425

controlled bombs which would go sailing down on their pre-selected targets.'

'And the flaw you mentioned?'

'The target,' said Taylor. 'A tiny church that was over a thousand years old? A church that at five in the morning should have been deserted? And only one bomb. It just doesn't make sense.'

'It does if you know that that little box was only brought here during the night and that the woman who brought it had no idea what it was.'

Taylor's eyes widened.

'The woman? *She* brought it? In the pram? You knew her, didn't you?'

'Yes, I knew her,' said Mackenzie grimly. 'And I know where there are two more boxes just like that one.'

CHAPTER TWENTY-NINE

Christmas Day

The rendezvous was for two o'clock on Christmas morning. It had been fixed as a result of a sealed message delivered to the British Embassy by a British officer who had been an ELAS prisoner since the first day of hostilities. The officer had been charged by his captors, as a condition of his release, to deliver the sealed envelope to the British Ambassador and no one else. The message inside was from the ELAS leader who called himself General Cephalus.

Its content was of a nature that could not be taken lightly.

Cephalus sought safe conduct for a personal emissary to meet the British Ambassador or his nominee. Total secrecy was necessary and must be guaranteed. The reason for the meeting could not be disclosed, other than to say it was directly concerned with the safety of the British Prime Minister during his visit to Athens.

Mackenzie, Preston and Drinkwater sat in the closed truck, waiting.

All three men were acutely aware of the isolation and vulnerability of their position. They had followed instructions precisely: driving west out of central Athens, across the Peristeri-Piraeus road and south-west along the main thoroughfare through north Piraeus. They were now deep inside ELAS territory, having passed through the most forward British positions a mile back along the road.

Their progress had been unimpeded. And the section of the front through which they had passed had been uncannily quiet. Both sides of the line in this area had been told that a twenty-four-hour Christmas truce would be operative locally from midnight, and that attempts were being made to extend the truce to other zones.

Mackenzie looked at his watch.

'It's two o'clock,' he announced.

The words were no sooner spoken than a man emerged from the shadows of a lane to the right. He walked out into the middle of the road and came towards the truck.

'This looks like our man,' muttered Mackenzie. He got out of the truck.

'You are punctual,' said the stranger in English. 'Is everything arranged?'

'We've kept exactly to instructions.'

'Good,' said the man. He stuck out a hand. 'I am Major Voutsas, special emissary of General Cephalus.'

Mackenzie shook the hand.

'I'm a British officer. I'll take you to the Ambassador's representative. We'll ride in the back of the truck.'

The man hesitated.

'You are not taking me to the Ambassador himself?'

'The Ambassador is not available. I can assure you that his representative has full powers.'

Voutsas still hesitated. Then, with a shrug of his shoulders, he followed Mackenzie round the back of the truck and climbed in.

Mackenzie thumped on the driver's partition.

'Home, James.'

Preston U-turned the truck and, at a cautious thirty miles an hour, headed it east towards Athens. There was no sign of ELAS troops anywhere along the road. The first sign of life they encountered was a British soldier stepping into the road and ordering them to pull into the side. They were quickly waved through.

Maitland's HQ had been stripped of wall-maps and there wasn't a document or scrap of paper visible when Mackenzie ushered Voutsas into the caravan trailer.

There was little preliminary discussion. Maitland said that he wished his three officers to be present and Voutsas raised no objection. Maitland eyed Voutsas in his lofty, school-masterly way.

'Perhaps you will state what you have come here to say, Major Voutsas.'

'I have come to give a warning,' said Voutsas.

'Go on,' said Maitland.

'General Cephalus, like all Greeks, deeply regrets the present hostilities between our forces. Like all Greeks, he wants the British to leave us to govern our own affairs. He says that if the British do leave, he will do everything in his power to restore peace and prosperity to all sections of the Greek nation and seek harmonious relations with all freedom-loving peoples.'

'Most admirable intentions, I am sure,' said Maitland. 'But you mentioned a warning.'

'I am coming to that,' said Voutsas. 'First, I want to make clear the reasons for General Cephalus taking a great risk in bothering to make a warning when it is not incumbent on him to do so. His own interests might be better served by silence. Since, however, he is a man of goodwill and politically moderate, he feels impelled to act and avert possible tragedy. He is a realistic man who realises that, sooner or later, our two sides must stop fighting and start talking. When that happens, he trusts that you will remember his goodwill and moderation.'

Maitland smiled.

'One good turn deserves another, eh, Major? General Cephalus wants to do us a good turn now in the hope that we shall return the compliment at a future date?'

'He does not want the country to become a puppet of the Russians any more than he wants Greece to be a puppet of the British. He is alarmed by some of the extreme elements in EAM with whom, by necessity, he had to ally himself to rid the country of the Nazis.'

'Very well,' said Maitland, 'let us agree that you have established that General Cephalus is a reasonable man with moderate aims. What does he wish to warn us about?'

'He has discovered that an attempt is to be made on the life of Winston Churchill when he arrives in Athens tomorrow.'

Maitland's expression did not change.

'How? When? Where?'

'The man behind it is General Spiro. He is backed strongly by Moscow.' Voutsas paused and ran his tongue around his lips. 'It is believed that Churchill will be staying at the Grande Bretagne Hotel, where Papandreou and most of his puppet Government are already staying . . .'

'Yes?'

'Spiro intends to blow up the Grande Bretagne.'

'Is there any way you can prove this?' asked Maitland softly.

'Yes. A large quantity of dynamite has been hidden underneath the hotel. If you want to make a thorough search, you will find it.'

'How was it to be set off?'

'Spiro has spies in the city. One of his men was to place a small time-bomb near the dynamite tomorrow. That is all we know. I have no other information.

Maitland stood up.

'Major Voutsas, we are deeply indebted to you and General Cephalus for telling us this. You will find that the British Government is not unmindful and far from unappreciative.

Mackenzie was about to say something but Maitland

silenced him with a look. Preston and Drinkwater were given the task of escorting Voutsas back to Piraeus. When they had gone, Maitland lit a cigarette and inhaled the smoke deeply into his lungs as if he could not have survived a moment longer without it.

'I'm beginning to feel the strain,' he confided. 'I found it difficult to talk to that man and keep up a show of being cool, calm and unflappable. Christ, to hear him talk, you would think that Kirkos is a candidate for canonisation. I wanted to throw up.'

'So did I,' said Mackenzie. 'Does this alter our plans?'

'No,' said Maitland, drawing another lungful of smoke. 'Operation Snowdrop goes on and I want you to get on to the details right away. Fix up a meeting with Squadron-Leader Garrett at Kalamaki. He's promised a back-up fighter strike if necessary. He'll make available all the weapons you need from the RAF Regiment armoury. If you have any problems, contact me.'

'Do we still aim for sunset tomorrow?' Mackenzie had a sudden thought and looked at his watch. 'I mean *tonight*. Do you realise, sir, that it is now half-past three on Christmas morning?'

'And what a bloody way to spend it!' said Maitland with feeling. 'No, Mac, getting this operation off the ground as quickly as that is pushing things. I'll do my damnedest to keep Winston out of Athens for the next forty-eight hours. So, you aim to be well under way by first light on Boxing Day. That will give you and others time to get things properly organised and get some rest.'

'Right, sir. Anything else?'

'Yes. Wake up the chaps next door and tell them I want to organise an immediate search of the Grande Bretagne. I also want a lift to the Embassy, preferably in an armoured car. A sniper damned near got me on the way down here and I don't particularly want to be killed before I give His Excellency the low-down on our little chat with Comrade Voutsas.'

'Right, sir. Happy Christmas.'

'And the same to you. Oh, and Mac . . .'

'Yes, sir?'

'Sorry about the woman and the little boy.' There was an awkward silence, and then Maitland added: 'Why do you think she had that transmitter gadget in the baby's pram?'

'Because I said we wanted to lay our hands on one. I think she was trying to find me.'

'Maybe you're lucky she didn't find you. You could have been dead, too.

'Part of me is,' said Mackenzie. He went out, leaving Maitland staring thoughtfully after him.

Mackenzie managed three and a half hours' sleep. It was a sleep troubled by images of Christina Kirkos and Eleni Binas. He had arranged to see Squadron-Leader Garrett at Kalamaki at nine, and it was just before eight when he left the Grande Bretagne.

The hotel was in an uproar. A search of the premises which had started at four-thirty in the morning had led to a frightening discovery. Several tons of explosive had been discovered in the basement. Since daylight, soldiers had been carrying out crates of dynamite and loading it into trucks. There was enough of the stuff to have blown up half of Athens.

The revelation to the British that explosives were hidden in the Grande Bretagne had been a calculated gamble on the part of George Kirkos. It had two aims. The first was to make the British aware that at least one ELAS commander with a formidable army at his back was not aligning himself with the Extreme Left of EAM and was, therefore, a possible alternative leader of Greece to Papandreou on the one hand and an out-and-out Communist on the other. The second aim was to lull the British into the belief that the main thrust of any plot against Churchill had been foiled and that, if

432

anything now happened to the British Prime Minister, the suspicion would fall on Spiro, not Kirkos.

'You did well,' he told Voutsas. 'You say that the British Ambassador's man stated that his Government would not be unappreciative.'

The pair were on the balcony outside Kirkos's headquarters at the Paradissos Hotel.

'They will have found the dynamite by now,' said Voutsas.

'Yes,' nodded Kirkos. 'Now they will have no reason to doubt my credibility or good faith if anyone should point a finger. What about my invitation to Spiro?'

'He suspects nothing. He is coming here at noon to see you. And the Russian, Karolov, is coming with him.'

'Good, good. Spiro has never been able to resist conspiracy. You just hinted, I hope?'

'I told Spiro that you were unhappy at the way Natsinas always seemed to be playing the pair of you off against one another and that you wanted to talk about it.'

'Both Spiro and Karolov would love to clip Natsinas's wings. And mine.'

'That's why they're coming so eagerly,' said Voutsas. 'They hope that you will help them to topple Natsinas and that they'll be able to send you down with the wreck.'

Both men turned at the sound of a light step behind them.

'How do I look?'

The girl pirouetted like a fashion model, so that they could admire her.

'You look wonderful, Petrea. Wonderful!' Kirkos clapped his hands in approval.

She was dressed in a neatly tailored khaki uniform of tunic and skirt, a cap daintily perched on her blonde hair. A tab on each shoulder had the letters UNRRA

433

embroidered on them. Immediately below was a colourful patch miniature of the American flag.

'I'm ready to go,' she announced. 'The jeep is loaded up.'

'Where is Stratou?' asked Kirkos.

'He is ready – but jumpy. Do you think he is the right man for this?'

'He's the only one,' said Kirkos. 'I told him that I have no one with his command of English. Perhaps it is the disguise, he does not like.'

'He is much to tall and slim for the part. He should have been fat and jolly-faced,' said Petrea.

Kirkos laughed.

'I am dying to see what he looks like. I think it was a stroke of genius on my part. Who would have thought to find such an outfit with all these British Navy stores? Go and get Stratou, so that Voutsas here can see him.'

She returned a few minutes later with Nikos Stratou, whose sheepish expression was concealed by a white false beard and whiskers. He wore the red hood and coat of Santa Claus.

Kirkos's unrestrained laughter at the sight of him did not amuse Stratou.

'It is magnificent!' cried Kirkos.

'I feel like something from a sideshow,' complained Stratou.

'No one will question you in that,' said Kirkos. 'You will be cheered wherever you go by those sentimental British.'

'And the blood won't show if you are shot,' said Petrea scornfully. 'Are you afraid?'

He flashed her a look of malevolence.

'Yes, I am. The troops guarding the Parliament Building are from the Rimini Brigade. It only needs one of them to recognise me and the game will be up for both of us. Do I have to remind you that your life is at stake, too?'

434

'I am not afraid to die for Greece,' Petrea snapped back at him.

'Just so long as you know the risks,' said Stratou. 'That uniform you're wearing came off the back of a very pretty little American girl who came into Piraeus a couple of days ago to hand out lollipops to starving kids. Her friends over the other side of the river won't be overjoyed if they ever find out what happened to her.'

'They never will find out.'

'Of course they won't,' said Kirkos. 'Everything will work like a charm, you'll see. Have you both got your identity documents and passes?'

'Yes,' they chorused sullenly.

'It's time to go then, said Kirkos. 'Where did you leave your sacks, Nikos?'

'They're downstairs.'

'Let's get them then. I don't trust my men to keep their hands off all those cartons of American cigarettes. It would be too bad if Father Christmas had no bounty to distribute to the gallant British soldiers.'

In the courtyard of the Paradissos several of Kirkos's guerrillas were grouped round a jeep, speculating amongst themselves on what use this prize of war was to be put to. Kirkos ordered them away without enlightening them.

The vehicle had Stars-and-Stripes placards tied over the radiator and tail. The doors, too, were emblazoned with the American flag. Stanchions had been fitted to the body in the mid-section and these supported a white wooden frame above and behind the front seats. On the white frame in black letters were the initials UNRRA.

The back seats had been removed and the area was piled high with wooden crates. These carried Red Cross labels and had been stamped: AMERICAN RED CROSS – EUROPEAN RELIEF.

The crates also bore stencilled clues to their contents.

More were marked 'Disinfectant' and carried warnings such as 'This Side Up' and 'Glass – Handle with Care'.

Beside the cargo, Nikos Stratou deposited two Santa Claus sacks. They bulged with American cigarettes which had been plundered from the British during the capture of Piraeus.

Stratou climbed into the passenger seat. Petrea took the wheel. Kirkos stood by the driver's seat, his eyes aglow with excitement.

'You know what to do?'

'We've been over it a hundred times,' said Petrea. 'All going well, we should be back here by noon.'

'Good luck, then.'

Petrea revved the motor of the jeep. She gave a tight smile and a wave of the hand. Kirkos raised a hand in answering salute as the jeep moved forward up the gentle incline into the roadway.

They were quickly passed through three guerrilla strong-points commanding road intersections. They emerged eventually on the Athens road close to the point where Mackenzie had picked up Voutsas in the early hours of the morning.

Petrea's foot on the accelerator faltered slightly at the sight of British uniforms ahead. There were soldiers in view on both sides of the road. Some moved out to bar the middle of the road, guns raised, as the jeep approached.

'Leave all the talking to me,' snapped Stratou. He stood up in the jeep, his hands on the top frame of the windshield, as the vehicle slowed to a stop.

'Merry Christmas, boys. Merry Christmas,' he shouted.

A young lieutenant – who had been as nervous as a kitten during an uneasy minute of the local truce – advanced towards the jeep. He felt that the end of the truce could come at any minute and would be announced by a sniper's bullet from the building occu-

436

pied by ELAS guerrillas just five hundred yards away. He didn't want to be the target of that bullet.

'Do we get back to Athens this way, Lieutenant?' the Santa Claus was saying to him. The young officer stared at the figure in the jeep, uncertain and bemused. He became aware that several of his men, off the road, were directing wolf-whistles at the jeep's pretty driver. He did not immediately answer the Santa Claus. Instead he shouted back over his shoulder:

'Sergeant Leach, tell those men to stop that whistling.'

He looked up at the Santa Claus.

'You're on the road to Athens all right. Where have you come from?'

'We got kinda lost. We've been touring the lines giving out smokes. Would your boys like some cigarettes, Lieutenant?'

'I don't know. I . . .'

His words died away as Stratou fished in his sack and, producing a two-hundred carton of Chesterfields, threw it in his direction. The Lieutenant caught it and looked at it in surprise.

'Thanks. This is jolly decent of you.'

'There's more,' said Stratou, and tossed three cartons towards the soldiers blocking the road.

'Happy Christmas, boys. Sorry we don't have a case of beer to go with the smokes.'

The men dived for the cartons with whoops of delight.

'Share 'em out now,' shouted Stratou. 'A twenty pack for everybody.' He glanced down towards the young officer. 'D'you want to see our papers, Lieutenant? Mine were issued for the North Pole.'

The Lieutenant smiled shyly.

'I wouldn't dream of holding up Santa Claus. Thanks for the cigarettes, Santa. And a very merry Christmas.'

He waved his men out of the way.

Petrea drove the jeep slowly forward. The soldiers

on the road had already opened the cartons and were throwing twenty packs to comrades manning gun positions on the roof of a low flat building above the road.

Cheers and more wolf-whistles came Petrea's way as the jeep gathered speed.

Several times on the way into Athens, Stratou threw cigarettes from the jeep to knots of soldiers. Constitution Square was like an armed camp. Every corner was fortified and bristling with armed men – but the jeep's progress was as stately as a Roman triumph. Stratou continued to dispense cigarettes and greetings to warmly appreciative troops, making sure that one such distribution was made in full view of the guards entrenched around the Government buildings.

The men on guard-duty did not leave their posts to claim a share of the cigarettes being so freely handed out in front of their eyes, but the looks on their faces proclaimed their misery at being left out. Stratou, standing in the jeep, indicated to Petrea that she should drive between the banks of sandbags leading to the Government complex. They were promptly halted by an immaculately turned-out soldier. He wore British battledress with blancoed webbing and shining boots. A red tab at his shoulder bore the word 'Greece' in white letters and, beneath it, was the chevron of the Eighth Army.

Stratou handed him a carton of cigarettes and wished him a happy Christmas in English.

The soldier indicated that he should wait. He kept the cigarettes and called round the corner of the sandbag wall. A portable hut with a single window stood beyond the sandbags. From this emerged an elderly man in plain black uniform. He strapped a British-style steel helmet on to his head as he came.

He goggled in surprise at Stratou's Santa Claus outfit,

438

ogled Petrea briefly, and then beamed at the Stars-and-Stripes placard on the front of the jeep.

'American?' he inquired, nodding his head.

'That's right, General,' Stratou beamed in reply. 'Have some cigarettes with the best wishes of Uncle Sam. Do you speak English?'

'Sure, I speak good.'

He took a carton of cigarettes from Stratou. 'You want come inside offices of Government?'

'We sure do,' said Stratou. 'We got some stuff to deliver to . . . Now where the hell is it?' He fished inside his robe and hauled out a sheaf of documents. He selected one. 'I got here papers of identity but this bit of paper here tells about this stuff we got to deliver. It's for the office of the Foreign Ministry.'

'Ah, yes – office of Foreign Ministry,' said the man.

'I'll need some help,' said Stratou. 'Have you got any men who could help me unload these crates?' he jerked a thumb in the direction of the boxes in the back of the jeep. 'This stuff is from the International Red Cross. See – Red Cross!'

The man nodded eagerly.

'Yes, yes, I am knowing. Red Cross!'

He turned to the soldier and spoke to him in Greek.

'These Americans are crazy, eh? What do you think they've got in those boxes?'

'Ask him,' said the guard. 'Maybe it's more cigarettes. Or maybe whisky.'

'What you got in boxes?' the official asked Stratou.

Stratou prised a spare from the top crate, stretched a hand inside, and pulled out a bottle. He exhibited it to the man.

'Disinfectant.'

'What is this disin . . . What you said?'

Stratou mimed the action of pulling lavatory chain and then made a sprinkling motion with the bottle.

'It's for cleaning the john,' he said.

439

The man laughed. He turned to the guard.

'Whisky, eh? Maybe you'd like to get drunk on that stuff?' He described the function of the bottle's contents in an accurate but colourfully vulgar manner. The solider made a face.

'I show you where to go,' said the official.

He climbed on the step of the jeep and gave Petrea a friendly pat on the back of the neck. 'I would sooner sleep with her than you,' he shouted in Greek to the guard.

Stratou winked at Petrea as he sat down in the passenger seat. Her cheeks were crimson, but, otherwise, she gave no indication of understanding the comment.

Directed by the official, she drove the jeep round to the rear of the Foreign Ministry building. The man disappeared inside and returned moments later accompanied by two more elderly men. They wore dark suits which were shabby and threadbare. One man had a white apron around his waist.

The two newcomers seemed to be on the caretaking staff of the Ministry. They had not been told of any consignment of disinfectant but had no intention of arguing about gifts from America, whatever the commodity. With luck, they might be able to trade it for much-needed kerosene later on. Kerosene had been worth its weight in gold in Athens since the power-supply had been cut off.

'Where is all this stuff supposed to go?' asked one of the caretakers.

'We have no orders.' The gate official translated the query to Stratou.

'There is one case for every lavatory,' said Stratou. 'The Minister himself made a special request to the American Embassy. He has been afraid of an epidemic ever since the guerrillas blew up Hadrian's Reservoir and damaged the water supply. Apparently, there is a big conference in the Ministry tomorrow or the day after and the Minister is worried by the smell of the drains.'

The caretakers were all for putting the disinfectant in a basement store and leaving it there for someone else to sort out. Stratou began to swear a bit. The production of more cigarettes, however, won the caretaker round. He threw one of his sacks on the ground. There were still about forty two-hundred cartons in it.

'We're supposed to be handing these out to the soldiers,' he said to the gate-keeper, 'but I don't see any reason why you and these boys there shouldn't share them out between you if you saw that our orders were carried out. One crate of Pinefresh for every john on the premises was what we were told. If you guys don't do it, maybe I should speak to somebody on the Minister's staff.'

The gate official immediately took charge. He shouldered the sack and angrily told the caretakers that they wouldn't get a single cigarette if they didn't do exactly as the American wanted.

Stratou unloaded the crates while the two caretakers, carrying one load at a time, disappeared into the Ministry for periods of five minutes at a time. Forty minutes later, there wasn't a toilet or wash-room which did not have a case of Pinefresh sitting in one corner.

The second crate to be unloaded had been placed, as luck would have it, in the toilets adjacent to a ground-floor conference-room. It contained one of the X24 pilot transmitters. Another was in the last taken from the jeep. It had been placed in a wash-room used by female workers from the kitchen.

A cold wind was sweeping down from the mountains. From the window of Squadron-Leader Garrett's office hut at Kalamaki airfield, Mackenzie watched the bomber taxi to a halt. Two Spitfires flew in low after it

441

and then, with a tilt of their wings, soared away to the west.

A convoy of trucks and armoured cars moved out to the corner of the field where the bomber had taxied to a halt. The doors of the bomber were opened and a ladder placed against its side.

Maitland, huddled in a borrowed Navy duffle-coat, sat in the passenger seat of one of the trucks out on the field. He watched the small party troop aboard the aircraft. Field-Marshal Alexander was followed by the British Ambassador and then by Harold Macmillan, the British Government's political overlord for Italy and the Balkans. Maitland, who was not a superstitious man, found himself crossing his fingers and praying that one or all three would persuade Winston Churchill to stay out of Athens for the next two days.

Maitland looked at his watch. It was three minutes after two. He lit a cigarette and settled down to wait.

He had smoked nearly a complete pack of twenty before there were any more signs of activity from the aircraft. When the doors finally swung open again, a familiar figure in the uniform of Air Commodore of the Royal Air Force appeared at the top of the ladder and raised his left hand in the V-sign. He clutched a cigar in his right hand.

Troops and aircraft technicians in the vicinity raised a cheer. Churchill climbed down the ladder, followed by Anthony Eden, the Foreign Minister. They made their way towards one of the armoured cars.

Maitland got out of the truck and walked towards the Prime Minister. Churchill was wishing the driver of the armoured car a merry Christmas and shaking his hand. Recognising Maitland, the Prime Minister turned and proffered a hand.

'Compliments of the season, Maitland. I hope you are not going to have a go at me now. I have just survived two hours of the most persuasive counselling.'

'I trust you were receptive, sir. Welcome to Athens and my sincere wishes to you for a peaceful and happy Christmas.'

The Prime Minister glowed with good humour.

'Happy, I shall endeavour to make it,' he replied. 'Its peace I cannot guarantee.'

'Do you intend to stay, sir? The Ambassador promised to pass on my fears that it would be dangerous to stay in Athens, either at the Embassy or at the Grande Bretagne.'

Churchill smiled.

'That worried frown commends your concern for my welfare – but it sits heavily upon your countenance, Maitland,' he said roguishly. 'Do not worry. I have agreed to avail myself of the unfailing hospitality of the Royal Navy. Eden and I are off now to HMS *Ajax*. Perhaps you will come aboard this evening? I'd like to talk with you.'

'I shall make myself available, sir.'

'I am expecting Monsieur Papandreou and the Archbishop of Athens aboard at seven. Macmillan and others think everything will be solved if His Beatitude would publicly agree to becoming the Regent of Greece.'

'Damaskinos is a remarkable man,' said Maitland.

'So I have been told,' beamed Churchill. 'But I intend to find out for myself.'

Maitland watched the armoured car and its escort drive off the airfield and swing out on to the coast road to Phaleron Bay. The news that Churchill intended to spend the night aboard HMS *Ajax* was a considerable relief.

Maitland could not envisage the Prime Minister coming to any harm aboard the cruiser which had so distinguished itself at the Battle of the River Plate. The greatest risk aboard *Ajax* would come from exposure to the Royal Navy's traditional Christmastime hospitality.

Indeed, Christmas celebrations had been taking place

on *Ajax* since early morning. Other ships in the Saronic Gulf had been astonished to see crew members leap from the decks and swim around in the icy waters with much shrieking.

A measure of understanding came when binoculars focused on the spectacle revealed that the swimmers were being rewarded for their foolhardiness. When the swimmers scrambled back aboard, their skins purple with cold, death from exposure was averted by the induction of generous quantities of rum from casks on the after deck.

The enthusiasm with which the navymen were indulging their festivities had by no means abated when Maitland arrived at *Ajax* in the same launch as the Greek Prime Minister, whom Maitland knew and admired very much, and His Beatitude, the Regent Designate.

Papandreou went aboard first. Maitland waited until the Archbishop and a Government official had scaled the ladder before following them. The sight which greeted him at deck level made his eyes pop out.

A burly Welshman, dressed in what appeared to be a tutu, was playing rugby with the Archbishop's hat. His fancy dress, as Queen of the Fairies, did not flatter Leading Stoker Dai Evans. Nor was it apparent that sobriety was one of his outstanding characteristics.

'Come on now, boys,' he was yelling. 'Let's get a good three-quarter movement going here.' He tossed the Archbishop's hat to a half-naked Zulu warrior, who must have used several tins of boot polish to blacken his face and body.

Visualising an international incident of unprecedented proportions, Maitland took a deep breath, with the intention of using his parade-ground voice to acquaint the revelling sailors of their folly. Before he could utter a word however, there was a sudden movement to his left.

The black-skirted figure of the Archbishop was past him in a flash. The nearest sailors – dressed as a pirate, Tarzan and Little Bo-Peep respectively – fell like ninepins before the Archbishop's massive shoulders.

The Zulu warrior fell backwards, head over heels, surrendering the Archbishop's cylindrical head-piece and hood as he fell. His Beatitude retrieved his property and arranged it on his head. He righted the medallion of office which he wore on a chain round his neck and his bearded face split into a huge grin.

'*Hronia polla!*' he boomed, offering the traditional Christmas greeting of long life or, more literally, many years.

Leading Stoker Evans was gawping at Archbishop Damaskinos with surprise and admiration.

'Hey, bach, we could do with you in the front row at Pontypridd. Are you some kind of clergyman, then? I thought you was dressed up as Neptune, with that great beard and all.'

'*Hronia polla!*' repeated the Archbishop.

He was whisked away by a red-faced naval officer who muttered in an aside to Evans that keel-hauling was the least disagreeable fate which he and his mates could look forward to in the morning.

Maitland found himself staring at the Greek official who had preceded him up the ladder. The man wore a broad smile. Laughter was trembling on his lips and threatening to erupt uncontrollably.

Maitland felt his own face break into an answering smile. Then a laugh hiccoughed from him. Soon, both men were standing there laughing uproariously. Tears of merriment glistened in their eyes.

When, finally, the Greek was able to contain his mirth, he said:

'His Beatitude does not need a bodyguard. Did you know that as a young man his favourite sport was classic wrestling? They say few could match his strength.'

'I can believe it, my friend,' said Maitland. '*Hronia polla!*'

'*Hronia polla!*' replied the Greek and clasped Maitland's hand

Maitland's heart lifted. For the first time that day, something of the well-being and spirit of Christmas lit him from within. The good wishes of this stranger and the revealing human glimpse he had been given of the Archbishop warmed him in a strange way. He felt a sudden hope for starving, bleeding Greece.

In her long and chequered history, Greece had never been more in need of a heroic leader – a man of strength, humour, integrity and conciliating power, who could lead his people from the wilderness of hatred to peaceful unification. The thought occurred to Maitland that perhaps there was a God in heaven after all, and he had sent Damaskinos.

When Nikos Stratou and Petrea had failed to returned to the Paradissos by four in the afternoon of Christmas Day, a fierce demoniac fever seemed to descend on George Kirkos. The good luck which had smiled so constantly on his machinations appeared to be deserting him. For the first time in months, things were going seriously wrong.

It had been a bitter blow to learn – at the moment when he was orchestrating his final plans for the destruction of Churchill and the British-backed Greek leadership – that Wolarski, his ablest commander, was dead and that the British now held a quarter of the Piraeus. But he had accepted that. Some setbacks had to be expected.

Now, setbacks seemed to be occurring thick and fast.

The local truce which had allowed Voutsas and, later, Stratou and Petrea to pass into central Athens had given

Kirkos a breather to regroup his forces. But the cease-fire had been broken at eleven on Christmas morning – and there seemed no doubt to Kirkos that his own men were responsible.

Many of them had been drinking heavily – it was a national pastime at Christmas – and they had capped their celebrations by firing on the British command post where Stratou and Petrea had crossed into the British sector. Now, the guerrillas were being made to pay heavily for their folly. With the fragile truce giving way, the British had renewed their drive into Piraeus with steely determination. Half the port area was already in British hands and it seemed only a matter of time before the Paradissos would be cut off. A British drive towards the docks had turned north to link up with the forces pushing into North Piraeus from the east.

At just after four, Kirkos reluctantly made a decision. He decided to quit the Paradissos. Leaving a strong defence force around the hotel, he moved out with his personal bodyguard to direct operations from the hill above Piraeus, where his last seventy-five and the rocket-launcher were located.

Darkness was falling as the small party started their straggling ascent of the hill. With them went two prisoners: Karolov, the Russian agent, and Spiro. When the pair had arrived at Paradissos, Kirkos had ordered Voutsas to arrest both men. Then he had briefed one of his own men, Colonel Lougaris, on the timing of taking over command of Spiro's battalions in Peristeri. He had no fear of any resistance to the move on the part of Spiro's men, having prepared assiduously over a long period for the take-over. Indeed, many of Spiro's lieutenants had invited it. Spiro had always inspired fear and hatred in his men rather than loyalty, and Kirkos had never been in doubt that his way-going would provoke more cheers than tears.

In this, he had calculated correctly, but the ease with

which Spiro had been taken out of the game was cold comfort on a day when the bulk of Kirkos's army was being forced to concede far too much strategically important territory.

Looking out from the seventy-five emplacement at the top of the hill, George Kirkos was aware of an overwhelming loneliness. It ate like a cancer at the inner confidence which had been his strength over the past few years. This strength had grown with his ability to snatch at every blown reed of opportunity with unerring instinct.

Now, with the big prizes all within his reach, doubts crowded in. Was his sure touch deserting him? Had he made himself too dependent on weaker men to execute his plans with the will he would have employed?

From the moment when Kirkos had activated the first target-pilot for his death rockets, he had known he was committing himself to a course of action from which there could be no recall. All that had happened since had merely carried him further and further beyond the point of no return.

Making secret contact with the British, sending out Stratou and Petrea on their mission, arresting Spiro and Karolov . . . All three acts were simply emphatic endorsements of the irreversibility of his chosen course.

Each move had been a card played from the hand on which everything had been staked. Now, as the game neared its end, the tension was beginning to tell. It was a tension that had to be endured, and endured alone. There was no one to whom Kirkos could turn for help or reassurance. He had reached this point by believing only in himself and serving no one but himself.

He had always been sole witness to his own divinity. Suddenly, he longed for corroboration of the fact and it chilled him to realise that there was no one, not a single living soul, who could or would supply it.

What had happened to Nikos Stratou and Petrea?

More than anything else, it was the absence of any news of them which was unnerving him. They were now six hours overdue. Where were they? Had they reached the Foreign Ministry and accomplished their siting of the homing devices? Why had they not returned?

In fact, Nikos Stratou was at that moment approaching the limits of desperation.

He and Petrea had tried on four separate occasions since eleven in the morning to find a way back into Piraeus. Each time, they had run slap into street battles from which they had been lucky to escape with their lives. The American emblems on the jeep had cut little ice with the combatants.

On the first occasion, Petrea had reversed the jeep at top speed for nearly half a mile at the first sign of trouble. On the next two occasions, they had been ordered out of the battle-zone in no uncertain terms by irate British officers, one of whom had threatened to commandeer the jeep and arrest its occupants.

The fourth attempt had ended when a bullet had shattered the wind-screen and the jeep had careered out of control into a bank of rubble. Neither Stratou nor Petrea had been seriously hurt but both had been cut and bruised about the face.

Stratou had sweated blood getting the jeep back on the road and making sure that it was not damaged beyond use. Now, darkness had overtaken them and Petrea was urging him to make a fifth and final attempt to get through the British lines.

All Stratou's instincts told him to get back to mid-Athens and lie low until morning. There was a possibility they could reach the ELAS lines at night on foot, but to try it in the jeep was madness.

'Then I'll drive back alone!' Petrea screamed at him. 'You are a coward! I knew it from the very start.'

Stratou struck her savagely with the back of his hand.

'Shut up, you stupid bitch! You'll have every British

patrol in the neighbourhood down on us with that voice of yours.'

She cowered away from him, her lip bloody.

'Pig!' she muttered. 'Cowardly pig!'

He lifted his hand a second time but did not hit her. 'This is getting us nowhere,' he said.

They were sheltering a few yards from the jeep behind the crumbled walls of a shell-torn building. The street now seemed quiet and deserted whereas, only an hour before, one end had echoed to the constant bark of automatic weapons and the angry clump of bursting grenades.

'It is much quieter now. I think we should risk it,' persisted Petrea.

'Damn you,' snarled Stratou. 'I don't suppose I'll get any peace from you if we don't.'

He went over to the jeep and got behind the wheel.

'I'll drive,' he said. He had long since discarded the Santa Claus outfit. The UNRRA uniform, which he had been wearing underneath, was now torn and dust-bespattered.

He took the tyre lever and began systematically to knock the remaining glass from the windscreen. Petrea climbed into the passenger seat, her face sullen.

Stratou revved the motor. The sound bounced back at him from the buildings of the deserted street. The vehicle moved forward slowly.

They were on a down gradient. Stratou coasted the jeep. Ahead, the road curved right. As they neared the curve, Stratou could see figures moving. British soldiers were herding ELAS prisoners from a three-storey apartment block and urging them along the street towards the jeep. Stratou engaged the gear and gunned the throttle.

The jeep shot forward. Stratou got a glimpse of startled faces as he flicked on the headlights and powered the vehicle past the line of men. He was well round the curve now and could see a side street opening two hundred yards ahead on his right. The jeep shook as he double-declutched with the needle at fifty and threw the wheel round in a right-hand turn.

The manoeuvre nearly ejected Petrea but she clung on grimly. The new street was much narrower than the one they had left. The two-storey houses flanking both sides seemed to lean towards each other over their heads.

They had gone less than seventy yards when Stratou jumped on the brake. The street was blocked by two upturned flat wagons: the kind normally drawn by horses. Their shafts were slewed upwards against the houses at a crazy angle.

The jeep slid to a stop.

Stratou was dimly aware of something dropping from a roof-top above. The movement was caught at the widest extremity of his vision, somewhere behind his shoulder.

The object crashed on to the back floor of the jeep. Both Stratou and Petrea half-turned towards the sound and were consequently facing the wall of liquid flame which erupted and enveloped them.

Stratou threw himself instinctively away from the explosion of light and toppled out of the jeep. The top half of his body was a torch. He rolled on the ground, a hideous shrieking of sound bubbling from the fleshless hole which had once been his mouth.

Petrea's screams were no less blood-curdling. She thrashed around blindly in the passenger seat, blundering against the frame of the broken windscreen and falling against the door. Her blonde hair flared and shrivelled away to nothing as she tore at her clothes and face in an effort to escape the furnace of pain running molten over her.

The seats of the jeep were well alight and the oil smoke oozed black from the edges of the flame.

Two shadowy figures emerged from a doorway. They

were boys, barely eighteen. One was sobbing with horror, sickened by what he was witnessing. He tried to shut out the sound of screaming but the hands clamped over his ears could not stop the sound.

The other boy advanced round the jeep until the heat leapt out at him and made him recoil. He paused. Cradled in his arms was a long-barrelled rifle of greater age than himself. He pointed it at the writhing flambeau in the jeep and pulled the trigger. Petrea tottered and fell into the roadway. The flames which wrapped her sputtered and settled to a flickering uniformity along the blackened length of her corpse.

Circling the jeep, the boy tried to end Stratou's agony with a merciful bullet. Stratou, however, was still rolling and crawling and staggering and falling in the throes of blind pain. Twice the boy fired and missed. A third bullet brought the fiery writhing to an end.

The sound of running feet preceded the arrival from beyond the barrier of men in the nondescript garb of ELAS guerrillas. They carried tommy-guns.

The boy with the rifle was standing dumbly beside the blazing jeep, staring at Stratou's smouldering body. A guerrilla seized the boy by the shoulder and pulled him away roughly.

'The tank will blow!' he shouted furiously. 'You'll get killed!'

The group retreated to a safe distance just in time. They threw themselves flat as the jeep erupted in a pillar of flame. A rush of booming sound reverberated between the houses, shattering windows and rocking against the upturned wagons. The wagons lifted and fell as fire spewed over them, setting them ablaze.

The guerrilla who had grabbed the boy with the rifle grinned at him now as they lay on their bellies in the street.

'So, you got to use your petrol bomb after all, Stephanos? How does it feel to make your first kill?'

'One of them was a woman,' said the boy. 'One of them was a woman.'

CHAPTER THIRTY

Operation Snowdrop

The gale showed no sign of abating.

'You'll have to call it off,' said Squadron-Leader Garrett.

'We can't call it off. It has to be done today!'

Mackenzie paced up and down Garrett's office, his face thunderous.

'You can't drop on top of that bloody hill in this wind', said Garrett. 'You'd be blown half way to Egypt.'

'Well, we've got to find another way on to that hill. Maitland said that he can keep the Old Man out on the *Ajax* until about two but he's determined to come ashore this afternoon. They've fixed up a conference for half-past four ... Everybody will be at it ... Churchill, Eden, Damaskinos, Papandreou, half his cabinet, Alexander, people from ELAS if they turn up. We've got to knock out that bomb-launcher or whatever it is up on that hill before Churchill sets foot in Athens.'

'It's your show,' said Garrett. 'All I can suggest is that we get the Navy to help. ELAS don't seem to have any concentrations of men west of Piraeus. Maybe you could make a landing near Perama and strike overland?'

Mackenzie looked at Garrett and beamed.

'That's it! You're a genius. Where the hell's that map?'

He crossed the room and studied a big map pinned to the wall. Red pins denoted the known concentrations of guerrilla forces in Attica. Mackenzie rapped a stubby finger on the map.

'If the Navy could run us through the Straits of Salamis and put us ashore north of Perama, we could come in on Kirkos by the back door. Look, it's wide open high country to the south of Daphni. All we'd need to do is get across the road that runs up the coast and circle along the higher of the two hills here or go right over the top of it.'

Garrett peered over Mackenzie's shoulder.

'We were going to drop you here – on the Daphni side – so it won't mean much alteration to your basic plan.'

'Only that we'll have to slog eight miles on foot and most of it uphill. And we'll be making our approach in daylight now instead of in the dark. That could make it very dicey.'

The two men looked at each other. Mackenzie's brow was creased, his mind weighing chances. Garrett's expression was quizzical, expectant.

'You could postpone your drop until after dark tonight,' said the RAF man. 'The wind may not last all day – although the forecast isn't too encouraging. Gusts up to sixty knots over the next twenty-four hours.'

'We've got to go today!' said Mackenzie. 'How do we contact the Navy and ask them for a boat?'

'Leave that to me,' said Garrett. 'You'd better break the news to your lads.'

The adjacent room was thick with cigarette smoke. Mackenzie stood in the door and made a silent head-count. Preston and Drinkwater were playing darts at one end. They wore paratroop jump-suits and helmets. Nine other men in paratroop gear were congregated round a wood-burning stove, drinking tea and smoking.

The chatter died to a silence. Every face was turned towards Mackenzie, framed in the doorway.

'The jump's off, boys,' said Mackenzie.

The news was greeted with groans of disappointment.

'But Operation Snowdrop is still on,' Mackenzie added. There was a buzz of interest. 'Squadron-Leader Garrett is asking the Navy to run us round the coast and land us near the Perama-Eleusis road. It means we'll be sprinting up Grable Two instead of landing on the top.'

During the briefing on Christmas Night, the two hills behind Piraeus had been labelled Grable One and Grable Two because of a slight topographical likeness to a pair of mammary glands. The fact that Grable Two was considerably larger than Grable One had led Preston to observe that, well-endowed as she was, film star Betty Grable would not have been flattered to have her name associated with such an obvious implication of anatomical deformity.

The nine paratroopers were all volunteers. Two of them were from Clydeside and had been paid-up members of the Communist Party from the Depression days of 1931 until their enlistment in 1939. What they had seen in Greece in three short weeks, however, had so disillusioned them with Communism that their loathing of it was now as great as the passionate hope with which they had originally embraced the ideology.

One of the two, a barrel-chested man called McGovern, held up a hand rather like a schoolboy trying to attract the teacher's attention.

'D'ye mind if I say something, sir?'

'What is it, McGovern?'

The paratrooper looked at Mackenzie apprehensively.

'I was just thinking, sir, that from what we can see of those wee bits of mountain, there's a gey lot of snow up there. Would it no be a good idea tae tak sheets or something tae give us a wee bit o' camouflage?'

'That's a good idea,' said Mackenzie. 'I'll see what Squadron-Leader Garrett can drum up. There's no snow on the lower slopes . . . it's all above four hundred or so feet – but I reckon we'll have something like four and a half miles to travel when we get above the snow-line and we certainly don't want to be seen.'

Garrett's arrival to confirm that the Navy would provide transport for the short sea journey of about twelve miles was greeted with grins of approval. They had all been keyed up to make a dangerous parachute descent in darkness and should have been airborne half an hour before, at 0545 hours. Postponement had caused only frustration and nerviness.

'I have to deliver you at Phaleron Bay for embarkation at oh-nine-hundred hours,' announced Garrett. 'That means you've all got time for a decent breakfast before you go. I'll lay on a truck to get you away from here at oh-eight-hundred.'

There was also time for each man to be fitted, not with snow-suits, but with best quality officer's overalls of pristine white. A quantity of white sheeting was also provided so that the men could fashion white covers for their helmets and equipment.

At eight o'clock sharp, the truck containing the twelve men pulled away from the front of Garrett's office and joined the airfield's perimeter road. Operation Snow-drop was under way.

The bitterly cold wind, which permeated every corner of the hilltop bunker, and an inability to sleep had made George Kirkos abandon the bunk in his new head-quarters at five in the morning. He had prowled fretfully round his snow-enclosed eyrie until first light, then he had roused a squad to load the second X24 missile into the Javelin launcher. The sight of the long lethal cylinder with its shark-like fins afforded him some compensation for the depressing news that Voutsas had brought him in the cold grey light of dawn.

Nikos Stratou and Petrea were dead. Voutsas had

said they could not be one-hundred-per-cent sure – but there was no doubt at all in Kirkos's mind. It was yet another searing test of his nerve in the playing of the final hand. He tried to reassure himself that the game could still be won. You have to ride these setbacks, not make too much of them. When everything is staked on the last big play, every setback is magnified in proportion to the enormous risk. He had to keep his nerve.

It was too bad that Stratou and Petrea hadn't made it back. The consolation was that their deaths were not entirely in vain. The very fact that they had lost their lives on the return journey signified that they had already accomplished their mission. And that was something.

Voutsas had also brought word from Natsinas.

This was merely confirmation that the meeting with the British was timed for 5 p.m. that day in the Foreign Ministry and that Kirkos should meet the other delegates at 4 p.m. at the previously arranged rendez-vous.

Kirkos had promptly sent a runner to Natsinas to tell him that he could not possibly meet the other delegates at four. Because of the critical battle situation in Piraeus and the major offensive which the British had launched there, it was possible he might have to withdraw from the delegation. He asked Natsinas, however, to delay the delegation's departure for the Foreign Ministry until 5 p.m. If he hadn't arrived by that time, they should set off without him. For the benefit of the EAM hierarchy, Kirkos had added that it would be good tactics to keep Papandreou and the British waiting.

Kirkos also added a postscript. This stated that Kirkos was seriously disturbed by the activities of General Spiro and the Russian, Karolov, in his sector and that he would take action against them if it didn't cease forthwith.

He allowed himself a grim smile of satisfaction at this final touch. If, later, the Communists produced his handwritten message to Natsinas and tried to blame him for the destruction of the Foreign Ministry and the deaths of Churchill's and Papandreous's delegations, the document could rebound on them. He would have evidence of his own to produce: a 'Russian-made' rocket-launcher and the bodies of the assassins, Spiro and Karolov.

Christos Rafaelides had been in a sweaty panic for most of Christmas Night and the following morning. A plumber, employed by the City Department of Water Engineers, he had been called to the Foreign Ministry at four on Christmas afternoon to unblock a choked sink in the kitchens.

Because Christmas was his name day, he had been celebrating since mid-morning with members of his family. He was in a vile temper and more than a little drunk when he arrived at the Ministry building, cursing his luck at having his holiday celebration interrupted.

Most of the staff had gone home by the time he reached the Ministry, and he had been left to work alone in the draughty kitchen by the light of an oily lamp. When he had cleared the sink, the need to revenge himself on Authority had been sharpened by the liquor he had consumed. He looked around for something to steal, but his search of the kitchen environs had produced only one likely item – a wooden crate containing bottles, which he had found in a staff lavatory.

The crate was stamped in English, which he did not understand, but it looked promising with its Red Cross markings. He had seen a similarly marked packing case broken open by black-marketeers behind a taverna he frequented, and it had contained cans of corned beef.

Refaelides smuggled the crate outside to his tricycle. The machine had once been the property of an ice-cream vendor but, since the Occupation and the shortage of gasoline for motor transport, it had been acquired by the City Water Engineer's Department. The freezer box at the front had been replaced by a big basket pannier with a lid and, inside this, Rafaelides carried the tools and appurtenances of his trade.

As soon as he had got home, Rafaelides had taken the Red Cross crate from the pannier on his tricycle and prised the top spars open. His disappointment with the bottles he found was intense.

A sniff at the amber liquid was enough to tell him that it was some kind of cleansing fluid and undrinkable. But, because kerosene was so difficult to obtain for lighting purposes, he made his foul temper even more so by trying the disinfectant as fuel in his bedroom lamp. The experiment was a dismal failure.

The disinfectant would not even burn when he poured some into a saucer and dropped a lighted match into it. The match-flame just gave a hiss and went out.

Rafaelides had glumly decided that the only chance of profiting from the theft was to try selling the bottles individually to friends and acquaintances, even if he only got a modest price for them. In order to calculate his likely return, he started to unload the crate to count the bottles.

New excitement sparked in him when he realised the wooden crate held more than bottles. Cushioned by straw packing, a grey metal box rested at the foot of the crate.

Rafaelides took it out with wonder. He found there was no way of opening the box. He bent his ear to it. A steady high-pitched humming noise could be plainly heard. The plumber's wonder turned to fear.

His wife, who had been upbraiding him mercilessly since his return home over the worthlessness of his acquisition, now lashed him verbally on the need to get 'that thing' out of her house and get rid of it. But where? And what if it was worth money?

At ten the following morning, the box was still sitting on the kitchen floor. To Rafaelides, it seemed a live thing. It seemed to vibrate when he plucked up the courage to touch it with his finger-tips. It sat there on the floor and seemed to mock him.

Rafaelides could bear it no longer. He picked up the box, took it outside and placed it gently in the pannier of his tricycle. He pushed the machine along the dirt lane behind his house.

Reaching the street, he swung himself into the saddle. The bite of the wind made him screw up his face. Its force took his breath away. Cursing the tricycle's heaviness, he bent his back into pedalling the cumbersome three-wheeler towards downtown Athens.

He had no firm idea what he intended to do. Inside the pannier, the three bell-shaped heads of the tiny transmitter continued to generate high-speed heartbeats high into the atmosphere.

Kirkos, counting the minutes in his mountain-top bunker until he could play his final card, had no idea that Fate had dealt him a joker. And the joker was wild.

Boxing day was now ten and a half hours old.

The watery sun was at its noon zenith as the LCM glided shorewards. Mackenzie had ordered everyone to stay out of sight in the well of the landing-craft during the agonisingly slow journey through the Straits and round the headland of Perama.

The strong wind and a fiercely choppy sea had militated against a speedy run round the peninsula of Piraeus from Phaleron Bay, causing Mackenzie to fume with impatience.

The LCM was heading for a narrow strip of gravel which was sheltered on two sides by elephantine protuberances of rock. Beyond the landing-place, the heights of Grable Two looked stark and forbidding in the noonday light.

The landing-craft grounded and the ramp dropped with a thunderous metallic crunch on the stony beach. The twelve men, ghostly in their white equipment, moved quickly ashore. The last man was no sooner on the beach than the ramp was being raised and the LCM was backing off, water boiling around it as it went full astern on both engines.

The landing-place was less than a thousand yards below the road which skirted the footslopes of Grable Two. The men waited, pressed against a bank, until a convoy straggle of three carts pulled by oxen passed north going towards Daphni. When the road was clear, the raiders moved across it quickly and began the ascent of Grable Two.

It was hard going. There was thin snow below four hundred feet: a light powdering which made the ground slippery underfoot. Higher up, where the slope was much steeper, the snow was quite thick; frosted crisp on top and soft underneath.

It was well after one 'clock when Mackenzie indicated a change of course. Instead of heading directly for the summit of Grable Two, the small band began to circle north and east at the six-hundred-feet level. They marched along the contour in single file, marvelling at the breathtaking splendour of the mountains of Parnassus to the north-east and of Eleutherae to the north-west.

They had been trudging for two and a half hours without a break when Mackenzie called a halt. Away below was the small town of Daphni. Ahead, the ground slipped down from the east face of Grable Two and facing them was the north-west side of their objective, Grable One.

The men carrying the field radio equipment and

heavier weapons were desperately in need of a rest. So was Mackenzie.

Preston dropped down beside him in the snow and eyed him anxiously.

'You don't look in very good shape.'

Mackenzie was lolling on his pack, his breath coming in wheezing gasps.

'I'll be all right.' He grinned at Preston. 'You would think there was plenty of fresh air up here to keep these old lungs puffing away, but I just can't seem to get enough breath.'

'You should have stayed back in Athens. You didn't need to come on this caper.'

'Oh yes I did.'

Mackenzie sat up, his good eye blinking fiercely. Preston shrugged.

'I suppose you did at that,' he conceded. 'An eye for an eye?'

'A life for a life,' said Mackenzie through gritted teeth. He got to his feet and surveyed the resting men with an air of impatience.

'OK, you airborne cowboys, let's be having you! On your feet before your backsides get frost-bite!'

It took them another hour to cross the valley depression between Grable Two and Grable One. As they neared the top of the north-west face of Grable One, Mackenzie waved Preston and three men off to the extreme right. Drinkwater indicated with a silent signal that he would take three others to cover the left approach

Fanning out, they crawled cautiously towards the gentle curve of the summit.

Mackenzie edged forward on his belly over the last few yards. The hill was almost flat on top. The wind whipped at his face as he levelled his binoculars.

The ground sloped gently down away from him and then rose steeply towards the east summit of Grable

One. Mackenzie knew that, from the far side of the crater-like hollow in front of him, the whole of Athens and Piraeus would be spread out below in bird's-eye panorama.

A track led back from the far summit to what appeared to be a terraced series of dug-outs and pill-boxes. Possibly, the Germans had had a weather or radio station there. The installations certainly hadn't been built overnight.

Whatever the constructions were, it was not surprising that aerial photographs had made little of them. They had been built into and under the natural contours of the hilltop. From Mackenzie's side-on position, the flat slab roofs were visible in elevation but he realised that, from above, they would be indistinguishable from the rest of the landscape — especially under snow.

Mackenzie could see men with rifles slung on their shoulders patrolling under covered catwalks. Only the top halves of their bodies were visible.

'What do you make of it, sir?'

Selby, one of the three paratroopers who had followed Mackenzie on his belly-crawl to his present vantage-point, was stretched close by, protecting his face from the icy wind with an upheld hand and peering sideways at Mackenzie.

'That's our objective,' said Mackenzie. 'Can't see much from here. We'll need to get nearer.'

A low ridge of rocks offered cover midway between their position and the bunker. Otherwise, the hilltop was as barren as the moon. With a signal to the paratroopers that they should follow him, Mackenzie crept down the slope before him towards the rocks.

The movements of the ghostly white-suited intruders were unobserved by the occupants of the bunker but one guard, patrolling a westfacing catwalk, had keener sight than his fellows and an alert mind.

464

He had been looking out at the surrounding snow-covered moonscape all afternoon and something about the hill facing him suddenly looked different from the last time he had looked in that direction. He tried to work out what it was that was different. Then it came to him. Where before he had seen an unbroken bank of snow, there now seemed to be lines on it.

He borrowed field-glasses to study the bank. He gave a sharp snort of disbelief. Unless his eyes were deceiving him, the lines were four sets of tracks descending from the top of the bank and disappearing behind a low rocky ridge only five hundred yards away. He summoned the burly Cretan captain who had taken over running the post the day before, when Stratou had been called away.

The Cretan studied the snow bank and the tracks.

'Goats,' he concluded. 'Perhaps goats have made these tracks. But go and find out.'

The sharp-eyed guard slung his rifle and clambered on to the concrete roof of the gun-nest beneath his catwalk. From the roof of the gun-nest he dropped to the ground. Kicking at the snow, he walked towards the rocks where Mackenzie and his three men were considering their next move.

The need to make any decision was removed by the sudden appearance above them of a tall figure in a sheepskin coat. The man reached to unsling his rifle from his shoulder but Selby, crouched back on his heels, had the speedier reactions. The Bren gun, cradled across one knee, came up and a sharp burst sent the guerrilla spinning backwards and out of sight. He died with a gurgling cry.

Selby, pushing the Bren before him, peered cautiously over the rocks towards the bunker. The dead guerrilla lay only a few feet away, his blood beginning to stain the snow. The paratrooper ducked quickly as a sustained burst of machine-gun fire swept the rocks.

'They've got us pinned down beautifully now,' he lamented. 'Anyone who wants to stick his head up for a shufti is going to get it shot off. Sorry I fired, Captain, but it was him or us. What do we do now?'

'We keep our heads down for the moment,' said Mackenzie. 'You had no choice about popping off that Bren, Selby, so forget it. I think we're going to need a little help from our friends.' He turned to another of his squad, who was crouched a little distance away. 'Corporal Harris! time to get that radio of yours working.'

Mackenzie waited, fury and frustration working in him. To get so near in broad daylight and then to be robbed of surprise at the last minute was the foulest of luck. He leaned against the rock and allowed his gaze to wander to the snowy bank down which they had recently come. He saw the tell-tale tracks. No use blaming anybody, he thought angrily. It was your own bloody fault!

Another burst of raking fire swept the rocks from the bunker. This time it was answered by twin bursts from two points on the west rim of the depression. Preston and Drinkwater had positioned themselves well to cover Mackenzie's central approach to the bunker and had quickly assessed his difficulty.

But it was a stalemate situation. Mackenzie knew that there was no way twelve men were going to cross that stretch of open ground and take the strong-point in broad daylight.

'How's that radio coming?' he called to Corporal Harris.

Harris had stripped his bulky equipment of its white sheeting and was crouched, headphones over his ears, speaking into the mouthpiece.

'I've got Kalamaki very faintly, sir. They've got a couple of Spitfires in the air and they want to know if we're close enough to mark a target for them.'

466

'Tell 'em we're close enough to spit. We'll mark the target with orange smoke. If they're going to strafe, they'll have to make their run from south-east to north-west. Got that? South-east to north-west. Tell them that if they make any error to the left of the approach, they'll get us!'

'Roger, sir.'

Harris began to repeat the message into the radio.

Mackenzie was already unstrapping a grenade rifle from his pack. Selby, who had been carrying a pouch of smoke grenades, crawled towards him.

'Orange, sir?'

'Orange.'

Mackenzie fitted the stubby dart-like bomb into the rifle. Resting the butt against his shoulder, he raised himself above the level of the ridge, deliberately measured the arc of trajectory, and fired. He dropped quickly down as a machine-gun in the bunker sprayed the ridge with another murderous burst.

'Have a look, Selby,' he said as the guerrilla gunner, now without a visible target, ceased firing. The paratrooper exposed his head above the ridge for five seconds, drawing more firing, but ducked down quickly before the machine-gunner could adjust his aim.

'Bull's eye, sir,' reported Selby. 'You landed right on the roof of one of them dug-outs.'

The words were no sooner out of his mouth than there was a roar of sound approaching from the south. Two Spitfires tracked across the hilltop, a hundred feet above their heads, and banked away to the north-east. They watched the aircraft climb away until they were distant specks. They circled high over Athens, turning south towards the sea and then beginning a new approach which would bring them across Piraeus.

The Spitfires were higher this time, small dots in the distance seeming to hover at about two thousand feet.

The dots grew larger as the aircraft powered into their diving attack.

First, one came in over Grable One, tracers streaming from the 20mm Hispano cannons mounted in each wing. Then came the second. Over a hundred shells were pumped into the guerrilla bunker on the first attack. Then the dose was repeated. The Spitfires disappeared to the north with a tilt of their wings.

Mackenzie trained his binoculars on the bunker. The orange smoke was now wisping to nothing, but black smoke billowed from the narrow jaws of one pill-box and the roof of another had collapsed. Across the open ground which separated him from the bunker, he could hear men shouting. There was the unmistakable cry of a fearfully wounded man.

The RAF fliers had carried out their attack with remarkable precision, but how effective it had been remained to be seen. The answer, to Mackenzie's despair, was all too soon apparent. He had to throw himself backwards as the snow-covered rocks to his right suddenly became alive with bullets and the angry rattle of their source spoke from the bunker.

The spectacle of the two Spitfires diving towards the hills behind Piraeus had been seen from many parts of Athens.

Archbishop Damaskinos, arriving at the British Embassy, had looked skywards and had seen the light-blue bellies of the aircraft wheeling south to make their approach.

In a room at the Embassy, Winston Churchill scorned warnings of the sniper who had been pumping away at the building every day, to rush to a window at the sound of the cannon fire.

Rafaelides had been parking his three-wheeler in the lane behind his home when the roar of the aircraft engines overhead had made him look up. A feeling of great relief was on him now at his success in disposing of the embarrassing metal box.

Just after noon, he had found himself in an alley behind Ermou Street, still at a loss over what he should do with the unwelcome object. The alley was quite deserted. So, too, was the building opposite him. It had, during the Occupation, housed part of the German military establishment and had been badly damaged by petrol bombs thrown through its windows in the first days of Liberation by a group of vengeful Athenians.

Scarcely one window had glass in it. The ground floor was a blackened ruin. The others had been ransacked by looters. Rafaelides had ventured through the rear entrance. The door lay on the ground, torn from its hinges. He had explored the interior in a tentative manner before returning to his tricycle and lifting the metal box out of the pannier. Clutching it gingerly, he had taken it inside the building and concealed it behind the charred remains of an office desk.

On the way home, he had stopped at a taverna to calm his nerves with retsina. As he parked his three-wheeler in the lane behind his home, he gave little thought to the aircraft which had roared briefly over-head. He was wondering who, amongst his friends and neighbours, might want to buy a bottle of Pinefresh disinfectant.

He heard the cannon fire away towards Piraeus. Then, a few moments later, the steady drone of the fighter aircraft as they flew wing to wing in steady flight, their mission over.

The fighters flying wing to wing were also observed at the British Embassy. The party hurrying to two waiting armoured cars looked up briefly as the Spitfires appeared to the east of Mount Lycabettos and droned south towards the airfield at Kalamaki.

The two armoured cars and their escort moved slowly along Vasilissis Sophias Avenue and headed east past the Royal Gardens. The procession wheeled through a side gate before reaching Constitution Square. It drew up outside the Foreign Ministry building.

The armoured cars disgorged their passengers, who hurried inside the Ministry.

Winston Churchill entered the conference-room with Archbishop Damaskinos. A huddle of people, already in the chamber, faced the newcomers expectantly.

Damaskinos was shown to a seat at the centre of the huge oval table. Churchill, in Air Commodore's uniform, took the seat immediately to his right. Anthony Eden, the British Foreign Minister, took the seat on Churchill's right.

The Archbishop was flanked on his left by Field-Marshal Alexander, Reginald Leeper, the British Ambassador, and Harold Macmillan, the political supremo for Italy and the Balkans. George Papandreou and his ministers grouped themselves on Churchill's right and beyond them were the official observers from the United States, France and the Soviet Union. A row of seats had been reserved for the ELAS delegates, four in all – but this part of the oval table remained unoccupied. The ELAS delegates had not turned up.

The room was chill, without heating of any kind. The only warmth came from the kerosene lamps sitting on the table. The time was one minute to five.

A low hum of restrained conversation rose as the group around the table waited. From beyond the windows came the crack of distant rifle and machine-gun fire. While the various delegates waited to talk peace, the war went on.

George Kirkos had been almost paralysed by shock at the discovery that British soldiers were within five hundred yards of his mountain-top bunker. The slow-mounting dread which had eaten at him for most of the day had threatened to develop into blind panic.

His orders had been screamed at his men, all semblance of calm leadership gone. The wilderness of his eyes had betrayed his knife-edge proximity to complete loss of control.

When the Spitfires had roared in with blazing cannon, the last taut strands of his overstretched nerves began to snap. Out of hand, he had shot dead one of his own men for failing to respond quickly enough to his command to investigate the damage caused by the aircraft.

Now, almost demonic with tension, he paced the narrow headquarters room of his subterranean refuge with one single thought dominating the boiling cauldron of his mind. The British intruders had to be held off until the Javelin could do its work. The two remaining missiles would be fired at five minutes after five o'clock and ten past five respectively. Thereafter, the British were welcome to the hill and the strongpoint. It would by then have served its purpose.

Kirkos drew comfort from the fact that the British forces on the west rim of the depression had not attempted to storm the bunker after the air attack. This meant that the force was probably no greater than patrol strength. It was likely, too, that the attackers had no idea of the bunker's real significance and would hesitate to risk high casualties in its capture.

A measure of calmness returned to him as the light of day quickly failed. The coming of dark meant not only the approach of zero hour for his rocket attack. It also meant provision of the cover by which he could escape.

There was no firing from outside now. He left his underground chamber and walked along the passage which opened into the well of the bunker. There, the undamaged Javelin was extended towards the heavens and the X24 missile rested in its frame cradle.

It was two minutes past five.

'Clear the well,' he ordered. He made his way to the control console on its platform behind the east-facing parapet. Voutsas hurried at his heels.

'You are going ahead with it?' queried the Major.

'Of course, you idiot,' snarled Kirkos. Voutsas shrugged. He was used to the other's tantrums, but his confidence in Kirkos had taken a battering as a result of his behaviour in the last hour or so. He seemed to be suffering from a combination of persecution complex and runaway megalomania and he had been lashing out indiscriminately in all directions.

Kirkos was looking at his watch, counting off the seconds aloud.

'Five . . . Four . . . Three . . . Two . . . One . . . Now!'

He pressed the firing button with the ball of his hand.

Five hundred yards away behind the low wall of rock, Mackenzie was in the act of loading a Verey pistol which Selby had handed to him. Harris was talking to Kalamaki on the radio and McGovern, the fourth member of the group, was crouched nearby.

All four men looked up in surprise as a bright red glow lashed out from the bunker and lit the broad depression in the skull top of Grable One. They peered over the rocks towards the bunker in time to see a fiery pillar lift from below the surface of the ground and climb high into the grey-black sky. Upwards it soared until the light had only the brilliance of a distant star. It seemed to hang and then fall like a stone, away to the east, towards Athens.

All seemed suddenly silent. The darkness of the hilltop was as intense as ever in spite of its white snowy blanket. Then a flash of light briefly lit the eastern rim of the hill and a clap like distant thunder rolled towards them.

A shiver ran down Mackenzie's spine. He did not allow himself to think too long on the implications of what he had witnessed. He had no doubts now that the bunker was a launching-site for rocket bombs but, uppermost, was the sickening realisation that Operation Snowdrop had failed. They were too late.

A cold anger followed the realisation. He looked at the Verey pistol in his hands, blaming himself for waiting until the last daylight had faded before using it to signal to Preston and Drinkwater.

He pointed the pistol high and fired. A bright green ball of light leapt in a parabola and fell slowly earth-wards. He returned the pistol to Selby, who replaced it in a pouch on his pack.

The grenade rifle was propped against a rock at Mackenzie's feet. He picked it up and handed it to Selby.

'Smoke,' he said quietly. 'I want a wall of smoke all around that strongpoint. Plaster it! We're going in.'

He called across to Harris.

'Leave the radio where it is, Corporal – and pay attention. You, too, McGovern. We're going to blow that hornet's nest over there clear off this mountain!'

'It looked like a bloody great rocket, sir,' said McGovern. 'Did ye see it, sir? Did ye see it?'

'I saw it,' said Mackenzie. 'Now we're going to hit it. Sling your weapons and leave both hands free to attack with grenades. Selby here is going to make some smoke. As soon as he does, we go over the top. Spread out. We'll keep about ten yards apart. We've got to get as close as we can without being seen. OK, Selby?'

The paratrooper had already loaded the grenade rifle. He raised it to his shoulder and sent the first smoke grenade lobbing towards the bunker. As quickly as he could reload and fire, a stream of half a dozen more bombs curled out across the snow. A sulphurous fog came swirling back at them, whipped by the wind.

The four men crawled from their protective cover and fanned out in a line. They moved into the smoke running low, bent almost double.

473

Already converging towards the bunker from their left were Preston's and Drinkwater's teams. Preston and his three men were well covered by the smoke because of the wind direction but Drinkwater's squad, on the left, were more exposed. Mackenzie halted and signalled to Selby, miming the firing of a rifle and pointing.

Selby reloaded the grenade gun and fired two smoke shells to the far left of the bunker. Now the curtain of noxious vapour was complete, but the wind was dispersing it quickly.

A machine-gun opened up from a pill-box slit. The guerrilla manning it was firing blindly into the smoke and aiming much too high.

Preston, on the extreme right, was bellying forward like a snake, sliding across the down gradients of the uneven ground with extra momentum where snow on polished stone provided a sledging effect. Between the bursts of machine-gun fire away to his left, he heard another sound.

It was a creaking noise.

In the well of the bunker, the third and last of the X24 missiles was being lowered on a chain block and tackle into the guide-rails of the Javelin. Under the parapet, some distance away, Kirkos was screaming with impatience at the time the reloading was taking. It was now 5.27.

When the creaking noise stopped, Preston halted. Still lying flat on the ground, he cocked his head to one side to listen. Although the creaking noise had stopped, he could hear voices – and they were near enough to tell him he was now very close to the bunker. The smoke which had hidden him was now thinning rapidly.

He unclipped a grenade from his belt, took out the pin with his teeth and threw the black sphere in a high arc towards the origin of the creaking sound.

The grenade landed on a flat slab of concrete overhang, less than a dozen feet from where the launchingrm of the Javelin protruded from the central well of he bunker. The grenade rolled forward against the lown-slope of hill into which the concrete had been •edded. Then it rolled slowly back again, spinning on he flat slab.

In the instant it exploded, several things happened. he blast from the grenade spread out laterally, bucking the top of the launching-arm as it spread in one lirection, and throwing up rocks and stones from the •illside in the other. Lumps of rock and fragments of tone rained down into the bunker well. This cascade nd the noise of the explosion drowned out Kirkos's mpatient scream for the well to be cleared and preceded •nly by an instant his pressure on the firing button.

There was a flash of flame as the rocket ignited and •egan to lift off. It moved only a short distance along ts rails before the entire frame began to shake as the wisted and buckled top of the launcher-arm arrested, nstead of guiding, its progress. All the power of the hrusting force now blazing from the white-hot rear jets vas not pitted against the atmosphere as the missile oared in untrammelled flight, but was exploding nstead against the frame which held it and blasting •ack against the unyielding cement and rock of the •unker well.

The shaking increased to a frenzy of shuddering as he rocket buffeted and strained to escape from the mprisoning metal. The base began to lift from the floor •f the well. It was the framed arm of the launcher, vhich first proved unequal to the multitude of stresses earing at every inch of its length. Weakened and nelting in the blast-furnace heat of the flaming jets, it •egan to twist and bend along its lower half. Then, with shriek of rending metal, it folded. The top of the aunching frame, holding back the entire thrust of the rapped rocket, fell backwards in a slow crazy movenent. Escaping fuel erupted in fountains of liquid fire.

The men, who moments before had loaded the projec
tile into its cradle and had been blasted back agains
the walls of the bunker well, were now incinerated i
a boiling flood of leaping flame. It ran everywhere i
devouring clouds of white heat. The nose of the missil
sank down into the glowing mass, then a tremor c
blinding light leapt outwards with a rush of sound. A
mushroom of fire shot a thousand feet in the air.

Shock-waves of blasted air exploded through ever
cranny and space of the bunker, tearing at every surfac
and shape with the force of a hurtling express trair
Great slabs of concrete and rock, shaken from thei
supporting pillars, collapsed inwards, crushing an
burying men in the catacomb depths of the bunker. I
one unlit compartment, Spiro and his fellow-prisone
Karolov – their last moments filled with a terror c
unexplained noise and shaking ground – were squashe
to pulp beneath three tons of wire-stiffened concre
crossbeam and an avalanche of limestone.

Lying flat on his belly, fifty yards away, a wave c
heat scorched the eyebrows from Preston's face as h
watched incredulously. To him, it seemed that, with on
grenade, he had triggered the end of the world.

The blast was heard in the conference-room of th
Foreign Ministry, nearly nine miles distant. It was les
frightening than the awesome noise which had shake
the windows almost from their frames exactly twenty
two minutes before.

A patrol of British infantrymen from the Fourt
British Division - who had disembarked at Phaleron Ba
only that morning and were making their first acquaint
ance with Athens – were the first on the scene of th
earlier explosion.

They had been filing along Ermou Street when, fou
hundred yards away, a tall building had disintegrate
with a thunderous roar, leaving a gap in the skylin
The soldiers had rushed to the scene, certain that i

476

such a populated area a terrible carnage in human life must await them.

In fact, the only casualties were some passers-by who had sustained minor injuries and shock. The building which had been hit had been empty and so, too, had been the office blocks on either side.

A piece of wooden boarding, twelve feet long – which had adorned the side of the destroyed building – had been blasted seventy yards away and smashed through the windows of a taverna. The only occupants at the time were the bar-owner and an elderly customer. The two men recovered from their shock sufficiently to haul the board through the shattered window. The board had two words painted in black letters over the white background. There was a certain ironic significance in the words which escaped the two men. The sign said: HOTEL ARTEMIS.

If the massive blast had alarmed any of the Ministers and high officials grouped round the oval table in the Foreign Ministry, none was prepared to show it. They continued to chat informally, speculating about the non-appearance of the ELAS delegates.

By the time the second and more distant explosion was heard, impatience and unease permeated the atmosphere inside the room. It looked likely now that the ELAS delegates had no intention of coming. A hush fell on the company as His Beatitude, the Archbishop of Athens, pushed his chair back and rose to his feet.

He spoke concisely, articulately and with great dignity. He regretted that their number was incomplete but hoped that fruitful discussion could still take place which would aid the agony of Greece and see restored the liberties and peace which were so near to the Greek heart. He welcomed the various delegates and observers, reserving a special welcome for Mr Winston Churchill, whom he now called upon to speak.

It was a bitter disappointment to Churchill that the

delegates of ELAS had not appeared but the bitterness did not show in his words, only a certain sorrow.

'I come to Athens,' he began, 'not with the sabre but with an olive branch. I come to Athens to heal the wounds of war, not to make them. I come not to exacerbate the divisions of men and nations, but to reunite them in peace and reason . . .'

An interpreter translated each utterance into Greek. Churchill had barely got into his stride when there was a loud knock at the door.

It opened and three men entered. All three wore British uniforms but their battledress tunics were devoid of British insignia.

Four ELAS delegates had been expected but the three newcomers offered no explanation of the change in number or their late arrival. The entire company in the room stood politely to greet them. The ELAS trio acknowledged the courtesy by bowing solemnly. The men round the table bowed in return.

When the three men were seated, the Archbishop rose to say that the conference would begin again. Consequently, he repeated his speech of welcome.

Again, Churchill followed him. He spoke for half an hour, stressing that Britain's interest in Greece was no more sinister now than it had been in 1941 when a cry from a friend in distress had been answered.

The priority in Greece was the feeding of the people. The country's greatest battles now were for the restoration of peace and the rehabilitation of the economy. These things could not be accomplished while bitterness and hate and bloodshed prevailed.

Speeches followed from Anthony Eden, Field-Marshall Alexander and George Papandreou, the Greek Prime Minister. It was some time before the first ELAS delegate rose.

Partsalides had the urbane charm and good looks which are often so helpful to the professional politician.

With an eloquence befitting a University don – which he was – Partsalides welcomed Churchill's expressed hope for peace between Greece and Britain.

'I hope,' he said with a smile, 'that as I gladly recognise Mr Churchill as the voice of the British people, he will acknowledge that I – as First Secretary of EAM – speak for the great mass of Greek people.'

At his side, Siantos – secretary of the Communist Party – sat unsmiling, his ferret eyes generating sneering contempt for the proceedings. He was sharply in contrast with General Mantakas, the rather jovial-looking ELAS commander who sat beaming on the left of Partsalides as if enjoying it all immensely.

A Greek Government member was next on his feet raising the question of representation at the conference. The British Foreign Minister replied that the composition of the conference was now for the various Greek interests present to decide.

Churchill endorsed Eden's statement.

'Ours has been the initiative in bringing you together,' he said, 'but the conduct of Greek affairs must pass now entirely into Greek hands. We have begun the work. You must finish it!'

He went round the table, shaking hands with every delegate in turn. Then he led the British delegation from the room.

In the hallway, he turned to Eden.

'I thought the ELAS were to be sending four representatives?'

'So did I,' replied Eden.

'I wonder what happened to the fourth man?' mused Churchill.

George Kirkos had survived the destruction of the hilltop bunker. He was one of five men who walked away from the smoking ruins.

Voutsas, who had been standing less than two feet

away from Kirkos when the bunker had exploded around their ears, had been less lucky. Both men had been hurled over the parapet of their observation-point by the blast but Voutsas had landed awkwardly on unforgiving rock in a manner which broke his neck. Kirkos, by a strange chance, had somersaulted high in the air and come down almost feet first astride the back of the unfortunate Major. Voutsas's body had broken his fall before pitching him forward on his face. The clothes had been torn from his body, which was blackened and bleeding from hundreds of small lacerations. Three fingers on his left hand and two on his right were broken, as was his left wrist. But he was alive.

Mackenzie found him on hands and knees, whimpering pitifully, and unrecogisable at first as the George Kirkos he had known. When recognition came and he realised who his prisoner was, there came to Mackenzie the image of a woman and child laid out dead on an Athens street. He could feel again, too, a hot enflamed pain in the region of his patch-covered eye. The desire to kill the snivelling wretch before him rose in him like gall.

But he stood stock-still, arms motionless by his sides.

'Mac, is that you?'

Preston materialised wraith-like from the smoke.

'Mac, what is it?'

'A prisoner,' said Mackenzie. 'He's hurt. Get one of the lads to take charge of him, Leo. Will you?'

He turned and walked away.

CHAPTER THIRTY-ONE

The Second Dawn

Sir Neil Maitland negotiated the jeep through knots of pedestrians in Constitution Square and accelerated into Stadiou Street.

'Where are you taking me?' asked the tall uniformed man sitting erect in the passenger seat.

'To Peristeri first,' said Maitland

'You're being very mysterious.'

'You could say that's an occupational weakness. Blame it on the business we're both in.'

Colonel Vincent Radmeyer laughed.

'OK, OK, I'll contain my curiosity.'

'You're not going to like what I'm going to show you,' said Maitland. 'Remember the last time we met?'

'Only too well,' replied the American sourly. 'You took a rather hot potato off my hands. How is that young man getting on, by the way? I owe you a favour there.'

'Correction,' said Maitland. 'You owe him a favour. And an apology.

'Now, wait a minute,' protested Radmeyer. 'This wouldn't be a little propaganda exercise, would it? This wouldn't be a little bit of British chicanery to put a certain point of view over to the State Department?'

'Only partially,' said Maitland cheerfully. 'Tonight, you are going to compose a long report about me and about Athens and about young Preston and you'll send it to Washington.'

'I wouldn't be too sure about that. You've got the wrong guy. Look, I know you think I carry a bit of weight, but if you think I'm going to stooge for the British and pressurise the State Department, you're making a big mistake.'

'I don't think I'm mistaken about you,' said Maitland. 'You're a genuine, true-blue American. You're honest, you play hard but fair. You're interested in truth and justice . . .'

'Flattery will get you nowhere – but thanks for the build-up anyway. Maybe you'll put it in writing.'

'I could have said you were incorruptible, too – ' Maitland's eyes twinkled mischievously – 'But I meant what I said. I don't want to influence your judgement by saying nice things about you. I just want to present you with some facts and leave you to make your own judgement.'

They drove in silence across the Ilissus bridge into Peristeri, arriving eventually at a street which was barricaded off and guarded by British soldiers.

Maitland got out of the jeep and showed an identity card to the Sergeant in charge. After a brief conversation, he returned to the jeep.

'We'll leave the jeep here,' he said to Radmeyer. He led the way past the barricade. Beyond, one side of the roadway had been dug up. A trench about four feet in depth extended for about fifty yards.

'Have a look in the trench,' invited Maitland.

The American, not knowing what to expect, walked over and gazed down. The colour drained from his face. He turned, his eyes horror-stricken and accusing at the same time.

'You bastard!' he said hoarsely 'Why? Why are you showing me this?'

'Take a good look at American foreign policy, Colonel. That's what ought to be buried there. We didn't abandon these people – but you did. We'll go on paying the price for a long time but, sooner or later, America is going to have to foot its share of the bill. You'll probably have to go on paying long after we've been bled dry and opted out.'

'You're a bloody bastard, Maitland!'

'I'm presenting you with facts, Colonel. Unpleasant facts. I can't make them go away. Even when you turn your head away as you're doing now, they'll still be there. Like the people in that grave. There are more than two hundred of them there. Men, women and children. Murdered – not to make Greece free, but to make it Communist.'

'For Christ's sake, stop!'

'No, Colonel. Not until you look at them – and take a good look. Note how they've all had their hands tied behind their backs – even the little ones who were scarcely old enough to walk.'

'Have you finished?' Radmeyer's voice was shrill with emotion.

Maitland's shoulders slumped.

'Yes, I've finished. I could take you to other graves. We've found fifteen hundred bodies just in this one part of Athens. But what's the use? If they can't say anything to you, what hope have I?'

Radmeyer turned away from him abruptly and walked back to the shallow trench. He walked along its entire length, his face white and grim.

When he returned, he went straight past Maitland. He went past the barricade and the soldiers to the jeep. He stood beside the jeep, took out cigarettes and lit one with a trembling hand.

When Maitland arrived, the American was calmer.

'I'm sorry,' he said. 'I wasn't prepared for . . . that! I shouldn't have cursed at you the way I did. I'm sorry.'

Maitland put a hand on his shoulder.

'I'm the one who should be apologising. It was a brutal thing to do. I'm sorry.'

'No, goddamn it, you were right! I'll be making a report to Washington. Just like you said. But maybe you'll tell me why it's so important to you that the State Department changes its tune over Greece? Is it because they've been making out that you British are the villains of the piece here?'

'No, Colonel. The really disturbing thing is the effect that Greece, or rather the situation here, has had on Anglo-American friendship . . . The distrust and suspicion it has caused.'

'You really and truly care, don't you?' said the American.

'Yes, I really and truly care,' said Maitland passionately. 'I want to leave behind to my grandchildren a better world than the one I found. I weep for what has happened in Greece.'

Radmeyer's anger had completely dissipated. His eyes shone with feelings almost of kinship with his British counterpart. He had been acquainted with Maitland for four years now but, not until this moment, did he feel that he actually *knew* the man.

'You've won your truce here in Greece,' he said. 'Things can only get better now.'

Maitland shook his head sadly.

'It's a very brittle peace. The Communists still hold twenty thousand hostages . . . Innocent families.'

'They have promises to release them now, surely?'

'I pray to God they do. They've also promised to surrender their guns. But I have had experience of Communist promises before. I fear they may just be biding the time for a fairer wind and it'll start all over again.'

'You think they'll try again to seize power?' asked Radmeyer.

'They don't give up,' said Maitland. 'Did you know that for all the size of the guerrilla armies, there are fewer than three thousand hardcore Communists in the whole of Greece? Their leaders know that they could not have held on to power here without the direct intervention and support of the Russian Army.'

'Instead of which, Stalin supported Churchill.'

'With words, not with deeds. Stalin is a political realist. He has sown the seeds of Revolution in Greece but he is in no hurry to gather in the harvest. Not while there are richer takings to be had everywhere else in Europe. He probably looks on the whole thing here like an exercise in logistics – a hundred divisions to make Poland a province of Russia but only a few thousand revolutionaries to take over Greece. I bet he's sitting there in the Kremlin rubbing his hands. He probably said to EAM; "Nice try, boys! You did very well but let's get the membership up and the organisation better before you have another go." '

Radmeyer was silent. Maitland smiled at him.

'Colonel, you look like you could use a drink. I've got some very good Scotch whisky back in the Grande Bretagne. I've also got somebody waiting to see you.'

Radmeyer brightened.

'Now that's the first happy news I've had today. About the Scotch, I mean. The visitor can wait. Unless . . .' He broke off. 'You haven't fixed an audience with the Regent of Greece? Not His Beatitude himself, the Archbishop?'

'No,' laughed Maitland. 'I'm talking about a good solid American who should rightly be in American uniform. He's got something to show you. You haven't forgotten Lieutenant Leonidas Preston?'

'Oh,' said Radmeyer apprehensively. 'You said I owed him an apology.'

'Well, your people did rather take the view that he was a coward or a liar or both. We have conclusive proof to the contrary.'

'You do, eh?'

'Yes, Colonel. Lieutenant Preston's account of what

485

happened during that infamous ambush near Agrinion back in nineteen forty-three has been substantiated by a British officer who was there.'

'I thought Preston was the only survivor,' said Radmeyer.

'There weren't meant to be any survivors, Colonel. We also have in custody the guerrilla leader who arranged the ambush with the Germans. He was working with both the Communists and the Nazis. He has told us everything. Perhaps you would like to interview him.'

'I might at that,' said Radmeyer.

'There's something else you should know about Preston. Yesterday, he was decorated by General Plastiras with the Medal of Honour for outstanding bravery in the field.'

'As a result of that ambush?' said Radmeyer, his eyebrows arched in surprise.

'No, for his part in the capture of Rimini last September.'

'Hey, wait a minute. I thought you were going to give the guy a job in the desert . . . As an interpreter.'

Maitland gave an embarrassed cough.

'Well, maybe I wasn't as specific as I might have been, Colonel. He did serve in Egypt with the Greek Brigade – but he moved to Italy with them. He didn't have to get mixed up in the Rimini battle, but he volunteered. He acted as artillery spotter with the Greek infantry and kept a radio link going with our heavy artillery which was supporting the Greeks.'

Radmeyer was thoughtful as he sat beside Maitland on the drive back to the Grande Bretagne.

Suddenly, he turned to Maitland, a fierce expression on his face.

'Look, Sir Neil, there's one thing I'd be mighty obliged if you would do for me.'

'If it's humanly possible, I will,' replied Maitland.

A grin spread across Radmeyer's face.

'My name's Vincent,' he said. 'When the hell are you going to stop calling me Colonel? My friends all call me Vince.'

Maitland grinned back.

'OK, Vince, you've got a deal – on one condition. You've got to stop calling me Sir Neil. My friends call me "Matey". From Maitland . . . "Matey". Got it?'

'Matey? Are you sure, Sir Neil?'

'Matey.'

'Holy cow!' breathed Radmeyer. 'Matey, for God's sake!'

He silently wondered if he would ever understand the British. Then he smiled to himself. He was sure as hell going to try!

The truce was now three days old and there were signs that it was going to hold. Athens was returning almost to normal. People were coming out into the streets. Tavernas which had been closed were opening again for business.

Preston and Mackenzie were sitting in a taverna near Omonia Square. A white-haired Greek with a face like a mahogany carving raised his glass in Mackenzie's direction.

'Many years,' he toasted.

Mackenzie and Preston raised their glasses in return.

'Many years to you, old one'

'It is over now, eh?' said the old man. 'We have peace.'

He drained his glass and stood up. He buttoned up his threadbare coat. There was a look of contentment on the old man's face.

'Peace is good,' he said. 'Peace is to see a stranger in your country and bid him welcome. Peace is to raise your glass to him and wish him many years. I had almost forgotten what it was like.'

He put a gnarled hand on Preston's shoulder.

'In richer days, I would have called for a bottle and told the waiter to put it on your table. I apologise that circumstances do not permit me to exercise such hospitality. Forgive me.'

'Have a drink with us, old one,' invited Preston. 'It would give us great pleasure.'

Pride flashed in the old man's eyes.

'You are very kind, but no. If we were in your country, I would accept – but we are in Athens. Do you understand?'

'I understand,' said Preston softly.

'You are American?' said the old man. 'Do you go home soon?'

'As a matter of fact, this is my last day in Athens, old one. I leave Greece tomorrow.'

'They say America is a wonderful place.' There was a wistful air to the old man's words. At the same time, there was the unspoken suggestion that American's wonders could exert no more than a passing fascination for the true Athenian. 'Come back to Athens in happier times,' he said. 'Journey safely, my young friend. May you go with goodness.'

Solemnly he shook Preston's hand, then Mackenzie's. He looked long in Mackenzie's face and at the eye with the patch over it. The old man's eyes said it all; the recognition of the warrior's badge, his understanding of it as one who in former years had borne arms in battle, the bond of respect it forged between comrades and, sometimes, between friend and foe.

He was a poor man, a humble man, but dignity was in his farewell and in the steady steps which took him to the door and out into the Athens street to be swallowed up by the city.

'There spoke the heart of Greece,' said Mackenzie solemnly. 'Aren't you sorry to be leaving, Leo?'

'I'll miss your ugly mug more than anything,' said Preston.

Mackenzie feigned offence.

'Here, just because they've let you wear an American uniform again and made you up to Captain, doesn't mean you can go around making remarks about my physiognomy.'

'What are you going to do, Mac?' said Preston. 'Are you really going to stay on in Greece?'

'Maitland wants me to hang on here for a few weeks. Then, if they'll let me have some time off, there's a certain island in the middle of a pretty lake where I've got to go.'

'Marriage?'

'If she'll still have me.'

Preston smiled a sad smile.

'May you go with goodness, old friend,' he said, offering the traditional wish of farewell.

Preston's departure left a strange emptiness in Mackenzie's life. He became impatient himself to be away from Athens.

There was one final task for him to perform. Since he had been presented with the opportunity of killing George Kirkos and chosen to walk away from it, he had become indifferent to the Greek's fate.

Kirkos had been handed over to military custody like any other insurgent captured in battle and made prisoner of war. He had become the responsibility of the military authorities. Mackenzie hoped that he would never see or hear of George Kirkos again. He was glad that he had not exacted the revenge which was his due.

It was a surprise, therefore, when Mackenzie received a message from the Commandant of the POW encampment at Kalamaki. This was to the effect that George Kirkos wanted to see him urgently.

Mackenzie made no move to visit the encampment

for two days after receiving the message. Then, on an impulse on the third day – a gloriously sunny January morning – he drove down to Kalamaki.

Major Hood, the Commandant, had passed on Kirkos's request without any particular interest in its outcome. He received Mackenzie affably in his office.

'You're only just in time,' he greeted Mackenzie. 'You know we've been busy trading prisoners with the ELAS since the truce, well, Kirkos has got us a deal that, for once, is in our favour.'

'I don't understand,' said Mackenzie.'

'Well, the exchange-rate has been pretty one-sided,' explained Hood. 'We've had to hand over twenty ELAS prisoners for every British soldier we've been able to get back. But we're getting forty RAF men for Kirkos.'

'They must value him pretty highly then. I suppose he was one of their most successful generals when you think about it. Are the powers-that-be going to let him go?'

'Yes. It has been cleared all the way up. When Churchill said amnesty was an essential part of the peace, he meant amnesty. No strings.'

'Why does he want to see me?' asked Mackenzie.

'I'm afraid I've got no idea. And you've got only about forty minutes to find out. The exchange takes place at eleven o'clock. At least, that's when he leaves here.'

Mackenzie was shown to a comfortable barrack hut where Kirkos had a room to himself. He was shaving when Mackenzie entered the room. The plaster had been removed from his broken wrist but it was heavily strapped. There was also strappings on the fingers of both hands.

Shaving was obviously a slow and laborious process to him but he was in better humour than Mackenzie had ever glimpsed in him. In fact, he was scarcely recognisable as the surly individual he had accompanied to

Greece or the whimpering wretch he had found on Grable One.

'Good morning, Captain. So you came?'

'Just in time, it seems. In an hour, you'll be a free man.'

Kirkos laughed.

'Is that what they told you?'

'You are to be exchanged.'

Kirkos lowered the razor and smiled at Mackenzie.

'Yes, I am being exchanged – but for what? If I am lucky, it will be quick – a bullet in the back of the head.'

Mackenzie drew in his breath.

'Have you mentioned this possibility to the Commandant?'

'No, he's a nice guy. He'd probably try to stop the exchange.'

'You mean, you don't mind?'

'No. I've had time to think about it. I gambled everything. I lost. It's as simple as that. This time I don't squeal for mercy.'

'Why are you telling me this?'

'Because I knew it would end this way. No, that's not true. I feared it. I saw it in your face all that time ago . . . That you would win. Christina knew it, too.'

'You know she's dead? You killed her.'

'I know. I'm sorry. It was not intentional.'

'The baby, too'

'And now Natsinas will have me killed. I'm afraid I have embarrassed him rather badly with Moscow. The penalty is death.'

'You're sure of that?'

'I'm sure.'

'What do you want of me?' asked Mackenzie.

'Nothing. Not your forgiveness. Not your prayers. I don't even expect you to understand. I just wanted you to know. At least one person should know the truth.'

Mackenzie sat down on the narrow metal bed. He stared at his hands.

'Where did you go wrong, Kirkos?'

The Greek splashed water on his face and then dried himself with a towel. He gave a short ironic laugh.

'Where did I go wrong? Now, there's a question. But I can answer it. I went wrong by always doing what suited George Kirkos and believing that I did it for Greece. Even now, I'm ready to welcome death but I don't have the consolation of knowing I'm doing it for Greece. I am doing it for George Kirkos. I don't want to live.'

He spoke soberly but his eyes suddenly twinkled.

'You can do me a good turn,' he said. 'You can perpetuate the myth of George Kirkos. If someone should ever ask you why I chose to die, don't disillusion them. Tell them that I lived for Kirkos, but I died for Greece.'

Mackenzie tried to dredge up the hate and bitterness he had once reserved for this smiling puzzle of a man. It wouldn't come. Not even his indifference of the past month could be summoned. He felt only a strange sorrow.

'I'm going to stop this,' he said at last. 'I'm going to speak to the Commandant and have the exchange stopped.'

'No!' said Kirkos fiercely. He relaxed again. 'It wouldn't do any good. I would deny all I've told you. I'd say you were out of your mind. Delirious. I would insist on being exchanged. They are handing over forty RAF men for me. That's quite a compliment – forty Englishmen for one humourless Greek!'

Mackenzie smiled grimly at his use of the word 'humourless'.

'Ah, I see you remember telling me once that I had no sense of humour,' said Kirkos.

'I remember.'

'I admit my sense of humour is not as sharp as God's when he looks down on us from his heaven. How he must laugh at our follies.'

Kirkos completed his dressing. He had been given British battle-dress without insignia of any kind. There was a knock at the door.

A boyish-faced soldier stuck his head round the door. 'The transport's here. Are you ready, sir?'

'I've been ready since the day I was born,' replied Kirkos. 'Goodbye, Captain Mackenzie. it was a pleasure to see you again. Thank you for coming.'

He gave a slight bow and, picking up a small canvas bag into which some belongings had been crammed, he walked out through the doorway.

Mackenzie rose wearily and followed him. He watched him climb into the waiting jeep and sit stiffly next to the driver. As the jeep moved off, he gave a tight smile and raised his hand in what might have been a salute.

Mackenzie watched the jeep out of sight. He never saw George Kirkos again. Nor did anyone else. The exchange was made near Tatoi, some distance from Athens, where a reception committee – which included Comrade Natsinas – was waiting to greet the liberated Kirkos.

The welcome was formal and subdued. Kirkos walked calmly to meet his former Communist associates. He was never seen again.

It was almost two years to the day since Mackenzie had arrived in Greece. Athens was *en fête*. After a month's negotiations, a Peace Treaty had been signed which promised a measure of policital stability in Greece for the immediate future.

The February sun came out to shine with the warm promise of spring. Athenians were abroad early, hailing the day as that of the 'Second Liberation'. The general excitement pervaded Mackenzie's room in the Grande Bretagne from the Square below. He, too, felt a sense of second liberation. He had been granted three months' leave of absence on full pay and Maitland had pulled strings to put a small utility truck and a load of petrol at his disposal.

There were a few formalities to complete in the office he had occupied during the past month. Mackenzie made it a leisurely day; saying goodbye to friends, eager to be off but savouring the final moments before the leash which held him was cut and he would be free.

Warmly happy but far from tipsy on a few farewell drinks, he went to his room to pack just after six. Below his open window, more and more people were crowding into Constitution Square. People were even thronging on the rooftops and balconies around the Square.

Greek soldiers lining the roads soon abandoned any hope of controlling the happy crowds. They just let them take over. Mackenzie estimated that there were sixty thousand people in the sardine squash below.

The sun went down in a sky of red, changing to violet, before the waiting crowds were rewarded for their vigil and the object of their patient congregation became evident.

On the balcony of the Regent's house appeared the Greek hero of the hour, the tall figure of the Archbishop Damaskinos. And there was a surprise. With the Regent was Winston Churchill, who had broken off his flight home from a conference in Yalta to spend a few hours in Athens and celebrate the new Peace Treaty.

The crowd cheered their approbation of the two men on the balcony, so dissimilar in life experience and background and yet so alike in qualities of courage, will and compassion.

The Regent stepped to the microphone and invited the blessing of God on Greece and her people. The crowd hushed as he solemnly declared his hopes and prayers for this historic day.

Then he pushed Churchill forward, obviously taking the great man by surprise. An interpreter joined the British Prime Minister, indicating that he would translate the words of the impromptu speech which the Regent had clearly invited.

Nor did Churchill's words fail him, although he was plainly in the grip of a deep emotion.

His rhetoric rang out a phrase at a time and then, for the benefit of the crowd below, the interpreter translated to Greek.

'. . . Let the Greek nation stand first in every heart, first in the thoughts of every man and woman. Let the future of Greece shine in their eyes . . . From the bottom of my heart, I wish you prosperity. From the bottom of my heart, I hope that Greece will take her proper part in the ranks of the nations that have suffered so grievously in this war . . . Let right prevail . . . Let party hatreds die . . . Let there be unity . . . Let there be resolute comradeship. Greece for ever! Greece for all!'

Tumultuous cheers greeted the words. The joyous acclamation went on.

Eventually, Mackenzie turned from the window. Bag over his shoulder, he left the hotel by a back door to where the utility van was parked.

It took him an hour to get clear of central Athens. He whistled cheerfully as he drove north on the Delphi road. A journey of more than three hundred kilometres lay before him. He planned to take his time, not rushing, but spinning out his tantalising expectancy so that his arrival should be in daylight.

The sun was rimming over the mountains of Roumelia when he got his first sight through a grove of olives of the sparkling waters of the lake. A dog was barking over on the island as he parked the truck and made his way to the jetty.

It was old Petros who came in answer to his call. The old man was almost falling about with excitement as he untied the boat and sculled it across the short neck of water. It almost drifted away as he clasped Mackenzie in embrace and effusively welcomed him.

The island was exactly the same. Nothing had changed. The soft grass was wet with dew as the pair made their way towards the house.

Next Agarista appeared. She stood at the door, shouting her excitement and spilling the contents from the cooking pot she still held in her hand.

Then Eleni was there. She stood still as a statue, more beautiful than ever, framed in the rectangle of doorway like a Botticelli painting. She took a few paces towards him. Then she was running. Then they were in each other's arms.

No words were needed. The beating of their hearts, their glistening eyes, the grip of their arms, the harmony of their beings . . . communicated all.

All of the joy and the sadness and the mystery of eternity was in the tableau: the aged pair, simple in hope and expectation; the lovers, no longer young but not yet old, so grateful for today and yet hopeful of tomorrow.

And the glory of Greece, majestic, timeless, was all around.